About the Author

Bruce Nicholls writes from an intimate knowledge of diplomatic and political affairs, having served in Australia's Foreign Service, with postings to India, Germany, Switzerland, China and Hong Kong. In the 90s, he returned to a corporate life in Australia, serving on the boards of several private and public listed companies, on the boards of major public corporations and in public policy and political advisory capacities. He chairs a bipartisan public policy think tank and is a prolific writer and advocate of free speech and democratic rights. His first fiction, 'Codename Sentinel', won the coveted Newspaper House Literary Award and was described as 'the standout entry from a field of over 70 manuscripts'. Like his first novel, this work draws upon extensive research into geopolitical affairs to add edge and poignancy to his plot. Bruce travels widely, speaks German, Hindi and Mandarin Chinese and is enjoying the autumn of his years with his wife, Annie, on their historic rural holding, Carlsberg, located near Melbourne, Australia.

Other contributions by the author:
  'A Briefcase in Transit'
  'The Austrade Story'
  'Code Sentinel'
  'The Plato Prophecy'

The Dongfeng Deception

Bruce Nicholls

The Dongfeng Deception

Publisher: Carlsberg Press
Melbourne, Australia

Publisher: Carlsberg Press, in association with Intertype Publish and Print
Unit 45, 125 Highbury Road
BURWOOD VIC 3125
www.intertype.com.au

Ordering Information:
Quantity sales. Special discounts are available on quantity purchases by corporations, associations, and others. For details, contact the "Special Sales Department" at the address above.

The Dongfeng Deception/ Bruce Nicholls.
2nd edition – date of Publication: 1 June 2022
ISBN 978-0-6454140-7-3

Dedication

I dedicate this book to peace in our times, as cartoon-like political leaders strut their preposterous puffery across a fragile, global stage and Western democracy struggles to retain dignity and moral authority!

Acknowledgements

I thank my wife, Annie, for her quiet support and encouragement, Ellie-belly, who keeps me grounded, Dolce, for loving me unconditionally, and Lucky, the stray tomcat, who is my new friend. But most of all, I thank Dr Wikipedia and Professor Google, who have made life so much easier for modern authors than it was for our quill-in-hand forebears.

PROLOGUE
Cold War - Isle of Dogs, London, 1981

Anatoly Pushkin, Second Secretary, Soviet Embassy, raised his bloody head and squinted through swollen eyes at the blinding stream of light. These were the last days of the Cold War, but a new cold front had swept in, casting its frost over east-west relations and heralding a dangerous escalation of the game.

A powerful, phosphorescent beam had been trained upon Pushkin's cowered figure, blinding him, making it impossible to discern any other features around him. He was their prisoner, trapped in a dark void which seemed to swallow light and distort all sense of time and space. They had taken him by surprise, jumped him from behind, subdued him with a chloroform gag and bundled him into a vehicle. They had pulled a sack over his head, ensuring that he could not see their faces, so he knew with a special clarity that they must be hostile agents, operating professionally in the same, murky espionage world as he did, where conventional rules and conventional morality had no meaning.

After ten minutes on the move, the vehicle he was in, a commercial van, he guessed, had jerked to an abrupt halt and he had tumbled to the floor. His hands had been tied behind his back, so he had been unable to brace himself against the fall or to right himself when he had nose-dived into the floor. Based upon the time it had taken to drive to this location, he reckoned he was no more than ten kilometres from the CBD. From his prone position on the floor of the van, he had heard the mechanical rumble of a metal roller-door rising, followed by the sound of the rear door of the van being thrown open.

Rough hands had dragged him from the van and bundled him into the building in which he was now held hostage. The vehicle and the voices of two of his assailants had retreated, and the roller-door had rumbled back down. The echoing quality of the one remaining voice suggested that he was now in a cavernous building, a warehouse perhaps, and the absence of any ambient noise or light told him the building was located in an isolated part of London. Only one voice, the voice which so stridently harangued him, now remained.

Although he had been blinded by the intense beam of light when the bag had been removed from his head, he was able to squint through the glare and discern the dark shape of a stocky figure standing over him, whose face was hidden beneath a woollen balaclava. His tormentor was muscular. A young male, he thought… with a deep, gravel voice and a pronounced American accent. 'CIA,' the Russian thought, calculating his survival odds. Just as his mind refocussed, the blurred image of his tormentor lurched forward out of the blinding light and landed a vicious blow to the side of his head. His tormentor's second blow was delivered at the end of a clenched fist. It crashed into the Russian's jaw like a freight train, knocking his head backwards and stunning him momentarily.

Desperate to avoid the next blow, the Russian ducked his head to one side, but he was trussed up like a Christmas turkey, and was unable to evade the blow, which collided just below his left eye, making him wince in pain. That side of his face was now feeling as raw as a piece of butcher's meat and the resultant swelling had almost completely closed his eye.

A river of sweat ran freely down his face, not because of the temperature in this cold, empty place but as an anatomical response to the trauma he was experiencing. He knew that this was just the way the nervous system reacted to extreme stress or abuse. Copious sweating was a physical response to fear, the fear that now gnawed at his guts, warning him that the beatings would continue until his interrogator had extracted the information he wanted.

The abuse was not just physical. His tormentor was also using mechanical means, sensors taped to his armpits and attached to leads running from a power source. Whenever he refused to answer a question, he received an electric jolt that made his torso twitch and jump like a rag doll. Whenever he dared to stutter an answer, his answer was cut short, deemed unacceptable, and the sharp jolt came again, sending pulses of pain across his chest, making his heart race and constricting his lungs in its vice-like grip.

'How fitting,' the Russian thought, 'that the sick bastard has chosen this method to torment me, made famous by Russia's own 'Pavlov' to condition obedience in dogs. 'I may be human,' thought the Russian, 'but right now I am as useless as one of Pavlov's dogs, and this American will soon have me barking like one. He means business!' As his consciousness began to fade in and out, the Russian doubted that he could hold out much longer.

Although he was losing any capacity for rational thought, Anatoly Pushkin understood that his choices were narrowing. If he toughed it out, he would be beaten to a pulp. If he spilled details of the missile, he would face a deadly rebuke at the hands of his own people. He was in a *no-win* position, he thought, perversely amused by the hopelessness of his situation. If he folded, his Moscow controllers would finish him off. If he resisted and died, they would make him a hero of the Soviet Union, but that corrupt State was now a fractured relic of the former superpower it had been, teetering and ready to fall. Then the gravelly voice came at him again, more conciliatory this time:

'It doesn't have to be this way, Anatoly,' his tormentor said. 'We know that your man has defected. We know that he has been turned. We know he took the plans to London with him, and we know that he has offered the blueprints to the Chinese. It's all there, in the coded message we intercepted from your London office to your First Directorate in Moscow. When Moscow hears that we're onto you, you will be finished. They'll shop you for a song.'

'I don't know what you are talking about,' replied the Russian, physically and mentally at the end of his rope, as the bright light began to fade in and out.

'You don't, eh? Let me refresh your memory! You terminated your missile program with the Chinese. Why? We know that your defector stole a blueprint. What blueprint did he steal? Was it the old CSS-2 or the CSS-3?'

'Nyet. You know I can't give you that. I don't haff those details. If I did, I'd already be a dead man,' he replied, bracing himself for the next shock.'

Tired of this charade, the impatient young CIA field agent stepped back, sighed, and withdrew a hypodermic syringe from his tote bag. He pointed its needle towards the ceiling and ejected a mist of spray, to exclude any air bubbles in the chemical fluid which might cause an aneurism.

'You know how this works, Anatoly. You guys invented it. I shoot you up. You go all warm and fuzzy and then you start telling me the truth. What d'yer say?'

'Nyet! I cannot tell you what I do not know,' the Russian protested, spitting blood from his swollen lips. 'I am a just a junior functionary, not a scientist or a missile expert. I am too junior to be trusted with those details.'

The Russian's evasive reply tested the limits of the young American agent's patience, prompting him to resume his task with even more zeal. In an overt display of temper, the athletic young agent seized his hostage's arm, twisted it roughly over and speared the syringe into the vein on the inside of the Russian's elbow. Allowing time for the drug to work, he stepped back, flicked open his cigarette lighter, directed its flame to the end of a cigarette and drew deeply on its silky tribute, luxuriating in the richness of its nicotine buzz.

The determined CIA operative contemplated the battered figure of the Russian with emotional detachment and disdain, as he waited for the sodium pentothal to penetrate. The Russian's body now hung limply from its bonds, inert and spent. 'A tough nut, this Ruskie,' thought the American. 'But he will break.' There was no way he was going to fail his first test and he was quietly confident that this chemical would be fail-safe. If what he had been told about the drug were true, the sodium pentothal would slowly invade the Russian's brain and induce a hallucinogenic state, removing any sense of moral outrage and replacing it with pure trust, compliance and reckless joy. However, when he resumed his interrogation, the drug had proved useless.

Not only did the American's demands fail to elicit any new information from the delirious man, but the brave Russian, barely conscious, had finally raised his bleeding head, opened one puffy eye and spat out a defiant rebuke:

'You think you are a goddamn clever bastard, American, that I will just roll over and giff you what you want. Go to hell!' he declared, spitting a stream of saliva and blood at the feet of his tormentor.

For a brief moment, the American felt a grudging respect for his victim. Then the Russian's taunting response struck a sadistic nerve, and the American snarled. Like the breaching of a dam, the young sadist felt a torrent of rage spilling from him, causing his face to redden and his eye to tick nervously.

His answer to the Russian's defiance was passionate and brutal. Taking a heavy steel mallet from his tote bag, he swung it into the Russian's kneecap. Intoxicated by the righteousness of his mission, he imagined he could hear bone splintering and tendons tearing, as a shrill cry exploded from the mouth of the Russian. Now crimson with rage, the sadistic young agent pressed on, marvelling at the thrill he felt at each blow and at each anguished cry from his victim. Looking down, the American found that he had developed an erection.

'Stop! Nyet! Please stop!' sobbed the Russian, as the leering American applied manual pressure to his victim's shattered knee. With each new assault on his victim, the rookie field agent was enthralled by the Russian's anguished cries and transported by the guttural screams which now reverberated around the chasm walls of the empty warehouse.

***

The following morning, behind the privileged walls of the American Embassy in Grosvenor Square, agent Charles Ritter resumed his more usual role as the US Cultural Attaché, a convenient cover for his clandestine assignment to London station. He was pleased with his first interrogation.

15

The Russian had finally sung like a mezzo-soprano. He had been tough to break and would be unlikely to survive his terrible beating. The probationary CIA field agent had been forced to clean up the mess himself. He had removed all ID from his victim's body and dumped it behind a row of disused warehouses in the remote Docklands precinct. The Russian would not be found for months, and no clues would remain on his battered body to explain who he was.

While this was mildly reassuring, Ritter had assumed that Pushkin's disappearance would be noticed quickly at his place of work, the Russian Embassy, with serious diplomatic repercussions. Uncertain how this might play out, Ritter had scanned the press over the ensuing months, but there had been no mention of any murder or victim in the Docklands. The Russian had simply disappeared.

It seemed possible a KGB 'cleaner' had been sent in to recover Pushkin's body, to avoid a major diplomatic incident. But how could that be... unless, by some miracle, Pushkin had survived... lived to fight another day.

On his return to the Embassy, Ritter invested much effort in drafting his first major intelligence report, which was transmitted in code to Langley, Virginia. His brutal but effective interrogation of Pushkin had produced extremely valuable and strategically important information. Ritter's report had therefore been received as a masterstroke by senior officers back home, sealing the young agent's fate and ensuring his rapid rise to prominence. Indeed, his rise had been so meteoric, that it had outpaced the annual psychiatric evaluations routinely required of new field agents.

At the end of his three-year posting, no such testing had yet been completed on Ritter, so his mentors in Langley, highly impressed with the results of his first field assignment, remained unaware of the disturbed nature of their young recruit's mind. Psychopaths rarely make good intelligence officers, but sometimes deviates, like Charles Ritter, slip through the cracks.

Thirty-five years later, after learning to control his explosive temper, the sadistic agent could feel smugly satisfied with his career achievements. He had been promoted to the top of his nation's intelligence community, directing its sensitive work, from Islamic terrorism to the Chinese military threat.

In his new role as Deputy Director of the CIA, Ritter discharged these important duties from the comfort of his plush, Langley office. On the wall behind him, a large shield proclaimed the CIA's famous motto *"And Ye shall know the truth and the truth shall make you free"*, taken from the holy bible.

Nanning, China - 2014

Major General Zhang Ming Wei's black Mercedes crunched to a halt in the gravel courtyard of the high security complex. As it came to rest, a platoon of security guards snapped to attention and saluted. A nervous orderly rushed to open the door of the senior officer's stylish limo. The formidable head of the People's Liberation Army, Second in Command, Joint Military Defence, was oblivious to all of this attention, as he alighted from the vehicle with a serene air, stretched his compact frame and turned to survey his surroundings.

Just forty-five years old, the diminutive General was extraordinarily young by China's leadership standards. His stocky frame, close-cropped hair and horn-rimmed glasses failed to diminish the commanding aura which emanated from him. This aura was accentuated by a resolute, bulldog's face and cold, impassive eyes, making for an intimidating presence. If his eyes left any doubt about his authority, it was reinforced by an imposing array of braid and stars on his summer dress uniform, chosen for his visit as a concession to the humid, sub-tropical climate in this part of China.

'Welcome to Nanning Missile complex, General,' stammered the nervous orderly. Colonel Liu is waiting for you in the map room.'

General Zhang gave a curt nod of acknowledgement, betraying no emotion, and followed the orderly into the complex. While he projected the military bearing of an old-school Prussian, Zhang was a thoroughly modern soldier, to say the least. He was archetypal of the new elite now being introduced across China's ranks to succeed a geriatric cohort of older men, who had been selected for loyalty and political allegiance rather than military capability.

The General's credentials were impressive, and explained his rapid rise to his present, senior rank within the Strategic Command. Having graduated with distinction from Whampoa Military Academy, China's *West Point*, he had been allowed to undertake postgraduate studies abroad, completing an economics degree at Harvard. On his return to China, he had completed a Master's degree in military command structures at the National Defence University in Beijing, under the leadership of the famous Weng Xibin, and post-grad courses at China's Naval and Air Force Academies.

Having acquired a taste for international discourse during his student days in the US, Zhang was determined to travel widely, appreciating travel-built knowledge and valuable overseas alliances. It had become his personal mantra that one should 'know one's enemies well and keep them close'. It annoyed him, however, that NATO counterparts still treated Chinese staff officers as junior members of their celebrated international military elite.

Obsessed with the fading glory of their British, Prussian, French, and American military traditions, the West seemed ignorant of, or simply unable to acknowledge, China's own, extraordinary military tradition. They failed to understand the timeless nature of that tradition or how deeply it ran in the Chinese military psyche. In Zhang Ming Wei's view, that was a major tactical blunder on their part; one that could be exploited to China's advantage.

In medieval times, China's military had no peer. Indeed, cavalry, canon, gunpowder, and missiles were all Chinese inventions. Since the 1700's, however, Chinese military genius had lost its currency and, by the middle of the 20th Century, been forgotten. It had finally been devalued by the Imperial Palace's humiliating defeat at the hands of British expeditionary forces during the Boxer Rebellion and further diminished by Mao's revolutionary long march, with its under-equipped and poorly-trained peasant-soldiers, trudging up mountains with mules. Finally, it had been dismissed as irrelevant during China's Cultural Revolution, which saw all intellectuals, technocrats and those who dared to question authority, banished to remote work camps.

In truth, it was only in relatively recent history that European powers had developed a cogent military science. They had done so when Portugal

19

had finally evolved a technology for casting cannon barrels which didn't explode and when a rampaging Napoleon had forced Europeans to join forces, think tactically and drastically improve their weapons, mobility and efficiency.

In their scramble to do so, European Generals had revisited the war tactics of the Romans and the ancient military genius of China's legendary General Sun Tzu, articulated in his 'Art of War' manuscripts. These had then become a sort of manifesto for contemporary military teaching and China's military genius had thus silently informed all western military thinking and logic.

A brilliant strategist and philosopher, China's great General had identified three principles which underpinned all warfare and which a very contemporary US General, Norman Schwarzkopf, had later conceded he relied upon in his storming subjugation of Iraq; Sun Tzu's principles of 'deception, speed and obliteration of the weak link' had become Schwarzkopf's 'Shock and Awe'.

It was Sun Tzu who, reflecting upon the tactics of Genghis Khan, had first identified guerrilla warfare, years before it was used by the Sikhs, by Mao (to harass the Kuomintang), by south American rebels and by the Viet Cong. Sun Tzu had said… "A military leader must be serene. He must be inscrutable. He must use diplomacy to enter the mind of his adversary, he must understand his enemy's unfathomable plans and he must live to fight another day."

General Zhang Ming Wei seemed to have each of these immutable principles etched into his very psyche and to wear them as a cloak in his daily interaction with others. Indeed, that was what made people around him so nervous. His inscrutability, which he used as a personal foil to disguise the shrewd intellect which was always at work inside his head, working like the feet of a duck below the calm waters of a pond, portraying serenity on the surface while he analysed and planned every decision in furious detail.

On this occasion, he was visiting Nanning to inspect the aging missile facility personally, having received unsatisfactory reports about its state of repair, its military relevance and the extent of recent flooding in its subterranean silos. That was the trouble with 'below-ground' systems. They were always flooding. Paradoxically, the enemy's ICBMs were all highly susceptible to flooding, but only because they were deployed in nuclear submarines, running silently beneath vast oceans. Western submarines were clearly superior. They did not leak! They ran silent, they were mobile and almost impossible to interdict.

When it was first introduced, the Dongfeng Missile system had been housed in another of China's great, but little-known construction wonders; its so-called 'Underground Great Wall'. General Zhang understood the proud history of this iconic project, but he understood its modern limitations even better. During the cold war, this labyrinth of inter-connecting tunnels had been meant to serve as a nuclear fall-out shelter for troops and to protect China's military arsenal. Later, the tunnel system had been adapted to accommodate missile silos, in a deployment chain stretching over two thousand miles, from Kashgar, on the north-western border with Kyrgyzstan, to Nanning on the border with Vietnam.

Now all that was about to change. In the brilliant young General's view, China's underground system was now a white elephant. Those defences had long since become sitting ducks and an embarrassing tribute to China's military obsolescence. Modern surveillance technology, anti-missile defence technology, bunker-busting armaments and other advances now meant that each silo had long since been carefully targeted by opposing military forces.

'Launch signatures' had been programmed to ensure immediate detection, retaliation and interdiction of any ICBMs launched from China's static silos.

This inspection was, therefore, a precursor to a bold decision by the young General to shut the whole system down permanently in favour of a more contemporary, mobile system, using aircraft carriers and nuclear submarines. Indeed, while the west was coming to grips with China's economic miracle, it failed to notice that China, under the leadership of General Zhang, was working a military miracle that might eclipse its economic achievements.

Upon entering the complex, the General found a fawning Colonel Liu waiting on the elevated gantry leading across the silo complex to the map room. Colonel Liu bowed his head low, like the court Mandarins of old, to emphasise respect. Then he snapped to attention, smiling obsequiously as he directed the General to precede him down the corridor. They entered the map room, which served as a sort of a board room, but with glass walls on two sides providing a commanding view into the labyrinthine cave containing the tall, gleaming Dongfeng VII ballistic missile. The Dongfeng rose, proud and erect, from its central launch pad. It looked innocent enough, but it carried the lethal sting of a billion vipers in its conical nose. There, a 3,000 kg 5-megaton nuclear payload lay inert, like a sleeping dragon, waiting for its master to press a button which would summon it to life and allow it to belch its fire.

A nest of service corridors radiated out from the central chamber surrounding the launch pad. These ran off at various levels, providing access for a miscellany of support personnel servicing the missile. Vulnerable to the explosive blast of a launch, these service corridors could be closed off during the launch phase by activating huge, hydraulic fire doors.

'Welcome to Nanning Missile Complex, General Zhang,' the beaming Colonel continued. 'I am very proud to show you my wonderful complex and to explain how it works. I regard this complex as the teeth of the tiger, which make our great People's Republic invincible. But first, may I offer you and your staff some tea?' asked Liu.

General Zhang walked slowly to the head of the table, strategically positioning himself at the most commanding seat in the room. Then he removed his cap and sat, as a chairman might at a board meeting. When he was seated, the minions around him descended upon the other seats, vying for a position close to the General. Even the small banality of the seating arrangements had been turned to military advantage by Zhang, affording him, as the head of the table, an opportunity to outflank those in his presence. He accepted a steaming tribute of green tea, took a careful sip and set it back down. Then he raised his head regally and directed a steely gaze at the Colonel.

'I wish I could agree with you, Colonel Liu, but only two possibilities exist. You are either totally ignorant of the current technological superiority of Western forces arrayed against us, or you are an imbecile; a pig-ignorant man lacking the wit to see how out-of-date your glorious missile silos have become.'

The General's words descended upon the unsuspecting Colonel like a thunder clap, leaving him wide-eyed and completely emasculated by their brutal logic.

'But General,' Liu stammered, 'we have invested a fortune in this system and it has been at the forefront of our deterrence, for as long as I can remember.'

'That is my point. These silos are almost as old as you, Colonel Liu. Like you, they have lost all of their menace and sting. They are tired, anachronistic and an embarrassment. The US forces and NATO have long since identified each and every one of our missile silos, provided an around the clock satellite surveillance of silo hatches, and programmed a launch signal, activating interdiction of each missile before it is more than 800 kilometres downrange.

'You will continue to man this facility, because it represents a huge, sunk investment and because I intend to use it to confuse our enemies, when I deploy new warheads on a more diverse, mobile front. That information is confidential, but you will kindly continue to mouth your asinine assurance that our underground silo network is our principal deterrence. I will choose my time, when I have completed my work on a new, more potent system, to ensure the west comes to know and appreciate it. Then we will see where China stands in the international constellation of military power,' he said.

With that, the General stood, turned and marched out of the map room in the direction he had come from. The Colonel and his minions scurried after him, feeling diminished by his powerful logic and in awe of his incisiveness. As his career developed, those traits would come to define the General, attracting wider attention and grudging respect from a growing audience of military observers around the world and from China's National People's Congress.

Treasury Gardens – Melbourne, Australia

A tall blonde, wearing black leotards and a baseball cap, rounded the final corner of the jogging path and huffed her way up the rise towards her accommodation. Birds flittered though patches of mottled light, seeking a flight path through lofty boughs, as shafts of morning sun penetrated the ancient oak canopy. The combination of mottled light and morning bird song lent a bucolic atmosphere to this quiet, botanical sanctuary in the middle of the Melbourne CBD, giving a lie to the frenetic honking of car horns and clanking of trams which played out, just over the rise, in Collins Street.

Dr Maggie King slowed and cocked her wrist to inspect the jogging monitor strapped to it, a metaphor for the order which ruled the fastidious academic's life. Satisfied that she had completed the eight-kilometre distance she had set herself, to ensure a high aerobic heart rate and keep her in excellent shape, she sprinted up the final rise. Her legs quickly resumed their former rhythm, pumping in sync with the sounds of Vivaldi's *L'estro* violin concerto, which rose majestically from her iPhone and resonated through earplugs into her beautiful brain. The whole was orchestrated, as a conductor might orchestrate a concert with his baton, by the rhythmic bobbing of her blonde ponytail.

Arriving at the ramp leading into her serviced apartment complex, she came to a halt, planted her legs apart, placed her hands on her hips, and sucked in deeply, allowing her heart rate to slow and her body to luxuriate in the oxygen-rich afterglow which always followed her run. Having regained her breath, she strolled into the sleepy Lobby of her building, retrieved the morning papers from the concierge, and disappeared up the stairway. At the top, she entered a light-filled studio apartment, took in its view over the beautiful parkland below, and charged the coffee machine in

24

the kitchen alcove with fresh coffee grinds. It could gurgle away and percolate while she showered, sending its reassuring coffee vapours through the small suite of rooms and beckoning her back to a lazy breakfast.

Today was special. She was a long way from New Jersey and her beloved Princeton University, where she directed the Master's program at the school of Political Science. She had briefly traded those familiar surrounds for a short sabbatical in Australia, at the invitation of the Institute of International Affairs. She would spend this day in her hotel suite, finalising a vote of thanks for the annual Sir Zelman Cohen Oration, which she had been invited by the Institute to deliver. The oration was a major event in the nation's political calendar. Important eyes would be upon her, giving her a unique opportunity to broaden her intellectual authority in front of a powerful, Asian constituency. She would have to choose her words carefully, but then, she always did.

The oration was always delivered by a senior statesman or academic, one whose celebrity extended beyond national boundaries. It always explored a controversial area of public policy, ensuring that it attracted wide media coverage, and it was always attended by an audience of international political, academic and business leaders, who were deeply interested in the insights it would offer about the region's political and economic future.

Tonight's oration would be delivered by no less a luminary than the world-renowned historian, Professor Julian Blainey, an eccentric genius and entertaining speaker, who would doubtless deliver a 'tour de force' on the subject of China's rapid economic and military emergence. His address would explore the impact of China's ascendancy upon the USA and, by extension, upon the nations ringing the rapidly changing Asia-Pacific basin.

Dr King was delighted to be delivering the vote of thanks to this august assembly. She had been asked to take extra time, to include her own observations, as a respected academic assessing the evolving new order from the objective distance of her American University campus. That privilege had rarely been given, as it would dilute the impact of the main speaker's address. However, Maggie King had made China a special focus of her academic life. She had studied and now spoke fluent Mandarin and had, for some time, been cautioning successive US Administrations that

25

they would need to reshape their relationships with the *sleeping dragon*, whose rapid emergence would radically alter the world all Americans lived in. Her early pronouncements on China had proven accurate, prescient and ahead of the general discourse, so she had rapidly become globally recognised as an expert on US-East Asian Affairs, even advising foreign governments on areas of foreign policy sensitivity. The Chinese, too, respected her for her measured analysis and had acknowledged her as a *Lao Pengyou* (old friend).

After showering, the attractive academic emerged from the bathroom in bare feet, faded jeans and a loose-fitting sweater and padded into the lounge area, winding a towel around her wet hair as she went. A delicate neck and flawless complexion complemented her large, liquid eyes and sensuous mouth. These traits, together, served to heighten her femininity and natural beauty, a beauty which needed no make-up or artifice of any kind to achieve a stunning effect.

She poured a steaming tribute of coffee into a mug and plonked down onto a large sofa, where a sheaf of scribbled notes had been strewn the night before. She always began this way, scribbling bullet-points to build a skeleton around which she would construct the body of her address. She adjusted her spectacles, shuffled her notes together and began reviewing them:

"How will a new Asian Superpower change our world? — Rebalancing relations with the US against the rise of China"

• *Professor Blainey has provided a valuable roadmap, but we must also hear the voices of other, Asian politicians, academics and professionals to understand how China's emergence plays out across the Asian social and political divide. The world will want a peaceful transition and one unified, regional voice, which distils unity from a chorus of self-interested nations.*

• *While the western alliance countries have experienced serious economic problems, China should not write them off or see them as a waning political force. Militarily, the US remains light years ahead of China. Its economic resilience is legendary and I am certain it will regain its more usual role as a global economic powerhouse.*

26

- *As China explodes onto the world stage, lesser Asian states will each recalibrate their relationships with China and the US, searching for a secure balance of interests. The chemistry of the region will be changed forever and Asia's feet will learn to march to a different set of geo-political drums.*

- *The assertion that the 21st Century belongs to Asia fails to value the roles America and Europe will continue to play. Australia might be right about China's rapid emergence, but it should not put all of its political eggs in one basket. If Asia does become the new locomotive of the global economy, and if you are to maximise your local advantage, you will need to shrug off the clichés of your colonial past and replace them with the language of a new, Asian-oriented diplomacy. Above all, show the US and China that you have an independent foreign policy mindset, based upon common political and economic interests, which can accommodate both China and the USA.*

- *An obsessive focus upon China could cloud the urgent need for a balancing strategy towards India, which is an important player in the policy mix. India's emergence will surely draw ASEAN eyes westward, across the Indian Ocean, transcending a short-sighted, myopic focus upon the South China Sea.*

- *In the newly emerging Asia, Australia, with its hybrid mix of eastern and western cultures and European system of law and justice, can be an ideal arbitrator of issues across the geo-political divide, providing neutral but careful leadership and bridging the gap between the east and the west.*

- *It is said that one must look to the past for lessons about the future, so when I was preparing for this oration, I did some research. I was dismayed to learn some inconvenient truths about my own country. Research into the relative hegemony of the two super powers, the US and China, reveals that America has invaded, been at war with or had major disputes with most of its allies, at some point in its comparatively brief history. America's penchant for breaching the sovereignty of other nations has been unmatched, except perhaps by Japan. China emerges as the world's most pacific nation, having preferred diplomatic solutions to military intervention for most of its history.*

- *However, for the first time in centuries, China may be drawn, unwittingly, into a militarily engagement beyond its own borders, not offensively, but defensively, to protect its burgeoning global interests. It might do so, for example, if a third party threatens the supply security of resources feeding its own, rapacious growth. It will want to protect long term arrangements with Australia, Africa and Brazil, since resources from those countries underpin China's economic growth. Should this inspire angst or make the case for welcoming Chinese investment? Will closer economic ties triumph over xenophobia? These are critical questions Australia must now answer.*

- *A SINAUSTRAL Defence Pact could complement the ANZUS Pact, but that would require a radical shift in defence thinking. Your Defence Minister has invited China to participate, as Indonesia does, in joint military exercises in your north, as a symbol of your neutrality in the emerging US-China dialogue. I think that a good idea, though the tea-drinking, conservative American lobby may be shocked by such a radical shift in your posture. The USA will need time to accept the new geo-political reality which compels Australia to be more integrated in the Asian community in which it is becoming immersed, and America will need reassurances from you that this new, realpolitik, does not, in any way, diminish the close friendship you have always enjoyed with your American allies; one that has been tested in the fiery cauldron of four major global conflicts, fighting side by side.*

- *Your Government's White Paper on the Asia-Pacific Century highlights a need for schools to teach more Asian languages, particularly Mandarin. I find that curious, since 38% of your population comprises first or second generation Asians, giving you a rich repository of native-speaking skills in those languages from within your existing citizenry. America would love to have your depth of native speakers in those Asian languages, but Spanish has become its second language, for all of the wrong reasons.*

• Australians of Anglo-Celtic extraction will need to gradually accept that their home is no longer a European but rather, a fully-fledged Asian nation, living in an Asian cultural flux. From the distance of my office at Princeton, a long way from this exciting new theatre of global development, being an Aussie and living in this part of the world should become a badge of honour. Your transformation into a fully integrated Asian nation could not come at a more propitious time in your history. History will record this development as a watershed that refreshes and greatly enriches your nation.

• Finally, most informed commentators agree that you are uniquely placed to benefit from the new world order unfolding on your doorstep. However, please don't jettison your long-standing relationship with the US, simply to counter the Chinese perception that you dance to our foreign policy on every issue. In your brave new world, you can seek a middle road, becoming the new 'Switzerland of the South'. Your decision to host joint naval exercises with China is a good first step. Culture-bridging diplomacy like that could resolve many new policy tensions and make Australia a haven, offering legal and fiscal security for distant investors wanting to access Asian markets.

Maggie King nodded thoughtfully, as her pen moved across her notes. Her views would not be welcome in some quarters. Ignorance and xenophobia always stalked ideas which challenged comfortable orthodoxy. However, she wanted her speech to resonate with her audience, and the new world she was describing would surely achieve that. If her speech received wide media coverage, she might be remembered as the first to advocate such a bold shift in thinking on China. Why not? She was an articulate and intellectually sound advocate; the new voice of a more questioning academia, as Asia made a rapid transition from the dark shadow of its under-developed past into the full sunlight of a new era of economic prosperity.

Satisfied with her summary, she sighed, slumped back into the nest of cushions on her sofa and reflected on the current shape of her life. Any outsider would think that she had her life in perfect balance, but there was a gaping, emotional hole. Although she was a natural beauty and should, by

29

rights, have had an army of men chasing her, there was no special man in her life. Indeed, her personal investment in work and career had come at a high cost. Over time, she had evolved a strong independence which most men now found daunting. There had been men in her life, both casual and more enduring lovers, but none had lasted very long. Each one had eventually come to realise that he could be no more than a satellite, rotating around her academic universe. It would take a special man, she knew, to subdue her spirit and rein in such a charismatic, intelligent woman.

Still, in a deep recess of her mind, Maggie imagined that there must be a man like that out there somewhere; one who fitted her exacting requirements. A tall, strong man, able to curb her strongly assertive nature and unlock the passionate, yet fragile woman inside. One who could penetrate her protective shell and touch her soul. In truth, the lack of a man in her life was a gaping void which she desperately needed to fill. As her body clock ticked on, she was becoming subliminally ready to open herself up to that possibility.

***

Later that afternoon, Maggie studied herself in the robe mirror one more time, adjusting her cocktail dress and smoothing out any creases in it. She had combined a figure-hugging navy-blue dress with matching stilettoes and a simple string of pearls, achieving a careful mix of academic chic and natural beauty. Her hair was piled up and fixed in a bun, accentuating her femininity and the slender lines of her neck and shoulders. She had added a subtle blush to her cheeks, a clear lip gloss and eyeliner to accentuate her large, intelligent eyes. Quite simply, she looked stunning and would turn lots of heads at the function.

Right on 6.30, a chauffeur-driven hire car pulled up outside. She gathered the small purse containing her speech and slid into the rear seat. Ten minutes later, the limo was cruising sedately up Williams Street towards the Georgian columns of an impressive sandstone building, pulling up in front of its stately, wide entrance. This was the exclusive *Australian Club*, a familiar home to a large constituency of Australia's business and

30

academic establishment and the venue for tonight's oration. Men in tuxedos and women dripping with diamonds made their way up the front stairs, receiving their name badges at the top before facing a phalanx of waiters bearing silver trays of champagne. Guests mingled in the foyer to the soothing strains of a string quartet.

A dignified looking gentleman, retired Senator Jim Hurst, was strutting about like a mother hen. He was a trustee of the Institute for International Affairs, the organiser of the oration and the author of Maggie's invitation to deliver the vote of thanks. For some time now, he had been searching for his esteemed American guest, expecting a more matronly, academic woman. He inquired of the lady manning the registration table whether Dr King's name tag had been collected and was horrified to learn that it had, and that one of his guests of honour had slipped past his guard. The lady pointed across the gathering at a tall, elegant young woman in a stunning, navy blue cocktail dress, standing by herself in a corner of the room. The Senator scurried over to her.

'My dear Dr King! How can you ever forgive me, letting you wander in on your own like that without a proper welcome? Please let me introduce you to some of our other guests. You are seated on Table 2, adjacent to the lectern and convenient to the stage. I am the host of that table and most of the others on our table are from academia or politics. I do hope they don't bore you. As you don't have a partner, I've placed you next to Colonel Tom Grant, a rather interesting soldier with a degree in Asian Studies and a Masters in Political Science. Oh, and he is a former war hero. Let me introduce you to him.'

Maggie followed the Senator as he worried his way through the throng of guests, heading for a tall, ruggedly handsome military officer, looking immaculate in formal mess uniform. This incorporated a white mess jacket, white cummerbund and black tie. His breast pocket sagged under the weight of military service ribbons and, around his neck, he sported a rare George Cross, the second highest bravery award in the British Commonwealth.

Grant was engaged in a lively exchange with another guest when Maggie and the Senator broke into his group. As they did so, all eyes focussed upon the arresting young woman, who made such a commanding

31

figure. Tom Grant's eyes turned nonchalantly from his discussion partner to the new arrivals, settling upon the large, intelligent eyes of the gorgeous American guest. The impact upon him was immediate and palpable. His eyes locked onto hers, as a homing missile might lock onto its target. Her captivating beauty and tall, physical presence took his breath away. His eyes must have communicated this strong attraction because she, too, was soon staring intently into his eyes, as if they were suddenly the only two people in the room.

'Allow me to introduce Dr Margaret King, from Princeton University,' said Senator Hurst. 'Dr King will be giving the response to the oration and moving the vote of thanks. Please make her feel welcome.'

The geriatric men in the group fell over one another, keen to demonstrate old world gentility as they jostled to shake Maggie's hand, while Tom Grant was lost in his own world, taking in her wondrous beauty, until she woke him out of his reverie with a beaming smile, addressing him though dazzling white teeth. 'You must be Colonel Grant,' she said with a mischievous look in her eyes.

'Senator Hurst tells me that you are a very interesting man.' Tom noticed that she concluded these remarks by gesturing at his George Cross.

'You must mean this thing hanging round my neck. They gave me this because I was too slow getting out of the way. I was trying to pull one of my blokes out of a hot situation in Afghanistan. Anyone would have done the same. Every man in my regiment should have received one of these.'

Maggie was amused by the Colonel's awkward response and impressed by his humility. She looked forward to learning more about him. Just as she was about to delve further, a gong announced that it was time to enter the main auditorium and be seated. They moved into the auditorium, where Tom was delighted to find Maggie standing beside him at his table. He pulled out her chair in a gesture of chivalry and they both sat, immediately continuing their conversation. Although she should have been nervous about speaking in front of such a distinguished audience, the tall, gregarious war hero seemed to have put her at ease. She was enjoying his company and was captivated by his deep, resonant voice, his subtle sense of humour and his strong, male sexuality. 'God,' she thought. 'I am really attracted to this man.'

When Maggie was called upon to speak, Tom Grant found himself hanging on her every word. He was impressed by her giant intellect and by her articulate delivery and wondered how anyone could be blessed with both the beauty of a catwalk model and the intellect of a Dean of Faculty at Princeton. Maggie completed her speech to thunderous applause and regained her place at the table beside him.

'That was brilliant, Maggie,' he said. 'I absolutely agreed with your analysis. You really do understand the challenges we face as China emerges, and that is a rare thing for a distant observer. I am doing some work in that area myself,' he added. 'In fact, that's why I am here.'

'How so?' she inquired.

'Well, I am a member of our Joint Forces Strategic Command, based in Canberra, where we are grappling with the military implications of China's emergence. They are deploying nuclear subs in our northern waters and have also just launched their first aircraft carrier. As a matter of fact, I am shortly to be posted to the States as a Visiting Fellow, at the invitation of your West Point Military Academy. I will be over there for a year, briefing your guys on what we think is unfolding down here and learning from them. I will be attached to our diplomatic mission in New York.'

There was a pregnant pause as Maggie digested this extraordinary news. She looked into the charismatic soldier's eyes and, for an instant, felt her heart surge. 'Had they been fatalistically drawn together?' she asked herself. Was he that special man she had been searching for and never found? '

Wow! What a coincidence. We should stay in touch,' she said. 'Who knows? We might bump into each other again, this time on my turf,' she joked.

Tom looked intently into her gorgeous brown eyes and said with genuine sincerity, 'I really, truly hope that we do, Maggie. I can't tell you how much this brief meeting has meant to me and what a delight it has been to know you.'

Maggie smiled broadly and allowed her hand to venture across the table and cover his. There was a genuine look of hunger in her eyes and Tom felt an electric charge as her fingers folded over his.

'I have a strong feeling we will be seeing more of each other, soldier,' she said. 'Call me when you are settled into New York. My campus is in New Jersey, just a morning's drive away, and I have some favourite restaurants I need to show you. I get to New York pretty often, so maybe you can introduce me to your diplomatic colleagues… or do you Aussies call them mates?'

Tom squeezed her hand and replied:

'That's a deal, Doctor. You are definitely on for lunch when I get to New York, but I won't be introducing you to any of my Australian mates. I'm not that stupid. I'd have to beat them off with a stick!'

CIA Headquarters, Langley, Virginia

There it was again, that Chinese word, jumping out at him from his computer, conjuring dark images from a distant past. '*A thorough review of China's Dongfeng missile program*' the instruction said, and it came from the desk of no less a person than the CIA's charismatic Director, Frank Angiotti. The Director's instruction went on to inform a select few agency staff (your eyes only personnel) that Ritter would lead the review. That was a surprise which the balding CIA veteran, the agency's Far East expert, had not anticipated.

Charles Ritter turned from his screen, sighed and looked down at the faded folder on the edge of his desk. When the Dongfeng missile had first come to the agency's attention, there were no desktop computers. Early intelligence reports had been hand-typed and transmitted by telex. Back then, hard copies had been stored in the agency's now dusty archives. Ritter recalled the day, thirty-two years earlier, when he had first seen the curious word. He would begin with the papers in this original, old file and work forward. He would have to cull the sensitive bits and manage the release of other details carefully.

Agent Ritter had personally retrieved the dusty old file from the basement registry. It was now 2017, thirty-six years after the file had first been opened. The sudden call for the inquiry had come from the Defence Appropriation Committee of Congress. It would surely open up old wounds. When he had first seen the directive, Ritter had winced. The word *Dongfeng* carried a dark meaning. It took him back to his time as a young field agent, when the enigmatic Chinese missile had drawn him into its vortex, introduced him to a world of Machiavellian intrigue and left him with a secret he needed to protect. A curious word, *Dongfeng,* with a curious meaning. Mandarin for *East Wind.*

It was a clever name, even back then, for a fledgling missile project, one that would send a chill wind from the Far East towards US and European forces aligned in the west. The missile's deployment, and China's rapid economic emergence, had since combined to cause a tectonic shift in global affairs. Looking back, Ritter realised that the Dongfeng had been the canary in the coal mine. He should have recognised it, when it was first deployed in a bizarre system only the Chinese could have conceived - a network of missile silos housed in an underground tunnel system stretching two thousand miles across China. When astonished Western intelligence services had first discovered the system, they had called it China's *Underground Great Wall*.

Work on the tunnel system had commenced in 1965, when fallout shelters were first conceived as a naïve device for surviving a nuclear holocaust.

China had hoped that this enormous, underground tunnel system might act as a giant fallout shelter, protecting its military leaders and the main part of its massed land forces, in the event of a full scale, nuclear conflict.

That futile, head in the sand response had later given way to a more pragmatic global strategy; a *balance of destructive power* which was perversely dubbed MAD (*Mutually Assured Destruction*). The only positive thing one could say of that insane stand-off was that it recognised the nightmare a nuclear conflict would unleash on an unsuspecting world; a nightmare which had almost found expression during the Bay of Pigs crisis.

When Kennedy had stood up to the attempted smuggling of Soviet missiles onto Cuba, the Soviets had escalated to Code Red and US forces had gone to DEFCON 1. Missiles on both sides had been activated and their warheads armed, and the chill in east-west relations, glibly referred to as the *Cold War*, had reached a terrifying crescendo. Back then, the agency had been fixed upon one adversary — the Soviet Union. China remained an enigma. Although it had over a billion citizens, it was a sleeping dragon, made impotent by its feudal society, its lack of sophisticated military capability and its third world economy. Back then, China was no more than a faint blip on the agency's security radar. Now, thirty-two years later, it was the name on everyone's lips.

Returning to the reality of the present and the new task before him, the balding espionage chief picked up the folder and flipped it open. After thumbing through the preamble, his eyes settled on an early despatch from London; his own despatch; the one that had followed his interrogation of the KGB agent, Pushkin; the despatch that had changed his life.

'**LONDON June 24, 1981 - TOP SECRET - Code DF1** - *Theft of Soviet missile blueprints by PLA'*... it began. He read on, hypnotised by the words he had penned all those years before...

'The Sino-Soviet Friendship Treaty of 1950 provided that Russia would help China develop an ICBM, resulting in the 'Dongfeng' or 'East Wind' project. It was a hollow treaty. Russia had only ever transferred obsolete technology to China and then, only after deploying a more advanced Russian missile itself.

Last month, two things happened to change all that. First, a Russian Embassy signal was intercepted by our London station indicating that Russia had abruptly terminated its missile program with China. Next, Moscow station reported that KGB agent, Anatoly Pushkin, had been assigned to the Russian Embassy in London as Second Secretary, Cultural, but with a covert mission, deciphered from later signals traffic, to locate and seek the return of the stolen missile blueprints. The blueprints are believed to be those of the Soviet's new CSS-3 missile.

Our mission at London station was to verify this intelligence. Attempts at further signals interception, targeting the Soviet's London Embassy, failed. Accordingly, probationary field agent R901 accepted the high-risk option of intercepting and interrogating Soviet agent Pushkin personally, under code orange conditions (hostile interdiction with government denial if exposed).

During the code orange interrogation at a remote London location, agent R901 finally broke KGB agent Pushkin, who confirmed that the stolen design was the Soviet CSS-3. This missile has a 7,000-kilometre range and a 3-megaton nuclear payload, making it a game changer in Chinese hands.

Pushkin confirmed that the blueprints had been stolen by a rogue Russian agent, disgruntled by corruption within the KGB. He also confirmed that the Chinese secret service, the 'Guojai Anquanbu', was a willing buyer, having been angered by the unilateral termination of their agreement with the Russians. The Russian defector is said to be seeking asylum in London.'

Charles Ritter paused to reflect on that extraordinary event, which had seen China suddenly emerge from military obscurity. Their damned missile had precipitated a huge reassessment of the CIA's geo-political priorities.

The theft of the Russian missile blueprints had preceded the appearance of the first cracks in the Soviet Union's giant military machine. When those cracks had opened, shortly after the Dongfeng incident, a watershed had been reached in global intelligence thinking, prompting a radical review of global threats and a redirection of resources towards north Asia.

Under the combined impacts of Russia's faltering economy, its bogus five-year plan achievements, which had been sugar-coated, its burgeoning debt and the blossoming corruption which had lined the pockets of decadent officials, Russia's military spending had become a giant sea anchor, bringing the sprawling Soviet economy to a stand-still. Then Gorbachev had introduced *Glasnost* and the first cracks had also appeared in Russia's iron-fisted central control, causing the mighty bear to stumble, small satellites to stand up to their distant master and finally, the once mighty union to slowly disintegrate. Now deeply invested in reading the historic document and the flood of vivid memories it evoked, agent Ritter read on:

'The Soviets are alarmed. If the blueprints are indeed in PLA hands, the Soviet design gives China a first strike capability against Moscow. If, indeed, these are the CSS3 blueprints, we can also expect to see production of a Dongfeng-4 ICBM fairly soon, cloning the Russian design, but with the range and capacity to reach Moscow and, critically, to reach US forces on Guam. Moreover, Beijing station has confirmed that China now has the engineering expertise to take ICBM development forward without Russian support and we have an unconfirmed report that China is now planning to equip this design, the new DF4, with additional thrust, to create a variant

for use as a space launch vehicle, under their Chang Zeng (Long March Rocket) program.'

By now, Charles Ritter was in an out-of-body state, as images of those heady days came flooding back, replaying in his mind with crystal clarity. It had been 1981. East-West tensions had been high and the ambitious young agent had been determined to prove himself. This intelligence report had given him his big break. It had built his reputation, resonating with alarming clarity and detail across the senior echelons of the CIA and, from there, escalating to the White House and setting the young field agent upon a meteoric rise to seniority.

Recruiting that explosive intelligence, however, had been at a secret cost. Ritter had broken all the rules, discovering in his testosterone-fuelled youth an enthusiasm and moral indifference that had surprised him; a quality which he later found he had in abundant measure. Keen to break the Russian and make him talk, he had allowed his passion to morph into a brutal rage, which he had since learned to control. If the agency came to know what he had done that night, his career, and his reputation, might well be at risk.

He recalled the night when he and two embassy guards - US marines - had taken Pushkin by force to the remote Docklands area of London. He had sent the marines off while he stayed behind to handle the matter personally, not wanting witnesses or their unit to be involved in his reckless breach of protocol. He had worked the Russian over a treat… gone a bit too far, in fact.

'I wonder if Pushkin ever survived?' he thought, as he reached for his coffee and looked down philosophically upon his pudgy girth - a middle-aged spread that belied the muscular, athletic young man he had once been '…or if they ever found his body behind that row of abandoned warehouses?'

While Pushkin's body had simply disappeared, the fear of its discovery had haunted Ritter. He had told London station that, after interrogating Pushkin, he had let him return to his Embassy with an undertaking, common within the 'trade', that there would be no acknowledgement of the exchange. For weeks thereafter, he had combed through the London daily

39

press, searching for an item about a body discovered on the banks of the Thames, a revelation which might have closed the door on his young career, but there had been nothing.

Someone had cleaned up. Pushkin had simply disappeared. Nonetheless, years later, the vision of that night still haunted him, replaying in his mind as if he were back in that empty warehouse, not his contemporary office, where that curious word, *Dongfeng*, continued to chew at his consciousness.

ASIO Headquarters – Canberra

A white limousine, bearing the green and gold insignia of Joint Operations Command, rolled to a stop under the portico of an imposing low-rise complex. It was a very contemporary, boomerang-shaped building, whose architect had combined glass and an earthy, marble façade to masterful effect. In its front courtyard, a gigantic flag fluttered in a gentle morning breeze, beckoning visitors into its reassuring embrace. In the vestibule, a silver sculpture, in the shape of an all-seeing eye, stood on a white marble plinth, a testament to the extravagant cost of the building and the resultant public ire it had attracted.

This was the headquarters of the Australian Security Intelligence Organisation (ASIO), the nation's premier intelligence service, built at a bewildering cost to the public purse to house some 4,000 intelligence operatives. The imposing structure had been hastily commissioned by a nervous government in answer to what its political apologists had neatly called 'the real and present dangers posed by Islamic terrorism and the fast-flowing geo-political developments on Australia's northern doorstep'. The single, most compelling reason, however, had been China's meteoric rise as a global superpower and pressure from the US, under its ANZUS Defence Pact, for Australia to ramp up its surveillance and intelligence contribution in the new, Asia-Pacific theatre of operations.

As the limousine came to rest, the driver, a Corporal from the Transport Corps, emerged from the front seat and opened the rear door for his passenger. Seated in the rear of the vehicle was a senior army officer, wearing a crisp khaki uniform bearing an impressive array of service ribbons. Two awkward legs appeared, one after the other, struggling to escape the tight confines of the rear seat, and were followed by the tall, willowy figure of Colonel Tom Grant. The former SAS officer and war hero emerged from the vehicle and stood to a commanding six feet four in height. He returned his driver's salute with crisp military precision and made his way towards the entrance foyer.

It was not difficult to appreciate why Maggie King had found him so attractive. Grant was a ruggedly handsome man, with sharply defined features. His strong chin and determined set of jaw were balanced by inquisitive blue eyes that suggested both sensitivity and calm reason. He moved easily, with an athlete's coordination, suggesting a natural, sportive flair. In his younger days at the Defence Academy, he had played rugby in the Army's First Division and represented the Defence Academy in national triathlons. Later, when he was undertaking his gruelling SAS training, he had shone through the ranks, demonstrating gritty determination and natural leadership. Now more mature, he remained extraordinarily fit despite his more sedentary, executive duties.

Tom Grant's military bearing and natural machismo belied the sharp intellect which operated beneath the surface. He was a graduate of the Australian Defence Forces Academy, the nation's elite officer training school, which also operated as a campus of the acclaimed University of New South Wales. Grant had graduated with honours in Asian Studies and been awarded the *Sword of Honour*, an accolade accorded to just one, stand-out trainee from each crop of ADFA graduates, in recognition of consistently high standards of leadership and academic achievement. The sword of honour was a passport to rapid promotion and, ultimately, to the rarefied atmosphere of the General Staff Officer Corp. Tom Grant had since added a Masters in Political Science.

While these were impressive achievements, Grant was essentially a modest man. He had always allowed his actions to speak for him, requiring few words, and the legendary status he had achieved within the military had been eked out of quiet tenacity and moments of bold leadership. During his deployment in Afghanistan, he had sprinted into a hailstorm of bullets to rescue one of his men. It was this selfless action which had earned the reluctant hero his George Cross for conspicuous bravery. The injuries he had sustained in that action, however, had resulted in his redeployment to Australia in a new policy role, attached to Joint Forces Strategic Command.

Despite this more intellectual work, Tom Grant's celebrity had continued to grow. After returning to Canberra, he had unwittingly become the target of an assassination attempt. It had happened as he travelled in a motorcade to a reception at Government House, where he was to be presented with his bravery medal. Terrorists had mistaken his vehicle for one carrying the Prime Minister and a visiting US Secretary of State. Grant had survived the attack and joined a national manhunt for the terrorists, finally running them to ground and achieving wide media coverage and national celebrity for his actions.

Although Tom Grant had been a central figure in the national manhunt, in his own mind, he had been no more than a functionary, guided by crucial intelligence from the Office of National Assessments, the premier intelligence collection and assessment agency, and by ASIO. It was ASIO's chief, Sir Robert Chandler, who had now summoned Grant to this morning's meeting, a meeting which Sir Robert had said could only be conducted 'unter vier Augen' (under four eyes). This was the term the eccentric intelligence chief often used to indicate a *top-secret* discussion. Grant had immediately agreed to the meeting, intrigued to learn about its purpose from the mercurial spy chief, nicknamed 'Lazarus' for his survival of a number of public inquiries into the cost of running his clandestine agency.

After passing through body searches and a microwave scanner, Grant emerged in front of a bank of lifts and took an elevator to the 4th floor, where Sir Robert's office was located. When the lift doors opened, the intelligence chief, a former High Commissioner, was there to greet him. Lazarus extended a gregarious hand, winked and greeted Tom warmly. Their acquaintance dated back to the national manhunt for the Islamic terrorist, Mushtak Ferraza, and had since matured into a close, personal friendship following Grant's secondment to the National Security Task Force, on which they both sat.

At first, Tom had thought that the meeting must be social, to wish him well for his first diplomatic assignment. Under the military exchange program with the US, he had been posted to New York, and would leave in a week's time. He would have a diplomatic passport and carry the title

Military Attaché, formalising his attachment to the Australian Consulate General in New York. Concurrently, he would enjoy *Visiting Fellow* status at West Point, America's leading Military Academy, and assist his US colleagues to understand the defence challenges associated with the emergent Asia Pacific theatre of military operations. The Australian military machine had, since the days of the Vietnam conflict, earned the respect of its American allies for its Asian language expertise and its capacity to analyse military threats in the unique, East-Asian theatre. Indeed, the Asian Languages School at Point Cook was a world leader, producing mandarin speakers for both the military and the Foreign Service. This gave Australia a particular niche of expertise within the western military alliance, which America now desperately needed to exploit.

The aging intelligence chief looked resplendent in an expensive, double-breasted jacket, which flowed gracefully over his voluminous girth. Somehow, Lazarus always managed to achieve an important, intellectual air, magnified by a flamboyant, silk pocket handkerchief and pink, pince-nez glasses.

Sir Robert directed Tom down the hallway towards his office and paused to exchange pleasantries with his secretary, Louise Adler. Unlike the romantic archetype of a spy-master's mistress, inspired by Hollywood fantasy, this spymaster's PA exuded quiet professionalism. She had a slim, linear figure, attractive for a woman of her years, a subtle but keen sense of humour, an exceptionally small bust and a huge intellect. However, she retained a healthy appreciation of attractive young men like Tom and enjoyed the irreverent banter which the charismatic soldier always exchanged with her.

'Morning, Louise,' said Grant with a smile and a wink. 'How's the power behind the throne?'

'Tell that to the boss,' she replied. 'And if you mean it, tell him I need a raise!' Sir Robert placed his hands around his enormous girth and laughed so enthusiastically that Louise thought he might have a convulsion. The two men then left Louise, whose real role was far more than a PA and who many conceded was the secret genius behind the nation's complex intelligence efforts, and disappeared into Lazarus' embarrassingly large suite of offices.

'First they insist that we need a much-expanded intelligence service. Next thing I know, they foist these grandiose headquarters upon us,' he cackled. 'Then they chastise me for the cost overruns associated with delivering their own monster,' he concluded. 'I wonder whether politicians ever address *function* rather than *form*. Our organisation needs good intelligence officers, not great architecture. We need good people, not a huge, fixed asset. You can't send bricks and mortar on intelligence missions and, as Ho Chi Min famously said, '*You can't eat money*!'

'Absolutely,' replied Tom Grant. 'But you *do* have the best office in the southern hemisphere, befitting the nation's most important public servant.'

Once again, Lazarus let out a loud guffaw and waddled towards the bar, situated adjacent to the lounge area in his uniquely private office.

'I know the sun is barely over the yardarm, Tom, but we could enjoy a quiet tipple, if you like. This is the only office in the entire public service where one can do so without being detected. How about a cold beer, old boy?'

'Not for me, Sir Robert. I never drink on the job. Your invitation seemed shrouded in innuendo and intrigue but, since you and I have come to know each other pretty well, I imagine it's just another one of your pranks and something much simpler, like a word of farewell,' replied Grant.

'Ah! Fair point, old boy. But I'm afraid this time there is no prank. I should have warned you that this meeting is serious business, not pleasantry. Incidentally, I do hate it when you call me Sir Robert. Everyone calls me *Lazarus* behind my back and, between you and me, I rather enjoy that. You could call me Robbie, as my close friends do. My Scottish forebears would enjoy that.'

At that point, Lazarus' laconic smile gave way to a more sombre face.

'I called you here after receiving representations from, er, let's just call them *people in high places*. What I am about to ask of you is sensitive. You may stop me at any moment. However, even though we are friends, I have to warn you that anything we say in this room is critical to our national security and nothing we discuss may be repeated. If you betray this confidence, you will be subject to the provisions of the Official Secrets Act.

Our Act is pretty punitive. It puts you behind bars for as long I need to keep you there. Is that clear?'

Tom Grant was taken aback. Up until this point in their relationship, the *Lazarus* that Tom had known had always been a jovial and eccentric security chief, whose roguish sense of humour had always defined his personality. This time there was unmistakable gravity in Lazarus' voice. His tone had changed, as suddenly as a spring dawn might change into a tempest when a storm front rolls in. Any social ease associated with his offer of a drink had vanished. Had that been another of Lazarus' cunning tests, calculated to ensure that he had a man of sober temperament in whom he could confide?

Lazarus proceeded cautiously, aware that this was a seminal moment in intelligence recruitment, when a man with no interest in clandestine activities and no need for the extra money it offered, was persuaded to serve his country as a patriot, in a dangerous and unrewarded role.

'So that's his game,' Tom suddenly realised. 'Lazarus is recruiting me. He has brought me here under false pretences, to schmooze me and win me over.'

'Lazarus... whatever you want me to call you... I came here as a friend, not an employee, expecting you to bid me a fond farewell and wish me luck, not to ambush me with some fanciful project of yours. I feel betrayed, and I have no interest in your murky intelligence work or your clandestine operations.'

Sir Robert eyed Grant thoughtfully, stroked his chin and pressed on.

'Just hear me out, Tom, before you judge me too harshly. You and I are essentially doing the same job. We would both consider ourselves patriots, striving as diligently as we can to achieve justice and equity in a corrupt world. I will understand if you simply walk away from this discussion... but, if you do, you will always wonder what it was that I called you here to discuss?'

'I don't think so, Lazarus. But since you've got me cornered in your office, I might as well hear what you have to say.'

'Good man,' replied Lazarus. 'But before I begin, I need you to sign this attest. It states that you understand and accept obligations under the National Secrets Act, including the consequences of your breaching them.'

Tom Grant was annoyed by this bureaucratic side-step and its implication that his personal integrity might be questioned by Lazarus, but he grudgingly scribbled his signature across the bottom, if only to hurry things along.

'Thank you, old man. I am sorry about these formalities. They don't detract from my high personal regard for you. They are simply necessary in the uncertain world we live in, where trust has become an out-dated concept.'

'Where do I begin? As you know, my agency, ASIO, is responsible for national security, largely based upon a domestic intelligence role, but also working hand in glove with ASIS, our Secret Intelligence Service, which has the running on the ground in foreign countries. In this particular matter, the PM has given me overarching authority in a joint operation with ASIS to get to the bottom of a vexing issue. Last week, Bob Murray, a trusted operative at the Office of National Assessments, passed on some intel about north Asia that rather worries us. As you know, Beijing recently carried out a geographical survey of islands in the East China Sea, whose ownership they are disputing with Japan. While this seems innocuous in the scheme of things, China's move has greatly heightened tension with Tokyo, whose new Prime Minister, Shinato Mitabe, is starting to shape up as a hawkish, right wing fellow.'

'I know Bob well,' replied Grant, 'and I would trust him with my life. But I am off to North America, not North Asia, and I don't see how I can help you.'

'Bear with me, Tom,' Lazarus continued. 'When China announced its plan to survey the islands, it sent a Chinese survey aircraft close to, but not inside, the islands' airspace, as if the islands were already part of the Chinese mainland. Next thing, Japan scrambled a squadron of fighter jets and the tensions have been building ever since, like steam in a pressure cooker.'

'Last week, Bob intercepted another disturbing piece of intel, confirming that China's Supreme Command had issued formal instructions to its armed forces, instituting a one-year training program for a battle they said 'must be won, to regain lost territories'. As if this were not sufficient evidence of a dangerous escalation, a field operative attached to our Tokyo station then confirmed that US and Japanese fighter jets would undertake regular airstrike exercises over waters adjacent to the islands, bringing American forces directly into the equation. We think this a reckless action and a real foreign policy blunder by the US administration. They ought to have known better.'

'As you will be aware from your work on the Joint Forces Strategic Command, Japan's new PM is a hawk. He is brimming with confidence, having won office by a landslide after promising to reinvigorate Japan's military alliance with America and to take a much tougher line against Beijing. Our Office of National Assessments suggests that we view this development through the prism of the US pulling its huge military machine out of Afghanistan but needing to redeploy it somewhere else to maintain the economic stimulus of the military spend. Part of that equation is brinkmanship to beef up the US military presence in Darwin.'

'This all adds up to a perfect storm, right on our northern frontier. The dispute over the islands, known as the Diaoyu group in Beijing and the Senkaku group in Tokyo, has simmered quietly for years. Now it has suddenly come to a head, following Japan's abrupt decision to nationalise the few islands it does not already control. You will probably have followed media reports about the angry demonstrations in China. China doesn't usually allow public protests, but this time the protests were condoned by the Communist regime, which saw them as bolstering China's claims to legitimacy, and fuelling condemnation of Japan's actions in the minds of its ordinary citizens, who have not forgotten the Japanese invasion of China in the 20th century.'

'China describes its cartographic survey project as *"part of a programme to map China's territorial islands and reefs and safeguard its maritime rights"*. In a massively naïve understatement, its National Administration of Surveying, Mapping and Geo-information has issued a

48

statement conceding that there could be "*difficulties with landing our survey teams on some of these disputed islands, and in surveying and mapping the surrounding sea areas, where some other countries have infringed and occupied these islands of China*". '

'Last week, our covert ops man at Tokyo station reported another round of joint operations, involving six US FA-18 fighters and around ninety American personnel, with four Japanese F-4 jets and an unspecified number of people. Our intel disclosed plans for a five-day war game, described internally as "*Japan's first military exercise designed to recapture a remote island invaded by an enemy force*". We have since learned that the US persuaded Japan to drop its plan for a "*simulated retaking of remote islands*", reportedly because NATO reacted angrily and told the US it should not provoke Beijing this way.'

'Although we are troubled by these developments, we think we have a good handle on what the Chinese and Japanese are doing. Our own intel resources in North Asia are second to none. What troubles us is the fragile state of the US economy, the massive loss of national face the US has suffered as its economy baulks and China's rapid emergence, which has challenged US superpower authority. As if to rub salt into America's wounds, China now owns almost one third of US foreign debt. The Yanks have never been much good at diplomacy, or at clever foreign policy, seeing every issue through the narrow lens of their own self-interest, so we are worried how all of this might translate in the minds of America's more hawkish politicians and Generals.'

'That's where you come in, Tom. We need you to get inside those minds and apply your well-proven analytical skills to determine what the Americans are thinking. You have the network of senior military contacts, you will be attached to our diplomatic mission in New York and we have arranged with our Ambassador that you be given free rein to travel regularly to Washington and given all the support you may need from our mission there. What do you say?'

'I say why the hell did you call me here? I report to a General. I certainly don't report to bureaucrats or spy chiefs,' protested Tom. 'What will the Defence Minister, or his mate, the Minister for Foreign Affairs, say when they hear about this reckless endangerment of our relationship with the US? How often does one close ally spy on the other?' he asked.

'Oh, much more frequently than you may think, my dear old thing. Since you ask, I can tell you that both the Foreign Minister and the Defence Minister *have* been consulted, at a meeting held in the Prime Minister's office two days ago, and they are all on board with the proposal. You clearly made an impression when you took down those terrorists last year. They all thought you were just the right man for the job,' countered Lazarus. 'The project was then approved by the National Security Committee of Cabinet. That should tell you how seriously we take this matter and the lofty heights to which I had to go to get the project approved.'

'Incidentally, you should be happy with the extra perks I have arranged for you. You will have a nice, spacious apartment in New York, opposite Bryant Park. It will be regularly swept by us but we will be as inconspicuous as possible. Its proximity to Bryant and Central Parks will satisfy your passion for an early morning jog,' concluded Lazarus with a smile. 'I have also arranged for you to have an aide-de-camp and a consular vehicle at your disposal. The aide is our man, under cover of course, and he will report directly to you.

He will be accredited as a member of the consular driving pool. He is really an IT boffin, with an SAS background, like yours. Thankfully, he is also a good driver. He will need to be. Your consular vehicle is a black, special edition Mercedes Kompressor. It will look like a sedate little street car, but it will have 5.2 litres of grunt under the hood, stabilisers and low-profile racing tyres, in case you need to put space between yourself and any adversary, though I think that unlikely. Oh, and we had to re-engineer the front seats to take your long legs, so there's just a narrow jump seat in the back. I love our creative boffins and their thoroughness! Most of the time you will just be a defence attaché, but one with extra perks to lighten your daily load,' chortled Lazarus.

Tom was impressed. Lazarus had thought of everything. The manipulative old scoundrel had added enough sweeteners to make Tom's New York posting more attractive than it might otherwise have been, albeit with some risks.

'Let me think about it, and I'll get back to you,' said Tom.

'By close of business today, if you don't mind, Tom,' Lazarus added with a rueful smile. 'And I really hope you don't disappoint me. God knows what that would do to my careful plans. Your aide-de-camp, our undercover man, is already in the air, you see, sent ahead to sort things out, and your new vehicle is on its way.'

'I hope I have not taken too much liberty in setting these arrangements in train, before asking you,' he said with a grin. 'Happy landings, Colonel.'

CIA Headquarters, Langley VA

It was Friday morning and the end of a busy week at the agency, so the prospect of the weekend break had everyone in a jovial mood. Deputy Director Charles Ritter turned to the next report, which had just come in from the CIA's London station. It was another, coded despatch from the desk of a loveable, if slightly eccentric field operative, Bill Robertson, who Ritter had personally assigned there with the single purpose of pirating British intelligence. Robertson was respected in the trade as a master hacker and known affectionately, within the ranks of the CIA, as 'Round-eyes Robbo' for his large spectacles. The hugely intellectual Robbo was not even vaguely reminiscent of the field operatives of old. His exaggerated proboscis and rotund figure made him an un-athletic enigma, belying the Bond-like myth that intelligence officers were all svelte and sportive types. Indeed, Robbo walked with a slight limp. Despite these deficiencies, no one in the agency had Robbo's uncanny knack for farming cyber space for new intel. He was an extraordinarily valuable asset and always came up with results.

'How things have changed,' mused Ritter, as he thought back to his days as a young agent attached to London station. In those days, recruits had been required to pass an exacting physical, favouring track and field types. These days, one hour's work by a clever computer nerd could produce a rich payload of intelligence, while a dashing, old-school field operative would take days, months or even years to produce the same result.

Ritter had researched the Dongfeng in depth, concluding that it was a fairly innocuous, outdated ICBM - one which appeared to offer only a limited threat in the constellation of much more potent missiles deployed around the globe. Wanting to confirm this conclusion, he had asked Robbo to find out what the Brits might have on the mercurial old missile. That message had, of course, been covertly delivered by Robbo's controller, a dapper attaché at the US Embassy in London. When one was a diplomat at London station asking one's own spies to spy on one's own allies, one had to do so discreetly!

As Ritter read through Robbo's report, hacked with characteristic efficiency from British SIS files (the Secret Intelligence Service), he realised that he was onto something big. The SIS was an overarching body directing a number of divisions, including the famous MI5, responsible for domestic security, and MI6, responsible for foreign intelligence operations. Robbo's report explained why research into the Dongfeng had come to a dead end. The Chinese had changed the missile's name, to recognise a new configuration and design.

Indeed, the accent in Robbo's report was not upon the land-based Dongfeng, deployed in China's underground Great Wall system, but rather, upon an upgraded version of it called the 'Ju Lang' or 'Giant Wave' missile, with global reach and under-sea launch capability, using nuclear submarines as the launch platform. Just as the old Dongfeng had been a game changer in its day, so too was this new, under-sea variant of the Dongfeng.

Ritter had always dismissed claims that US military dominance was being eroded by the Chinese and played down State Department reports, written by naïve young diplomats who wouldn't know jack shit, that the Chinese were bridging the military gap. The Agency had always supported colleagues at Defence, even at the level of Defence Secretary Leon Perry, who stubbornly maintained that the US military machine had no peer and could swat any adversary as easily as one swats a fly. Hadn't they proven that with Schwarzkopf's 'Shock and Awe' campaign in Iraq? Well, thought Ritter, Robbo's report might change that complacency. He began reading...

DONGFENG GOES UNDER-SEA – Source: MI5 Sct. 438 CHINESE TYPE 094 SUBMARINE USED as PLATFORM

Verification of source material:

(i) This report is distilled from British intelligence reports. The British, for their part, have included information farmed from Japanese covert surveillance reports, obtained clandestinely by British agents in Tokyo, and

from western satellite surveillance of China's State-owned Hulu Dao shipyards.

(ii) Executive overview:

In 2004, China commenced what it called 'The Dongfeng Under-sea Program', giving itself a horizon of ten years to achieve operational deployment, using upgraded, Jin Class nuclear submarines as the new launch platform. The project was the plaything of China's brilliant young military strategist, General Zhang Ming Wei. This development has been well guarded and details are thus still sketchy, most coming from British and Australian intel and from articles published in Jane's journal of warcraft, with vociferous denials from the Chinese.

The new, under-sea Dongfeng (East Wind) has been renamed the Ju Lang-2 (Giant Wave-2) missile. It comprises a two-stage, solid liquid fuel rocket design with a range of 7,000 kilometres for the basic version, 12,000 kilometres for the Mk II (JL2-Jia) version and 14,000 kilometres for the Mk III (JL2-Yi) version. However, its under-sea deployment, on a silent, infinite-power nuclear submarine platform, gives it a much improved range and strike capacity.

The new Dongfeng, underwater variation is thought to carry a payload of up to three warheads (MIRVs) of about 250 kilotons each, and therefore provides China with its first, credible, sea-based nuclear deterrent. Our hitherto flippant disregard for Chinese nuclear capability must now, therefore, be the subject of an embarrassing rethink and gives grounds for serious internal analysis and debate.

(iii) Summary of Nuclear Submarine platform:

The Chinese Jin-class is a ballistic missile submarine developed by the Chinese PLO's Naval Force. The first-of-class was constructed at Hulu Dao Shipyard in Hulu Dao, Liaoning, and launched in July 2004. A further six submarines are believed to have since been constructed and more are planned.

Type:	*094 ('Jin' Class)*
Builder:	*Bohai Shipyard, Hulu Dao*
Operator:	*People's Republic of China - PLO Navy*
Predecessor:	*'Xia' Class submarine (Type 092)*
Planned successor:	*'Tang' Class (Type 096)*
Date brought into service:	*2010*
Number operating in service:	*7*
Displacement:	*8,000 tons surface; 11,000 tons submerged*
Length:	*133 metres*
Propulsion:	*Nuclear reactor, using one drive shaft*
Speed:	*Est. Over 20 Knots*
Range:	*Unlimited*
Armament:	*Six 533 mm Torpedoes*
Missile payload:	*Fifty to fifty-two Jin Class (JL2) submerged launch ballistic missiles (SLBMs).*

Charles Ritter whistled, as the gravity of this analysis sank in. The Chinese were catching up fast, maybe even leaving the US navy in their wake, at least in the Pacific, as they ramped up to full deployment of their seven nuclear subs. On the positive side, this made the land-based Dongfengs obsolete and China's incredible underground Great Wall a vast, white elephant.

'That's good,' thought Ritter. 'This latest report clearly shows that the Dongfeng poses no threat. That should allow me to make a case for winding up the investigation. Thank God. That will put the past to rest, and my involvement with Pushkin need never come to light.'

Ritter resolved to use Robbo's excellent new intel as the basis for an attention-grabbing report to the Defence Appropriation Committee. He would send the old files on the old, land-based Dongfeng back to the basement, where his secret would lie buried forever, and release his new report about the under-sea variant and its deployment on nuclear subs. A report like that would resonate within government and earn him some high accolades, as the US administration came to terms with this new threat. Ritter adjusted his chair and began typing with new vigour, buoyed by the thought that this report would ensure his succession to the top job.

Excited by this prospect, he decided to make an immediate start on the report. That way, he could take his first draft home over the weekend and give it a final polish. He would need a peaceful environment to build a well-argued, skilfully worded case. He instructed his PA that he was not to be disturbed and turned to his computer, quickly becoming engrossed in his work and completely oblivious to time and space. Before he knew it, it was 6.50 p.m., and he was jolted back to reality by his PA, who knocked at his door, just as he was completing the last paragraphs of his report.

'Come in,' he called, unaware of the lateness of the hour.

'Excuse me, sir,' responded his PA. 'Your driver is wondering whether he should wait or whether you will drive yourself home. What shall I tell him?'

'Oh, thank you, Sally. I had no idea it was so late. Tell him to drop the keys in and you run along too. I have my late-night pass with me and a bit more report writing to complete before I lock up for the weekend.'

Ritter turned back to his report, as his PA busied herself with the ritual close-down procedure, which she repeated at the end of each work day.

Access to the executive floor, shared by the Agency's Director, Deputy Director and their respective staffers, was controlled by a five-digit password keypad. After 6.00 p.m., this measure was strengthened by the need to pass through a series of eye scan and thumb scan stations, which gave access, in turn, to the lift well on each floor, to the ground floor vestibule and to the executive car park, beneath the building.

Two hours later, Chuck Ritter completed a spell check, saved the document and closed the lid to his laptop. He was pleased with his report. It gave a comprehensive analysis of the emerging Chinese nuclear threat, in articulate language backed up by agent Robertson's excellent intelligence on the new generation *Giant Wave* missile. It was pretty much final text, as it stood, but he always liked to sleep on a report and to review it again more dispassionately later. He decided to stow his laptop in a secure, aluminium attaché case, the ones provided by the agency, with a wrist chain and digitally operated combination lock, and take the report home with him to review it more thoroughly over the weekend.

He navigated his way through the maze of security hurdles and emerged in the basement car park, where he unchained the security briefcase containing his laptop, threw it onto the passenger seat beside him and slid in behind the wheel. The car park exit would take him into a tunnel which emerged in the surrounding streetscape. There were lots of myths about CIA Headquarters. While it was described as being located in Langley, Virginia, its exact street address was never published. The old HQ had been at 2430 East Street NW, not far from Washington, but the new headquarters had moved to the George Bush Centre for Intelligence, not in Langley, but in suburban McLean. The centre had a tightly controlled public façade. Private, vehicular access, provided for senior executives, was located remote from the front driveway and not generally known.

Ritter emerged from the public exit ramp leading from the agency car park and turned right, heading towards his home, which was located in the upmarket, north-eastern sector of McLean. As he did so, a shadowy figure in a black Corvette, which was parked at the curb side diagonally opposite the exit ramp, turned his ignition key, fired up his sporty V8 and rolled quietly into the traffic flow behind the CIA Deputy Chief's vehicle.

Ritter rubbed the back of his neck and shook the cramp out of his tight shoulders. He had been at his desk all day and needed to loosen up. He had no family to race home to. His first and only marriage, to his college sweetheart, had ended badly. Whenever the young chauvinist had hung out with the boys for a drink, his child bride had accused him of ignoring her or of chasing other women, which he did. His response was always to arc up, assume a florid face and give her a burst of his famously quick temper. One day, when she had kept on at him, he had lost it completely and hit her with a closed fist. She had run to mummy and taken an AVO out against him, just two years into their marriage. What the hell. Life had been much better without that female crap, and he had since accepted that he was not cut out to be married, preferring his new, bachelor lifestyle.

He turned off the main drag into *Old Dominion Drive*. This was a longer route home, but it took him past *McKeever's Bar*, widely touted as *the best fake Irish pub in the greater McLean area*. McKeever's burgers were exceptionally good, too, and a wide screen TV usually played Ritter's favourite ball game to a rousing audience of beer-swilling, male patrons. Ritter pulled into the rear car park, killed the lights and began to exit his vehicle. Then he suddenly remembered the metal attaché case and its security chain, sitting on the passenger seat beside him. It contained the final draft of his report on the Dongfeng missile and its nuclear submarine variant. He could not leave it lying in full sight, in the public domain.

'To hell with it,' thought Ritter. 'I'll sling it in the trunk and fix the wrist chain around the spare wheel assembly. That should keep it secure.'

As Ritter completed these tasks, a black Corvette entered from the other side of the car park and pulled silently into a vacant bay. Its occupant watched from his shadowy position as the spy chief popped the trunk of his vehicle, slid the aluminium attaché case into it and leaned into the cavernous rear storage area to fasten the security chain to the wheel bay. He watched Ritter close the trunk on the highly secret report, saw him turn from the vehicle and followed his progress towards the popular night spot.

Two hours later, at approximately 11 p.m., Ritter re-emerged into the now largely deserted car park and made an unsteady path towards his vehicle. He pressed the door release button on his key ring and was reassured when the blinker lights flashed and he heard the characteristic click of the doors unlocking. He slid into the driver's seat, bent forward and fumbled with his key, which he struggled to insert into the ignition - clearly affected by too much alcohol. He finally found the ignition hole, inserted the key and settled back in his seat for the drive home. At precisely the same moment as he rocked back into his seat, a dark figure leaned over from the rear seat, pulled a sack over the startled security chief's head and instructed him, in heavily accented English, to place his hands on the dashboard. The disorientation Ritter felt as a result of the sack over his head and the determined voice of his assailant, made him immediately comply. No sooner had he placed his hands on the dashboard than he felt the sharp prick of a needle being jabbed into his neck. He tried to find the strength to resist, but his immediate response was nausea, followed by a rapidly growing weakness in his limbs and finally, a complete surrender to the darkness which flooded over his fading consciousness.

When Ritter's body finally slumped forward, his assailant settled back into the rear seat, retrieved his mobile phone and prepared an SMS message for his North-American field agent, Sergei Kerin, codenamed *Peregrine*.

'Package 1 - Nightrider - taken down. Package 2 - DF file - secured. Request assistance to transfer packages and stow vehicle' – Red Bear'

State Wildlife Reserve, John Mosely Highway, VA

As Ritter slowly regained consciousness, he became aware of a bright light, which he recognised as the penetrating rays of a late morning sun, burning through the windows of the small hunting lodge in which he was held captive. His head throbbed and his parched mouth protested to his addled brain that it desperately needed hydration. Was his splitting headache the result of his overindulgence at McKeever's the night before, he wondered, or of the toxic chemical which had been used to knock him out, and had left a bitter astringency on his tongue? A gag had been tied around his mouth, denying him the ability to express any protest and making it almost impossible to swallow. As his vision cleared, he squinted in protest at the brightness and peered through the window glass at the surrounding terrain. The small hut he was in seemed to be nestled in a clearing, ringed by huge Douglas firs, suggesting he was in the middle of a State forest.

He tried to move his arms and legs, finding that they were tightly bound. As his eyes adjusted to the brightness, he was able to assess his situation more closely, analysing his predicament. There was a haunting sense of déjà vu about his circumstances. He was trussed up in a medical straight jacket, whose sleeves were wrapped around his torso and fastened behind his back, restraining any attempt to move his arms. His body was strapped to a wooden chair, secured there by a rope around his waist and with separate ropes binding his ankles to the front chair legs, so that any attempt to move them would send him, and the chair, toppling to the floor. The room was bare of furniture, save for a wooden deal table, three other chairs and a bunk bed. A duffle bag had been left in one corner, with a torch, some clothes and other paraphernalia lying on the floor next to it.

Ritter suffered in his immobilising restraints for what seemed an eternity. The ropes around his ankles were cutting into his flesh and his

60

muscles cried out in pain. Through bloodshot eyes, he watched the sun slowly crawl across the forest canopy and sink lower, towards a dull twilight. By the time it had dropped below the horizon, Ritter had slumped forward, weakened and parched by the lack of water or sustenance and fighting to remain conscious in the prison chair to which he had been tied. Finally, the torment of his lonely isolation was broken by the distant sound of an approaching engine. He could hear the engine revving as it climbed the escarpment and drew nearer, finally bursting into the clearing and skidding to a halt in front of the hut. An elderly man, wearing a lumber jacket and a hat pulled down over his eyes, emerged from the vehicle and made his way towards the hut, dragging a crippled leg behind him. He was accompanied by a muscular, younger man.

Ritter heard a key turn in the door and the clunking sound of the crude lock releasing. Then the door was flung open and the elderly man entered and limped towards his victim, dragging his crippled leg behind him. He finally came to rest in front of Ritter and looked down at him through a badly disfigured face. The man's face seemed to be simultaneously smiling and scowling, so twisted were its features. One eye remained fixed, while the other moved. The fixed eye was set into a knot of damaged tissue surrounding the eye socket. Scar tissue also ran down the side of his face from the damaged eye, immobilising muscles on that side of the face, so that the mouth sagged a little. Ritter attempted to scream an angry protest, but his voice was muffled by the tight gag. All that he could manage was an unintelligible grunt. The crippled old man looked on impassively, while his younger companion checked the restraints around Ritter's torso, before standing behind him with a restraining hand on each of Ritter's shoulders. Then a tortured smile appeared on one side of the older man's badly scarred face and he began to mouth a heavily accented introduction.

'It has been a long time, Charles Ritter. Remember me? Your old friend from London. What is it… thirty-two years? It's me! Anatoly Pushkin, your friend from the Soviet mission. You should have finished me off back then, Ritter, when you had the chance. But you didn't, and I managed to claw my way back to the highway, inch by inch, dragging my shattered knee. Now it's my turn to have some fun with you, don't you think?'

61

'By the way, I have the attaché case. Nice job, Ritter, but I will be making a few changes before I give your report to your colleagues on the hill. We will be leaving your body as a calling card, making it look like the Chinese don't appreciate the terrible things you say about them. Sound familiar?'

Ritter's eyes bulged in disbelief. Sweat ran down his face, as memories of his torture of Pushkin came flooding back. He knew, in that seminal moment, that he would face a gruesome end. He attempted to cry out, but the result was another muffled groan, even more ridiculous than his first.

Pushkin, on the other hand, was relishing every moment. Now Director General of the FSBR (the successor to the KGB), Pushkin had personally sanctioned the interception of Ritter's Dongfeng report. As soon as he had known that Ritter would be its author, he had pleaded with Moscow station to let him run the mission out of their US station, so he could even the score with Ritter. Despite Moscow's initial reservations, his American station controller, *Peregrine*, had been forced to support the ageing spy chief's request, pledging local assistance with the take down and dedicating the resources of his field team. Codenamed *Red Bear* for this mission, Pushkin would direct the operation. He had directed this first stage magnificently, it seemed. Now he looked forward to the end game, when he would personally snuff out the life of the sadistic American. He was already relishing the astonished look in Ritter's eyes. And there was something else Pushkin had to look forward to – even more satisfying than exacting his revenge on Ritter. As a plausible cover for his visit to the US, Moscow had agreed that Pushkin might book into a famous orthopaedic clinic in Boston, for a knee reconstruction and prosthesis, at their expense.

Pushkin was exhilarated by the sadistic moment of what he planned to do to Ritter. It was much more humane that Ritter's treatment of him had been, all those years ago, but it was an intelligence master stroke, which would have far-reaching consequences. Limping to the corner of the room, he removed a small, electric soldering iron from a duffle bag. He attached it to an extension lead and plugged it into an outlet, watching a feather of smoke rise from its metal tip, which soon glowed red. Satisfied with this result, he placed the soldering iron on a heat pad, turned and limped back towards Ritter. His accomplice, the younger, more muscular agent Peregrine, stood aside as Pushkin approached. When Pushkin was positioned directly in front of Ritter, he calmly reached into his lumber jacket and produced a large, silver handgun, a Glock, with a kick like a mule. Ritter's eyes bulged in terror as the elderly Russian raised the weapon, pointed its huge muzzle at the centre of Ritter's forehead and calmly pulled the trigger. Ritter's head recoiled as the force of the Glock's bullet punched through his forehead, killing him instantly. His body rocked slowly backwards, twitched briefly, then slumped forward again, his eyes still fixed in a look of pure astonishment. The back of Ritter's skull was now completely missing and its contents, which had been expelled as a fine spray of grey tissue and blood, now coated the wall behind him.

Calmly passing his handgun to his assistant, Pushkin now rummaged in his pocket for a small slip of paper, with two characters written on it. He spread it on the floor and studied it carefully. Next, he motioned for his accomplice to hold Ritter's sagging torso in an upright position, retrieved the electric welding iron and began painstakingly burning the Chinese characters into Ritter's forehead. The coroner would later note that the first, 东, *Dong*, was burnt into the left occipital lobe, and the second, 风, *Feng*, into the right occipital lobe.

Just as Ritter had disposed of Pushkin's body on the Isle of Dogs, Pushkin would now dispose of Ritter's body. This time, however, he would place it strategically, at Ritter's home in McLean, to ensure that the message, apparently left by the Chinese on his forehead, found its way to Ritter's employer, the CIA. First, however, there was some cleaning up to do and some important foreign policy work to be completed.

Pushkin's accomplice pulled on surgical gloves, freed Ritter's corpse from its restraints and wrapped the agent's limp body in a large sheet of black plastic, securing its ends with tape to contain the coagulating blood still flowing from Ritter's gaping head wound. Next, he attached a rope around the package and dragged it onto the front porch. Then he returned to his vehicle, backed it up until its rear abutted the porch, popped its trunk and rolled the corpse into its spacious void. He replaced his bloodied gloves with a fresh pair of surgical gloves, to prevent any finger prints or DNA contamination. Then, he retrieved Ritter's metal attaché case from the back seat of the vehicle, along with the blue-tooth remote control used to enter its digital access code, and re-entered the cabin. Pushkin and his accomplice, *Peregrine,* had removed the steel wrist chain securing the case to the wheel well in Ritter's vehicle, using bolt cutters. However, the aluminium attaché case remained locked. In the centre of its top, there was a digital read-out panel, requiring a ten-digit access code to be entered using the remote control, which they had recovered with it. The correct security code would be necessary to make the lock yield. Without the code, Pushkin would have to open the metal case with an angle grinder, betraying the fact that the case had been tampered with.

Pushkin laid the metal case down carefully on the wooden table in the hut, not wanting it to show any signs of tampering, and pointed its front panel towards him. 'Ten digits,' he thought. 'What could they be? Maybe a word, followed or preceded by some zeros.' Pushkin started by punching into the remote control ten digits spelling *d o n g f e n g 00*. Nothing. Then he tried *00 d e n g f e n g*. Still nothing. He experimented with *c h u k r i t t e r*, but still the lock refused to budge. Finally, on a wild hunch, he punched in the word *i s l e o f d o g s,* comprising exactly ten digits. His face distorted into a beaming smile, as the security panel lit up, displayed the code in red digits, blinked twice and released the locking mechanism. He was then able to slide back the clips securing either end of the case and open it.

Still wearing the protective gloves, he removed Ritter's laptop from the briefcase, placed it on an adjacent table and powered it up. The familiar Microsoft desktop lit up, with its familiar array of desktop icons, and Pushkin began his search for any sign of the document which Russian intelligence had indicated must be there - Ritter's report to the US Congressional Committee of Inquiry into China's nuclear capability. His eyes quickly found a file labelled *Dongfeng*, which he opened. There it was; Ritter's draft, in all of its carefully-researched glory! Pushkin was ecstatic. All he now needed to do was creatively manipulate its contents.

Disinformation – the planting of plausible but false information – was the bread and butter of good counter-intelligence work, and Pushkin was a master of the technique. His mission was to sow seeds of political discontent between China and the USA, as the two nations were building a new, practical détente, while relations between the US and Russia were deteriorating rapidly over Russia's involvement in the Ukraine. Pushkin's counter-intelligence challenge was to find a means of creating new antipathy towards China. He would try to amplify China's growing belligerence in the South China Sea and, more generally, in the Pacific. The best way to achieve this, he had already decided, was to create and expose a new, Chinese military threat, but he had not yet decided just how that might be achieved. He would leave most of the narrative as it was, in Ritter's own, unmistakable words, and add some credible misinformation, calculated to distort reality and ignite American hostility towards China.

The words, moreover, must be inserted using Ritter's own keyboard.

Before proceeding to the task of introducing these creative changes, Pushkin beckoned his field agent, *Peregrine,* to sit with him so that they might go over the next steps in the delicate counter-intelligence operation, particularly those requiring the younger man's physical participation. Pushkin had insisted that he would deal with Ritter personally, but he realised that his crippled leg made it impossible for him to manage Ritter's transfer from the car and other physical aspects, by himself. Peregrine had thus been summoned to the nightclub carpark to handle those details. Now there was more physical work to be done by the younger Russian agent. Ritter's body would need to be relocated to his home and his vehicle needed to be sanitised offsite and delivered back to its position in Ritter's driveway. The vehicle would be the first thing the CIA would look for when Ritter failed to show up for work the following Monday morning.

Always meticulous in his attention to detail, Pushkin had thus instructed *Peregrine* to deliver Ritter's body back to his home and locate it in a slumped position in the lounge area. He was then to drive the CIA vehicle back to their safe house, sanitise it, return it to Ritter's home and routinely park it in Ritter's driveway. Peregrine and Pushkin would then have to find a hiding place for the attaché case and laptop, containing the altered report, somewhere inside Ritter's home. All of this needed to be completed quickly and discreetly.

When their work was completed, the presence of Ritter's vehicle in his own driveway would confirm that the CIA Deputy Director had made it home alive and subsequently hidden his report in a secure location. Investigators would conclude that he had been killed later, by an unknown intruder. The Russians would make it look as though all of these events had transpired inside Ritter's home, rather than remote from it, to lend credibility to the idea that the briefcase and the report it contained had not been found or tampered with. It would have to remain intact, with its contents still protected by the ten-digit access code, so the CIA would conclude that the report remained genuine. The Russian pair would also remove any trace of the wrist chain from the wheel hub, so that it would appear that Ritter had taken the attaché case home without its security chain attached. Having worried over these details with his younger field agent, Pushkin returned to Ritter's report, switched on a desk lamp and began scrolling through the text for logical holes in the narrative where he could insert a few, critical variations. His 'misinformation' would need to be inserted in such a way as to retain the essential flow of Ritter's report.

Pushkin decided to read the report from cover to cover, before returning to the section headed 'technical capability'. It was apparent from this section of the report that China's ageing Dongfeng missile, still deployed in the archaic, underground network of silos stretching across China's southern coastline, had become entirely obsolete both because of new, bunker busting technology and because the Chinese had since deployed a new, under-sea variant of the missile, able to be launched from its new fleet of nuclear submarines. Pushkin decided he would have to find a way to make the obsolete, land-based Dongfengs come to life again. He would have to give them a new upgrade and a menacing new purpose... but how?

Then a brilliant idea began to form in his mind. He recalled an intelligence report from the early 60s, when he was a young field agent, about the unintended consequences of a US nuclear test in the upper atmosphere. The detonation had sent an electro-magnetic pulse back to earth, upsetting electronic equipment, radio signals and a host of other electrical services in Hawaii. This had given rise to concerns, in both the

USA and the Soviet Union, that an upper-atmosphere detonation could be used as a tactical weapon. He determined that he must contact Moscow station as soon as possible, requesting detailed background on the upper atmosphere detonation, with a view to garnering credible technical data to insert into Ritter's report. If he could make it look like the Chinese planned to use their existing land-based missiles in that way, that would constitute a major, new Chinese military threat. That was what he needed to turn Western eyes toward China and away from Russia. He would need the data from Moscow within 24 hours to allow time to insert it into Ritter's report, creating a credible, new missile threat, and leaving enough time to secrete it back into Ritter's home before dawn broke on the next business day, Monday.

JFK International Airport, New York

The Qantas Airbus A380 'Superjumbo' banked gently and began its steep descent from 38,000 feet into JFK. Shortly thereafter, the two-storey, 550 passenger luxury airliner deployed its huge stabilisers and flaps, resulting in a characteristic braking sensation and a rumbling vibration. These subtle noises were followed by a metallic clunk as the sixteen-wheel landing arrays were lowered into the turbulent airstream and locked into place.

Colonel Tom Grant peered out of his business class window at the spires of the sprawling metropolis below him, which would become his home for the next year. New York was the financial heart of the world's most successful experiment in free-wheeling capitalism. A capitalism which had become a pervasive, global economic fundament, but which had recently faltered dramatically. Greedy Wall Street traders had ventured into unchartered waters, financing their taste for malt whisky, Bentleys and ever larger annual bonuses, by leveraging new levels of debt and securing it with bogus security instruments which had no value or enforceability.

'Why the hell don't governments let banks fail when they do things like that?' wondered Grant, recalling the unprecedented bailouts required to rescue Freddie Mac, Fannie Mae, Lehman Brothers and other insolvent icons of the banking and finance sector. Terrified of losing their banking system, the Federal Reserve had no option but to rescue them, grudgingly reinforcing the reality that the banks considered themselves above governments. Apparently, they were. Tom deplaned and made his way towards Customs and Immigration but was intercepted by an athletic looking young man in weekend casuals holding a placard with Tom's name on it. How the hell had he gotten through all of the barriers, thought Tom, as he approached the man with the placard and introduced himself?

'I'm Tom Grant. You must be from the Consulate.'

'Welcome to the Big Apple, Colonel Grant. I am Mike Stephens; Corporal Stephens, when I am in uniform. I am listed in the Diplomatic directory as your aide-de-camp and will be your driver during your short term posting here as Defence Attaché. I understand we have a mutual friend in Canberra, a Lazarus-like gentleman who will have told you a bit about my background in the SAS and my other role here,' said Mike with a wink, extending a firm handshake and greeting his new boss warmly.

'Indeed we have,' replied Tom. 'And he speaks highly of you. He sends his regards and says you should not "Ace" me too often, whatever that means.'

'Oh, that! Lazarus nicknames me 'Ace' because I play tennis, but I have heard that you play a mean game of tennis too,' replied Mike. 'We'll have a chance to test that soon. As a member of the senior consular staff, you are entitled to memberships of the New York Health & Racquet Club. If I'm a good boy, you might even agree to sign me in occasionally,' he joked. 'It has a great gym, squash courts, indoor tennis… the works. And it is within jogging distance of your apartment. But the *real* reason Lazarus calls me *"Ace"*,' he explained, lowering his voice, but confident that he could speak freely on this remote piece of tarmac, 'is to make fun of the clumsy codename for my American field work, which is 'Tennessee'.

Stephens led Colonel Tom Grant through a side gate designated '*VIPs, Diplomatic Staff and Flight Crews Only*', where his documents were stamped and he was summarily ushered through with a courteous nod.

They wheeled Grant's baggage to a curb side zone marked 'CD', where his modified diplomatic vehicle, a black Mercedes, waited to spirit him through the approach roads to Manhattan. Grant would take up temporary residence at the Andaz, on 5th Avenue, until his effects arrived by sea, and then move into permanent accommodation just around the corner.

'The Andaz is a great little boutique hotel, opposite Bryant Park,' explained Stephens, as they made their way into the city. 'Its location gives you a chance to get to know your neighbourhood better and Bryant Park doubles as a great jogging track. Each lap of the park is exactly one kilometer, so you can measure the distance you run by the number of laps. Oh, and opposite the entrance, in 42nd Street, there is an Irish Pub which screens rugby tests, something unique in the States, where everyone follows American football, baseball and basketball. Hope that works for you.'

'Sounds ideal,' said Grant. 'When we get to the Andaz, I hope you'll excuse me if check straight in and crash. I've crossed the dateline and arrived in the States a day before I left, after nearly 29 hours in the air, waiting for domestic connections and all. What time do we start tomorrow?'

'Up to you, sir. We defence attachés work pretty independently. We are not bound by the same work hours as career diplomats or, for that matter, by their office routine. However, you will need to make a courtesy call on the Consul General before you settle in. He's a good bloke, is security cleared to top secret and has been briefed about your mission here. He is very keen to help. You should probably also attend Happy Hour on Friday evenings, so you get to know the consular and support staff. Although we're not really part of their foreign relations show, we need to maintain a close collegiate relationship with them all. That makes our cover role more credible and ensures that we look like real *dipos* to any outside observer. There's also *Prayers* every Friday morning. That's when section heads gather around a large table with the head of mission and share any major developments in their areas, though we won't be doing much sharing. It's safer if the other staff remain blissfully unaware of our work,' he added.

'Good work,' said Grant. 'That's a really useful briefing for a bloke like me who is new to the game and wouldn't know a diplomat if he tripped over one. Pick me up outside the Andaz at about 8.50 a.m. and see if you can arrange a meeting with the Consul General sometime tomorrow morning.'

'Will do, Colonel,' replied Stephens. 'I also have a heap of paperwork for you to sign. Applications, accreditations to various defence groups, formal request for a diplomatic ID pass and your entry in the diplomatic register, incoming mail for you via the diplomatic bag and so forth. We'll knock that stuff over first, if you don't mind Sir, and then you will be free to begin your round of personal calls on local agencies, friendly missions etc.'

'Sounds like a good plan, Mike,' replied Grant, impressed with the quiet efficiency of his new aide-de camp. Grant had already decided to use a familiar tone with his more junior work colleague, well aware that Mike Stephens would have his back and be his closest comrade at arms; a dog in any fight, rather than a subordinate, despite their differences in rank. The powerful Mercedes surged up 5th Avenue in low gear and turned into West 42nd, pulling up in front of the hotel's entrance, where a doorman in smart livery appeared to open its doors and assist with the baggage.

'I'll check in and let you get moving,' said a flagging Grant, disappearing into the hotel lobby behind a man pushing a trolley loaded with his bags. Ten minutes later, with his body clock struggling to keep pace after his long flight, Colonel Tom Grant had showered, pulled on loose shorts, slipped between the fresh sheets of his welcoming hotel bed and fallen into a deep, palliative sleep.

Red Bear's Safe House, McLean VA

Before Tom Grant's head had hit his pillow in New York, Anatoly Pushkin was already studying the interesting information supplied by Moscow on electromagnetic pulse technology and its potential use as a tactical nuclear weapon. Most of it was now publicly available from Wikipedia or other sources. He arranged the information in chronological sequence, and began reading it, to understand it and extract realistic paragraphs.

"During British nuclear testing in 1953," the report began, *"there were instrumentation failures that were attributed to "radio flash", the early British term for an electromagnetic pulse (EMP). Then, in July 1962, the US tested a 1.44 megaton nuclear device in space, which was detonated precisely 400 kilometres above the mid-Pacific. That test demonstrated that the effects of a high altitude nuclear explosion were much greater than previously estimated. Indeed, the test caused extraordinary electrical damage in Hawaii, about 1,445 kilometres away from the detonation point, knocking out about 300 streetlights, setting off numerous burglar alarms and damaging a telephone microwave link.*

"Recalibrations were made, based upon this detonation. They showed that, if the warhead had been detonated over the United States, the pulse would have been much greater, because of the strength of the Earth's magnetic field at that aperture. These new calculations, and the advent of smaller, microelectronics into millions of electronic appliances, both public and private, heightened awareness of, and significantly increased the military threat posed by, a hostile Electromagnetic Pulse Device.

"A nuclear electromagnetic pulse differs from other electromagnetic pulses because it produces 3 different pulses all at once. The E1 pulse is the fastest component of a nuclear EMP. It creates a brief but intense

electromagnetic field that quickly induces very high voltages in electrical conductors. It destroys computers and telecommunications equipment.

"The E2 component is an 'intermediate' pulse that lasts from between one microsecond to one second. The E2 pulse has many similarities with the pulses produced by lightning. Because of these similarities and the wide use of lightning protection technology on buildings and communications systems, the E2 pulse is considered to be the easiest to defend against.

"In 2004, recognising the potentially catastrophic effects of nuclear EMPs, the United States established an 'EMP Commission'. The Commission's initial Executive Report stated that... "An E2 pulse would not be critical for public infrastructure, since most items have existing defences against lightning strikes. However, there is a significant synergistic risk, because the E2 pulse appears a fraction of a second after the first, E1 pulse, which does have the ability to destroy many protective devices. The energy from the second pulse might thus still pass into and damage other systems.

The E3 pulse is much more worrying than the first two. It is a very slow pulse, varying in duration from ten seconds to several hundred seconds. It is caused by the nuclear detonation forcefully heaving the Earth's magnetic field out of the way, basically pushing it out of shape. This is then followed by the impact of the earth's massive magnetic field snapping back into its natural balance. The E3 pulse is like a very severe solar flare. It can induce currents in long electrical conductors, and damage large infrastructure items, such as power lines and transformers.

"Several factors govern the impact of a Nuclear EMP attack. They are:

1. The altitude (height above sea level) of the weapon when detonated;

2. The yield of the nuclear device, and its method of construction;

3. The distance the impacted area is from the weapon when detonated;

4. Geographical shielding or intervening geographical features (hills);

5. The local strength of the magnetic field of the Earth.

"There are worrying reports that the US, China and India have developed a 'Super-EMP' weapon that exceeds the previously accepted physical limits of a pulse weapon, set at 50,000 volts per metre of electrical intensity. Nuclear physicists conjecture that they have done so by achieving an instantaneous burst of gamma radiation of higher intensity than is normally produced by second-generation nuclear weapons.

"According to the Federation of American Scientists... a high-altitude nuclear detonation pulse can easily span an entire continent the size of the US, Australia or China, and can affect systems on land, sea, and air. They say that a large device detonated 400 kilometres above Kansas would affect all of continental U.S.A. Moreover, there would be no protection if the explosion were visible just below the tops of mountains.

"The ideal altitude, quoted above, is greater than that of the International Space Station and many low-Earth-orbit satellites. Large weapons could thus have a dramatic impact on orbiting satellites and communications.

"The United States military has developed a number of hypothetical EMP attack scenarios, as war games. In a written testimony delivered to the United States Senate, a senior staffer from the EMP Commission noted:

"The EMP Commission finds that the physics of EMP phenomena and the military impacts of EMP attacks are now widely understood internationally. Chinese scientists have mastered the principles behind EMP weapons and are said to have developed a design which could generate an enhanced-EMP effect; what they call a "Super-EMP" weapon. "SuperEMP" weapons, according to foreign intelligence, could destroy even the best protected US military and civilian electronic systems, and would wreak havoc, destroying entire societies and creating an infrastructure and communications winter that would result in the loss of millions of lives and require years of rebuilding and trillions of dollars of new investment."

Pushkin was deeply affected by the power of these final words, not because they were a calculated deception, but because the science they described actually existed and the potential for an EMP holocaust was real. Essentially a deep thinker, and still in touch with his basic humanity,

74

Pushkin was in awe of the dreadful threat this technology posed to world peace. Had scientists gone mad? When they accidentally discovered this phenomenon, did they experience the same feeling of dread as Einstein and others had, when the power of the atomic chain reaction was first understood? Why was it that man, in his quest for a better life, had such an unerring talent, instead, for inventing the means of his own extinction?

Somewhere deep in his psyche, a small fibre of moral outrage tugged at Pushkin's conscience, making the hard-nosed espionage practitioner baulk at the monstrous risks associated with his elaborate deception. He knew he was unleashing a monster, one which, if taken to its logical conclusion, might leave an indelible stain on the pages of history. Sobered by this thought, he turned from his own computer to the CIA agent's laptop and focussed upon Ritter's Dongfeng report. His surgical gloves danced over the keyboard of Ritter's laptop, scrolling down though the CIA agent's report to the words '...*making China's Dongfeng missile, deployed in the land-based, underground silos, effectively redundant*'.

He deleted these words and began composing his own, creative narrative, to replace them. A credible EMP threat would raise eyebrows, not just in the Pentagon but across the western military world. Pushkin was sure that his brilliant deception would turn all heads towards China, taking pressure off Russia's waning defence budget. When he had proposed this strategy to Moscow station, they had roundly applauded its brilliance and dubbed his mission the 'Dongfeng Deception'. He would have to follow through now, whatever the risks, or lose his credibility with Moscow. His fingers began dancing across the keyboard, the words flowing as if by magic, subtly changing Ritter's report while adding a terrifying scenario:

"With the deployment of the new, under-sea variant of the Dongfeng, we might be forgiven for thinking that the old, land based Dongfeng, deployed in China's underground silos system had, as a consequence, become redundant. That may be precisely what the Chinese wanted us to think.

"However, intelligence from our Far East desk, working in collaboration with Japanese and Australian Intelligence services, confirms that the Chinese have recently perfected a new 'Super Electromagnetic

75

Pulse' (SEMP) device, a nuclear device engineered for maximum destructive power if detonated in the upper atmosphere above the United States. The Chinese are re-arming their redundant Dongfeng VII rocket with new, super EMP warheads, and using them as a land-based delivery system. This re-values their sunk investment in the silo network very intelligently. It achieves a much-increased threat – one which amounts to a clear and present danger, requiring a western response. The Pentagon's ICBM experts estimate that, in a first strike scenario, 32% of the 160 new generation Dongfengs, which are also capable of launching satellites, could evade our interdiction measures and deliver their SEMP payloads into the upper atmosphere over designated US targets, producing a pulse wave capable of destroying the entire North American continent.

"Research by our own EMP Commission into the likely effects of an ICBM attack using EMP warheads indicates that we would likely see a complete breakdown of American society, including massive failures across the nation's electrical power grid, the failure of a wide range of industrial, commercial, retail and home technologies (including refrigerated food products in supermarkets), disruption to the delivery of a wide range of critical supplies and essential services, and a nationwide failure of other appliances upon which society depends, like mobile phones, small and large computers, bank teller machines and medical equipment. The consequences are unimaginable and would take our nation back to the dark ages. The wider impacts of a breakdown in law and order, leading to street violence and aggressive contests for limited supplies of food and water by an angry and disorientated civilian population, are self-evident."

Pushkin completed the last sentence and slumped back, physically and emotionally drained by his task, and disgusted with himself for being the agent of this potentially catastrophic deception, which could well be the catalyst for a nuclear confrontation with China. If the Dongfeng deception achieved that outcome, a largely innocent world would pay a high price.

He completed a spell check, rationalised the text so that it flowed, in identical case and typeface, and pressed SAVE. Then he replaced the laptop in its special attaché case, closed it and locked it by pressing the 'lock' icon, which scrambled the access code. Still wearing surgical gloves, he checked his watch and calculated that he had half an hour until midnight, the deadline he had set himself. That gave time for him to rendezvous with *Peregrine* and return the attaché case to Ritter's home. Agent *Peregrine* had left some time to complete his part of the work. He would be waiting for Pushkin at Ritter's house, after dumping his body in the lounge room, sanitising the car and returning it to Ritter's driveway, and placing the keys casually onto the coffee table in the lounge area. When the two had hidden Ritter's attaché case in his home – creatively, but not so creatively that a forensic search would not find it - *Peregrine* would drive them through the night to Boston, where Pushkin was scheduled to book in for his surgery. Then the devil's clock would start ticking.

***

Pushkin and agent *Peregrine*'s vehicle glided along the interstate towards Boston. In the still night, Pushkin felt ready for sleep, but he had one final formality to complete. He plugged his mobile phone into a code scrambler, typed in an SMS message, in Russian Cyrillic script, and sent it to his station chief at the Russian Embassy in Washington. Translated, it read:

> *'Intervention successful. Maintain watch. Confirm bait taken.*
> *Medical phase commences.*
> *Red Bear'*

From his desk at the Russian Embassy in Washington, Pushkin's station chief would understand from this message that Ritter had been executed and his report on the Chinese Dongfeng missiles had been successfully intercepted and edited. He would also understand that Pushkin was en route to the Boston clinic for the planned corrective surgery on his knee. While Pushkin underwent his treatment in Boston, Russian field agents would monitor the CIA's reaction and response to Ritter's death. They would use both physical surveillance and cyber-hacking techniques to confirm that the Americans had discovered Ritter's corpse and found his hidden Dongfeng missile report, in pristine condition. Their next task would be to confirm that the Americans had swallowed the bait. To do so, they would monitor signals from defence and foreign relations sources, including the CIA, the Pentagon, the State Department and others.

Cyber hacking was now a formidable weapon in Russia's espionage armoury. It had been augmented with massively increased funding and was now yielding excellent results in a number of foreign jurisdictions. While this ramping up of Russian capability was happening under their noses, the US, obsessed with the Chinese cyber threat and angry about their recent cyber penetration of US secure traffic, had remained blissfully unaware of the more potent cyber-hacking now emanating from Russia.

CIA Headquarters

Sally Ormiston was a highly competent Personal Assistant. She was extraordinarily loyal to her boss, Chuck Ritter, and fussed over him like a mother hen, so that his life as the Agency's Deputy Director seemed to flow effortlessly. She knew that her boss was deeply engrossed in his latest project, so she had elected to come in early, expecting to find him at his desk this Monday morning. His failure to show up on this frenetic, first day of the week was therefore out of character and increasingly curious.

Monday mornings were religious. They always began with a 10.00 a.m. 'heads of division' meeting in the 4th floor conference room. The meetings were chaired by the agency's chief, National Director Frank Angiotti, so Charles Ritter was always at pains to be well prepared for them. Today, however, the hands of the wall clock above Sally's desk were nudging 9.45 a.m. and there was still no sign of her boss, making the fastidious assistant increasingly nervous. This was not supposed to happen.

Sally felt certain there must be a simple explanation. She dialled Agent Ritter's home number again, allowing the phone to ring out and divert to his message bank. The lack of any response suggested that Ritter must be on his way, caught up in traffic perhaps, or delayed with a flat tyre. Who could say? She then tried his mobile for the umpteenth time and was again unable to reach him. As time marched on, she developed a strong intuition that something was seriously wrong. Her instincts in such matters were usually reliable, and she needed to share them with someone she could trust. As 10.00 a.m. drew nearer, she elected to call her close friend, Nicole Price, Personal Assistant to Director Angiotti

'Nicky, this is really out of character. Chuck never misses the Monday morning wrap sessions and today's is a really important one for him. He always phones if something has delayed him. What the heck should I do?'

'Don't worry too much, Sal. I am sure it will be something simple. I'll let the boss know that Charles is held up and we'll see where that takes us.

'Meantime, why don't you ask one of Mr Ritter's senior staff to sit in for him at the meeting until he gets here? Danny Lovett might be good.'

Satisfied with this compromise, Nicole Price continued collating the meeting agendas, shuffling a bundle of supporting papers and placing them neatly to one side of her desk. Getting last minute papers ready for Monday's meeting was always stressful, and she decided to complete that task before addressing the more mundane issue of Sally's boss being late. In doing so, she was unwittingly costing the agency valuable time.

Just as department heads began arriving for the Monday wrap session, she finally remembered to buzz her boss, Frank Angiotti, to pass on the seemingly innocuous news that his deputy had failed to show for the meeting and was proving difficult to contact. Angiotti was an astute man, with considerable experience in running the nation's intelligence agency. His brow creased, as he processed this unusual, last minute advice, realising immediately that agent Ritter had been working on an extremely sensitive matter and that his report was due to be tabled at this morning's meeting. Something about this highly uncharacteristic circumstance told him there must be a more sinister reason for Ritter's failure to show; one he needed to eliminate. Although the department heads had already begun milling outside the conference room, Frank Angiotti was more concerned about Ritter's absence. Electing to ignore the clock he summoned Nicole Price into his office and issued an urgent instruction.

'This is worrying, Nicole. Deputy Director Ritter can be mildly obsessive about his work, and he never misses our Monday meetings. He has been working on a sensitive matter, with *top secret* classification, which I know he was keen to table at this morning's meeting. I need to be sure that he and his report are in safe hands. You will have to brief the security guys in Special Ops about the situation and have them send a team to Ritter's home immediately. Get them out to his place right away and have them report back to my office if they have anything on Ritter's whereabouts. Interrupt me if you have anything.'

80

Down in Special Ops, the phone on Bruce (Macka) McKenzie's desk buzzed and he nonchalantly picked up. The former field officer found his new head office duties boring. His role as a flat-arsed bureaucrat was a sinecure and nothing exciting ever happened any more. When he took the call and realised it was the Agency chief's Personal Assistant on the line, he immediately straightened in his chair, as if an officer had walked by and demanded a salute, and his face assumed a more intense expression. His mood darkened as the substance of the director's request became clear.

'Deputy Director Ritter was working on a secret matter,' Nicole Price began. 'He failed to show this morning and could not be contacted. While it remains likely that there is a simple explanation, foul play seems a remote possibility, one that you and your team must eliminate quickly. This work must have top priority. You are to report back to Director Angiotti within the hour.'

Macka responded with a tense 'Yes, Ma'am!' and immediately spurred his special assault team into action. He was ecstatic that this opportunity had presented. It would showcase his real talent as a physically engaged field officer rather than a desk-bound flat-arse. Within seconds of receiving the director's call, he and his team had kitted up, raced to the basement car park, fired up their pursuit vehicle and were streaking through downtown McLean, towards agent Ritter's home. Their blue assault team uniforms bulged over Kevlar, bulletproof vests, which they each wore underneath their jackets. Macka and his 2IC, Louis (Louey) Ambrose, carried Beretta M9 side-arms, the Rolls Royce of close quarter combat pistols, while the third member of their team, (Wild) Bill McCabe, carried a Ruger tear gas canister and stun grenade launcher. If there was any operational threat, the experienced agents were ready to meet it.

'Listen up, guys,' barked Macka as they sped towards their target. 'We play this by the book. We will assume that we have a bad situation here until we are able to confirm otherwise. That means being ready for an aggressive interdiction against a hostile agent. We might even find a perp still lurking on the premises. When we reach Ritter's street, we will pull over well short of his driveway to drop Louey off and allow him time to cover the rear. When he is in place, Wild Bill and I will approach from the front of the property. That way, if there is a situation, we can contain it.'

When agent Ambrose was in place, agent McKenzie and his colleague made a stealthy approach to the front of the property without incident. Everything seemed orderly, with no sign of any forced entry or other disturbance. Ritter's black Lincoln was parked in the driveway, looking innocuous and quietly at home. They mounted the front steps and approached the front door of the premises. Just as McKenzie was about to ring the door-bell, the door opened and a startled agent Louey Ambrose appeared in the entrance foyer, beckoning them urgently inside.

'I managed to make it to the rear of the property, through the neighbour's garden, and was able to progress undetected right up to the back door,' he said. 'When I got there, the door was wide open and there were signs of damage to the lock, suggesting it had been jemmied, so I walked right on in. That's when I found Ritter's body. Not a pretty sight, Macka. Bloated, and starting to smell. Been there for about two days, I reckon. Gunshot wound to the centre of the forehead, execution style, and two weird images burned into his temples. They look like Chinese characters.'

Special Operations agent, 'Macka' McKenzie, absorbed this information grimly. Reacting instinctively, as a field commander rather than a bureaucrat, he pushed past Ambrose to inspect the corpse of the CIA boss slumped back, the face upturned with a startled look in its eyes, on the sofa in the lounge area. McKenzie stood over the corpse and recoiled slightly at the sweet smell of death. Ritter's face was barely recognisable. His skin had assumed a purplish hue, his lips were swollen and cracked, his bloated tongue projected through angry teeth and his dull, plastic eyes stared in astonishment from either side of a gaping hole in his forehead. 'Don't touch or move anything until the forensic guys and photographers get here, and don't send any public signals. No voice, digital text or other record of this event. I will pass this to our counter-intelligence guys. We don't want the local police involved in any way. Not until the agency has worked out the dimensions of this problem and where it takes us. We will need all of our cunning to keep this under wraps and in-house, at least while we work out what the fuck is going on. That is especially important in light of the top-secret project Chuck Ritter was working on and because he is a very senior officer in our national intelligence service. No one is to touch the body, the surrounding environment, his personal effects or his vehicle. Arrange a truck to collect Ritter's vehicle and have it loaded using protective gloves. Get it straight over to our techs at the works depot. Their forensic team will need to go over it with a fine-tooth comb,' he said.

It took less than half an hour for a CIA forensic team to take photographs of the scene, recover fingerprints, sanitise the site and wrap up and transport Ritter's corpse and all of the evidence they required for an offsite, forensic analysis of the event. The agency's work would, of necessity, include a secret, illegal autopsy of the body and an examination of all of the physical assets that surrounded the circumstances of their Deputy Director's death. One glance at the gruesome corpse made it clear to McKenzie that Ritter had not died of natural causes, or even been the subject of an accidental or random tragedy. He had clearly been targeted, cornered and executed - brutally and with clinical precision.

Moreover, the manner of Ritter's execution suggested a sinister motive, and the intervention of a clandestine, foreign agency. The causal chain of evidence made these truths plain. All of the evidence pointed to an espionage operation, which must have had its genesis in Ritter's secret intelligence work or in something potentially explosive connected with it. McKenzie was shrewd enough to recognise that this thing was bigger than the agency's own, narrow intelligence mandate and needed to be escalated immediately. If his instincts were correct, news of this event would go all the way to the White House, so Macka was determined that Frank Angiotti, alone, should be apprised of this explosive development in the strictest confidence and given an opportunity to calculate how he chose to pass on the news and navigate the tricky political waters ahead.

Contrary to the usual practice, this American spy chief was neither a politically appointed hack nor a 'yes man'. McKenzie realised that people like Angiotti rarely succeeded to high public office without some other, special charisma, transcending political patronage. The Scot was therefore a little nervous about phoning this revered, God-like leader for the first time. The Scot was accurate in his assessment of the man he had not yet met in person. While, in the American context, most appointees to the head of the premier spy agency had enjoyed political patronage, Angiotti shunned such partisan bias. He had a more valuable attribute, his political astuteness, and was protective of his staff and fiercely defensive of his agency's political independence. That made him one of a rare breed and a 'natural' leader. Moreover, Angiotti was both a man of few words and of unquestioned personal integrity. If those traits were not enough, his background as a highly decorated soldier had given him an aura of quiet authority and of respect, on both sides of the Congress, for his patriotism.

When told of Ritter's failure to make the meeting, Angiotti had displayed those leadership qualities in a nanosecond. He had smelled a rat, insisted that agents be sent immediately to Ritter's home to investigate, and insisted that he be interrupted with the results of the investigation. These were decisions which most people would worry over. They entailed risks, which ordinary men and women found unpalatable. Angiotti embraced risk, without hesitation, and fearlessly followed his own conviction.

When the call came from agent McKenzie, Angiotti's secretary fetched her boss from the conference room and patched the call through to his private desk phone. The CIA Director listened grimly to McKenzie's account of what he had found. Angiotti reacted with calm, ordered intellect. In the face of this crisis, he instructed McKenzie to come straight up to his office, to give a detailed, first-hand account of what he and his team had found. Next, he instructed Nicole Price to convey his apologies to the heads of division and inform another, senior agent, Bruce Lovett, that he should take over as chair of the meeting. While he waited for McKenzie, Angiotti contacted the National Security advisor at the White House, Bill Nordish, and gave him a heads-up on the rapidly evolving situation. That single action, while it was a responsible one, would be a match lighting a torch paper of intrigue which would spread like fire across the administration.

Minutes later, McKenzie, knocked on Angiotti's door. It was a quiet, self-effacing knock, signalling the nervous discomfort the gentle giant felt in his new office environment. Macka was more comfortable in the field, dodging bullets, than in this alien, wood-panelled bureaucracy. When he had been a field officer, Macka had been a confident, swashbuckling man. Now considered too old for field work, he had been kicked upstairs and made to wear a suit and ride a desk, and that had rattled his confidence.

Despite his initial reservations, McKenzie quickly discovered a positive chemistry between himself and his charismatic agency chief; one which allowed no hierarchy, seniority or pretence to intervene in their man to man discussion. His boss beckoned the athletic old field agent into his office, fixed determined eyes upon the rugged Scot and took his hand in a vice-like grip, a signal of respect between men of action.

Building upon this chemistry, the CIA chief then used familiar language and an intensely personal style to put his more junior officer at ease.

'Take a seat, Macka. I want you to give me your personal take on this,' said Angiotti. 'I've had extremely positive reports about you and your team and I am looking for an unvarnished interpretation of what we have here; not some carefully worded, bureaucratic bullshit. You OK with that?'

'Yes, sir,' replied agent McKenzie with a grin. 'I'll give it my best shot. All of the signs point to an execution-type slaying. You can't put a neat hole between someone's eyes if they are struggling to escape the muzzle of your handgun, so I'm betting the forensic guys will find gunshot residue around the entry wound, confirming that he was immobilised and shot at close range. Looks like physical incursion with a strong element of surprise. My guess is they were lying in wait for him inside his house when he got home, since his car was parked, apparently routinely, in his driveway. They must have jumped him, tied him up and drilled him for information they wanted very badly; so badly they were prepared to go to any lengths to get it. He must have been onto something really sensitive.'

'He was, Macka, and that is an understatement. Agent Ritter's personal assistant tells us it was so hot that Ritter had insisted on handling the matter personally. He became so absorbed in it that he worked back last Friday and then took the draft of his highly controversial report home with him, to give it a final polish over the weekend. He had told me that he would be tabling his report at this morning's meeting. He must have been desperate to finish it. Taking it home was an extraordinarily foolish thing to do – in breach of

85

every code of good intelligence practice. As an experienced intelligence officer, he should have known better.

'For your ears only, his report was about a foreign missile system which could threaten the United States. Our agency was asked to recruit the best intelligence we could find on the subject, then to analyse the national security risk and to submit our findings to the Defence Appropriation Committee of Congress. Ritter would not let anyone else near it. When I asked him why, he said something strange… "this investigation will rake over old coals and unearth stuff that might embarrass the agency" …or words to that effect. We have two options; find Ritter's report or, in a worst-case scenario, concede that it has fallen into hostile hands. Did your guys check Ritter's home, his office or den, for any signs of the report?'

'No, sir. That was not a part of our brief. We raced to the scene in record time, but our mission was to establish whether Deputy Director Ritter was OK… whether or not there had been any foul play. We were not given information about the Deputy Director's intelligence report,' replied Macka.

'I see. Never mind. You did well in quickly securing the scene. Was there anything else you wanted to report or that you think I need to know?'

'Hell, yes, sir! I haven't even gotten to the crazy bit yet. Agent Ritter's forehead had two symbols embossed into it. They looked like Chinese characters, and they seemed to have been *burned* into his skin, leaving brownish burn marks, much like the marks you see when a rancher brands his cows. The characters were permanently seared into his flesh. Why would they do that? Why leave us a calling card… in Chinese?'

Frank Angiotti stroked his chin quizzically and gave a measured reply. 'That's a bloody good question, Macka. What the hell would motivate anyone to do something like that? And why the Chinese characters?'

As he spoke these words, the intelligence chief was struck by a chilling thought. For the first time in his long and illustrious career, he might be dealing with a Chinese intelligence operation, boldly undertaken *inside* the United States. For decades, the CIA had been focussed upon the Soviet's KGB and the East German counterpart, the STASSI. Then they had shifted their focus to the newly emerging threat of Al Qaida and other Islamic terrorist groups. For some inexplicable reason, China had never been more than a remote blip on the agency's intelligence radar. Angiotti realised that the agency may have been underestimating a major new adversary. If so, he would have trouble explaining why. The Chinese had well-documented intelligence capability. They were world leaders in cyber interception and at hacking into foreign data bases. The west had been slow to concede that China might one day compete in that area.

Angiotti was generally aware that Ritter's report was about China upgrading its aging ICBMs in favour of a new missile, with greater range and potency. Ritter's report would have seriously embarrassed the Chinese but the burning of Chinese characters into the forehead of an American Intelligence Officer was highly provocative. Could it be a signal from the Chinese that they had had enough of US intervention in their affairs? That was, after all, not so very different from the over reactions the US had displayed when it was displeased with other nations. It had invaded Iraq, attacked the Taliban in Afghanistan, used drones in Pakistani air space and sent in a team to kill Bin Laden, violating the sovereignty of those nations. If the US could justify these actions as legitimate responses to remote, hostile threats, why should the Chinese not be equally capable of doing so, to protect their national interest.

Angiotti was angry with the way his country tended to manage those issues. He considered respect for another nation's sovereignty an article of faith. How could the US claim to be a defender of free and democratic ideals without respecting that principle? Too often, that principle was now sacrificed on the bonfire of political expedience. Perhaps America was now getting a taste of its own medicine. It had long been established that China's hackers had no peer. At first, their monitoring of cyber content was driven by a need to censure political expression at home, to preserve the authority of the State. China had now developed hacking skills which it could migrate to international cyber traffic. As they became increasingly adept at their craft, they were routinely interdicting western cyber traffic, and hacking secure sources, heralding a new frontier of intelligence risk.

'Maybe the Chinese hacked into Ritter's computer and found some disturbing content in his Dongfeng report?' thought Angiotti. After all, in

2011, the CIA had found hard evidence that the Chinese had hacked into Pentagon files, resulting in an official protest by the State Department and a denial from Beijing. Maybe the agency's legendary cyber nerd, based in London, who was working with Ritter, had tried to hack into intelligence on China's nuclear capability and been caught with his fingers in their pie.

Angiotti realised that a hostile intelligence operation by the Chinese on American soil, targeting a senior US Intelligence official, was a highly provocative event, with potentially catastrophic consequences for China - US relations. However, international convention provided that covert actions were deniable unless the plaintive was able to prove, beyond any reasonable doubt, that the act was State sponsored. That applied to US actions abroad, in places like Iraq, Syria and other rogue states, where US teams worked covertly in a host of hostile locations. Why should China not want to enjoy the same privileges? The simple fact was, no one had ever considered that China would dare undertake such a thing on US soil.

If the agency could prove that this act had been sanctioned by the Chinese, that would give rise to an explosive, international situation. If, however, the matter languished in the murky protocols of the intelligence underworld, there was nothing much that could be done. Angiotti decided that he would cover his arse by briefing the White House, the National Security Adviser and the Secretary of State and asking them to keep the information under tight wraps until further investigations were concluded. In the meantime, he would have his forensic team go over every inch of Ritter's home to determine what had happened there, to recover Ritter's report and, above all, to learn what explosive information it contained.

Dep Director Ritter's Home - McClean VA

Agent Susan Longworth was head of the CIA's counter measures unit. She was highly respected for her work in covert communications and her team were experts at providing what was termed 'protective services', sweeping for listening or monitoring devices and cleaning up after what were termed 'dark ops'. They were equally adept at what was termed 'offensive measures', involving the planting of those same devices in a hostile environment. Angiotti had become increasingly agitated that, despite a forensic search of Ritter's home, no one had found his report, or the computer that his PA had said he had used to draft it. Angiotti had thus decided that, in addition to the second sweep by his forensic team, he would send in Susan Longworth's team for one last, painstaking sweep of Ritter's residence. If this last effort failed, he would be forced to the conclusion that Ritter's report was now in foreign hands.

Susan Longworth agreed with Angiotti that it was quite likely that Ritter had, himself, hidden his laptop, conscious that it contained highly sensitive information and might attract hostile interest. That theory was a bit of a long shot, but the best way to test it was to search for the tell-tale electronic signature which always radiated from a laptop computer. A computer could be traced if it generated even a microscopic amount of current. To that end, agent Longworth had brought with her some highly sensitive equipment, designed specifically for detecting faint electrical currents or electromagnetic fields. She and her team all wore white lab coats and surgical gloves, standard wear for a forensic sweep of this sort.

'Over here, Susan,' called one of the techs. 'I think I have a faint signal in the right frequency range. 'Seems to be coming from behind the air vent; from behind the mesh screen set into the air conditioning duct, up there.'

89

They congregated under the vent and one of the men climbed onto a step-ladder, reached up and pulled the mesh cover away. His arm delved into the dark void of the air-conditioning duct and he withdrew it, smiling broadly as he produced the elusive aluminium attaché case, with its digital lock still in place. The weight of the case confirmed that it still contained something solid, probably Ritter's laptop, with his top-secret report hidden somewhere in its labyrinth of files, so there was euphoria at the discovery. Even in death, it seemed, the heroic Deputy Director of the CIA had cheated the hostile agents seeking to muzzle his report.

'Bag the laptop before you handle it further, so we can dust it for prints and confirm that only Ritter's or other familiar CIA hands have been on it. After the lab guys have dusted for prints, we will need to open it and let Director Angiotti take a look at what agent Ritter had to say in his report. Whatever it was, it was explosive enough to cost him his life. I will check with Ritter's PA in case she can help with the ten-digit access code.'

Forty minutes later, the aluminium security case was on the desk of the agency's chief. Standing around his desk, eager to learn more about the contents of Ritter's report, were Acting Deputy Director, Bruce Lovett, special agent Susan Longworth, Macka, from field ops and Ritter's PA, Sally Ormiston, who was still distraught after learning the gruesome details of her boss's murder. Sally had recovered a slip of paper from her boss's wall safe, where his highly classified documents were always kept, and advised Angiotti that she was sure it was his secure access code.

'Alright folks. Let's see what Deputy Ritter had to say that was of such compelling interest to our unidentified enemies. Each of you has signed our agency's non-disclosure document, making you subject to the provisions of the Official Secrets Act. You are trusted to keep anything you see or hear in this room to yourselves. Anyone who repeats any of this, even to a spouse, a close friend or a trusted colleague, will be liable for prosecution under our national security code. Its provisions make a treasonable act punishable by death or life imprisonment. Is that clear?'

Each staff member nodded assent, moved by the gravity of their chief's remark and believing that they were about to hear something truly significant, affecting America's national security. Angiotti turned to Sally

Ormiston and asked her to read out the ten-digit access code, which had been scrawled on the slip of paper taken from Ritter's wall safe.

'The code Mr Ritter has written is really strange,' said Sally. '*i s l e o f d o g s*', it says. Sounds like the name of an island. Lucky he saved it. We would never have cracked such an obscure code without a record of it.'

'It was a smart choice,' replied Angiotti. 'Its obscurity, and the fact that the only record of it has been kept in Ritter's wall safe, gives us a high degree of certainty that no one has accessed the briefcase or read Ritter's report, although whoever wanted it so badly must have had some inkling of its contents. That might mean they learned about it by hacking into his internet traffic, or intercepting intelligence reports from one of his agents reporting from abroad. We will need to follow up all of those possibilities.'

Sally Ormiston handed chief Angiotti the digital remote and he punched in the obscure access code, *i s l e o f d o g s*. When the last digit was entered, the digital read-out panel blinked red and the locking mechanism released with a hum. Just as Angiotti was about to open the case, Susan Longworth leaned over his desk and raised her hand in a 'stop' motion. 'Just a minute, boss. Probably best if my technical guys remove the laptop from the security case, using protective gloves, so we don't contaminate any part of the laptop. We need to be sure that it hasn't been tampered with. If Ritter's report has been saved as a file, I can find it in his laptop and download it onto a memory stick, so you can read it in private, at your leisure. We can also encrypt it, to provide another level of security and more tightly manage its selective distribution or disclosure.'

'Good thinking, Susan, but don't keep me waiting. Download Ritter's report and get the memory stick back to me as soon as possible.'

The team was then dispersed, disappointed that they would not be privy to the contents of Ritter's report and anxious to learn more about it.

Within half an hour, agent Susan Longworth had returned with the memory stick, which she plugged into Angiotti's desktop and opened as a 'read-only' file. Angiotti instructed Nicole Price that he was not to be disturbed, locked his door, settled back with a coffee and began reading Ritter's report. He found the first couple of pages, recounting the early history of the Chinese-Russian development of the Dongfeng missile, interesting but unremarkable. His interest increased, when he read about China's deployment of a fleet of nuclear submarines carrying the new generation Dongfeng, renamed the 'Great Wave' missile, which was capable of under-sea launch and had therefore given China an elusive, mobile nuclear platform. He suspected, however, that this intelligence was already well known to key US agencies; by strategists at the Pentagon, by US Naval Command and by the Joint Chiefs of Staff.

Finally, he came to the section headed... *Re-arming of land-based Dongfengs with Electromagnetic Pulse Warheads*. He read on, ashen-faced, pausing to reread the final paragraphs detailing the devastation which would be wrought, should such a weapon be exploded in the upper atmosphere over North America.

"...deployment of such a nuclear device would see a complete breakdown of society, including massive failures across the nation's... electrical power grid, the failure of a wide range of industrial, commercial and domestic machines, massive disruption to the delivery of essential goods and services, and a nationwide failure of appliances, including mobile phones... computers, telecommunications devices and refrigerated food shelves in supermarkets across the nation. The consequences are unimaginable and would take our nation back to the dark ages. The social impacts of a likely breakdown in law and order, including... street violence and... contests for... food and water by an angry, frightened and disorientated civilian population, are self-evident."

Angiotti paused to imagine a modern, nation State in which lights were suddenly extinguished and millions of lives were suddenly, brutally disrupted. A nation in which frightened mothers, dependent on their landlines, mobiles and iPads for communication, were suddenly unable to phone or text a child left waiting at a kindergarten, or a frail relative in a nursing home. In his mind's eye, he saw rows of refrigerated meat and dairy products rotting, as their rancid chemical signal wafted from a myriad of supermarket freezer cabinets. Ritter's report had brought that nightmarish prospect into stark parenthesis. This was a shocking, game-changing military development, which had extraordinary implications for America and for wider, global security. Deeply troubled by the report, Angiotti called Nicole Price into his office and addressed her stoically.

'I need to arrange urgent meetings in the next couple of hours with each of the following people: the President, the National Security Adviser, the Secretary of State and each of the Chiefs of Staff, in that order. Get each of them on the line now. If they obfuscate or suggest that I call back later, tell them this concerns an explosive development affecting our national security. Tell them it will require an urgent meeting of all key portfolio heads, at a secure venue, ideally in the President's Situation Room.'

'One more thing, Nicole. We need to test Ritter's intelligence against any intel our closest and most trusted allies might have on this. We could start with Sir John Ruddock, at MI6 in London, but what I really need is some Australian expertise. They and their army of mandarin speakers are much better informed in the China theatre. See if you can get me my old friend *Lazarus*, you know, Sir Robert Chandler, head of the Australian Security Intelligence Organisation. Let's get his people rolling with us on this one.'

'We'll need to wait until 7 p.m. Langley time, to get Sir Robert on the line. That will make it ... let's see… 9 a.m. Canberra time. Sir Robert will just have arrived at his desk in Australia,' concluded Nicole, disappearing into the anteroom to arrange the dial ups. She would use s*ecure-squawk*, a special, voice-scrambling protocol, which enabled a normal phone conversation to be switched to *scramble,* at the sender's end, and the voice signal reassembled at the recipient's end, if the recipient had a secure-squawk protocol with the US. Both MI6 and ASIO had one and used it frequently for sensitive matters.

With each of these calls, CIA Director Frank Angiotti was conscious that he might be lighting a bonfire, one whose flames would steadily grow until they engulfed the west in a security conflagration, the likes of which had not been seen since Kennedy's face-off with Russia over the Bay of Pigs affair. Back then, had Kennedy blinked or Khrushchev been more obstinate, the course of history might have changed, leaving a legacy of nuclear destruction and human misery. Such was the potential impact of Charles Ritter's report. It would surely usher in an era of dangerous new brinkmanship with the rapidly emerging Chinese super power. That would mean a return to cold war and the threat of a third great conflict. China's global intentions, like its mercurial writing, spoken language and ancient culture, remained unfathomable to most Americans, and therefore a source of suspicion and distrust. Understanding this dynamic, Angiotti saw a real danger that Ritter's report could fuel a new xenophobia towards China, based upon ignorance and raw emotion, which could percolate up to the senior echelons of the US government. That sort of xenophobia would skew objectivity and needed to be avoided at all costs. It would require careful management, to ensure that cool heads prevailed.

At 7 p.m. that evening, after a harrowing day of further investigations, the phone buzzed on the CIA Chief's desk, turning Angiotti's thoughts to the wider implications of Ritter's execution, and he picked up.

'I have Sir Robert on the line, sir. Scrambling and putting you through,' finished Nicole. Angiotti waited for the 'squawk' signal before speaking.

'Sir Robert. Thank you so much for taking my call, and my apologies that it comes so early in your day down there. Got a moment to speak?'

'I always have time for old friends, Frank. What is it at this early hour? Must be something quite pressing.'

'You've got it, Robert. I can't give you the whole nine yards, but we have just unearthed some really troubling intel concerning the Chinese, whose military footprint is getting bigger every day. One of our agents was looking into that when he was taken out; clinically executed, that is.'

'For the first time ever, it looks like the Chinese secret service might have been active on US soil, right under our noses. Has all their hallmarks, but we don't want to jump to conclusions. Our man had just completed a report on a new weapon system they have developed that threatens our continent. Looks like the Chinese were trying to prevent our man's report coming to light. We'll give you everything we've got and let your Asian guys look at it. We don't want to escalate unless this thing is on the level.'

Sir Robert, *Lazarus* within the trade, processed Angiotti's words carefully before framing his response. The Yanks were generally good in their own front yard. Their new Homeland Security organisation had been a model for Australia's own counter-terrorism structure, but their credibility in the foreign policy area was in tatters after Iraq, Abu Ghraib and Guantanamo Bay. Lazarus had sensitive foreign policy antennae. He would not be setting any hares running without compelling evidence of the gravity of the issue and its consequences for Australia. China had become Australia's largest trading partner and its politicians were quietly moving towards a more neutral position on China. This also reflected the reality of Australia's proximity to a rapidly evolving, Asia-Pacific power shift. Always thorough and risk averse, Lazarus recalled that Colonel Tom Grant was on assignment in the USA. Tom would be ideally placed to sit down, face to face, with the US intelligence agencies and could give Lazarus an accurate, objective account of what was really going down over there.

'Well, Frank, old man,' he replied, 'it seems you are in luck. We have just sent one of our best men on a short-term assignment to the USA. Colonel Tom Grant, a former SAS Officer and member of our high-level Joint Services Strategic Planning Committee. He is there as a visiting 'Defence Fellow', sharing his ideas with your blokes as part of the exchange program between our militaries. He is especially literate on defence issues around the Asia-Pacific and will share views on that with your people at the Pentagon and West Point. He is cleared to Top Secret and has diplomatic immunity. You will find him listed in your diplomatic directory as the Defence Attaché seconded to our mission in New York. I will instruct him to contact you a.s.a.p. to manage the exchanges between us.'

'Hey, that sounds... what do you *blokes* say, a *super* idea!' said Angiotti.

'I think you might be confusing us with the Brits, mate, and that is a serious error. When it comes to intel on the Chinese, they are good but they are '*missing a few wallabies in the top paddock*', as we say here.'

'They're missing what?' replied Angiotti, wondering what the hell his Australian colleague had said and thinking he might need a translator.

'It's just a local expression to describe someone who is not altogether across the issues. Our version of '*all hat and no cowboy*', I should think. I shall try to use a more '*Hollywood*' vernacular in future, old boy. In the meantime, you must consider all of our resources, including those of ASIS, ASIO and ONA, at your disposal, if this is as big as you suggest.'

Frank Angiotti roared with laughter, thanked his counterpart from *down under* and rejoiced that Lazarus had provided the response he had hoped for. There was a long history of close cooperation between the two agencies, who even shared confidences about their British counterparts. British motives were not always clear. Somehow, the Brits still managed to treat the two members of their former empire as colonial underlings. A shared, healthy cynicism about British intelligence motives had served as a bond between Australia and America, cemented by a laconic Australian sense of humour which most Americans seemed to share. Angiotti looked forward to meeting this guy Grant, and to having him on his team.

Bryant Park

A tanned Colonel Tom Grant turned through the bottom corner of New York's Bryant Park, his *Nike* joggers squealing in protest as they skipped around the top of the stairway leading to the subway. His well-muscled frame propelled him effortlessly over that obstacle and he swerved to avoid the familiar figure of a bag lady, who responded to his cry of 'Morning, Joyce' with a toothless grin and a wave of her grimy hand, as she bent over a cartload of trash she seemed to be protecting. While his body responded mechanically to its jogging task, his mind was busy replaying his recent phone conversation with Lazarus and reworking the coded instructions which had followed, detailing his new assignment as an official liaison between the two intelligence organisations on the Dongfeng affair. After rounding the final corner, Grant upped the pace as his legs pumped him up the final slope towards to his 5th Avenue Hotel suite. This lap would complete his morning routine of six. Small beads of sweat now appeared on his brow, but he seemed otherwise unstressed, as he pushed harder up the rise, sucking in regular gulps of New York air.

About forty metres from the end of the rise, the footpath was occupied by a work detail, where pedestrians were diverted off the footpath to a narrow walkway around the work site. Grant moderated his pace and swung into the narrow diversion, then came to an abrupt halt as his path was blocked by the approach of another, female jogger. The two joggers came to an embarrassing impasse, narrowly avoiding a collision, looked at each other and locked eyes. This innocent confrontation was followed by a sudden flash of recognition, as Dr Maggie King's face broke into a beaming smile.

'My God! It's the long-lost Aussie Colonel! You're a long way from your Gentleman's Club in Melbourne and your kangaroos, aren't you Tom?'

'Dr King! What a surprise, running into you like this. I thought you were based at Princeton, in New Jersey. What brings you to New York?'

'I'm here for three days. A seminar, sponsored by the State Department,' replied Maggie. 'Checked in last night. I'm staying just around the corner.

'Don't suppose you fancy a morning coffee and a catch-up somewhere? I'm not due at my seminar until 9.00 a.m., and it's quite close by.'

'Sounds like a plan. I'm just across the road, at the Andaz Hotel. I could use a quick shower, though, before heading back out and I'll have to leave in time to make a 10.30 shuttle from O'Heir,' he said.

'OK. Why don't we nip back to our rooms, freshen up, and meet here again in, say, half an hour? I can highly recommend the coffee and bagels at the *Bryant Park Café*. How does 8.00 a.m. sound? I'm dying to hear how you've settled in and what you think of my favourite town.'

As they walked along the final stretch of footpath towards the level crossing, Tom Grant found his eyes returning to the attractive figure of the tall, rangy academic. Their first meeting in Melbourne had been at a black tie affair, where Maggie had displayed conservative elegance and chic. Now, Tom was treated to another aspect of this engaging woman, as she sauntered along the footpath in a loose-fitting, cotton singlet and lycra tights, which accentuated the lines of her pert behind. The sweat glistened on her well-toned body, giving her a different, animal allure which Tom found strangely attractive, though he tried to appear indifferent. Maggie, too, seemed to be stealing the odd glance at the athletic Aussie's body, as the duo made their way toward the crossing and split off towards their respective hotels, agreeing to meet up again at the café in half an hour.

When Maggie returned to the café, she found the rugged Australian already seated at a table. He wore a charcoal business suit, a pale-blue, open-necked business shirt and designer sunglasses. His straw-blond hair was still wet and had been tousled by the morning breeze, lending a rakish quality, at odds with his otherwise business-like demeanour. On the chair beside him, a trendy man-bag containing his iPad and a business tie, rolled into a ball, prepared him for some more formal contingency. Maggie appeared in an equally stylish smart-casual outfit, comprising white pants, a striking marine-blue linen shirt, loafers and sunglasses. To the uninitiated observer, the pair could have been a Mediterranean couple dining at an Adriatic resort. Maggie dropped her bag next to his and slid easily into her chair, as he beckoned the waitress to their table.

'So,' said Tom, 'What's a girl like you doing in a place like this?'

'Nice line, soldier. An oldie but a goodie,' she joked. 'I'm really loving this visit. They call it work, but it's a bit of a sinecure. I have to deliver one of the opening seminar papers, direct a couple of break-out sessions and join the panel of experts on the last day, when we sum up our findings. That leaves lots of time for shopping in the Big Apple, my *real* mission.'

'Our seminar will be close to your heart, I suspect, since you guys are members of the *coalition of the willing*. We will look at the impact of a western troop withdrawal from Afghanistan. Our government thinks it will all be fine, but I am backing the negative scenario that, as soon as we're gone, the Taliban will flood back in to fill the void. If they do that, you can bet they will reintroduce their Islamic fundamentalism, make women wear veils and scrub floors and generally fire up the old, anti-western sentiment that was the root cause of the whole misguided thing in the first place.'

'It's a bloody mess! I sometimes wonder why governments don't start by planning how to get *out* of the countries they invade before they go *in*. If they calculated that in advance, and understood how difficult it can be to extract an army, they might think twice about invading in the first place.'

'Couldn't agree more,' said Tom. 'Did you know I was in Afghanistan? Wrote a paper on precisely that point'.

'Of course I did. You were introduced to me as the *war hero*, remember. Seriously though, I would be really interested in having a copy of your paper,' replied Maggie. 'But first I want to hear what you are up to here in the States. Have you had many military exchanges with our guys yet, or with the guys at West Point? Are we all on the same page?'

'Matter of fact, I haven't gotten into that yet. There's been a lot of briefing and I'm still waiting for my personal effects to arrive from Australia. The strategic stuff begins soon, including war games based upon some pretty weird scenarios, including one involving a conflict between North Korea and the Japanese. That looked like a creative fantasy a few years ago, but it starts to look more plausible every day, with that crazy new leader they have. I will be in digs at West Point for about ten days, where they have a really high-tech war game simulator. Coincidentally, they tell me they have an excellent Officer's Mess, so it should be a lot of fun and a good opportunity to build contacts. Meantime, something unexpected has come up. I can't go into the details right now, but Canberra has asked me to fly down to Virginia for a meeting with one of your senior intelligence guys. Something about a better understanding of the Chinese military build-up in the Asia-Pacific, which is a subject I am supposed to know all about. Probably just another junket, to make me feel useful,' he lied.

They exchanged pleasant banter for another half hour, enjoying an increasingly easy rapport, before Tom interjected.

'I had better watch the time. Your seminar starts soon, and I have a flight to catch. It's been lovely seeing you, Maggie. Hope we do it again soon.'

'I insist on it, soldier, and I intend delivering on my promise to show you a good time in the Hamptons, where I plan to subject you to some really bad cooking. I'll give you a call at the Consulate and set something up, that is, if there's room for me in the diary of a bachelor in uniform?' she laughed.

'Absolutely! I look forward to it,' replied Tom, gathering his bag and leaning over the table to deliver a polite kiss to Maggie's cheek. There was a special chemistry there, one that was palpable to both of them, and Tom felt sure that they both needed to explore it further.

Just as he and Maggie stood to leave the park-side café, a car horn sounded and a black Mercedes slid into the curb side, pulling up adjacent to them. It was Tom's aide-de-camp, Mike Stephens. Mike wound down his passenger side window and called out to his boss:

'You ready to get started for the airport, sir? Traffic's a bit heavy this morning, so I thought we should try to make an early start.'

Tom climbed into the front seat of his consular vehicle and waved a hurried goodbye to Maggie, as his driver gunned the vehicle into the traffic stream. The specially modified sedan surged forward, responding to its driver's adept hands on the wheel as it glided smoothly through gaps in the dense traffic towards the outskirts of the city and the airport freeway.

'Nice looking lady, sir, and a nice job of saying goodbye,' said Stephens, with a larrikin smile on his face. 'If I may say so, sir, you're not doing too badly for a bloke who only arrived in New York a couple of weeks ago.'

'You may *not* say so, Mike. She is a beauty alright, but she's just someone I met professionally, at a function in Melbourne last month. I promised to look her up when I arrived in the States. Incidentally, how the hell did you find me? Didn't we agree to meet outside the Andaz at 8.30?'

'We did, but I make it my job to know where you are at all times. You are important diplomatic cargo, sir, and about to become an important field asset. Lazarus said I should cover your back, 24 / 7, as your bodyguard, though he forgot to mention that you could handle any opponent better than I could. I have some additional briefing papers he has sent for you to read on the plane - some background on CIA Director Angiotti and some suggestions on how you should play the first meeting with him. They're in the diplomatic briefcase on the rear seat, sir. It is a carry on size and immune from inspection. The combination is in this envelope.'

An hour later, Tom Grant boarded an American Airlines flight and settled back into his business class seat for the one hour trip to Ronald Reagan airport, about eleven miles from the Langley CBD. He had been told that he would be met on arrival by a CIA representative and transported to the meeting with Angiotti. Until then, he had plenty of time to read and absorb the extra material sent by Lazarus. He was sure it would be couched in general language, to avoid direct reference to the subject matter of their meeting and prepare him subtly for his discussion with the CIA chief.

As he scanned the text, Tom recognised Lazarus' unmistakable hand in the crafting of the briefing, which described Angiotti as a shrewd and highly effective intelligence chief who Lazarus considered a close and trusted friend. He did not, however, think the same basis of trust extended more generally to others in the CIA, who often treated correspondent agencies in other western countries as junior partners. Lazarus explained that Tom would need to work in tandem with an ASIS agent attached to the Australian Embassy, Washington (ASIS being the international arm of Australia's intelligence services), but that ASIO would remain the lead agency, because it had seniority in matters impacting international relations and national security. Tom was to work on building a close, personal rapport with Angiotti and to establish a contact framework with the CIA's other operatives involved in the investigation. He should also try to monitor whether the CIA retained principal carriage of the issue within the US Administration or whether authority was devolved to others, like Defence, State or Homeland Security. If that were the case, he was to try to identify the personnel in each other agency critical to the investigation and seek Angiotti's assistance in securing regular access to them as well.

If Angiotti attempted to interrogate Colonel Grant about Australia's intelligence assets, either in the USA, in North Asia or in Europe, or to farm Australian Intelligence on the Chinese military build-up, Grant was to be guarded in his comments, simply reinforcing the fact that Australia had excellent intelligence assets on the ground in North Asia and would support any reasonable request from the US for information. He should state that he expected an equal exchange of intelligence from the US.

Tom Grant finished reading the brief and returned it to his diplomatic briefcase, just as the aircraft banked and began its descent into Reagan. With no baggage to collect, he was soon through the baggage area and approaching the footpath. There, he found an African-American wearing Marine Corps fatigues bearing the rank of sergeant, holding a placard displaying Tom's name. He approached the man and identified himself. This prompted a smart salute from the marine sergeant, though Grant was not, himself, in uniform. After receiving the curt instruction 'this way, sir', he followed the marine to the concourse and climbed into a waiting military vehicle for the twenty-minute drive to Langley. They soon left the industrial precinct around the airport and entered a more residential quarter, which seemed much too urbane to be home to the intelligence headquarters of the world's most powerful nation. Perhaps that was precisely why it had been located here… to be an invisible presence in the chaotic, urban sprawl. Just outside of the Langley CBD, the vehicle slowed, veered off the freeway into a private driveway and rolled down a ramp leading into an underground tunnel. The vehicle eventually emerged from the end of the tunnel into a well-lit, cavernous underground car park.

'We take a lift from here to the lobby, sir,' advised the marine. 'Someone will come down, clear you through security and take you to your meeting.'

After completing security formalities in the lobby, Tom Grant was approached by a smiling young woman who introduced herself as Nicole Price, Frank Angiotti's personal assistant. She shook his hand vigorously and led him to a lift, requiring a secure access code to access the top floor suite, where CIA Director Frank Angiotti was waiting to greet him.

'Welcome to Langley, Colonel Grant,' said Angiotti, extending a hand and shaking Tom's firmly. 'It's good of you to come. Your people down under speak very highly of you. We are pretty thin on the ground in Asia, where you guys seem to be fairly well deployed, which is why I contacted your ASIO head, Sir Robert Chandler, and suggested we join forces and try to sort this thing out together. I guess you know some of the details, but I hope to fill in the gaps and bring you up to speed. Let's get started.'

Tom Grant settled into Angiotti's sofa, and Nicole reappeared, took orders for coffee and departed again, closing off the area's heavy glass doors. Grant was sure the area was regularly swept for bugs and cleaned.

'First up,' began Angiotti, I'd like you to take a moment to read this extract from my deputy, Charles Ritter's, report. He seems to have prodded a hornet's nest with it, since it has cost him his life. You and Lazarus will receive the full report, but I hope the short extract I have provided for this meeting will raise your eyebrows and make an impression,' he added.

Tom Grant read through the extract, becoming deeply absorbed in the horrific picture it painted of the effects of an electromagnetic pulse weapon exploding in the upper atmosphere. He was shocked by its final observation that *"the consequences are unimaginable and would take our nation back to the dark ages. The social impacts of a breakdown in law and order, including street violence and contests for food and water by an angry, frightened and disorientated civilian population, are self-evident".*

'Good Lord,' said Tom. 'Since the shocking scourge of mustard gas in the First World War, the Geneva Convention has been strictly enforced by all governments. Severe economic sanctions and other harsh penalties have been imposed to prevent further development or use of any such weapons. We all fear that, one day, an evil nation-state might use weapons based upon chemicals, like sarin gas, or germs, like anthrax, but no one ever imagined that a civilised nation state like China would ever stoop that low. Nor did we ever contemplate such an extraordinary weapon, capable of attacking an entire continent. This electromagnetic pulse is a new frontier of madness. The fact that it can be launched atop an ICBM by an adversary on the other side of the globe and detonated a couple of hundred kilometres above its target must make it difficult to detect in time and to interdict. However, if your military guys know where the launch sites are, they should be able to monitor them, using satellite surveillance, and take them out when a launch is initiated, before any missile is very far down range, shouldn't they?' said Grant.

'I thought so, too, Tom, so we looked at those options more closely. However, our military analysts tell us that, if the Chinese were to launch all of their Dongfengs simultaneously, at least 15% would get through our counter-measures. They have 600 of these Dongfengs. That means ninety would get through. They only need one to reach its predetermined aperture over North America to achieve their objective,' said Angiotti. 'Now that you've got a handle on the EMP threat, let me show you some photographs taken at the crime scene. They show how fiercely our enemies must have wanted to prevent disclosure of this development.'

Angiotti handed Grant a folder of photographs including the gruesome images of Deputy CIA Director Charles Ritter's purplish corpse. Grant noted the neat, round bullet entry hole between Ritter's startled eyes, with its dark ring of gunpowder residue, which he recognised as the hallmark of a close range, execution-style shot. But what really shocked him were the two Chinese characters embossed into Ritter's forehead.

'Bloody hell!' said Grant. 'Looks like some sadistic Chinese bastard has left you a calling card... but why do that? What possible motive?'

'Crazy, isn't it? That's the part of the riddle we are anxious to solve. First up, we sent the photos to an associate of ours at Princeton, a woman who heads up the school of Political Science there. She specialises in Asian studies, is a fluent Mandarin speaker and reads Chinese. She tells us the symbols are *Dong* and *Feng*, meaning *East* and *Wind*. Together they form the name of the Chinese ICBM which Ritter's report claims China has rearmed with EMP warheads. Like you, our Princeton expert found these images gruesome, out of character for the Chinese, and hard to accept.'

This gratuitous piece of information captured Tom's full attention. He knew of only one head of the School of Political Science at Princeton.

'I don't suppose your Princeton expert is Dr Maggie King?' said Grant.

'That's right,' replied Angiotti. How the heck did you know that? She was recruited four years ago, not as a field operative but as an 'accredited advisor'. She has been given special security clearance to provide advice and expertise to the agency and is working with our analysts to improve their understanding of the Far East. She also consults on a case by case basis and gives us information on promising students, with a gift for oriental languages, who might be recruited as we work to build up our Far Eastern intelligence assets. She's an important member of our team.'

'I know the same Dr King, but in another connection. When she is not involved in clandestine work for you, she is a highly regarded commentator on foreign policy and its effects on east-west relations. I first met her at an annual public policy oration in Melbourne, Australia, where she assessed the impact upon the Asia-Pacific balance of power of China's rapid emergence. Since then, we have stayed in touch. In fact, we hope to catch up socially during my stay here in the US.'

'Excellent,' replied Angiotti. 'She might be useful in helping us understand the political fallout from this thing; you know, advising how we should play the situation to make our point with the Chinese, while limiting damage to the bilateral relationship. Why don't I ask her to work in with us on this?'

'If you don't mind, Frank, I think we should avoid telling Dr King about my involvement, unless you really need her in on this. We need to keep this thing tight, given its implications for both China-US and for wider, global relations. I really don't want to betray my involvement in it. I am supposed to be here under our military exchange program with the US and it's best if people continue to think that is the *sole* purpose of my visit.'

'I agree,' said Frank. 'You are much more valuable to us under cover.'

'Meantime,' continued Grant, 'I am uneasy about this whole thing. I smell a rat. The Chinese might be communists, but they are deeply Confucian in their thinking. Historically, that has made them a pacific people, who rarely engage in aggressive behaviour beyond their shores. I hope you are wrong about them. On the other hand, they have been fairly belligerent towards the Japs lately, over the disputed islands in the South China Sea, and we still haven't seen the colour of their new military leadership. Their president has recently cemented his power and is assuming a Mao-like permanence, and one of their military leaders is quoted as having said "*if China attacked Japan, the Americans would run like rabbits*". Our analysts consider that a loose remark, for domestic consumption, and the man was later rebuked for making it. I'd like to review everything you have on this thing and run it past our China analysts before we jump to conclusions. It would be helpful to know more about Ritter's involvement in the Dongfeng missile thing. Maybe there's some history we are missing; some snippets about the people he contacted or the intel sources, both here and abroad, he used in his report, which could point towards the people who did this.'

'That makes a lot of sense,' replied Angiotti. However, in the light of the execution of one of our most senior intelligence officers, I was obliged to pass on details to Bill Nordish, the National Security Adviser. It wouldn't surprise me if Bill recommends that the President calls in the Chinese Ambassador. He is a hawkish bastard and might opt for confronting the Chinese with the facts and requiring a formal government response.'

'I sincerely hope he hasn't done that yet. That would be both premature and provocative, given the political volatility of the matter, and I promise you that the Chinese won't appreciate being shirt-fronted in public,'

'We'll see,' replied Angiotti. 'These may be difficult times – politically and economically - for America, but we are still the world's most potent military power. We need to remind people about that every now and then. It's a question of how forcefully we do that. I'll try to get you a meeting with Nordish. You might be able to persuade him to take a more conciliatory view, before he gets the President all steamed-up about this thing.'

Although this was their first encounter, it seemed to Tom Grant that the two men had quickly developed a strong personal rapport. They were two blokes who didn't mince words or stand on formality and would work well together. When they had finished, Angiotti had shaken Tom's hand firmly and promised the Aussie intel officer that he would have unfettered access to him at any time, for any information or assistance he required.

As Tom Grant made his way back to the airport, his thoughts returned to the Chinese characters burnt into Ritter's forehead, and he was deeply troubled by them. It was improbable that the Chinese would commit such a brazen crime on US soil and it made no sense that they would incriminate themselves in that way. He decided that, as soon as he was back at his desk, he would contact Lazarus and provide a comprehensive, confidential report on his discussions with Angiotti. He would ask his government's security agency to lodge a formal request for as much background on Ritter as Angiotti could provide. He would also share with Lazarus his serious reservations about Chinese involvement and ask for a forensic effort by Australia's intelligence agencies – ASIS, ASIO and ONA, to confirm or deny China's alleged deployment of EMP warheads.

White House – Washington DC

Lt. General Bill Nordish entered the 'Situation Room', a secure conference room in the West Wing of the White House set aside for Presidential briefings on sensitive political or military developments. The Situation Room was made famous as the place from which an earlier President had viewed live coverage of the commando operation to capture and kill Osama Bin Laden. Nordish found the Secretary of State, Elizabeth Rankin, the Chiefs of Staff and the Vice President already gathered there. They would be joined by the President. Then Nordish would brief them on the execution-style slaying of Deputy CIA Director Ritter, on the contents of his intelligence report and on its likely implications for national security.

Nordish was a big man with a gregarious nature, traits which had quickly made him a commanding presence around the White House. He was in his sixties and balding, but he still possessed the rugged good looks and athleticism of a former college footballer. His appointment as National Security Adviser followed a distinguished military career and he had been rewarded for his strong support for the President during the election primaries. In the army, he had been a firm, charismatic commander, making difficult decisions easily. However, while these traits were virtues in the military, in his national security role they were seen by some as a bit blunt. His predecessors had been people of thoughtful temperament, with a consultative, rather than an emphatic, opinionated style of leadership.

National Security Advisors were personally appointed by the President, using his executive powers, so their appointment required no public sign off by the Senate. As a result, they were seen as God-like figures, who had the President's ear. Nordish's appointment put him in the company of other, titanic figures in American public life, including Henry Kissinger, Condoleezza Rice and Colin Powell. Like them, Nordish enjoyed an office near the President's, in the West Wing of the White House, giving him ready access to the nation's leader in the course of his daily duties. At length, his commander in Chief, US President James Kennelly, entered the Situation Room, and they all rose to acknowledge his arrival.

'Please remain seated, folks, and let's get this underway. I'm due out of here by chopper in about forty minutes. Over to you, Bill. It's your meeting.'

'Thank you, Mr President. Yesterday I received a call from CIA Director Frank Angiotti, who had some quite disturbing news. His Deputy, Charles Ritter, had failed to show up for an important meeting, whose principal purpose was to share his latest intelligence on the Chinese military build-up, looking particularly at their Dongfeng ICBM program. Ritter had been leading the investigation into this highly sensitive matter, so when he failed to show, Angiotti immediately sent a team to Ritter's home to investigate what might have happened to him and, above all, his report.'

'That's all very interesting,' said the President, 'but are you saying that there are national security implications? Was the report stolen?'

'Bear with me, sir. I am coming to that. When Angiotti's team reached Ritter's home, they found his corpse in the lounge room. He had been executed, gangland style, by a single bullet to the forehead, leaving an entry hole between his eyes. That extraordinary event was, however, eclipsed by the discovery that Ritter's forehead had also been branded with two Chinese characters, *Dong* and *Feng*, meaning *East* and *Wind* in Mandarin, the name of the Chinese Intercontinental Ballistic missile.'

'What if this was just a sadistic, criminal act, by some disaffected troublemaker wanting to get even with Ritter,' countered the President.

'We considered that, sir, but the evidence supports a much more sinister motive. Ritter was working on a report about the rapid increase in China's military capability, and it focussed upon their Dongfeng program. The report had a political twist, as it had been commissioned by the Defence Appropriation Committee of Congress and was to have been made public yesterday. Imagine the global outrage, and the political difficulties for you at home, sir, if Congress had come to learn about this new military threat, being developed right under our noses? Even worse, what would a world audience think when they learned that we had lost such a sensitive report.'

'Dear God,' said the President. 'I see what you mean.'

'Yes, sir, and that's why we are desperate to reschedule the tabling of the report, to buy time, and why the CIA is so desperate to track it down.'

'But surely you have secure copy in the agency,' said the President.

'That's just it, sir. Given its controversial nature, Agent Ritter decided to manage all of the sensitive intelligence aspects personally. He insisted that there was information which could embarrass your government and which needed his personal supervision and vetting. Against his better judgement, he took his draft report home over the weekend to give it a final polish. When we learned this, we immediately instituted a forensic search of his house, wanting, above all, to retrieve the report and confirm that its highly sensitive contents had not fallen into foreign hands.'

'And did you find his report?' inquired the President.

'Here's where it gets interesting. After sending in two teams and combing the place twice, Angiotti's people finally discovered Ritter's security-coded briefcase, containing his report on the Dongfeng missile. Computers emit a faint electromagnetic signal and Angiotti's team was able to exploit this technology to locate the report. It was hidden in an air-conditioning duct, so he had gone to extraordinary lengths to protect it. Ritter must have known that foreign powers wanted to get their hands on it, or wanted to prevent its publication, so he went the extras mile to protect it. The code needed to open his attaché case was an incredibly obscure one. The code turned out to be a ten-letter word... *i s l e o f d o g s* ...which was a strange arrangement of letters written on a slip of paper. We found it in the wall safe in his office at CIA headquarters and used it to open his attaché case and read its explosive contents. The attaché case was intact, with no unexplained fingerprints on it or signs that it had been tampered with. We are therefore confident that, even in death, Ritter managed to deny his assailants access to the report.'

'And his report?' asked the President. 'What did it say?'

'His report was dynamite; more shocking than we could ever have imagined. I have provided an executive summary of its contents in a single page brief, which I will hand to each of you now. You must return it to me before you leave this meeting. Ritter's full report, which contains a more complex, scientific explanation of a new weapon the Chinese have developed and of its likely impacts, will be provided separately. However, it is probably best if I try to explain all of this in layman's language,' he concluded, pausing to let the group digest his dramatic introduction.

'Ritter's report confirms that the Chinese have armed their Dongfeng ICBM's, 600 of them, with SEMP warheads. SEMP stands for *Super Electromagnetic Pulse* – a pulse triggered by a nuclear detonation in the upper atmosphere which is capable of bringing the entire North American continent to its knees. Computers, most electronic devices and even high voltage power lines would fail, leaving the continent in darkness and creating a communications 'winter'. Imagine life with no phone lines, no mobile phones, no television broadcasts and no wireless communication. No ATMs, no electronic banking, no share trading, and electronic record systems wiped. In short, our modern, organised society would cease to exist, the economy would crash and the civilian population would panic, reduced to animals fighting for survival. Unrefrigerated food would rot in supermarkets across the nation, untreated water and sewerage would spread disease, traffic lights would fail, causing road chaos, and so on.'

'I see,' the President said grimly, as he processed this horrific scenario.

'Well, Bill, we can't let that happen. This SEMP thing may signal the start of another conflict, something our nation can ill afford at the moment. Let's go around the table and have your ideas on a possible response. I will cancel all of my other appointments until we get to the bottom of this thing. Let's start with you, Bill, then I want Elizabeth's view, setting things out from the State Department's perspective. If this thing is as serious as you say, we need to tread carefully. I want to understand how best to deliver a firm response through diplomatic channels before we start rattling sabres. I don't want to call upon the Chiefs of Staff, unless we face some sort of military brinkmanship. You first, Bill. What do you think we should do?'

'Well, Mr President, I think we could start by calling their ambassador in and demanding an explanation. If we were dealing with the North Koreans we would not mince words, but these guys are a different kettle of fish. 'We've never been in this space with them before. They are, how can I put it, *inscrutable*, to say the least. That's why I favour a strong retort. They might be on the ascendancy economically, but we need to remind them that we are still the big guys in town when it comes to a shoot-out.'

'I agree, Bill, but I wouldn't use that sort of language on a sensitive issue like this,' replied Kennelly. 'What's your view, Liz?'

'I agree about controlling the language,' replied Liz Rankin. 'And I also agree with Bill that the first step is to call in their ambassador. We could hand him a *demarche* - diplomatic jargon for a *please explain* letter - less strong than a *Note Verbale* but still short of an ultimatum. If that fails, we can front them in the UN by calling a special meeting of the Security Council and threatening sanctions, but that would be very aggressive.'

'If we challenge the Chinese and cause them an international loss of face, might they do something stupid? You know, react militarily? And do we have enough assets on the ground if that happens? asked Kennelly, raising the spectre of a possible military escalation.

'They'd be crazy if they did, sir,' replied Nordish. 'They got their fancy new Jin Class nuclear sub, with an 8,000-kilometre range, and their shaft speed is pretty much up to ours across all naval classes now. But we've been consolidating our *Operation Asia Pivot* for two years now, and we got much better feet on the ground. Pivot is all about rebalancing in the Far East, both on a rotational and forward station basis. The Chinese don't like it, 'cause they want to control the South China Sea. They got a long way to go before that happens. Hell, our Military Sealift Command, based out of Singapore, has forty-eight ships able to lift thousands of tonnes of equipment and supplies into that theatre at a moment's notice and we're beefing up the deployment of aircraft, subs and missiles in that theatre. I reckon they'll react diplomatically.'

'They'd be crazy to try anything else,' insisted Nordish, 'but I'll get our forces to go to DEFCON 3, increased readiness, just in case.'

'I hope you're right Bill,' countered the President. 'OK. Let's begin with a response from the State Department. Manage it out of your office, Liz. Start by drafting your *demarche* and arranging an interview with the

Chinese ambassador. Run the wording by me before you get it out there but do it quickly. We need to stop this thing now, before it's too late.'

The group broke up and set about their respective tasks. Bill Nordish felt slightly aggrieved at the public put down he had received for his use of aggressive language and disappointed that he would not take the lead on the issue. However, he was pleased that his suggested approach had been adopted. Wanting to regain lost ground with the President, he returned to his office and prepared a carefully worded report on the key points raised in the Situation Room and the actions to be taken by each of those present. He included, as an attachment, the full text of Charles Ritter's recovered report, and added a postscript about CIA Director Angiotti's call on support from friendly intelligence services, which he described as a helpful initiative, reinforcing the US position...

"Respecting their superior intelligence on the ground and specialist language assets in North Asia, we have shared agent Ritter's intelligence with ASIO and ASIS, the two key Australian intelligence services, and have sought their support to investigate and report back on Ritter's assertions about the Chinese use of SEMP warheads. Colonel Tom Grant, who is visiting the US as an Exchange Fellow under our military exchange program, will serve as the liaison between our respective intelligence services and assist our investigation. His intelligence codename is 'Archangel' and his diplomatic cover role, Defence Attaché."

Satisfied with this tidy summation but, in his zealousness, underestimating the security looseness of even an internal email, he pressed *Send*.

Three hundred kilometres south of Washington, in his New Jersey safe house, Russian station chief *Peregrine* studied the cyber-intercept report, conveying Ritter's report and General Nordish's summation of the meeting in the White House Situation Room. He read these with great delight. The Americans had swallowed the bait. If events were allowed to run their likely course, there would soon be a major diplomatic blow up between Washington and Beijing. The Chinese Ambassador would be called in, sparking an immediate escalation of tensions between the two States and a heightening of aggressive sabre-rattling and blunt diplomacy. It looked as though Pushkin's strategy, though risky, had been a masterstroke.

***

While Secretary of State, Elizabeth Rankin, was composing the diplomatic demarche with her senior advisors at the State Department, Tom Grant was busy at his desk in New York, digesting a coded message from ASIO in response to his report on the meeting with the CIA's Frank Angiotti.

Grant's report to 'Lazarus' had focussed upon facts, avoiding unfounded speculation. It had reported Ritter's brutal execution and the evidence provided in Ritter's report that the Chinese had acquired an SEMP warhead and were fitting it to their land-based Dongfeng missiles. Grant had recommended that ASIO and ASIS use their assets in North Asia and Europe to investigate the credibility of the American report. He had also asked that they look into Deputy Director Charles Ritter's background, to see if there was anything outside of his present intelligence duties that might have triggered the brutal attack. Grant had also recommended that they investigate Ritter's use of the curious code '*i s l e o f d o g s*' for any clues it might provide. Finally, he had added his assessment that a covert Chinese operation on US soil would be highly unusual, entirely at odds with Chinese historical practice and thus needed careful examination.

Tom Grant's first intelligence report had attracted an immediate reply from Lazarus. The SEMP issue had such major international implications that time was of the essence. Hence, it had been sent directly to Grant, electronically, in cypher, rather than through the usual embassy diplomatic channels. Lazarus' reply was the first communication with Grant using the charismatic young Colonel's new ASIO codename, '*Archangel*', a name which Tom Grant found amusing in the context of his more mundane cover role. As Grant was new to the intelligence game, Lazarus had interpreted all acronyms used familiarly by seasoned intelligence officers to identify various agencies, like the US Intelligence agency (Uncle), the British domestic intelligence agency (Mother) and the Russian FSBR.

"FOR ARCHANGEL'S EYES ONLY," it began.

"Have instructed field agents Europe and North Asia to investigate SEMP and DFAT and ONA to assess Chinese actions. The following will inform a cautious response to Uncle, under intelligence sharing arrangements:

1 Ethical considerations - need for caution:

- *This belligerent action is totally at odds with Chinese thinking and practice. Recommend caution while both sides investigate further.*

- *Aggressive response from Uncle could lead to 'Amber' conditions, (escalation in our region) and should be avoided at all costs.*

- *Remind Uncle that the US was first to develop EMP warheads following its own early, upper-atmospheric testing over the Pacific.*

- *Remind Uncle that the US has a credibility issue. It has established an EMP Commission, giving a government imprimatur to this worrying WMD technology and provided funding for its further development.*

- *For your eyes only, ASIO Intel confirms that US Air Force has secretly developed a new EMP weapon, described as a precise beam which can be 'concentrated, targeted and delivered surgically by fighter aircraft to take out discrete targets - e.g. office buildings, factories, etc.'*

2 Possible Third-Party Intervention / Deception

- *Following an all-stations search for linkages to the code word 'i s l e o f d o g s', we have positive feedback from London station. The 'Isle of Dogs' is a freight terminal located on an island in London's Docklands.*

- *While protecting the reasons for its request, our London station thus asked Mother (MI5) to research any linkages it could find with this site. Mother reports that, in 1981, she intercepted signals from US Embassy Attaché Charles Ritter to Uncle, reporting code red interdiction and interrogation of Anatoly Pushkin, Second Secretary, Soviet Embassy.*

- *Pushkin, at that time a suspected KGB agent, was later medically evacuated and replaced by Tatiana Petrovic, Second Secretary.*

- *Pushkin is the present Head of the Central Asian Directorate,*

Federal'naya sluzhba bezopasnosti Rossiyskoy Federatsii (FSBR) the new Russian espionage agency which succeeded the KGB and was established following the collapse of the Soviet Union.

- We think the historical linkages between agents Ritter and Pushkin and the geographic linkage in use of the security code 'i s l e o f d o g s' more than coincidental. We must thus explore Russian involvement.

- Our analysts think it possible that a Russian espionage mission on US soil may have been undertaken to implicate China in a wider threat, as a means of distracting attention from its attempts to annex the Ukraine.

- If so, and allowed to succeed, a mission of this sort has potential to ignite military tensions between the US and China while neutralising the threat of China's rapid emergence on Russia's southern border.

- Dongfeng was originally the Soviet CS missile, transferred to China under a post-war joint development program which the Soviets ceased in 1981. China has since improved the missile's range to take in Moscow, causing Russia to closely monitor its further development."

***

Due to the fourteen-hour time difference between Canberra and New York,

Lazarus' coded message did not reach Tom Grant's office until late on Friday evening. Fortunately, his aide-de-camp, Mike Stephens (codename *Tennessee),* was still at his desk. Understanding the importance of the transmission, Stephens had immediately contacted Grant to advise that he had received the transmission and would call by his boss' hotel with a deciphered copy.

Around midnight, Mike Stephens met his boss outside the Andaz hotel lobby. Grant returned to his room where, in the relative security of his isolation there, he digested Lazarus' report, tore it up and flushed it down his hotel toilet. At precisely the same time, 127 kilometres to the south, in his New Jersey safe house, FSBR station chief Sergei Andropov, codename *Peregrine,* was digesting the same text, relayed to him from Moscow's cyber interdiction unit. Appreciating the moment of its disturbing message, he prepared an urgent, encrypted message for his visiting intelligence chief, Anatoly Pushkin, codename *Red Bear*, outlining the threat posed by the meddling Australian intelligence agencies:

"CIA has invited friendly intelligence assets to investigate claimed use of SEMP warheads by China. Australian intelligence assets in North Asia seriously question the US claim, holding that the Dongfeng program is obsolete. A joint British and Australian investigation into Ritter's use of a security code - isleofdogs, a wharfage area on the outskirts of London - has since linked Ritter to his 1981 interrogation of FSBR chief, Anatoly Pushkin, to extract intel on Chinese theft of Russian ICBM technology for use in their Dongfeng program. The Australians have connected the dots and suggested Russian involvement in Ritter's murder. Imperative that we prevent ASIO's US operative 'Archangel' (Col. Tom Grant) delivering this intelligence to the CIA until after the US demarche is delivered, accusing China of using EMPs warheads and engineering the desired military tension between the two States. Critical we hold or eliminate Colonel Grant, New York-based ASIO operative, before he can relay his intelligence. Request that you sanction extreme measures – Peregrine."

In his Boston condominium, the disfigured Russian Security Chief, Anatoly Pushkin (codenamed *Red Bear),* studied Peregrine's report with alarm. He had not yet undergone corrective surgery on his leg or cosmetic surgery on his facial disfigurement. His surgeon had first insisted that he wear painful callipers to align his twisted leg. Surgery would follow, one procedure at a time, with a hiatus between each operation. Although he was geographically remote from Moscow, this allowed time for him to share in and direct his team's covert espionage mission. As he read Peregrine's report, his mood darkened. The bloody Australians were about to rain on his parade. His orders were short and emphatic:

"Imperative you delay submission of ASIO report. Use extreme measures, including elimination of Archangel, to buy time and ensure Americans can lodge their diplomatic complaint with the Chinese – Red Bear."

Andaz Hotel, 5th Ave., New York

It was 8.00 a.m on a splendid autumn morning. Tom Grant sat in the ground floor coffee shop, enjoying the rich vapours rising from his cup and looking out of large picture windows at a rising tide of pedestrians and vehicles, as New York's sleepy morning came to life. Right on time, the silver Mercedes, with its distinctive diplomatic plates, pulled into the curb and Corporal Mike Stephens emerged. Tom had persuaded his aide-de-camp to lend him the diplomatic vehicle for the weekend, insisting that he could drive himself to Maggie's beach house in the Hamptons. In truth, his driver would have relished the trip to the exclusive Hamptons, but Tom needed to spend quality time, alone, with this special woman. Taking his driver along would have cramped his style. It would also have seemed a bit pretentious. Though Mike Stephens was disappointed that he would not visit the scenic Hamptons, and would feel a little naked without his much loved automobile, he approached the coffee shop with a wide smile, saluted and handed the keys to his boss.

'She's gassed up and ready to go, sir. Easy on the accelerator. You'll find she has a fair bit of grunt when you want it, a real muscle car,' he added proudly. 'A five litre V8 under the hood, wide mags, low profile racing tyres, so if you get into any trouble she'll give you a quick pair of heels.'

'Thanks for your concern, Mike, but what can happen on a quiet weekend in the Hamptons? If I get into difficulties with Maggie, they'll be the sort of difficulties a big boy can handle himself,' he said with a mischievous grin.

'I'm sure you're right, sir, but you never know in this business. I've left a tourist map on the seat, but Ms King will probably direct you, since she will know the best routes. Have a great weekend and we'll see you on Monday.'

Tom Grant took the keys, slid his long frame into the driver's seat, which had to be adjusted back to its fullest extent, turned the ignition key and felt a surge of power as the innocent-looking little Merc leaped forward. A short way down 42nd Avenue, he turned into an underground parking station, where he would park the car until Maggie's arrival. As he steered the nimble machine down the ramp, he reflected on Mike Stephen's comment about a 'quick pair of heels'. Mike's experience with covert operations had made him naturally overcautious, and Tom wondered how he might have reacted had he known that Maggie, too, was an advisor to the CIA. He had been amazed to learn of this extra-curricular aspect of her work and wondered what other surprises she might have for him.

They had agreed that Maggie would drive up from her campus in New Jersey and leave her car in Tom's parking spot, so that they could travel together in one car. She would need time to travel the fifty miles from New Jersey to New York, via Edison and Newark, and hoped to arrive around mid-morning. When she arrived, she would ring up to his room. With time to kill, Tom made his way back to his hotel for a lazy breakfast. After breakfast, he returned to his room, packed an overnight bag and changed into a marine blue shirt, white slacks and a sweater, appropriate wear for a visit to the highbrow area, which was home to the rich and famous.

At 10.30 a.m his phone buzzed, and Maggie's chirpy voice greeted him. He found her waiting in the foyer, looking casually stylish in faded jeans and an oversized sweater, which highlighted her tanned physique and dazzling blue eyes. She smiled widely, scooted over to him and offered her right cheek. Tom bent forward and greeted her with a gentlemanly kiss, feeling immediately comfortable with this gorgeous, if mercurial, new woman in his life. Maggie took his hand, as naturally as a wife might, and walked him to the curb, where her small Volkswagen Golf stood idling. She beckoned him into the passenger seat, jumped in and drove them to the adjacent underground car park, where they had agreed to transfer to Tom's car.

'I'm a bit of a novice when it comes to finding my way out of this city,' said Tom. 'Why don't you drive until we get out of the CBD? Then we can stop somewhere for a morning coffee and change over.'

'Sounds good to me,' replied Maggie. 'It is a bit of a task getting out of New York, but I think I can handle it. Once we're through Manhattan, we swing onto the freeway and it becomes much easier. The freeway takes us to the outskirts. Then, if you like, I can show you the lazy route. It winds through seaside villages. It will add two or three hours to our journey to my place at Gibson beach, but it's worth the detour.'

'Sounds excellent,' said Tom.

'Most people travel down on the Long Island rail,' she continued. 'It's much faster, but a bit boring if you ask me. We have lots of time and I think we should just cruise. First, I will get us onto the Long Island Expressway. Then, near the end of the peninsular, we can turn onto Sunrise Highway, route 27 East, which takes in most of the cute hamlets. From there, it's a cinch. You'll love the quaint little shops and coffee houses, the great beaches and the smell of salt in the air,' she added.

Once seated behind the wheel, Maggie marvelled at the power of the compact sedan, as she touched the accelerator and it leaped forward.

'What the...!' she exclaimed. 'This car is a bit nippy, isn't it?'

'I meant to warn you,' said Tom. 'It has been modified. I'm a bit of a car freak, so I ordered a sports package, with a bigger engine,' he lied.

Maggie made her way cautiously through the underground car park, dodging its tight corners as she found her way towards the exit ramp, then swept up its sloping surface towards the dazzling sunlight above.

Further down the street, a late-model SUV idled at the curb side. Behind its wheel, Russian agent Peregrine watched the smiling couple emerge from the underground car park and turn into 42nd Street. He shifted his dark grey rental vehicle into drive, allowed two vehicles to intervene and made a U-turn into the traffic, joining the procession of cars. He would remain a calculated distance behind Grant and tail his Mercedes as it made its way out of the city. Half an hour later, both vehicles were making good time along the Long Island Expressway. Traffic had thinned now, and Maggie was clearly enjoying the responsive little machine.

'What a great car!' said Maggie. 'If it were not for the regular parade of motorcycle cops, I'd risk putting my foot down and winding her out.'

'I was just thinking the same thing,' said Tom. 'Why not? This is my consular car and it has diplomatic plates. They can't touch me. Why don't you pull over and let me drive and we'll see what this baby can do?'

Maggie seemed genuinely amused by her companion's mischievous suggestion. He was revealing himself as a man with a keen sense of humour and an irreverent disdain for convention. Maggie pulled into the shoulder and they changed places. Farther up the freeway, surprised by this unexpected manoeuvre, Peregrine slowed, then realised that he would have to roll on by them and wait for them to catch him up. He wondered how long that might take and worried that he might lose his tail. Now he was the one being followed, but those concerns were soon allayed. A break appeared in the traffic and Tom pressed the accelerator to the floor. The sporty little Merc surged forward, sending a spray of gravel flying and fish-tailing out of the layby, as its powerful engine propelled its wheels across the loose surface. Finding the bitumen, they gripped with a shriek of rubber and launched the nimble sedan into the traffic stream. Tom stitched a route through the slower cars, traversing three lanes of traffic and settling into the fast lane. Then he shot forward, leaving the tide of general traffic in his wake. Maggie tossed her head back and roared with laughter as they rocketed along.

It had taken mere seconds to reach and overtake Peregrine's SUV. They had streamed by it as if it were standing still, catching Peregrine by surprise. Startled by this manoeuvre, and unable to match the speed of the sleek Mercedes, the Russian watched helplessly as his prey darted in and out of the traffic stream in front of him, until it disappeared into the horizon. Forced to stay within speed limits, Peregrine spent the next hour scanning the traffic ahead, trying to identify his elusive targets. At length, fearing he had lost them, he lifted his handset and dialled Red Bear.

'Pree-vyet, Red Bear. Archangel is driving a souped-up vehicle and has left me in his dust. He sped off suddenly, as if he were trying to shake my tail. But why? There was no way he could have seen me. He's never seen me or my vehicle before and he can't know that we are following him, not unless he's bloody clairvoyant. I will just have to continue my pursuit and hope that I can re-establish contact. There is only the one, main trunk

121

route. It eventually feeds onto the single lane route, taking day trippers through the villages. I reckon they will head that way. In any case, there are too many people out here to risk an intercept on a busy freeway and I don't fancy a contest on a freeway against that quick vehicle of his.'

'Calm down, Peregrine. Any attempt to take him on a public road would be sheer lunacy,' replied Red Bear. 'You must choose your moment carefully, when the opportunity presents, to take him quietly. Use the girl. She is his Achilles' heel. He is the chivalrous type, and I'm betting he'll do whatever it takes to protect her. Wait until they stop for a break. Let them leave their vehicle. Then tail them and see if you can intercept the girl and use her as a pawn. He will have to play along. You might have to take some risks, but for God's sake, be subtle. Try to get them both back into his vehicle, not yours. You then cover them from the rear seat, and leave your vehicle parked. That way, you can force them to drive you to the old potato farm, hide their vehicle in the barn and stymie any police search when they fail to return. We only need a few days… enough time for the Americans to deliver their diplomatic tirade to the Chinese. To achieve that, you may have to eliminate them, but be discreet. Keep me posted. Dosvidaniya.'

'Da. Da,' replied Peregrine. 'Dosvidaniya, Red Bear.'

After a burst of exhilarating speed, Tom had slowed to a more sensible pace, conforming to the general speed limits. The Long Island peninsular was now becoming noticeably narrower, with the seascape intermittently visible, as small bays and inlets cut into its narrowing girth. They took the exit onto the Sunrise Highway and followed its picturesque course through Southampton and on to East Hampton. Having made good time, Maggie suggested that they stop for lunch when they arrived there. Presently they approached the beautiful hamlet, cruised to a stop on its outskirts and examined Mike's map to better understand the maze of small roads and one-way lanes criss-crossing the village. As they idled on the roadside, Peregrine breasted the hill behind them and immediately spotted the silver Merc glinting in the distance. Relieved that he had re-established contact, Peregrine closed the gap, pulled over and waited for their next move.

Maggie and Tom moved off again, having decided to turn into James' Crescent, in search of Maggie's favourite inn, aptly named 'The Hampton

Inn'. It was a delightfully English B&B set in picturesque gardens, which offered coffee, Devonshire Teas and light lunches, served on its rustic terraces. They drove down a side driveway, parked the Merc in the car park at the rear of the property and walked to the rear of the cottage, where an open door took them through a hallway to the side terrace. The air was crisp and the mood relaxed, as Tom directed Maggie to a table overlooking the cottage garden, seated her and beckoned a waitress.

'I have heard that the Hamptons is a domain reserved for rock stars and billionaires,' said Tom. 'How does a humble academic like you have access to a weekender in this splendid place?'

'Most people could never afford a place out here, but Dad bought the place years ago, before it was fashionable, back when it was dotted with struggling vegetable growers and potato farms. It was a smart investment. Mom was grateful that he kept it all those years and left it to us. He loved it out here. When I am here I can feel his presence,' replied Maggie.

'Tell me about your Dad?' asked Tom.

'Well, he was one of those men who managed to find time for his family despite a demanding career. Dad began life in a middle-class home, but he was one of those driven individuals. He had a gift with people and he was smart. He became the managing partner of his law firm, specialising in litigation, and made lots of money. In the early part of his career, when I was a little girl, Mom complained about the hours he worked, but he was always special to me. He would come home late and look in on me, even when he thought I was fast asleep. He would tuck the blankets around me, kiss me on the forehead and whisper 'sleep tight, my little darling', and I would snuggle deeper, knowing, simply, that my dad loved me.'

'When he became more senior and had lots of staff working for him, he had more time for us. He bought the weekender in the Hamptons, and it became our special retreat. He loved it here, and Mom and I spent many weekends following him along the beach, digging up clams with our toes for him to use as bait, and watching the sun go down as he stood in the surf with his big beach rod, pulling in flathead and whiting until it got dark. Then, about twelve years ago, mom told me he was ill. He had cancer and it didn't look good. He died shortly after that. I miss him terribly. Mom doesn't come here anymore, because it reminds her of a good man she loved dearly and it makes her sad. She could sell our beach house for a lot of money, but she knows how many memories it holds, how much it meant to my brother and me, and it remains an important way for her to remember Dad. That's why she can't bring herself to sell it. So, there you have it. I hardly know you, but here I am, bearing my soul and spilling my innermost thoughts to a virtual stranger, as if we had been friends for life.'

Tom found this sudden release of emotion endearing. How had this strange young woman from another country touched him so deeply, he wondered? She evoked a strong, protective urge in him. He couldn't help imagining Maggie as a little girl, running and gurgling along a beach, while her dad fished in the evening tide. It was an important moment, when the latent sexuality that had brought them together gave way to a more fundamental humanity, exposing the softer sensibilities of this ostensibly strong and successful woman, and he found her immensely attractive.

'I am touched that you shared that with me, Maggie. It makes you more real to me. I don't know if I would ever have the same courage to share my innermost emotions. My story seems trite by comparison,' said Tom.

'Try me,' said Maggie. 'If I can share in that way, so can you,' and with that, she reached across the table and took his hand. That simple gesture was electric for them both. Tom found his hand closing around hers and they looked deeply into each other's eyes, crossing a new frontier.

'Well, it's a long story. As a young SAS officer and later, serving in Afghanistan and other places, I couldn't allow myself to get too close to any woman. Life was too fragile and the risks too high. Unlike yours, my British father was an austere man who could never show emotion. I spent most of my youth yearning for a sign of approval from him. The only sign that I had pleased him came when he said 'well done, old boy' and shook my hand. I don't think he could ever have held me, let alone kiss me on the forehead, but somehow, I know he loved me. That stern upbringing, and a lot of macho military training, which promoted a tough guy culture, made me terrified of showing emotion, or getting too close,' he confided.

'Life in the army was tough and, for many of my colleagues, pretty short. To his credit, my dad encouraged me to read, study and improve my mind. I worked hard at uni, graduated with Honours and then did a Masters. After Afghanistan, that gave me some extra skills to draw upon. I was rapidly promoted and posted back home to my current, cushy job in strategic command. I had a nine-to-five role at a desk and, for the first time in years, a normal social life. Completely by chance, I met a beautiful woman, a member of our Foreign Service, who was involved on a project with me. We fell in love, but I lost her tragically. She was badly burned in an accident and very self-conscious about her scars. Later, she took her own life. She thought the fire had disfigured her face, but I still thought she was beautiful,' he added. 'She broke my heart, and I thought I could never love again. That was three years ago,' he replied, 'and I still find it hard to talk about.'

Maggie was deeply moved by Tom's confession and could see how his tragic loss had left him emotionally fragile. She was starting to develop feelings for the tall, rugged Aussie, but she would need to take it slowly, one day at a time, if she were to kindle the fire she felt was flickering in their souls. The waiter appeared with their food and a carafe of wine and their conversation became much lighter, turning to her academic research into China's emergence as a superpower and its impact upon the west.

That work paralleled Tom's work in strategic command, so they had soon swapped their intimate exchange for an easy discourse in a more relaxed world of their own making. When they had finished their meal, Maggie looked at her watch and suggested it was time that they moved on, before the afternoon passed them by. She excused herself to visit the rest rooms, while Tom agreed to settle the bill and re-join her in the car park.

From his well-hidden position at a small table on the adjacent veranda, Peregrine peered over a newspaper. Through the building's old, refractory glass windows, he watched a distorted image of the couple on the next veranda as they prepared to leave. He rose quickly and followed Maggie's progress toward the rest rooms. 'Perfect,' he thought, as she disappeared into the ladies' convenience. He moved on past the rest rooms and turned into an alcove further down the hall, which Maggie would have to pass on her way to the exit. Presently, she re-emerged and made her way down the hallway towards the rear car park. As she approached Peregrine, he stepped into her path and pointed his Makarov semi-automatic pistol at her, a small but lethal weapon which packed a deadly punch. Before she could protest, he addressed the startled woman in an urgent tone.

'Not a word, Dr King. Any sound you make will be your last!' With that, he moved behind her and pushed the barrel of his gun into the small of Maggie's back, prodding her with it towards the exit. 'Make your way quietly to the car park. Do exactly as I say and no one will get hurt.'

There was a steely menace in the Russian's tone and his eyes burned with quiet fury. His body chemistry and a determined set of jaw told Maggie that he was deadly serious and not a man to be trifled with. She dropped her head in a gesture of resignation and made her way quietly toward the car park, with the Russian following closely behind.

'Is this something to do with my work for the CIA?' she asked. 'You obviously don't understand. I am simply an adviser on foreign relations, a consultant, like any other, not a spy. I am here with a visitor from abroad, a friend who knows nothing about my work for the CIA. He needn't be involved in this. Just take me and leave him here,' she suggested.

'Don't patronise me, Dr King. We know about Colonel Grant's work with ASIO and his cooperation with your precious CIA. It is Grant that we want, not you. You are small fry. We only want to talk with him, so just do as I say and no one will get hurt,' he repeated.

Maggie was surprised to learn that Tom was involved in covert activity, if what the Russian had said was correct. She would never have picked him for that. Her mind whirred with confusion as the Russian marched her to the Mercedes with his pistol thrust into her back. Once there, they turned around to face the rear of the B & B and wait for Tom to emerge. 'Smile as Colonel Grant approaches. If you try to warn him, you will both die. Just tell him I am a colleague and you are giving me a lift up the road. Understood?'

Maggie nodded her agreement, believing that the Russian was fully capable of carrying out his threat. Nonetheless, she felt a compelling need to warn Tom, by some subtle facial expression perhaps, a distorted smile or a roll of her eyes, anything. After settling the bill, Tom finally emerged onto the rear veranda and made his way across the car park towards Maggie, noting the stranger standing beside her and wondering who he might be. When he was just metres away, Maggie flashed a suspicious look and addressed him in a stern, remote manner, totally at odds with their familiarity, causing Tom to question what the hell was going on.

'Colonel Grant, allow me to introduce a colleague. He has a place just down the road and I have agreed that we will give him a lift,' she added.

The tone of Maggie's voice and her stilted body language convinced Tom that something was seriously amiss. As he drew closer, he realised that the stranger's arm was directed at Maggie's back. His military antennae and her defensive demeanour told him that she was a hostage, with a gun to her back. Not wanting to antagonise the man or endanger Maggie's life, Tom feigned innocence, offering a greeting, and extending a handshake. The stranger recoiled, sensing something dangerous about the athletic Aussie's demeanour, and kept a safe distance between them.

'Forget the niceties, Colonel Grant, or should I call you *Archangel*? As you can see, I have a gun in Dr King's back. Do exactly as I say, or she gets it. Front passenger seat for you, Grant, and you, Dr King will drive. Get in!'

Seeing no alternative, the couple climbed into Tom's vehicle as directed.

Peregrine climbed into the rear seat behind them with his pistol trained on Maggie, and Tom was directed to punch coordinates into the Mercedes' Satnav system to lead them to the village of Sagaponack. Maggie knew this to be a more sparsely populated area and was filled with dread. Once home to a remote community of traditional potato farmers, whose farms had dotted the landscape fifty years before, Sagaponack was now wedged between the old money of Southampton and the nouveau-riche billionaires of East Hampton, leaving small pockets of rural isolation.

Tom looked nervously over his shoulder, his mind working feverishly to calculate how he might overpower the Russian. As if by some telepathic thought transfer, Maggie felt the same urge. Suddenly, she slammed her foot down on the accelerator, sending the powerful Merc fishtailing across the car park and causing Peregrine to lose balance and lurch to one side.

Grant chose this moment to spin around and lunge at Peregrine's gun, but the Russian quickly regained his balance and his fist, holding the cold steel of the hand gun, came crashing down onto Tom's skull. The last thing Tom remembered was a distant, shrill cry of protest from Maggie, as dots began to dance before his eyes and everything went black.

Dept of State, Washington DC

Chinese Ambassador Liu Qixin, Political Counsellor Sun Maomin, and an Embassy interpreter followed the American desk officer, Far Eastern Affairs, to the 10th floor conference room, where US Secretary of State, Elizabeth Rankin, was waiting to receive them. Ambassador Liu had been greatly puzzled by the call from Rankin's office requiring, rather than requesting, his presence at the 9.00 a.m. meeting on this pleasant autumn Monday. As a seasoned diplomat with fluent English and several earlier postings to western capitals, Ambassador Liu understood that the circumstances associated with calling in an Ambassador were special and often signalled a serious problem in the relationship between the nations. In the normal course of events, it was incumbent upon his office to go through diplomatic channels to seek an appointment with the host country's officials, particularly when they were senior political leaders.

Anticipating something out of the ordinary, he had brought with him two other Embassy colleagues, Political Counsellor Sun Maomin and translator Xiao Lin. This was a routine measure in such circumstances, to ensure that there were Chinese witnesses to the exchange. Counsellor Sun was a well versed, senior political officer, able to assist Liu with any deficit of knowledge about issues currently at play between the nations.

When Ambassador Liu entered the room, he found US Secretary of State Rankin even more heavily supported by a retinue of senior State Department officials. In this way, Rankin hoped to underline her status as the senior diplomatic spokesperson for the world's leading superpower and, for her part, to ensure that there were American officials present to record the exchange. Although the two were good friends, she received the Ambassador coolly, extending a handshake and beckoning him to sit beside her at the head of the conference table. She had decided in advance of the meeting that the two would sit together at a corner of the long table, rather than in the usual configuration of each team being aligned along opposite sides. The wily head of State realised that seating the two groups opposite each other tended to generate a confrontational atmosphere, particularly if a terse exchange was necessary, and she preferred to soften the chemistry of the meeting by changing the seating.

'Dear Madame Secretary of State,' began Ambassador Liu, bowing his head with exaggerated politeness, 'How can I be of assistance?'

'Thank you for coming, your Excellency,' began Rankin. 'I wish I could say that the purpose of this meeting was cordial, but unfortunately, I have to inform you otherwise. Let me get straight to the point. Intelligence channels, both here and abroad, have provided what they regard as irrefutable evidence of a very disturbing and, might I say, provocative development associated with your county's military disposition in the Far East. While we accept that China now has the resources to upgrade its military capability and a legitimate military role in its own domain, around the South China Sea, that political latitude does not extend to military initiatives which threaten a much wider theatre, including North America. We are informed that you have recently refitted your Dongfeng missiles, which have the range and capability to reach the United States, with so-called SEMPs, Super Electromagnetic Pulse warheads. SEMPs are explicitly outlawed as WMDs under UN regulations. Deploying them puts China in breach of its international treaty obligations. Our weapons experts inform us that your SEMPs have the capacity to take down our entire North American electronic systems, including telecommunications and the power grid, with wider implications for public infrastructure. That provocative action, and the stealthy way it has been introduced without the required international notifications, has created a new threat which is unacceptable to the United States. We are, therefore, left with no option but to issue this diplomatic demarche, requesting that you immediately remove and destroy these warheads. We also seek your agreement to our weapons inspectors verifying their removal and destruction, as outlined herein,' concluded Rankin, handing over the formal demarche letter.

'You will be aware that a demarche only amounts to a firm, diplomatic request. It is a subtle first step, so to speak, along the path to reconciling this problem. It does not have the force of a demand or an ultimatum, but I would encourage you to instruct your Premier that, should China vacillate in responding positively to this firm request, we will have no hesitation in escalating our concerns to the next level. That would also include an address to the UN Security Council, and a UN enforcement motion, which would make your provocative action a matter of global public record and a political embarrassment. Should you not respond positively to our demarche, we will move to an ultimatum. The President has been briefed on this proposed course of action and I have his and his Government's complete support for it. The President shares with me a wish that we might enjoy a long and cordial relationship with the People's Republic of China, but that relationship must always be founded upon openness and trust, not upon deception. China must now demonstrate those qualities.'

Liu Qixin was not amused by Rankin's forthright manner. His gregarious mood quickly vanished and was replaced by a more sombre tone. He seemed visibly shaken by Rankin's accusation, a state of mind which Rankin had not witnessed before in the warm, highly intelligent diplomat, with whom she had enjoyed regular diplomatic exchanges. Liu had always seemed comfortably in control, exuding the confidence of one whose appointment to the United States was evidence of the high regard in which he was held by both Governments. Liu requested a pause to review Rankin's remarks and assess their implications, resulting in an embarrassing silence while he consulted with his two advisors in guarded whispers. The meeting thus degenerated into a private, side dialogue.

In the absence of any advance briefing on the matter, Liu realised that he would need to stall, allowing time to contact Beijing to obtain verification or denial of the American claims and give his Government time to prepare a carefully worded response, the protocol required of China in response to a formal demarche from one nation to another. Beneath his calm façade, Liu's mind worked furiously through a range of options. He struggled to understand why he had not been briefed on such a provocative military initiative. China's new military whiz-kid, General Zhang Ming

Wei, had certainly turned China's military fortunes around, making its detractors sit up and think. This development sounded entirely consistent with the aggressive young general's work to rapidly modernise China's military and elevate its global military standing. For a brief moment, Ambassador Liu felt a flush of pride, enjoying the possibility that China had finally captured America's undivided attention with its new, super weapon. However, he had come to like the Americans and was a cautious man who favoured peaceful negotiation and an intellectual process, above threatening language. He was simply not in a position to confirm or deny the facts outlined by Rankin. If they were true, the issue could escalate dangerously. He would make it his priority to confirm the facts first, retain a calm and inscrutable façade and buy time for his government to respond more formally. After several minutes, he turned back to the charismatic stateswoman seated beside him and offered her a guarded response:

'Madame Secretary, I am merely the humble servant of my Government. I am not party to the intricacies of our military establishment. I am, therefore, not able to offer you a response at this time on this matter. It is not in my province of expertise. But I can assure you that China has always been a peaceful nation, preferring diplomatic dialogue to any form of aggression. Indeed, we have often been the subject of invasions, in ancient times, by the Mongol hoards to our north, and more recently, by the Japanese, who still rattle their swords at us over islands off our coast, which have been the haven for our fishermen for over a thousand years. China has always believed that there is room in our world for all nations to exist in harmony. I assure you, Madame Secretary, that this remains China's policy and my wish. I will see that you receive a formal response to your demarche. In the meantime, I would ask you to avoid any over-reaction or escalation of your concerns until I have had a chance to explore details more fully.'

'Thank you, Mr Ambassador,' replied Rankin. 'I will expect a response from your Government within twenty-four hours. That is all,' she added. Upon concluding with that final, terse remark, Elizabeth Rankin stood and left the room, leaving a bewildered Chinese team still seated at her table.

Rankin had played her cards well. She had learned that, when flexing diplomatic muscle, a bit of bold theatre often achieved more than mere

131

diplomatic words. Bolstering the display of strength and providing a soft undercurrent of anger would have made the message unambiguous. In the mind of this strong, charismatic woman, blinking or showing weakness would be counter-productive. A weak-kneed approach was not an option for a superpower such as hers, particularly at this critical time in its history, when it was beset by so many other distractions, sent to dilute its national resolve. There were the global economic uncertainties, war in the Middle East continuing to drain the public purse, divisive politics at home and now the spectre of a new superpower testing the boundaries of its global influence. In Asia, the US was still an interloper rather than a potent, visible military presence. Perhaps this latest development would change all of that, particularly now that America's European cousins and its NATO allies were reeling from their own economic meltdown. Whatever the challenges, Rankin would not see America humiliated on her watch. She would let China know that she meant business.

If the first, relatively subtle step of issuing a demarche failed to elicit rapid compliance by the Chinese, she would call an emergency meeting of the UN Security Council. Publicly outing China's belligerent action would ensure wide, international consternation. If China did not remove their SEMP warheads, the next step in the exchange was an ultimatum, a final precursor to declaring the deployment of SEMP missiles an act of war.

***

Ambassador Liu Qixin wasted no time in returning to his desk at the Chinese Embassy and preparing a scrupulously accurate account of his meeting with US Secretary of State Rankin, for immediate despatch to Beijing. In it, he questioned why he hadn't been told of this provocative development and asked whether General Zhang Ming Wei might assist his inquiry. His message went in cypher to the Foreign Ministry, but was also copied to Vice Premier Wei Jintan, bypassing the trivial desk officers in the Foreign Ministry, in deference to the seriousness and urgency of the matter. The Chinese *Guangxi* system ensured that close acquaintances always enjoyed special access. Liu was confident that he had the ear of his close family friend and schoolmate, now China's Vice Premier, and that he would be rewarded for reporting to him directly.

Wei Jintan, in turn, wasted no time reporting the development to senior colleagues in the political hierarchy. He also contacted the central committee Secretariat and requested an immediate audience, which he suggested should include the charismatic young General Zhang, to seek confirmation that the PLC had indeed armed its Dongfeng missiles with SEMPs. The matter would ultimately require a council of senior party and military officials to determine a response to America's provocative action.

At 14:00 hours Beijing time, General Zhang Ming Wei left his Beijing office and made his way to the confidential briefing convened by Vice Premier Wei Jintan. When he arrived, he found he was in good company, including two senior members of the Central Committee of the National People's Congress, the Foreign Minister, with three of his senior advisers, and the PLO's ranking Air, Naval and Ground Force Commanders, who made up China's High Command. The assembled group sat around a modern conference table awaiting General Zhang's arrival. The modernity of the conference room belied the external landscape in which they found themselves, at the rear of Beijing's ancient, Forbidden City. The Forbidden City had, for centuries, been the national seat of power and a focal point of political intrigue in China. Security was tight and access only available to those with exalted rank or special passes. When General Zhang had extended polite greetings and taken his seat, the Vice Premier moved to his place at the head of the table, signalling that it was time to get down to business. His intelligent eyes made contact with each of the assembled officials through a thin mist of steam, issuing from their collective cups of green tea. Satisfied that all those summoned were now present, he ordered the doors closed, and brought the meeting to order.

'Tongshimen', he began, in the gruff Mandarin of a *chende Beijingren*. '*Womende jintiande gongzuo ...*'

'Comrades, our duty today is to clarify a most pressing issue, which has potentially dangerous consequences for our relationship with the United States of America. You will each have received copies of a top secret report from our Ambassador in Washington, outlining a meeting he was summoned to attend by the US Secretary of State, Elizabeth Rankin. At that meeting, she accused our nation of a provocative act in arming our Dongfeng ICBMs with electro-magnetic pulse warheads, classified as WMDs by the UN Security Council and therefore putting us in breach, they allege, of our international treaty obligations. I have asked General Zhang Ming Wei to brief us on this weapon technology, on whether we possess it and have deployed it, as the Americans claim we have. I am hopeful, General Zhang, that you will have a good explanation for this, as it has created a serious diplomatic incident and brought us to a sudden and dangerous impasse with our major western military adversary. Please enlighten us, General.'

Eyes turned to the wily young General, who disappointed his audience by removing his tinted glasses and polishing them slowly with a cloth, a device he had perfected, much as a British diplomat of old might have used his pipe and tobacco, to buy time while his fertile mind weighed the issues and calculated a careful response. Those close to the highly intelligent young General had long since come to recognise that his military wisdom was only surpassed by his political cunning, which had been a major factor in his rapid rise to prominence.

'My dear Vice-Premier, let me put your mind at rest on the question of arming our Dongfeng missiles with so called SEMP warheads. We have not done so, and the fact that the US believe we have raises more questions than it answers. It is true that we are up-grading our Dongfengs, as we consider them old technology. However, even when their range is upgraded, they will represent little more than a marginal deterrent.'

'The Dongfeng was deployed some years ago. It is a high-altitude missile, but not sufficiently high to penetrate shallow space and is therefore vulnerable to American interdiction technology. Its deployment in our old, underground "Great Wall" silos, established at the beginning of the cold war, means it lacks mobility. In today's high-tech environment, that is a fatal flaw. It means that we can't disguise our launch sites by regularly changing their location. Foreign powers understood this problem thirty years ago and developed mobile launch platforms. However, let us ignore that issue for the moment and return to the vexing question before us. If we

134

choose to refute the American claim, we will still have to comply with their request to inspect our facilities, and I am strongly opposed to doing that.'

'If we don't have SEMP warheads, we should simply say so and allow the inspection. Why should we baulk at that?' insisted the Vice Premier.

'The issue is rather more complex, but let me try to explain. While the current fleet of Dongfengs have outlived their usefulness, one variant of the Dongfeng has been modified to launch satellites into low orbit, and I have initiated inquiries with a view to replacing the existing, limited altitude Dongfengs with that variant, giving us a much-improved deterrent. The upper atmosphere variant enables a vertical launch path into space, the shortest and quickest way to avoid interdiction. Those missiles which make it into upper orbit produce a circulating threat to specific targets, if we program their launch trajectories and global paths to fly over discreet targets. Perhaps foreign intelligence services have somehow come to know that we plan to upgrade the Dongfengs in that way and have made some grandiose assumptions about our intentions,' replied the General.

'Could we not simply deny the accusation and allow an international group of inspectors, including some of the neutral powers, to inspect the silos and satisfy themselves that they are not armed with SEMP warheads, but rather, just with usual, conventional warheads?' inquired the Vice Premier.

'My dear Vice Premier, that is precisely the problem. There is really no such thing as a SEMP warhead. In simplest terms, a SEMP warhead is just a large nuclear payload, but one programmed to explode at a precise apogee in the upper atmosphere so that it sends an electro-magnetic pulse - a shock wave - back to earth, taking out electrical appliances and installations. Theoretically, and practically, our space launch Dongfeng variant has that capacity, though we haven't contemplated using it that way. While our physicists know about the magnetic pulse effect and can replicate it, we are light years away from perfecting practicalities - re-entry control technologies and other scientific aspects necessary to position our warheads accurately in relation to the earth's magnetic field.'

'To be effective, a Super EMP has to be detonated precisely, that is, at a precise altitude above the earth, at a precise juxtaposition to the intended

135

ground target and at a precise point within the earth's magnetic field, so that it can distort the field and create a powerful shock wave,' replied the General. 'Hence, the American assumption is half right but is extremely flattering in its assumption that we have the capacity to read the earth's magnetic signature and position the detonation precisely so that it impacts North America. Do we tell them we don't have that capacity, and look like a third rate power, or equivocate and win the metaphorical victory of having them believe that we *do* have that game-changing capacity?'

'I asked you here to help me solve a problem, General, and you have given me a new headache. When will the new, space-launch-capable Dongfengs be in place?' inquired the Vice Premier.

'I think it may take ten years. It is not a question of technology, Mr Vice Premier, but of accommodating the nation's budgetary appetite for such an ambitious program, one which, in the light of this development, must now be considered urgent,' replied Zhang. 'But the impact upon the Americans, and their NATO allies, in their believing that we have that technology already, provides China with a 'Great Leap Forward', to quote Mao - an effective military deterrent now, not ten years later, and will save our defence budget billions while we buy time to catch up.'

'So where do we go from here?' replied the Vice Premier.

'I know it is not my place to suggest this,' responded the young General, as those around the table listened in silent fascination, such was the power of his personal magnetism. 'I am not a diplomat, but rather a pragmatist who hopes to offer clumsy advice. However, the committee should know that it has a brilliant and unassailable diplomatic response.'

At that point, the assembled throng was silenced, enthralled by Zhang's masterful understatement, which had captured everyone's attention.

'Point one: The Americans, not we Chinese, developed the SEMP effect. They must answer to an anxious world... not us. When they were testing their early nuclear devices in the Pacific, they exploded one in the upper atmosphere and created an electromagnetic pulse, by accident, taking out the electronics on their own Island of Hawaii and accidentally discovering the potency of this technology.

136

Point two: Like the A - bomb over Hiroshima, they were the first to introduce and use the technology.'

'Since then, instead of keeping this development under wraps or rejecting it as a sinister weapon of mass destruction, the US has chosen to create a national SEMP Commission, funding further research into the magnetic effect and giving the technology legitimacy within their own government.

'Point three: This technology is available on the internet. Any nuclear country can, theoretically, employ it. At this time, however, only the USA and Russia, have the capacity to deliver it, so the American's belief that we now have that capacity makes us a member of a very elite club.'

'Those are three compelling reasons why we should not feel any moral compunction to bend to America's demands. Rather, if they press the issue in the UN, we will have an opportunity to explain to the world that the US invented the technology, was the first nation to use the technology, and that it gave the technology legitimacy by establishing a Government funded, SEMP Commission. Moreover, they have recently tested an airborne variant of a pulse beam which can focus energy on a discreet target - a high-rise building or a manufacturing facility, to strike it surgically and take out its electronics. This exposes American hypocrisy.'

'In diplomatic terms, this means we can counter the American claims by noting their own use of the technology and asking for a countervailing inspection of their own silos, of their own SEMP Commission and of its research facilities. This would highlight their own inappropriate action and expose their own, practical military applications of the technology. Ideally, we should signal that this will be our diplomatic response, and that it will be made public. They will surely then choose to withdraw their demarche. In the meantime, as a precautionary measure, in case this diplomatic response fails to dampen their zeal, I propose that we place our nuclear submarine fleet on high alert and program our air-interdiction arrays to monitor all US or allied moves in our region, including from Japan and Guam. In military jargon, that means bringing our forces onto an 'Amber Alert' footing, a move which their military observers will quickly detect and interpret and one which will tell our American friends that we do not kowtow to their demands in our own front yard,' he concluded, fascinating his audience with the audacity and brilliance of his response.

The usually stern Premier, Wei Jintan, smiled in acknowledgement of the young General's elegant solution to the problem, before replying.

'Once again, General Zhang has done his homework and come to our rescue with a clever proposal. General, I will instruct the Military High Command and the National Security Committee of the People's Congress to formally give you their approval to bring our forces to *Amber Alert*. You should have it within the hour.'

'Mr Foreign Minister, you may begin preparing our response to the American demarche, in the terms outlined. I will require clearance from the Executive Committee of the National People's Congress, which will take a few days, and we will then arrange for our Ambassador in Washington to deliver it. In the meantime, Mr Foreign Secretary, please instruct our Ambassador immediately to advise the Americans that work on our response has begun and that they should have it within one week, a reasonable time period for our political system to digest and approve it. Remind them that approvals from their congress can rarely be obtained in such a short time and beg their indulgence politely for the slight delay. That is a necessary bureaucratic inconvenience they will have to live with.'

***

At 23:00 hours, Beijing time, the Chinese Naval Command ordered its fleet of nuclear submarines to come up to *Amber Alert*, which entailed arming missiles, dispersing sonar arrays, and maintaining silent running beneath the surface. While most of China's nuclear submarines had nuclear power plants and nuclear launch capability, some still ran on diesel, not nuclear power. They required the support of surface tankers. This made any change in fleet status easy to interpret. Diesels were noisier than western nuclear subs and could only remain submerged, with occasional snorkelling, for several weeks. US satellite surveillance and covert monitoring of the Chinese fleet's movements immediately picked up these subtle variations in the Chinese fleet's disposition. Hence, by 23:40, the US Pacific Naval

Command had reported the Chinese elevation of alert status and commanded its own fleet to move their DEFCONs (Defence Readiness Conditions) from DEFCON 5 (Fade-out, the lowest state of readiness) to DEFCON 3 (Roundhouse, increased state of readiness, pursuit and monitoring). This upgrading of US alert status was immediately detected by China's Naval Commander, South China Seas, and reported back to General Zhang. Pistols on both sides were now, relatively speaking, cocked and loaded.

In Moscow, First Secretary Vladimir Vyacheslav received a report from Commodore Valery Kutznetsov reporting that both Chinese and US Naval forces had come up to a higher state of war readiness. Vladimir wasted no time in reporting this to Russian Supreme Command and to the national security service. Anatoly Pushkin's deputy, who had admired the brilliance of his boss's plan to escalate tensions between the two powers, was delighted with this evidence and passed it immediately to Washington station for covert transmission to Anatoly Pushkin, codenamed *Red Bear*.

'Sunrise' Potato Farm, Long Island, USA

Tom Grant slowly regained consciousness in what seemed a dark, musty place. He winced at a sharp pain in the back of his skull and instinctively attempted to reach up and explore his wound, but found that his wrists had been tied behind his back. As his senses returned, he discovered that his feet were also tied. He was in some dusty old cellar, he guessed, a dark abyss where vision was limited. Although he was now fully conscious, his senses were dull and slow, telling him that he must have been drugged. Despite this lethargy, he recognised the stench of rotting vegetation and an unmistakable smell of rope, a queer combination which puzzled him at first. As his eyes adjusted to the dark, he was able to make out the blurred shapes of sacks filled with lumpy produce, probably hessian bags loaded with rotting potatoes, he reasoned. Now fully conscious, he recalled the struggle in the car, when he had tried to disarm their strangely-accented assailant. The stranger had brought his gun down brutally onto the back of Tom's skull. A sharp pain had followed, then blackness, making everything since that event a mystery.

When he attempted to move his head, he found that his hair had become attached to the sack behind him. A matted, blood-soaked clump of hair had adhered to the spot where his head rested. He eased his head painfully forward until the matted clump released its grip, freeing him to turn his head and survey his surrounds more completely. His mental processes were still dulled and slow, but he was able to discern important little things, like the stillness and solitude of his location. There was no sign of Maggie, so he assumed that she, too, must be captive somewhere else. There was no sense of any other presence, either in his dark prison-cellar or the rooms above.

Years of training in the SAS and lessons learned from his military service in Afghanistan had taught the former commando to use each of his senses as tools of assessment. He also knew instinctively to search for any weaknesses he could exploit, but his mobility was seriously impaired, making that a difficult challenge. He rolled onto one side, slumped to the floor, and used his feet to propel his body through the rows of sacks, as an inchworm might, two feet at a time, in a calculated search for any point of escape. As he rounded a large pile of potato sacks, his attention was immediately drawn to a faint light, coming from a spot high up in a corner of the cellar. The light seemed to be escaping from a rectangular hatch located at the top of a wooden stairway. He propelled his torso across the cellar floor towards the bottom of the stairway, where his proximity to the light source gave more definition to his surroundings. Breathing heavily from his exertions, he propped himself against the bottom step and paused to assess his situation. He established that he was, indeed, in a farm storage cellar, and that there was no obvious way out, apart from the hatch at the top of the wooden stairway.

From where he lay, he could now hear the muted sounds of a voice speaking what seemed like Russian. Although he could not understand the language, Tom judged from the tone of voice that there was a heated exchange taking place between his captor and someone on the end of a telephone.

Above him, oblivious to the fact that his captive had regained consciousness, Peregrine was in an intense discussion with Red Bear about what to do with his hostages. His controller's initial instructions, the day before, had been unambiguous. They had required that the two be eliminated before they could deliver Grant's intelligence report to the CIA. Then, shortly after their first exchange on the motorway, Red Bear had called back to say that he had now had second thoughts. The decision to eliminate Colonel Grant and Dr King had been made precipitously, in the heat of the moment, and he now considered that a dangerous option. While it remained imperative that Grant be prevented from delivering Lazarus's report to the CIA, any action which suggested interference by a foreign agency must be studiously avoided. Indeed, any action which gave grounds for doubting the accuracy of Ritter's report on the Dongfeng missiles would be catastrophic, so disposing of the two, high-profile hostages required

141

careful thought. After reflecting further upon this dilemma, Red Bear had instructed Peregrine to hold the two securely until they had developed a fail-safe way to deal with them, without evoking any suspicion. A motorway accident, or a drowning, perhaps. This had resulted in a stay of execution, and Red Bear and was now discussing those more considered options with Peregrine.

'Are they absolutely secure and under your control?' inquired Red Bear.

'I have them locked up at the old potato farm. Grant is a pretty athletic man. He made a grab for my gun so I had to slug him with it. Since then I have kept him sedated with propofol injections. He is sleeping like a baby, tied up in the storage cellar with a swelling the size of a rock on the back of his skull. The girl was hysterical, so I had to give her propofol as well. They are both drugged to the eyeballs. I am holding the girl in an upstairs bedroom and topping up their dosages every couple of hours to keep them heavily sedated. Renting the old potato farm was a smart move. It is remote from traffic and there are no neighbours for miles. I could eliminate them right here and dump their bodies somewhere later. They wouldn't be found for some time and it would be difficult to link their disappearance to us,' suggested Peregrine.

'Don't be so sure. If their bodies are found, there is sure to be an autopsy, given their high profiles and their connection with Langley. An autopsy will reveal puncture marks in the skin from your propofol injections and chemical traces in their bloodstream, you idiot. We will need to think about those. And if you dump them on Long Island, the CIA might trace the vehicle from public security cameras, and then link the car rental agreement back to us, even allowing for the fake identity you gave. If the bodies are found anywhere near the old farmhouse, the CIA will put two and two together and we will have a full-blown catastrophe. Both of these people have links to the CIA, so we need to come up with something much more subtle. We will have to make their deaths look like an accident, or simply destroy every vestige of evidence of their bodies, so that they simply disappear. We cannot afford any connection with us or with our network. That would be catastrophic to our mission.'

'The car crash idea might work,' suggested Peregrine, 'but it would be difficult to stage one in this flat terrain. Maybe a moonlight swim and a drowning, but I would have to submerge them in water first, park their car at a remote beach and get them into the surf undetected. I would need help, not just to move the bodies, but to arrange the accident. Could you send Alexei to assist? I will keep them on ice until tomorrow night to give you time,' said Peregrine.

'A good idea, comrade. You will need help, and we need to think this through carefully to ensure there are no mistakes. A road accident or a drowning still leave the problem of an autopsy and the risk of a finding of misadventure. If that happens, we will have the law all over us. I will send Alexei to work with you on the problem. You might think about chartering a small vessel and arranging an accident at sea. There are lots of charter businesses at marine jetties along the coast. You could book a one-day charter, posing as a tourist or, better still, rent a motor launch. Then you could rendezvous with Alexei further up the bay to take the bodies on board, make your way offshore, arrange a fire on board and have Alexei bring you back in a second boat, at nightfall. If we think through the details and do a thorough job, there will simply be an accident at sea and some charred bodies. Although they would be charred beyond recognition, with nothing to connect us to their deaths, we will need to ensure that some personal articles remained, allowing easy identification of the two,' added Red Bear, happy with this neat suggestion.

From his position at the foot of the stairs in the cellar, Tom Grant was able to overhear snippets of the conversation above him. He had no Russian and was thus unable to understand the conversation he was overhearing. However, the unmistakable cadence of the Russian tongue had given him a new insight into his captors, confirming the Russian connection which Lazarus had suspected. That connection and the common ground around China's development of the Dongfeng, using Russian technology, and Ritter's interrogation of a Russian agent years before, provided a clear motive for Ritter's murder. However, there must surely have been a more serious purpose in taking such a public risk. The murderer's crude act of embossing Chinese characters into Ritter's forehead made Chinese involvement an obvious conclusion, but it seemed too clever by half. If the CIA knew about this latest Russian twist, they would have grounds to suspect that Ritter's death had been stage-managed. If that were so, what was the motive? Ritter's report on the Dongfeng had to be the key. It was the only motive that made sense. The Russians must have corrupted Ritter's report, creating a deception to frame the Chinese for some obscure reason. That was a dangerous game to play with an emerging superpower.

Tom Grant knew that he must find a way to contact the CIA boss, Angiotti, as soon as possible. It was essential that Angiotti receive the Australian intelligence suggesting Russian involvement in Ritter's assassination, before the international incident got out of hand. By now, Ritter's report would have resulted in emergency meetings in Washington and quite possibly caused an aggressive response to the Chinese action, heightening tensions between America and China. As his mind processed these thoughts and their likely consequences, Tom Grant knew with absolute conviction that he must escape from this place and warn the Americans. If things went pear shaped, many lives would be at risk. At the same time, he felt a deep, personal need to find Maggie and protect the special woman who had come into his life, if only he could establish what the Russian bastards had done with her. If she were still alive, he would find her and make them pay. Either way, he had no alternative but to find a creative way to break out of his present predicament. If he did not escape, he would be trapped in the cellar, in a drug-induced stupor, while a potentially deadly game played out between two of the world's biggest military powers. That was an option he could not accept.

Before he had completed these thoughts, Tom Grant heard footsteps moving across the floor above towards his position and decided that he must be about to receive a visit. He shuffled back through the darkness, resumed his previous position and slumped back against the sacks. He would feign unconsciousness and try to learn more about his captors. Any attempt at aggression, in his drugged state, with arms and legs bound, would be futile.

Presently, the doorway at the top of the stairway opened, a cellar light clicked on and Peregrine's feet clumped noisily down the wooden stairway. He made his way over to Grant, who was slumped back against the potato sacks, and knelt beside his hostage. Peregrine's hand grabbed Grant's wrist and twisted it over, as he prepared to insert a needle into the prominent vein in the crook of Grant's arm. Grant felt his heart rate quicken in protest, as every fibre in his body urged him to lash out at his captor. However, he knew that this would only result in heavier sedation whereas feigning unconsciousness would give his captor a false sense of security and result in a lighter dosage. He felt the pin prick in his arm, followed by a sweet relaxing sensation as the chemical made its way into his system, invoking warmth and an irresistible urge to sleep. Then everything went black again.

On board USS Delaware, South China Sea

Commander Hank Vandenberg stood under the green overhead lights illuminating his command deck, quietly managing business as his beautiful new sub slid effortlessly through tepid, tropical waters northwest of the Philippines. The navy's newest acquisition had been christened at its stateside dockyard by the nation's First Lady, who had smashed a reluctant bottle of Veuve Clicquot against its arrogant prow just three months earlier and sent it sliding gracefully down its slipway into the embrace of its new, vast, ocean home. With the latest upgrades having been added to the Virginia Class sub, the Delaware bristled with world-leading technology. Displacing 7,800 tonnes, she had room on board for 134 officers and men. Her 377-foot-long hull was both an aerodynamic and an aquadynamic masterpiece, enabling her to cut through the stream of sea water surrounding her hull, which exerted huge hydraulic forces against it, at an astounding twenty-five knots, or forty-six kilometres per hour, a speed most surface vessels would envy.

While the USS Delaware was technically still 'trying out', her sea trials had been brilliant, confirming her place at the forefront of the fleet and her potency as a silent harbinger of death. The most critical elements of her performance during sea trials had been measured by a fleet of surface vessels, attempting to interdict her, and by sister subs seeking to ferret her out and tail her. She had come up trumps on all counts. The most important new aspect was her underwater hull signature, measured by her ambient sound and the turbulence set up by her propeller wash. It was so low that it heralded a new nadir of silent running which no other sub could emulate. Her nuclear turbines gave her a range measured in years (thirty-three years), not miles, and her missiles, designed for undersea deployment, were a potent nuclear deterrent and a final solution no sane person would ever wish to invoked.

USS Delaware had received instructions from Pacific Command to go to DEFCON 4 and was now following subsequent orders to close in on and shadow the Chinese Jin Class, ICBM- equipped subs in the surrounding international waters. The Jin Class was a sub which the Chinese had, themselves, designed after poaching all of the available technology they could from US, British, Russian, Scandinavian, Italian and Spanish designs. This gave China a 'smorgasbord' of options and was a brilliant strategy for an emerging power wanting to catch up quickly. The Jin Class thus had a much quieter hull signature than its predecessor, the 0-92 Xia Class, which sounded like a beached whale.

The Jin Class was a game changer for the Chinese. It carried the highly intimidating JL-2 nuclear missile, capable of undersea launch and with a range of 4,600 miles. China's earlier class of diesel-powered subs could achieve underwater speeds approaching those of their US counterparts. However, while their single driveshafts were quieter, their diesel engines made them much noisier. They required regular refuelling and snorkelling for clean air, leaving them light years behind the US. The new Jin Class, however, was powered by a nuclear reactor, driving its quieter single shaft and huge propeller smoothly and giving it much improved range. Its single shaft meant that its wake signature quietness was better than the American's and made it a formidable opponent in its own, home waters. There was now not much between them, except perhaps for the human command factor.

Delaware's Commander, Hank Vandenberg, was at the top of his game. He had won the contest for command of this beautiful new sub from an eager field of experienced, senior Naval Officers vying for the honour. The big Yank, of Dutch origin, had the muscular frame of a gymnast, a laconic sense of humour, a keen intellect and a slavish commitment to task, typical of a Hollander. He was also a born leader.

'Maintain silent running. Come to course two three zero. Maintain high crawl speed of eight knots while tracking Manila Trench,' Vandenberg announced over the on-board comms system. His First Officer repeated the order as Commander Vandenberg loped over to his helmsman's cramped sonar pit. O'Brian was glued to his deep scanner, viewing the surrounding seabed in extraordinary detail, as the sub turned its nose gently towards a course bisecting the Manila Trench. The trench was an underwater Grand Canyon, giving 2,000 metres of clear water below Delaware's keel, and ringed by subterranean cliffs which rose majestically from the volcanic floor of this unfamiliar, Asian seascape, a new frontier which the US Navy was keen to master.

An ethereal, green light was projected from a miscellany of computer screens around the command deck, making the submariners and their Commander look like actors in a Greek tragedy. Vandenberg's height meant that he was always slightly hunched over when working in tight areas on the sub and he tended to carry that stoop with him around the command deck, despite the more generous headroom there. Around him, his Exec Officers monitored running procedures while submariners and techs went quietly about their business, their labours punctuated by the intermittent 'pinging' of the sub's sonar, which was broadcast throughout the vessel. The background ping was ubiquitous, but it was not an irritant. Rather, it was a reassuring pulse, like a steady heartbeat. Any change in the regularity of the reassuring ping would sound *general quarters*, indicating a foreign intrusion or impending collision, and forewarning the crew that it must assume action stations. When that occurred, each crew member's pulse rate would rise.

Behind the Delaware, a 'sonar array' streamed through the placid waters. Its sensors, called hydrophones, were deployed along a cable stretching up to one kilometre behind it. They recorded every nuance of ambient, underwater noise. On-board software had been progressively refined to identify tell-tale sound signatures, including those from the ubiquitous marine life surrounding the sub, like fish, dolphins, whales, and noises from a host of other sources, including the hull and propeller signatures emanating from commercial trawlers, frigates, yachts and even seals. Every sound thus had its own, unmistakable signature. In this high-tech environment, a noise signature was a death sentence.

Twenty-eight kilometres north-west of USS Delaware, in the lower quadrant of the South China Sea, a PLO *Jin Class* sub, the *Giant Turtle* (

148

巨龟) was also running silent. Under the command of Captain Fu Gao Feng, it had been engaged in routine patrols around the Straits of Taiwan, where the People's Republic was asserting sovereignty over several islands, whose ownership was contested by the Japanese. Chinese fishing junks had moored at and fished off those islands for millennia, causing some international observers to remark that China had a genuine case, since Japanese sovereignty claims followed the annexation of the islands by the Japanese during their invasion of China, in the early 20th Century, rather than by international treaty.

When the order to go to a higher combat readiness had come from Chinese Strategic Command, the Giant Turtle had been instructed to move further south, to shadow and monitor US naval movements out of their strategic base in the Philippines. The Philippines had become the epicentre for America's new *Asian Pivot* strategy, designed to address a shift in global military influence, as China expanded its power and influence in that area. Since acquiring its second generation, Jin Class subs, China had been asserting more visible naval authority in its own regional waters. Under the direction of China's Commodore LIN Ting You, China had enunciated two central planks of its naval philosophy. One: introducing a column of coordinated sweeps to achieve what was termed a 'dragon in a bathtub' effect in the region, and two: coining the phrase 'blue national soil' to describe the task of defending China's legitimate territorial rights over waters bordering its mainland, which were host to numerous offshore oil and gas deposits and therefore highly strategic. Captain Fu entered the command bridge of the Giant Turtle, turned to First Officer Wan, and picked up the intercom:

"*Wan Xiansheng, quing dao youbiar…*" 'Officer Wan, give me right full rudder. Come to course 219, depth thirty-eight metres and bring hull speed down to eight knots. Hold for twenty-six nautical miles, following the Manila Trench south-south-east, with 2,000m clear bottom. Calculate coordinates for our next mark, at the end of our next sweep, and commence a parallel, return sweep after allowing for execution of a safe, 180 turn.'

Those two separate orders, given independently by commanders from two different nations, had set each crew on a fateful journey towards global

149

celebrity. Other, celebrated accidents of fate - at the battles of Marathon, Culloden Moor, Waterloo, Normandy and in other global theatres - had changed the course of history. In this instance, the two commanders had unwittingly set their nuclear subs upon a direct collision course. This would normally be a worrying development. However, at routine patrol speeds, collision could be easily avoided, as each sub's sensitive on-board detection hardware would, within a separating range of three kilometres, enable them to detect each other. Silent running would be a different matter, making that detection range much closer, but would require an order to come to a higher war footing which could only be issued by the two group's area commands.

***

While China's Giant Turtle and America's Delaware glided silently towards each other, back in Washington DC, Secretary of State Rankin and National Security Adviser Nordish were receiving Ambassador Liu Qixin, who had come to deliver an informal, advance message which Liu had been instructed to convey to the US State Department. After exchanging pleasantries, the group, assisted by their respective aids and note takers, assumed their seats around Rankin's conference table, where Secretary of State Rankin opened the conversation.

'Well, Mr Ambassador, I am delighted that your response has been so rapid and hopeful that we can put this unfortunate matter to rest. Please proceed.'

'Madame Secretary,' began Liu deferentially, for that was necessary to soften the message which would follow. 'I wish that were the case. My Ministry is preparing a formal response to your demarche, but that will take a little longer than expected to approve through our political process. I am sure you can relate to that regrettable obstacle, since your own congress is famously slow in approving such matters. Those delays are, however, essential checks and balances, which serve to prevent precipitous or ill-considered action. I do hope you understand. Because you have given us such a short time to frame our response, I am instructed to informally convey the gist of our likely response,' he continued. The Vice Premier himself has instructed me to do so. He thanks you most earnestly for raising your concerns with us, but he has difficulty with the facts outlined in your demarche and the assumptions it makes. That is why we beg your indulgence, while my government frames a more considered response. Upon receiving your diplomatic request, my Premier immediately sought advice from our military experts. It appears that the transgression you accuse China of committing is already well-entrenched in your own military practice. This makes China's actions no more or less legal than your own. In other words, ours is no more than a matching response,' he began.

With that calm but politically charged reply, the Chinese Ambassador had achieved his Government's goal. He had neither confirmed nor denied China's possession of Electromagnetic Pulse weapons and his words had been calculated to leave the idea in the minds of the American's that China might, indeed, have such weapons and have deployed them. It took the sagacious US Secretary of State no more than a nanosecond to understand the consequences of Ambassador Liu's response, and the colour rose in her cheeks. His obfuscation was typically Chinese. It frustrated the hell out of her, but the implications of what he had said, if it were true, did seem to imply a double standard.

Beside her, the hawkish Lt General, Bill Nordish, was bristling with undisguised anger. While Liu's answer was couched in diplomatic language and was evasive, it amounted to a rebuttal of the US request to allow an inspection of China's Dongfeng facilities or, if the SEMP warheads were subsequently found to be in evidence, to inspect their removal. The atmosphere in the room changed, as surely as if a chill wind had entered the room, making all of its occupants shiver a little.

'How do you reach that absurd conclusion, Mr Ambassador? Can you categorically state that China has not deployed SEMP warheads on its Dongfengs, because I can assure China that the United States has no such weapons in its arsenal. How, then, is yours a matching response, as you so elegantly put it?' she replied coolly, satisfied that she had outmanoeuvred the wily diplomat and landed a telling blow.

151

'Madame Secretary,' replied Liu smoothly, 'I beg to differ. It was the United States who first identified the magnetic pulse effect, when its atmospheric tests over the Pacific created an electromagnetic pulse over Hawaii, which took out most of the island's electronic systems. That discovery so impressed your scientists and your Government that you established an SMP Commission. It receives regular Government funding for research and development into the technology. Just last month, you deployed an application of EMP technology for stealth aircraft, which can deliver a high energy beam to take out all electronic systems over a discreet target, such as a single, high rise building or a factory. This surgical application is far in advance of any technology we may possess. By financing the use and development of electromagnetic pulse technology, your government has shown that it condones the technology and lends its imprimatur to it. The United States can scarcely condemn another power for a military technology which it condones itself,' concluded the articulate Chinese diplomat.

Politicians have keen antennae but they lack the consummate skills developed in career diplomats. Deep within the psyche of every politician lurks the instinct for electoral survival and an accompanying need for an aggressive response, however calmly articulated. It can rise to the surface when their backs are to the wall, as it did on this occasion. Rankin was a clear thinker and a cautious politician, but her patience was being sorely tested. This exchange was rapidly assuming the character of a Bay of Pigs moment, when a steely retort was demanded and blinking, or showing indecision, would, paradoxically, produce a national loss of face, something the Chinese understood better than most. Rankin stiffened, her eyes narrowed and her body language communicated more than any words could express. 'Mr Ambassador, your response is little more than clever obfuscation. Our position remains the same. If we do not have your cooperation on this matter, we will have no option but to proceed to the next stage, at the United Nations. While I appreciate that China has a right of veto, we are bound by international law to pursue that route first. If, after we share this knowledge with the international community, China maintains its current position, we reserve the right to pursue all options, as

152

we have on many occasions when the UN lacked the resolve to act. That, Mr Ambassador, is our non-negotiable position. Please inform your Vice Premier, and your Government, that the Unites States requires the removal of all SMP warheads from Chinese missiles and insists that its weapons inspectors be granted access to observe their removal.'

The usually implacable Chinese Ambassador was visibly shaken by the strength of Secretary Rankin's answer and resorted to his instinctive practice of polishing his glasses while framing a measured response.

'My dear Madame Secretary,' he replied, sounding foppish by American standards but behaving entirely correctly by Chinese standards of civility, genuinely moved to diffuse the growing rancour in the room.

'If you will permit me, I should like to speak off the record,' he continued. 'China's military expansion has nothing to do with territorial design or hegemony. The need for a larger presence is forced upon us as we grow, just as America had to assume a global leadership role as it grew. Our only wish is to maintain peace in an uncertain world and to protect our vital economic interests. I have lived in your country and studied at your universities. I have come to admire your people and your culture. I am no more than a messenger, and my fervent wish is that our two nations can live peacefully together and prosper. Our economy has expanded rapidly and, while Europe and America struggle through a period of economic stagnation, we hope for an early recovery, so that trade and economic prosperity can flow to all of our people. But you must see that the world around us is changing. China is now a large economic force in global markets, perhaps larger than the USA, since we now own some 30% of your nation's foreign debt. If we hadn't taken up that debt, your economy would be in even more trouble. I implore you to seek a solution to this problem with me, but you must understand that China is no longer a supplicant nation. Like the USA, it has become one which has to carry a heavy leadership burden. I assure you that we do so reluctantly and with peace, not aggression, always at the front of our minds,' concluded Liu.

At that point, Lt General Nordish offered an unsolicited comment. 'Now see here, Liu, we are talking missiles, not economics. We want those damned SEMPs scrapped, and that is the beginning and the end of this discussion, wouldn't you agree, Madame Secretary.'

'Well, Bill,' replied Rankin. 'I wouldn't have chosen that tone or those words, but I have to agree. Ambassador Liu, please convey my message to your Government, undiluted. It must either accept our request for access for our weapons inspectors or prepare for an international stoush in the UN. On a personal level, I want to express my thanks to you, my regret that it has come to this and to acknowledge that you are only doing your job,' she concluded.

Ambassador Liu and his entourage stood, bowed to the American officials and left the room. When they had left, Rankin turned to National Security Adviser Nordish.

'Bill, I respect your right to a view about military issues, but I insist that I take the running on international affairs. We will both have to agree about how to deal with this latest response. What's your take on it?'

'Goddamnit, Liz, those Commies…'

'Just a minute, Bill. Don't you dare use that word with me, or anyone else. It's unfair to China and it is inaccurate. These are pragmatists, not Russians, and they have a point about our own position on SEMPs. I need you to get back to me as soon as possible about that. Is it true what Liu said about our latest deployment of a surgical pulse weapon?'

'Alright, Liz. I'll look into it and get back to you on that. You can pussyfoot around with your diplomatic language, but I have a more pressing national security responsibility and I'm not gonna let these guys pull the wool over my eyes. Who knows where this thing is headed. Liu just confirmed, by his omission, what we all feared. He didn't deny the allegation about their Dongfengs and he wouldn't allow an inspection of them. That means he's got something to hide and that is all the proof I need. I'll be damned if I am going to let a jumped up Asian military outfit challenge American authority. I have no option but to prepare orders to bring our Asian pivot forces up to a higher DEFCON status. I need your support with the President on that. It will send a signal that we won't be bullied.'

154

'Alright, Bill, but I'll only support you on that if you promise to tread carefully. We have invested years in building this relationship. We don't need another Cold War, especially not with these guys. We need China to help our nation trade its way out of its current economic mess.'

While Bill Nordish left the meeting with a spring in his step, Elizabeth Rankin did so with a heavy heart. She sensed a testing period ahead and a deep sense of moral responsibility for navigating a safe path through this highly sensitive issue. Nordish, however, seemed to revel in the idea that the Chinese had pushed him too far and forced his hand. Rankin could exchange fancy words all day, he thought, but he would put teeth on his rhetoric and give it traction, even if it meant mobilising the most potent military force on the planet.

Within one hour of the adjournment of the meeting, Lt General Bill Nordish had ordered the US *Asian-Pivot* Command to come up to DEFCON 3. On the other side of the world, grimly reading these new orders on his command bridge aboard the *Delaware*, Commander Vandenberg felt a cold shiver. Coming up to DEFCON 3 required that he arm warheads and position six of his twelve ICBMs in their launch tubes. It also meant invoking silent running procedures, which required use of passive sonar and reducing hull speed to eleven knots, to minimise hull signature and detectable after-wash sound.

Advice of the US command fleet's change of battle status was interdicted by the Chinese and travelled at warp speed to General Zhang Ming Wei, who immediately brought his fleet, in the Southern Waters Command, up to an equal battle readiness, which included silent running and use of passive sonar, to avoid detection. In the vastness of the South China Sea, the chances of the two hulls colliding underwater was a million to one, and therefore not really a remote possibility, but tensions on board would, none the less, be high as the respective crews trolled for foreign hulls and asked themselves what circumstances might have caused the escalation of their alert status.

Australian Consulate General, 42 St., New York

Mike Stephens was beginning to panic. The former Commando turned ASIO field agent, whose cover role as Tom Grant's aide-de-camp was to watch his boss's back, was beginning to concede the possibility that Grant had met with foul play. He recalled his boss's fateful words, just prior to his departure for the Hamptons. *'What could possibly go wrong... on a romantic weekend?'* Those words now came back to haunt Stephens, and he was angry with himself for letting Grant make the trip alone, particularly in light of Lazarus' report on the Dongfeng affair. He had agreed that his boss would keep the consular car for the entire weekend, then return it to the Consulate General the following Monday morning. But where the hell was he?

Mike looked nervously at the hands of his wristwatch as they closed in on 10.00 a.m.. He had tried his boss's mobile phone several times. Each time it had rung out and defaulted to Tom's message bank. He had left several voice messages. Then he had sent several text messages, but there had been no reply. That could mean that the phone was switched off or out of range, he reasoned. Either case was possible but both seemed unlikely. Tom Grant was an early riser, always waking at dawn, going for his ritual morning jog and arriving at the office early, so his late arrival on this important day was totally out of character. After all, it was the day when his boss would urgently contact CIA Director Angiotti to share with him the critical, new ASIO intelligence on the Dongfeng.

As an intelligence agent, rather than a career diplomat, Stephens was not free to share his concerns with his consular colleagues. In doing so, he would blow his cover. Consulates, in commercial centres like New York, did not operate in the same, rarefied atmosphere as embassies in national capitals, whose diplomats were accustomed to international intrigue and the attachment of undercover intelligence operatives to their missions. Embassies were home to career diplomats who managed sensitive international relations and were accustomed to much higher levels of confidentiality. Consulates were different. They operated at a more open, practical level, promoting trade and commerce, providing immigration assistance and renewing passports. Consular staff were therefore less used to colleagues operating under cover. Indeed, with the exception of the Consul General, nobody at the Australian Consulate in New York was aware that the Military Attaché and his aide were, in fact, under-cover intelligence operatives.

Mike Stephens considered sending a communication in cypher to his area desk in Canberra, but it was midnight in Australia and he would expect a protracted delay before they could respond. If Colonel Grant was being held hostage somewhere, time was of the essence. Given the explosive nature of the Dongfeng matter and the importance of ensuring that Lazarus's report did not fall into the wrong hands, he resolved to take more decisive, local action. He would contact CIA Head, Frank Angiotti, directly and share his concern that something was seriously wrong. He would tell him that Colonel Grant was missing, having failed to return from a weekend visit to the Hamptons, and explain that Grant had, only the day before, received a highly sensitive report on the Dongfeng missile program from ASIO's security chief, Sir Robert Chandler. He would tell Angiotti that Grant planned to share this new intelligence with Angiotti and that he believed it was possible foreign agents had learned of this and decided to interdict. Tom Grant may have been taken out, to prevent him passing his report to the CIA.

Resolving to contact Angiotti was one thing. Doing so was quite another. Mike Stephens realised that he would have to navigate a complex protocol path to do so. Angiotti could only be contacted via a go-between, set up by the CIA for Tom Grant's exclusive use when liaising with the US Administration on the Dongfeng affair. Tom Grant, not Mike Stephens, was to initiate communications, using codename *Archangel,* and would then be directed to a covert CIA operative codenamed *Prometheus*. Prometheus, for his part, would ensure that Archangel's messages were passed confidentially to the CIA boss.

This process was an immutable rule within the CIA. No CIA Director was permitted to be directly linked to a field operative, a field action or a covert communication, however innocuous. This protocol was well understood and served as a circuit breaker, protecting the agency's Director from any association with politically sensitive or legally doubtful practices. That protocol also gave the agency deniability and was an important tool in averting the fundamental risks faced by any public organisation charged with managing clandestine operations.

Despite these complexities, it took ASIO agent Mike Stephens just twenty minutes to be cleared through to Angiotti's office, such was the priority accorded to the Dongfeng affair. Upon receiving the worrying news, Angiotti agreed to fly Stephens immediately to Langley, Virginia. His office arranged priority transport for Stephens on the agency's private Lear jet, out of La Guardia, departing thirty minutes later. The Lear jet required just under an hour's flight time to Langley, where Stephens would be met on arrival by an agency man and spirited off to his meeting with Angiotti. The entire process would take just two hours.

***

Two hours later. CIA Director Frank Angiotti greeted the young ASIO field officer warmly and ushered him into the small conference room adjoining his office. This area was designated a 'cone of silence' zone, making it an area which was regularly swept, both physically and electronically, for eavesdropping devices and protected by 'white noise' preventing any audio intrusion during a conversation. Once seated in the secure conference room, Angiotti began more grimly.

'Alright, Mike, start at the beginning and tell me as much as you can.'

'Thank you, sir', replied Mike Stephens, conscious of his much lower rank and wishing to appear as deferential as possible. 'As you know, I work as Colonel Grant's aide-de-camp…'

'Cut the crap, Mike,' replied Angiotti. 'We know you've been operating here as an ASIO field agent for the last two years, and that you were an SAS-trained combative prior to that. No problem. We've got our people in your country, too, attached to our missions there, but we're basically on the same side and share most of our intelligence with your people.

'That's what this meeting is all about, so I want you to feel free to lay it on the line, without any artifice or pretence. Just tell it like it is.'

'Thank you, sir. I will. Last Friday we received a report in cypher from Canberra summarising our separate investigation into the status of the Chinese Dongfeng missiles. The report drew upon intelligence provided by our Asian and European intelligence networks. I decoded the report and loaded it onto a memory stick for Colonel Grant. He took it home to study before deciding what aspects he might share with you.'

'That was good of him. The report was basically prepared at my behest, following a discussion with my old friend Sir Robert Chandler, your ASIO head. I believe you guys use his internal nickname, *Lazarus*. We respect that you Aussies have somewhat better networks in Asia, but I don't expect you to hold anything from us and I am keen to get my hands on Lazarus's report. I don't suppose you can tell me where the report is or what new information it contains?' inquired Angiotti.

'Well, sir, my office is in a private wing of the Consulate, next to Colonel Grant's, and I manage the encryption of all messages there. That doesn't mean that I read every word or understand them, but I do recall the main thrust of it. The message came in late on Friday afternoon. I encrypted the report, captured it in clear text and held it securely at the office. When I drove the Colonel back to his hotel that evening, he had chosen to take the original, coded text on a memory stick, along with his laptop, which has software for decoding it. That would protect its security. He wanted to study it that night, before heading off to the Hamptons, so I'm guessing he has locked the coded text in the wall safe in his room at the Andaz. He should have locked both his laptop and the memory stick in his safe before leaving.'

159

'OK, but I'm very uneasy about that report floating about, whether it is coded or not. I'll need to get someone over to the Andaz fast and see if we can recover it, analyse it and hold it more securely. What can you recall from the clear text version?'

'Well, there was a lot of bumf about the EMP technology, pointing out that you guys had basically developed it first, which may or may not be an embarrassing issue for you. Hard to lambast another power for simply doing something you have done yourself,' he added sheepishly. 'I guess that's the sort of stuff Colonel Grant would have edited out, so as not to cause offence,' he added carefully. 'After all, it is our intel, not yours, and Colonel Grant made the point that we make the decisions about how we share our intel,' he concluded.

'Fair point,' replied Angiotti. 'But the US is the central figure in this play and, unlike you guys, we carry a huge burden as global custodians of yours and other nation's freedoms. Our national interest is at least as important as yours and I have the international jurisdiction here. I guess I'm flattered that you and Tom see me as someone you can confide in,' he added, impressed with the intellect of the junior officer and amused that he had the balls to address a senior US official so directly.

'Yes, sir. That's right. But Colonel Grant doesn't always feel he enjoys the same access to your intel. Anyhow, to continue, there was a curious section in our intel report I will need to share with you. It contained information from our London station about an old, MI6 report on the Dongfeng. It described a field operation, back in 1981, when Charles Ritter, your deceased Deputy Director, was a young field agent attached to your London Embassy. The Brits say he was charged with investigating the theft by the Chinese of a new, Russian ICBM. Turns out this was the Dongfeng. Apparently, Ritter produced a groundbreaking report on the termination of the joint Soviet-Chinese missile programme, including details of the design the Chinese had stolen from the Russians and of how China planned to further develop it.'

'However, the CIA didn't share Ritter's report with the Brits until two years later, when he had completed his posting, since his covert action had amounted to an abuse of diplomatic privilege. Only then did it become clear to the Brits that Ritter had extracted the information under so called *code orange* conditions - *hostile interdiction with deniability* - meaning the sort of brutal interrogation used back then, but which would be in breach of conventions nowadays. The victim of Ritter's interrogation was… wait for it… a Russian diplomat Anatoly Pushkin, then serving as First Secretary at the Soviet Embassy. Here's where things get interesting. Fast forward thirty-three years and the same Anatoly Pushkin has become head of Russia's National Security Agency, the FSBR. The presence of all of these factors at the same time and place, in London in 1981, and involving Ritter, Pushkin and the Dongfeng affair – cannot be coincidental. That's why our analysts think the events surrounding Ritter's murder are somehow connected – a revenge perhaps. There is no other explanation.'

'Pushkin's torture at the hands of Ritter, when he was a junior field agent, provides a clear motive for Ritter's execution-style slaying. It's seems likely that Pushkin has never forgotten or forgiven the beating he received from Ritter back then. Maybe Pushkin has crafted a clever way to exact his revenge on Ritter and used the operation to also frame the Chinese for something they didn't do. After all, they are as nervous about China's rapid military expansion as we are.'

When Mike Stephens had finished speaking, a profound silence followed. Frank Angiotti looked agape at the young intelligence officer as the terrible implications of his report became apparent.

'Dear God!' whispered Angiotti. 'I hope, for all of our sakes, that you are wrong about this. I had hoped that our administration would find a diplomatic solution to our problems with the Chinese, but what sort of a nuclear nightmare might we unleash if you are right about the Russians being involved in Ritter's assassination. How will that go down on the Hill… a Russian spy murdering a senior US Intelligence Officer. I am already up against it, trying to diffuse this mess. General Nordish, our hawkish National Security Advisor, has an itchy trigger finger and is looking for any excuse to attack the Chinese if they don't kowtow to our demands. He is definitely prejudiced against them and their expansion.'

'You've got to help me, Mike,' Angiotti continued. 'Any proof you and your people can find to show that the Russians are behind this, or that the Chinese are innocent in this matter will be critical to averting a major international crisis. Tell Lazarus we need to pass his latest report, and any other intel you have, to the President and the Secretary of State as soon as possible, before that crazy National Security Advisor of ours loses his cool and we have a full-scale incident.'

'Yes, sir! I am sure Lazarus and his team will pull out all stops.'

'Let's go about this logically. First, get an urgent signal to Lazarus, briefing him on our discussion. Then we'll recover his report from Tom's hotel safe. Meantime, I'll get a team of agents down to the Hamptons to commence a search for Colonel Grant. I hope we're not too late.'

'We also need our people here to comb through all traffic signals and to analyse all direct or indirect arrivals over US air and sea ports during the past three months, searching for any Russian linkages. If your theory is right, Pushkin or one of his agents must have planned and executed the attack on Ritter's home. It seems likely a Russian team entered the States. Finding Tom Grant will be like looking for a needle in a haystack, but we need to start somewhere,' he concluded grimly.

'What about Dr King?' asked Stephens naïvely, forgetting that he hadn't mentioned her at all when relating these events to Angiotti.

'What the hell do you mean by that?' shot back Angiotti. How the hell is Dr King involved and how does she figure in this thing? Is she the Dr King who sometimes works for our agency?'

'I don't know about that, sir. Dr King is a female academic, from Princeton University. She was the one who invited Colonel Grant to spend the weekend with her at her family's home in the Hamptons.'

'Dr *Maggie* King?' shot back Angiotti. '*Our* Maggie King? From Princeton?' inquired Angiotti, as Mike Stephens nodded his assent.

'I don't follow, sir,' replied Stephens.

'Dr Maggie King is retained by this agency for classified assignments. International relations stuff… foreign political intrigues… for opinions on political power-shifts, etc. She's one of ours! Is she missing too?'

'I can't say for sure, sir,' replied Stephens, 'since we don't have her contact details, but I'm guessing that, whatever is going down, Colonel Grant and Dr King are in it together.'

Even before Mike Stephens had completed his last sentence, Frank Angiotti was dialling up agent 'Macka' McKenzie to get him to assemble a crack team of field operatives, brief them and get them deployed in the Hamptons. If anyone could make sense of this thing, it was Macka.

Deserted Potato Farm, Long Island

Tom Grant's head throbbed, his back ached and all of his joints were stiff. This was the legacy of lying prostrate, semi-conscious and hogtied on the cold, hard floor of the cellar for three days. It had been some hours since his last sedation. He was still very groggy, but he had regained a small measure of mental awareness. Each time he regained this small window of consciousness, he hauled his exhausted body back into a sitting position, flexed his muscles, propped himself up against the sacks of produce, and attempted to stimulate his circulation. Having been in a heavily sedated state for three days now, his brain felt like mush, but he knew he must push through the mental and physical barriers and use these brief moments of lucidity to plot an escape.

During each brief phase of lucidity, when the drugs were wearing off, he had manoeuvred his body - his shoulders, his cheek or perhaps a calf of his tethered legs – against the rough walls of his small corner of the cellar, searching for any sharp protrusion that might be used as a tool. Finally, he had found the jagged edge of a stone block, set into the bluestone wall of the cellar, and was able to use its sharp, abrasive edge to try to sever the bonds behind his back. If his wrists had been secured with rope, his bonds might have given by now, but the Russian had used heavy-duty, PVC cable ties, which were proving stubborn.

He wriggled his way again to the now familiar spot against the wall, felt in the dark for the jagged stone edge and repeated the painstaking, rubbing process. The abrasive surface of the stone had cut into the soft tissue around his wrists, leaving his skin torn and bleeding, but the pain associated with this had now become a friend. He found that he could use the pain as a way of elevating his awareness and heightening his resolve. The pain spoke to him. It told him he was doing something purposeful, not just surrendering to a cowardly submission. He used the pain, just as he did the jagged edge of the stone block, as a tool, a friend and a comforter, to break the mindless monotony of his drug induced stupor. After a time, his shoulder muscles screamed in painful sympathy with his wrists, fatigued by the repetitive sawing action and the contortion required to bring his bonds into contact with the stone surface behind him. Still, he pressed on, gaining ground, inch by inch, with each pass of his wrist across the jagged stone edge. Then, suddenly, the cable tie gave and his arms swung free.

His euphoria was immense, as a new sense of freedom changed all of the negative energy in the dark cellar. This small victory had given hope that his flagging spirits could feed off. He stretched out his cramped arms and felt the circulation come flooding back. The previous numbness in his wrists and fingers was initially replaced by a tingling sensation, then pain, as feeling was restored to them.

His euphoria, however, was short lived. Just as he was extending his arms to work on the next cable ties, those constricting his ankles, he heard the familiar shuffle of boots on the floor above him, tracking towards the doorway leading down to the cellar. This was the signal that his Russian tormentor was returning, with his evil syringe, to inject the next dose of his sleep-inducing chemical. If he repeated this process faithfully, the Russian would squat beside Tom, force a needle into the crook of his arm and then look on sadistically as the proud soldier slid back into a dark oblivion.

Anticipating a repeat of this scenario, and conscious of the approach of his Russian tormentor, Tom Grant sank back into his foetid corner of the cellar, intent upon assuming his ritual position, with hands tied behind his back, before he was discovered. He managed to achieve this just as the door above the stairway opened, permitting shafts of light to penetrate into the dark domain of the cellar. Tom Grant's feet were still bound and his arms had been returned to a position behind his back, creating the powerful illusion that he was still firmly manacled. As the Russian left the stairway and made an uncertain path through the dark towards him, the still dazed ASIO agent assessed his next moves. The Russian's eyes would be unaccustomed to the dark, and Grant could use that to advantage. It always seemed to take the Russian a few minutes to adjust to the dark cellar and this gave Grant a small window of opportunity which he decided he must exploit. Then suddenly, the Russian was leaning over him, repeating the mock greeting which always seemed to precede the medication process:

'Ah, Colonel Grant. You are back with us again. Never mind. Nursie is here to put you back to sleep. Where would you like this next shot, Thomas? In the arm, or is that starting to feel like a pin cushion now?'

Tom Grant's head drooped in apparent defeat. His eyes were mere slits, and he kept them half closed, feigning a semi-comatose state. His body language indicated feeble submission and was calculated to lull the Russian into believing that he could offer no further resistance. Reassured by Grant's apparent state of helplessness, the Russian squatted casually beside him in the dark, placed his revolver carelessly on the floor beside him and fumbled in a small tote-bag at his waist for his syringe. He pointed the syringe upwards and depressed its plunger, ejecting a jet of clear fluid to remove any air bubbles; then bent forward to inject the powerful sedative into Grant's forearm.

Although he was still very weak, Grant chose this moment to pounce. A rumbling volcano of energy exploded from within him, ignited by molten anger and a primordial instinct for survival. His SAS training had given him an armoury of lethal skills which his enemy could never have imagined - and these now found full expression, guiding his actions as if preprogramed. In his weakened state, Grant knew that he must focus his remaining energy efficiently, making every ounce of it count. In one, lightning-fast action, both of his hands emerged from behind his back, reached up to the startled Russian's face, locked around each side of his mandible, and twisted the man's head violently. There was a loud snap, like a whip cracking, as the vertebrae at the top of the Russian's spinal cord gave way. The wide-eyed Russian's head flopped to one side, signalling instantaneous death. His torso followed, tilting slowly forward and finally toppling, like a tree falling in a forest, as his lifeless trunk slumped to the cold cellar floor.

Exhausted by this manoeuvre, but relieved that it had succeeded, Grant paused to draw breath, shook his head to clear it, and slowly went back to work. He retrieved the Russian's handgun and stuffed it into his belt. Then he ran his hands through the Russian's pockets, in search of any ID or other

165

clues to his identity. He found a mobile phone in the Russian's breast pocket and placed it in a small tote bag, which he removed from the Russian's waist and attached to his own.

Armed with the handgun, but with his legs still tied at the ankles, he crawled from the dark corner of the cellar towards the circle of light at the top of the stairway, which beckoned like a beacon of freedom. At the bottom of the stairway, he used his arms to elevate his rump onto the bottom step and swung his bound legs out in front of him, so that he could inspect the cable tie around his ankles in the better light. The thick cable tie would require force to break it. He looked for some lever or tool to use and finally settled upon a loose spindle in the side of the stairway. He managed to prise it free and inserted its tip into the gap between the cable tie and his ankles. Then he rotated the spindle, using it as a lever to prise the cable tie apart. He winced in pain as the pressure multiplied and the tie cut into his flesh. Finally, it gave way and his legs parted, freed from their constricting bonds.

This small measure of exertion had again exhausted him, but new feeling was now returning to his lower legs, as circulation flooded back into his extremities. While feeling had returned to his legs, his feet were still bloated and swollen inside his footwear. He unlaced and removed his shoes, so that he could massage his feet, then elevated them to disperse the coagulation that had settled in his lower body over three days of inertia. When feeling returned to his toes, he replaced his shoes and attempted a wobbly stance, finding he needed the support of the handrail to stand up. He remained groggy, but his mind became clearer with each passing minute and his thoughts began to turn to Maggie. She must be held in another part of the building, he thought, and if she were still alive, she too was probably in a terribly state. His first priority was therefore to locate her as quickly as possible.

He made his way painfully up the stairway towards the open door at its top, not certain whether the farmhouse was now empty or still occupied by other hostile agents. Since he had overpowered and killed his Russian jailer, he had heard no further sounds from above, suggesting that the farmhouse was now deserted. Holding the Russian's handgun in front of him, he peered around the top of the stairway into a sparsely furnished lounge area, whose curtains had been drawn shut to exclude prying eyes. Even in this dimmed room, Grant's eyes protested at the light, having been in complete darkness for the past seventy-two hours. Through swollen eyes, he squinted about the room to assess any new threat, then moved tenuously into the centre of the room on wobbly feet, still finding it difficult to maintain his balance. Steadying himself against the wall, he slowly pulled back the curtains, recoiling at the brightness of the daylight which streamed in from outside. As his eyes adjusted, they took in a panorama of vegetation. An overgrown lawn led down a slope to the front of the property. The expanse of lawn was hemmed by a perimeter of she-oaks and smaller trees which provided a natural screen between the property and a distant motorway. There, he saw traffic moving in a silent column, like an army of ants on the move. The sight of the motorway was exhilarating. It provided a direct link to the sanity and safety of the civilised world beyond the farmhouse and he was drawn to it powerfully as a place of refuge and comfort.

Grant noted that a dirt driveway led into the property, with one spur swinging around to the front of the house and the other continuing on to a barn located at the side of the property. He made a mental note to check the barn for any vehicle which could be used for his escape. Turning back into the lounge room, he noted that a hallway led off one end and guessed that this must lead to bedrooms. Maggie could be a hostage in one of them, he thought. Steadying himself with one hand, he felt his way along the lounge room wall towards the hallway. Then, just as he turned into the hallway, he heard the sound of a car's engine approaching, revving up a steep section of the driveway towards the farmhouse. It looked like he was about to be joined by another visitor; one who would be expecting the deceased Russian agent to greet him.

With no ability to make it out of the house in his weakened state, Tom Grant needed a place to hide, somewhere to lie in wait for the new arrival. He hobbled across the room and took up a position behind the front door. He would open the door and leave it ajar, he decided, enticing the Russian to enter and providing an opportunity to surprise him from behind. Presently, the vehicle swung into the front of the farmhouse and came to a halt. The door opened and a voice called out:

167

'Privyet, Sergei, Kak u tebya dela …'

From his very basic understanding of Russian, Grant recognised *privyet* as the standard Russian greeting, the English equivalent of *hello*, and decided he must return the greeting, so as not to give rise to any suspicion, or alert the newcomer to a potential problem.

'Privyet,' he called back from inside the house, as boldly as he could, hoping his poor accent would pass for an acceptable response.

Russian agent Alexei Dolgorukov seemed reassured by the return greeting in his own tongue, emanating from inside the farmhouse, and continued up the steps leading to the front porch, pausing at the open door to knock and call again to his covert colleague, Sergei.

'Yest' kto-nibud' doma,' (Is anyone home?) he called, curious that Sergei was not at the front door to greet him.

Maybe Sergei was busy somewhere in the farmhouse, he thought, and had left the door open for him. Satisfied with this logic, the Russian stepped through the open doorway into the lounge room. As he approached the middle of the room, he heard the front door slam shut behind him and spun around to address the source of the sound. Instead of Sergei, agent Alexei Dolgorukov found a dishevelled Tom Grant propped against the wall with a handgun levelled at him.

'Sergei is dead, and so will you be if you try anything foolish,' croaked Grant, his throat gravelly and dry but his tone quietly determined. After his ordeal, Grant was certain of one thing. He would truck no nonsense from the Russian. He was in no shape for a physical confrontation.

'On the floor, face down, with your hands behind your back!' croaked Grant, his throat too parched to mouth the words more clearly.

At first, the Russian merely blinked, then a faint smile curled at the end of his lips as he studied the wreck of a man standing in front of him.

Grant's eyes were black and swollen, his wrists were bleeding, their flesh torn, and his filthy face spoke of total defeat. How could a man in this state represent any threat? Indeed, Grant appeared so weak and unsteady on his feet that the Russian seriously doubted he was capable of raising the handgun which drooped from his limp wrist. The Russian bent down, as if attempting to comply with Grant's request, then launched his body at Grant.

Having assessed the risks, he had decided he could overpower his weakened adversary. In doing so, he had greatly underestimated Grant. The former SAS officer's reaction was swift, clinical and automatic. It was honed and seasoned by the combat conditions he had experienced in Afghanistan. Levelling the Makarov at the Russians lower torso, Grant squeezed off a round, which penetrated the Russian's thigh, shattering his femur. Crying out in pain and clutching at his shattered leg, the Russian crashed to the floor, as blood oozed from a large exit hole.

'Now, Ivan, let me explain this again,' instructed Grant. 'Remove your belt and throw it here. Then roll onto your belly, with your hands behind your back. Any more nonsense and I'll take out the other thigh!'

This time the startled Russian complied, writhing in pain as he tugged off his belt and assumed a position face down on the carpet. Grant hobbled across the room and squatted beside the Russian, who continued to groan. He took the man's belt and wound it several times around his wrists, folding its end back through the gap between them and pulling it so tightly that the Russian cried out again, as the leather strap cut into his flesh. Grant saw irony in the Russian's protest. Having endured greater abuse for the past three days, he felt no sympathy for the indignant Russian. When he had secured the man's arms behind his back with the belt, Grant retrieved a plaited cord used to tie back the curtains. He tied one end to the man's injured leg and the other to the front door handle. Any movement by the Russian would disturb his leg and project excruciating pain through his shattered thigh. Satisfied that the Russian was immobilised for the time being, he retrieved his handgun and made his way down the hallway in search of Maggie.

He found a padlock dangling from one of the bedroom doors and decided that this must be where Maggie was being held. When he threw his shoulder against the door, the lock offered little resistance, its bracket splintering under the force of Grant's charge. Inside the room, he found Dr Maggie King lying unconscious on a bunk bed, her arms and legs bound, her hair dishevelled and her skin a deathly pale. There were no obvious signs of physical abuse, but she had clearly been heavily sedated, probably just before the Russian had descended the stairs to the cellar to inject Grant.

That meant it would be some hours before the propofol injection began to wear off and normal function and thought returned.

Tom looked down on Maggie's wretched form and cursed himself for embroiling her in his clandestine world. He felt deep shame at having involved this wonderful woman in his problematic work and a strong need to protect her. He found scissors in the bathroom and cut the ties from her wrists and ankles, then used warm water and a sponge to wash her face. Finally, he rearranged her on the bed as comfortably as he could and drew a blanket over her, leaving her to sleep off her drug- induced lethargy. He made a wider sweep of the house to ensure that they were alone, and then paused to calculate his next moves.

As he moved about the farmhouse, he slowly gained better control and coordination of his limbs. Finding a small kitchen at the end of the lounge area, he filled a glass with water and lifted it nervously to his lips. After days of privation in his prison-cellar, his parched throat found the sweetness and clarity of the water irresistible and he had to fight the urge to gulp it down. Instead, he drank carefully, in small mouthfuls, allowing his body to absorb the sweet fluid slowly and re-hydrate. He filled another glass, took it to Maggie's room and placed it on the small table beside her bed, so that it would be the first thing she saw when she regained consciousness. Then he made his way across the farmhouse towards the front door.

Stepping contemptuously around the groaning Russian, he crossed the porch and headed for the barn, which was situated a slight distance from the house. Upon reaching the barn, he paused to regain his breath before wrestling its heavy wooden door open. There, inside the barn, was the Consulate's Mercedes, serenely oblivious to the turbulent events occurring around it. His mobile phone sat in its cradle, offering an instant lifeline to the outside world. The vehicle was unlocked and its keys dangled from the ignition. He slid in, lifted the handset and dialled Mike Stephens, scarcely believing his good fortune. After several rings, the familiar sound of Mike's voice answered his call.

'Colonel! My God! We had almost given up on finding you. Where the hell are you?' exclaimed Mike, ecstatic that his boss was still alive.

'I wish I could tell you. Somewhere on Long Island, I think. Looks like an old potato farm. A hostile agent jumped us on Saturday morning and we have been his prisoners ever since. I was trussed up in a cellar, so I am pretty disoriented, but I managed to break out a short time ago. I'm OK, but not in great shape. We will need back-up pretty quickly, in case any more *hostiles* arrive on the scene. Can your guys trace this call?'

'No need to, Colonel,' replied Mike. 'In the Merc, left hand side of the steering column, there's a toggle switch. If you flip it on, it activates a GPS beacon, like those used on marine vessels. Make sure the Merc is in open ground, so it gives the satellite a direct line of sight. With the GPS beacon activated, we will be able to track you immediately. I am already in the field with a team of Frank Angiotti's men. They have put any resources we need behind our search for you and Dr King. We will get a chopper airborne and should be with you soon. Hang on, boss, and we'll have you out of there as soon as possible.'

'Bring a medic with you,' Grant replied. 'Dr King is still out of it - pretty much comatose, after being heavily drugged - and she will need urgent medical attention. There's also a bit of housekeeping to attend to. I can't go into details on the phone, but tell Frank there are a couple of Ruskies for his men to deal with. One of them has a slight problem with his neck - he won't be needing it anymore. The other is still alive, but he has a gunshot wound to his thigh and will need a medic. Take care of the one with the gunshot wound. He will have information which can lead us to his accomplices and help us clear up this mess,' said Grant.

'Oh, and when I get out of here, I will need you to set up an urgent meeting with Angiotti and a secure dial-up so we can talk with Lazarus and his people in Canberra. We need to stop this thing escalating.'

***

Tom Grant ended the call and turned to the immediate task of backing the Consulate's Merc out of the barn, to give clear transmission to the satellite. Then he activated the car's GPS beacon, climbed out of the vehicle and made his way back to the farmhouse. He found the Russian groaning where he had left him, pushed his way past him and returned to Maggie. Clearly still heavily sedated, she was comatose and would require some time before she would regain consciousness.

As he made his way back to the lounge area, the characteristic, juddering sounds of chopper blades could be heard approaching from the distance, followed by the shrill sounds of police and ambulance sirens streaming behind it. Within minutes, the helicopter and a convoy of pursuit vehicles had descended upon the abandoned farmhouse. The vehicles skidded up the narrow side access road and burst into the forecourt, where they formed a semi-circle around the front veranda.

Three FBI officers, wearing combat fatigues, Kevlar vests, helmets and earphones, leaped from their vehicles. Each of them brandished a high-powered, automatic rifle. They approached the front porch with their weapons raised in front of them, staring through their telescopic sights in anticipation of any hostile contact. As they drew nearer, Tom Grant emerged through the front door, his hands raised high above his head. Having survived one traumatic ordeal, he had determined to make himself clearly visible and submit passively, before some trigger-happy commando burst into the farmhouse and shot him by mistake.

'On the ground!' barked the FBI men, directing their aim menacingly at Grant. Before he could respond to their demand, Corporal Mike Stephens strode forward, placed a hand over the leading FBI agent's weapon and pushed its barrel to one side.

'Relax, mate,' said the laconic Australian soldier. 'He's a good guy; one of us, the Aussie Colonel, who has been held hostage here. We have him to thank for overpowering the hostiles and taking them down.'

The FBI men lowered their barrels and advanced cautiously towards Grant, who now assumed authority, barking orders at them, causing them to stop in their tracks as the chemistry between them changed.

'Get me to your command vehicle, so I can brief our people on the way back to town. Time is critical. Detail a team of your men to stay behind here and secure the scene. They will need to mop up, remove the body in the cellar and take the injured man into custody. Don't let them touch anything until a forensic team has been in and had a thorough look at all the evidence.

172

You'll need to get the surviving Russian, the one with the injured leg, patched up. Then hold him for interrogation.'

Despite the apparent authority and bravado behind these words, as the FBI officers mounted the steps towards him, Tom Grant's world suddenly began to spin. His vision blurred and dots appeared before his eyes. Then his legs buckled and he tumbled forward off the veranda into a black abyss. The FBI agents dropped their weapons and ran towards him, arriving too late to do more than kneel over his slumped figure. Severely weakened by his ordeal, Tom Grant had exhausted his last reserves of energy. There was simply nothing left in his tank.

Manila Trench; South China Sea

On board the *Giant Turtle*, China's newest Jin Class nuclear submarine, First Officer Wan was huddled over a small map desk, deep in conversation with his navigator. The two submariners were viewing a screen showing a green, phosphorescent image of the ocean floor and surrounding seascape. They were tasked with plotting coordinates for the end of their current, south south-easterly sweep of the Manila Trench. They needed coordinates for a spot in the trench which would permit the huge sub to make a safe turn through 180° to commence the next, return sweep, from the southern extremity in a north north-westerly direction, towards the familiar waters of the South China Sea. Parallel sweeps were standard procedure in the Chinese submarine fleet; a part of China's undersea surveillance of national and adjacent waters and a central plank in Commodore Lin Tin You's *dragon in a bathtub* strategy.

There was much more complexity to underwater reconnaissance than most people understood. *Sound* was the key. It was both the search weapon of choice and the greatest enemy of submarine patrols seeking to avoid detection. The speed at which sound travels under water varies with depth and water density. Moreover, the walls created by undersea canyons and mountain ranges, and the sea bed itself, operate to amplify sound, channelling and intensifying it. The Manila Trench was a huge, natural amplifier, with all of those subterranean traits, and made submarines particularly vulnerable to detection by sound signature. The *deep-layer zone* was where sound travelled fastest and was thus a danger zone for subs, almost as dangerous as the shallow waters of the *surface layer*. Advances in thermal imaging and aerial surveillance had now rendered submarines travelling in that shallow zone, *the surface layer,* highly vulnerable to detection by reconnaissance aircraft and surface vessels with thermal (heat seeking) probes. Commodore Lin Tin You had thus ordered his sub commanders to conduct their surveillance sweeps in the *median* or *thermocline zone,* safe from surface detection but above the deep zone, where underwater sound travelled much faster and sonar systems operated over a greater range.

These were the three *layers* which guided every sub commander's thinking. The *surface layer* ranged between fifty and a hundred fathoms below sea level (300 to 600 feet deep) and was the shallow zone in which submarines were most vulnerable to surface detection. The *median layer* stretched from 100 to 500 fathoms below sea level, ending at the so-called *peak thermocline depth,* where sound waves travelled at the slowest speed through sea water. The *deep layer* extended from that optimal, slow-sound zone down to a zone feared universally by all submariners, not only because sound travelled faster with each new metre of depth but also because the pressure exerted by the atmosphere on submarine hulls rose exponentially, becoming so immense that it could crush them like a giant fist crushing a tin can.

Running *beneath the layer* was thus the most strategic practice and meant operating in the *median zone.* This practice was combined with silent running procedures to minimise or supress sound transmission beyond the hull and make subs harder to detect. However, running *beneath the layer* made communication with naval command and support vessels difficult, as that required coming up to the surface layer and deploying aerials attached to buoyancy devices, able to break the surface to send and receive. Everyone knew that, in a hostile environment, nuclear subs could remain submerged for months. However, in a peacetime context, Commodore Lin had allowed his fleet to come up, or *snorkel,* once a day, at an agreed time, to send and receive data and exchange routine messages. Now that the Americans had come up to DEFCON 4, China had to match their status. Chinese Naval Command had thus suspended daily snorkelling, ordering that daily reports must cease unless there was something critical to be communicated.

After reviewing the terrain over the map table, First Officer Wan finally nodded in agreement with his navigator, jotted final coordinates onto

175

a plotting pad, and returned to the bridge, where Captain Fu Gao Feng awaited him.

'Have you calculated the return sweep coordinates, Officer Wan?' he asked.

'Yes, sir! We estimate distance to the end of this sweep at forty-eight nautical miles. At our current crawl speed of eleven knots, corrected to eight for ocean currents, we should get there in about 3 ½ hours. Our turn coordinates will bring us over a deep part of the Manila Trench and give us a safe arc of radius for a turn through 180 degrees. We will resume our return sweep after levelling at 500 fathoms, peak thermocline depth, to minimise our sonar signature, and then run parallel to and some five nautical miles west of our current line of sweep. Our return sweep will follow the direction of the ocean floor through the trench, in a south south-easterly direction. Permission to lock in coordinates, sir?'

'Permission granted,' replied Captain Fu. 'We are now in deeper waters and tracking south. Come to 500 fathoms and maintain silent running. Switch to passive sonar and advise the crew that this is no longer an exercise. They must maintain discipline and meet our higher state of operational readiness. Remind the crew that these waters are no longer exclusively ours. Ever since the Americans adopted their 'Asian Pivot' strategy - increasing their naval deployments to the Philippines - their sub patrols are more frequent and have started encroaching further north, into our waters. Now that they have come up to DEFCON 4, they will be actively stalking us, and we will need to be on guard. Our chances of engaging directly are extremely remote, but the crew must be ready to assume battle stations should we establish contact.'

'Aye, aye sir,' replied First Officer Wan, who then turned to the command bridge intercom and relayed the Captain's message to his crew, beginning with the universal, naval call to order: 'Xianzai ting …(Now hear this!)

***

176

Four nautical miles south south-east of the Chinese *Giant Turtle*, Commander Hank Vandenberg of the *USS Delaware*, pride of the American nuclear submarine fleet, was enjoying a coffee break in the exec room with Petty Officer Jake Collins. Although the Asian Pivot Command had come up to DEFCON 4, a fellow commander just back from the States had told Hank that the change in alert status was no more than a diplomatic ploy, intended to send a strong message to the Chinese, rather than imply any real threat of engagement. Nonetheless, that higher alert status meant invoking a number of additional operating procedures, ones which had only been simulated on the new sub during sea trials. Delaware's crew had been hand-picked from the navy's elite, but its crew members had only been working together for a short time and were still becoming familiar with on-board systems and building new working relationships. Indeed, some systems on the state of the art sub were totally foreign to them. Delaware bristled with new technology. If the game of stalking, which *USS Delaware* was required to play when operating at Defence Condition (DEFCON) 4, had become a game of cat and mouse, USS Delaware now had new, high-tech claws and teeth to bring to the game.

There were important differences between the two classes of submarine. China's new Jin Class was improved in many aspects, but it was rumoured to still be *noisy*. *Delaware,* however, was the latest version of the Virginia Class sub and her technical innovations had made her almost invisible. Both carried the usual arrays of underwater hydrophones, but *Delaware's* internal fit-out had been modified to maximise use of high-strength plastic components, to minimise her magnetic signature. Her outer skin had also been coated with new, anechoic (echo-retarding) tiles, increasing her hull's sound absorption and dampening sonar wave reflection. *Magnetic anomaly detection* devices were now employed universally to locate subs, so *Delaware's* new, reduced magnetic signature and tiled hull gave her a distinct advantage. Despite its many other advances, China's *Giant Turtle* had neither of these innovations.

Like most submarines on patrol, however, both were still heavily reliant upon sonar, both *passive* and *active*, to locate underwater targets, though active sonar was only used in friendly waters, as it immediately gave away a sub's position. As they were both on higher alert, both subs were now using passive sonar and running *slow and silent*. If the Chinese were lurking in these waters and their new Jin Class was as noisy as the Americans believed, Hank Vandenberg was confident that his new, high-tech sub would find them first, gaining an immediate tactical advantage... unless, of course, the Chinese were perched on Delaware's nose, the sonar *blind spot* on a sub.

At 09:50 Eastern Standard Time, Commander Hank Vandenberg was just finishing his morning coffee in the executive break room. As he downed the last gulp, the gentle, rhythmic pinging of the passive sonar suddenly changed. Experienced submariners found the rhythmic ping of the sonar a calming agent, like the slow, resting heartbeat in an athlete's breast. It had quickened and inclined in pitch, automatically triggering a call to *General Quarters*. Claxton-like alarms sounded down the length of the sub, as crew members looked up in surprise, dropped whatever they were doing and scurried to their action stations. Vandenberg instinctively reached for the nearest handset on the command network and barked an urgent order.

'Commander to Bridge. Acknowledge, XO, and report!'

The Executive Officer, Lieutenant Chris Jackson, was on the bridge. His was a metaphorical bridge, since a sub's bridge had no lofty height or architectural merit deserving that name. As 2IC, Lt Jackson assumed all executive functions when the Commander was absent from the bridge or indisposed.

'XO to Skipper. Positive contact. Dead ahead. Sonar Tech O'Brian confirms large submerged mass, four kilometres downrange at 500 fathoms, tracking directly towards us at a closing speed of sixteen knots. Noise and hull signatures strongly suggest a Chinese Jin Class, probably on patrol. Over!'

'I'm on my way, Chris,' replied Vandenberg. 'Sound action stations and await further orders!' Seconds later, upon reaching the bridge, Commander Vandenberg regained the command handset. He immediately issued several orders in his trademark calm voice, with crisp, clinical professionalism.

'Stop engines. Deploy drag planes to arrest speed. Come to zero knots. Activate weapons control systems. Load live fish in tubes 3, 4, 6 and 8, but with tube doors closed!' These orders were standard for a DEFCON 4 contact and usually also included arming of underwater-launch ICBMs, but Vandenberg stopped short of this.

'Aye, aye, sir!' replied the XO, repeating the orders to each department, whose crew members had overheard the orders and were already acting upon them. In the few seconds since the approaching sub had first been detected, the Americans had brought their sleek, 7,800-tonne underwater fighting machine to a complete standstill and made it invisible. Meanwhile, the longer and, at 9,000 tonnes, much heavier Chinese sub, the *Giant Turtle*, continued its unrelenting momentum towards the *Delaware*, still oblivious to its presence.

'Permission to speak, Skipper,' said the XO.

'Go ahead, Chris,' replied Vandenberg.

'I know we have made ourselves invisible out here, or at least simulated a stationary underwater obstacle, but what if the Chinese sub doesn't deviate and continues on its close pass trajectory? They might even hit us.'

'I hear you, but we need to hold our nerve. If we move, we will betray our position and lose our tactical advantage. Then they will be all over us. If we sit tight, they will pass us by. The chances of a collision are miniscule out here, in millions of cubic-feet of ocean. Their sonar will see us as a large, stationary submerged object, and their captain will plot a path around us. I'm sure of it. I look forward to telling Naval Command that we made our first contact with a Jin Class in the South China Sea and they didn't even know we were here.'

'Roger that, Skipper,' replied Jackson, reassured by his skipper's unassailable logic. Meanwhile, sonar technician First Class O'Brian continued monitoring and providing the bridge with progress reports, as the *Giant Turtle* closed in.

'Two thousand eight hundred metres and closing... PING... Two thousand seven hundred metres and closing' ...PING...

The crew of the *Delaware* stood stony-faced at their action stations, arrayed down the length of the sub; at weapons control stations, at the helmsman's wheel, at sonar screens and in the engine room, where *Delaware's* nuclear reactor was impatient to provide silent, instant power to the sub's stationary drive shafts. The crew listened into the internal comms network, as voice commands between the sonar tech and their skipper punctuated the steady ping of the sonar. Meanwhile, the huge Chinese sub continued to close in on *Delaware*, failing to alter course. When it had closed to 800 metres, XO Chris Jackson was now clearly agitated about the prospect of a collision and decided to interrupt the silence with a measured, operational response:

'Two hundred metres to critical turn point, Skipper. If the Chinese don't turn now, they will overshoot their escape window and be positive for hull impact!'

'Roger that, XO. Sit tight. It's cat and mouse. The approaching sub *must* have recognised our signature by now and will deviate. Hold your nerve. Over!'

Meanwhile, on board the *Giant Turtle,* all hell had broken loose. At 1,800 metres, the Chinese sonar tech had reported what appeared to be a stationary object but suggesting correctly that it could also be the front profile of a US Virginia Class submarine. The Chinese crew had little experience of stalking submarines, and had never stalked an American sub, many of whose crews, they grudgingly conceded, were more experienced at manoeuvring in hostile waters. The two subs were now positioned nose-to-nose, so *Turtle's* side-angle sonar was useless for detecting the overall size of the object in front of it, and its forward-angle sonar could only detect the front profile of *Delaware,* making it seem a smaller mass than it was.

Captain, Fu Gao Feng, was a very senior commander, having joined the navy two decades before. However, this meant that his early training had been on cruder, diesel subs and he was thus considered by some ready to pension off. The geriatric commander was not used to instantaneous digital systems or the tighter time windows required for decisive action in this new, high-tech environment. He was initially paralysed with indecision and wasted valuable minutes anguishing over his next order. Despite the

180

clear indications from his sonar officer, he was not convinced that the contact was an American sub.

'Comrade Gao, your Sonar indicates a stationary, submerged object with an ambiguous profile. This could be a steel shipping container or a geophysical prominence. If it were a Virginia Class sub, why would it block our path?

'These are our waters, not America's. They should acknowledge contact and commence avoidance measures. However, if they are provoking us, we must call their bluff. Reverse engines and slow to four knots. If they are Americans, we will give them time to move out of our way and avoid a collision. Over!'

The younger members of *Giant Turtle's* crew were the pick of the crop. They had only recently graduated under General Zhang Ming Wei's modernisation program, and trained in contemporary, underwater engagement tactics. They understood the risks associated with their pompous old Captain's strategy but were too junior to speak out. Tension in the sub was thus palpable. The crew waited, grim-faced, as the sonar ping indicated an impending collision. Each crew member knew that a mistake at this depth meant certain death. As a collision became increasingly likely, and in the absence of an over-riding order from their commander, some of the young officers began to lose their nerve.

'Tai gui-de Laoban... ('Precious master'),' the Chinese number two finally protested. 'I beg to differ with your analysis. If we do not divert in the next few minutes, we will collide, allowing the Americans to make fools of us in our own waters! A collision would attract global media coverage and be very difficult for you to explain to your shore-based commanders, sir.' The Chinese number two's logic was clever. The old captain blinked and reconsidered the effects on his career of a catastrophic collision, exposing his incompetence.

'Alright, number two. 400 metres and closing. Dive! ...Dive! Come to left full rudder!' he barked, hoping to save face and avoid a collision. This order compounded his error. Changing the 9,000-tonne sub's course over a 400 metre window was impossible, and diving would make it a side-on missile and increase the chances of a collision. Still, the desperate order

181

offered a slim chance of avoiding annihilation, so his crew reacted immediately, initiating the 'dive and turn' procedure which, commenced earlier, would have saved them.

On board *Delaware*, tensions were equally high, as the giant Chinese sub continued its relentless course towards the American sub. On the bridge, Hank Vandenberg was now losing his composure. While struggling to project quiet competence and calm leadership, he was no longer confident that the Chinese could deviate in time, and his experienced 2 IC was now sweating profusely, as the awful prospect of a collision became a reality. Finally, Hank Vandenberg's concern for the welfare of his crew and the preservation of his valuable, new naval asset overcame his stubborn naval pride. He blinked in disbelief, reassessed the risks and decided to blow cover.

'Those Goddamn Chinese haven't seen us! They're holding their course!' he barked. 'They are either ballsy sons of bitches or just pig ignorant,' he added, confusing *Giant Turtle's* ineptitude for a stoic determination to win the bluff.

'XO. Go to active sonar and betray our position! Quickly!' ordered the anxious US Commander. 'They may still be able to avoid us. Their sub is moving, while ours is stationary. Only they can now prevent a collision!' he concluded.

'Aye, aye, Skipper,' replied XO Jackson, immediately switching to active sonar and sending a loud, unmistakeable PING into the surrounding waters. Reacting instantly to *Delaware's* betrayal of her position, the white-knuckled Captain of the *Giant Turtle* gasped in horror, then ordered a power dive and a change in rudder-plane, in a frantic attempt to avoid the US sub. This hurried decision further compounded his error, widening the collision profile.

'Three hundred yards and closing,' screamed *Delaware's* sonar tech, as the distance between the two subs closed. 'Brace for impact!' he shouted, as the *Giant Turtle's* momentum took it beyond any chance of a radical change in direction. 'Two hundred and closing... One hundred and closing...'

'Open ballast tanks! Flood ballast chambers and incline trim blades for a steep, reverse dive!' barked Vandenberg. 'With a rapid descent, we just might get away with a glancing blow,' he added. Reverse engines! Full astern!' With this last, fatal manoeuvre he hoped to avoid a direct collision with the *Giant Turtle*. However, this bold tactic entailed serious risks. In committing his sub to a full ballast, reverse dive, Vandenberg knew he was propelling his sub to treacherous depths, where pressure on her hull would be immense.

Just as *Delaware*'s propellers began to churn, a deafening crunch signalled first impact with the giant Chinese sub. The American sub was jolted viscously and her crew members were thrown off their feet. This first impact was then followed by the grinding, twisting sounds of protesting metal, as the US sub's outer-skin was peeled back. In attempting to dive under *Delaware*, the *Giant Turtle* had torn strips of metal from *Delaware's* under-belly before bulldozing an exit path across her stern. As the huge Chinese hull ploughed forward, it caught *Delaware's* propellers, leaving them bent and dangling in its wake.

Delaware's lights flickered, died, then blinked back to life, as her emergency generators cut in. With no propeller thrust, however, *Delaware* resumed her fatal dive towards the deep layer, where her hull would be torn apart.

'All decks! Report!' barked Commander Vandenberg. 'Engine Room! Report!'

'Reactor is still delivering full power, Skipper, but we seem to have lost all thrust. The drive shaft is shrieking. Serious trouble here, Skipper. Over.'

'Stay with it, Chief! Aft compartment! Damage report!' barked Vandenberg.

'CPO Stein, sir. We're badly holed and taking on water fast. The first mate is now underwater, attempting to close the aft hatch. Flooding fast... Can't...'

'Come in, Stein!' shouted Vandenberg. Come in, son' ...but the aft report had come to an abrupt, gurgling halt and Vandenberg had to assume the worst.

'Get some men down there fast!' screamed Vandenberg. 'Close rear air-locks, for Christ's sake! We're taking on too much water and it's pulling us deeper. Blow all ballasts! Reflate! Chief, can you try to give me some thrust, to arrest our backward-slide? We need some upward drive, urgently!'

As the emergency unfolded, discipline gradually gave way to panic, and then to grim silence, as the surviving crew members, trapped in the air lock created in the three forward compartments of the sub, studied the spinning dials of their depth gauges. The now vertical hull slid backwards towards the bottom of the Manila Trench. The profound silence which now gripped them all was finally broken when the Chief's voice came booming from the engine room.

'Chief to bridge! I have full power now, Skip, but the drive shafts are steaming and water is still rising. Still no positive thrust. I reckon the propeller blades have been damaged. At these high revs, the shaft and bearings will seize. The reactor room is flooded now and we will go under soon. No way out. Sorry, Skip. Looks like I'm a goner too! Should I shut down the reactor?'

'Roger that, Chief,' replied Vandenberg. 'Try to stay with us, buddy,' he added, knowing that the order to shut down the reactor, while standard procedure in the event of a catastrophic failure on a nuclear sub, signed a death warrant for his Chief, his vessel and every member of his crew.

'XO. Release data recorder,' came Vandenberg's last command, signalling resignation to their gruesome fate. Like the black box on an aircraft, a nuclear sub's data recorder was its final testament. It would find its way to the surface, where its GPS signal would attract US support vessels. They would rush to retrieve it, before it fell into enemy hands. Later, they would study its data and listen, in stunned silence, to its record of *Delaware's* final minutes.

The proud *Delaware* seemed to pause in defiant protest, as she jettisoned her data recorder, then continued her majestic slide towards the ocean floor. At critical depth, her hull groaned angrily, then emitted one last, defiant shriek, like that of a dying beast, as the massive atmospheric pressure on her hull caused her to implode. In that instant, her proud crew members had the life crushed out of them, as their bodies were compressed. *Delaware's* hull plates were twisted and fractured, exposing her white-hot plutonium core to the surrounding ocean currents. The world's worst nuclear submarine disaster would have but one redeeming outcome. The planet's vast oceans would endlessly quench *Delaware*'s white-hot reactor core, neutralising its massive potential for overheating and preventing a serious meltdown. The Manila Trench, for its part, would beckon 134 brave souls – each one a husband, a father, a brother or a son - into its watery embrace, for eternity.

The White House, Washington DC

National Security Adviser, General Bill Nordish, was in full, indignant flight. He paced back and forth in front of his desk, as if addressing a parade ground of troops. Issuing a tirade of abuse to no one in particular, his verbal barrage was, however, directed at the only other person in the room, Defence Secretary Richard (Dick) Kraus, appointed by the President to this key role because of his reassuringly calm nature. The DEFSEC was now cringing in embarrassment as his colleague fulminated about *Nancy-boys* in the State Department, and a cowardly Congressional Committee on Defence procurement, which had ignored his earlier warnings about the Chinese.

Nordish had just digested the contents of a *top-secret* report from his Asian Pivot Commander, which he now brandished in his left hand. As its contents had become clearer, the General's mood had grown progressively darker, until the vein in his temple had begun to throb and his left eye had developed its characteristic tic. The report had confirmed his worst fears. The Chinese were getting too cocky by half and needed to be brought to heel. China's new military had pulled a provocative stunt, like Kruschev had, back in the 60s, with his attempt to base missiles in Cuba. China was flexing new military muscle and challenging US naval supremacy. Back then, when the *Ruskies* had challenged American resolve, Kennedy had not blinked. A grateful nation had worshipped his tenacity. Nordish, too, would not be intimidated by this latest Chinese move. If he had his way, China would have a taste of American resolve before the day was over. Having given vent to his indignation, Nordish flopped back into his swivel chair, donned his glasses and scanned the report again, to ensure details were clear in his head before issuing his instructions.

TOP SECRET (COMMAND EYES ONLY)

Urgent Attention: Commander in Chief, Security Adviser, DEFSEC and Joint Chiefs. Sinking of USS Delaware: (Virginia Class Nuclear Submarine)

At 10:34 hours, Eastern Standard Time, our naval surface vessels received a submarine distress signal from an antenna buoy deployed at coordinates placing the distressed sub in the Manila Trench. They converged on the coordinates and recovered an SOS beacon and data recorder jettisoned by the navy's latest, most sophisticated nuclear submarine, the USS Delaware. Delaware, recently commissioned by the First Lady, has only recently completed its sea trials and was on its first patrol in the South China Sea.

The data recorder was immediately delivered to the Commander, 'USS Freedom', our newest, 'Littoral Class' anti-submarine destroyer. It provided a detailed picture of the last minutes of Delaware's operational life. The data recorder was decoded on the Command Bridge and reviewed in the presence of senior Exec Officers. It revealed sonar tracking results, intercom voice data, hull pressure data, reactor core temperatures and other critical operational information, including evidence of a hostile naval engagement.

If this evidence is confirmed, it will signal a bold challenge to US naval forces deployed in the Far Eastern theatre, one which borders upon an act of war. The data recorder indicates that, at 10:15 hours, EST, Delaware's sonar picked up a large, approaching vessel, whose hull signature indicated, with an 89% probability, a Chinese Jin Class nuclear submarine. In line with normal 'hide and seek' protocols, Delaware came to a stationary hover, some three nautical miles in front of the approaching sub, commenced 'dead-in-the-water, silent protocols', killed engines and deployed counter-measures to confuse hull signature and minimise visibility. This was a copybook response by Commander Hank Vandenberg, one of our most experienced commanders.

What ensued remains open to conjecture. However, the Chinese sub would certainly have seen Delaware on its sonar as a large, stationary,

187

underwater obstacle. Despite this, it continued an unremitting path towards Delaware, suggesting it recognised the mass as a US sub and was challenging it to declare its position. Commander Vandenberg held his ground, not wishing to betray his position. The Chinese submarine continued on a collision path, beyond the window for either vessel to implement avoidance procedures.

The on-board data recorder repeated the last words between Commander Vandenberg and his crew, confirming that the Chinese sub had collided with the aft section of Delaware, breaching her hull and damaging her props, so that she took on water, lost forward thrust and was unable to prevent a fatal descent to the ocean floor. There, the deep pressure zone induced sudden, catastrophic hull failure. We have to assume that she is lost, with all hands.

While this appears a deliberately hostile engagement, perhaps calculated to assert Chinese authority over Asian waters, logic must allow for the remote possibility that the collision was accidental. It may have been occasioned by the Chinese crew's lack of operational experience with stalking protocols, a new tactical area of operations for China's young fleet. The fate and identity of the Chinese sub and its crew remains unknown, though work is in train to fix her identity. The Jin Class is a larger, heavier sub. We have no evidence of its disposition and must therefore assume that the Chinese vessel was less critically damaged and able to limp back to its home port. We are seeking all available Intel, including aerial surveillance of naval traffic around Chinese ports, floating dock repairs and other data, to confirm this possibility.

Given the loss of US lives and wider military-strategic implications, this event must be seen as a national tragedy, a naval catastrophe of epic proportions and a potentially explosive international incident. I therefore seek advice on preferred naval-military responses, particularly those involving my command. As Commander, Asian Pivot Fleet, I recommend escalation to Defence Condition (DEFCON) 3: Undersea launch readiness: intelligence maximums.

Finally, there is the serious matter of Delaware's nuclear reactor, which now lies on the ocean floor. We must anticipate global concern about

188

this nuclear accident and an angry response to the resultant radioactive pollution of the surrounding oceans. These will demand a careful political response, which ideally sheets home responsibility to the Chinese aggressor, where it belongs.

You will no doubt wish to review broader military-strategic implications for our other forces, particularly our Ground and Air Commands in the Asia-Pacific theatre, and to review their DEFCON status. You may wish to register a strong diplomatic protest and consider the military implications of a rebuttal.

Commodore J G Hosking, Commander, Asian Pivot, United States Asia-Pacific Naval Command

***

Satisfied that the report gave him the authority he needed, the red-faced General turned to his Defence Secretary and issued a clinical set of instructions, through gritted teeth, as the tic in his left eye quickened.

'We must respond swiftly, Dickie. Not diplomatically, but militarily. We must commend Commodore Hosking on his calm, reasoned analysis of the incident and then approve an immediate escalation of naval alertness in the Asia-Pacific Command to DEFCON 2, one level above that which he recommends.'

'Just a minute, Bill,' protested the Defence Secretary. 'You can't be serious!

'That is just one level below DEFCON 1, when the Defence Chiefs ask the President to give nuclear launch approval. Since the DEFCON series of alertness was introduced, no US force has ever been brought to DEFCON 1.'

In demanding this extreme response, Nordish was invoking a rarely used authority granted exclusively to the National Security Adviser to meet an unheralded development. This response could only to be invoked if the Commander in Chief, POTUS, was uncontactable or indisposed. This gave the DEFSEC authority to 'jump' forces to high alert for a short interregnum, buying time for a later, more reasoned response, once POTUS had been located, briefed, and his orders were passed down the chain of command. Nordish's order to come to DEFCON 2 could only remain in force for five hours without ratification by the President at an emergency session of the Joint Chiefs. That would now be called as a matter of urgency, and Nordish had no doubt that, when all the facts were known, his decision would be supported.

In this judgement, Nordish was seriously mistaken. As any student of China could have told him, the last thing one did with an Asian adversary was to rattle swords and threaten a public loss of face. Causing an international loss of face was the surest way to inflame an already dangerous situation.

'Goddamit, Dickie. I have the authority to do this under my interim provisions,' bellowed Nordish, not wishing to be outflanked again on this issue. 'We have to project strength, not weakness, to the Chinese. You will have your damned Commander in Chief's ratification within five hours. Just do it, damned you!'

Each step in the chain of events which followed was, of itself, small. Taken together, however, each was alarming in its explosive potential. The clearly anxious but deferential Defence Secretary hurried back to his office to implement the National Security Adviser's instructions. This resulted in a directive to all US forces in the Asia-Pacific basin to come up to DEFCON 2.

The directive to come up to DEFCON 2 was immediately detected by Chinese Intelligence, prompting a *Xiang Chengde Bao* (Code Amber) signal to China's young General, Zhang Ming Wei. General Zhang, in turn, called an emergency session of the National Security Council of the People's Congress. At that meeting, convened just forty minutes later, General Zhang persuaded his National Security Committee, chaired by the Chinese Premier, to come to *Gaodu Jingbao* - High Alert. *Dongfeng* missile silos, along China's 2,000 kilometre *Underground Great Wall*, then opened their hatches in launch readiness. This move, in turn, was immediately detected by US satellites.

United States 'eye in the sky' satellite intelligence was, in turn, relayed to US Central Command and thence, to Field Commanders, including the

'US Asian Pivot' Commander, based in the Philippines. Like all other field commanders, he had been briefed that China's Dongfeng ICBMs were now armed with warheads capable of inducing an electromagnetic pulse over North America, bringing American cities to their knees. Anticipating the seriousness of this escalation, US Air Command immediately directed that a squadron of stealth bombers, armed with bunker-busting technology, be scrambled with orders to stay aloft and be ready to take out the Dongfeng silos if theatre conditions escalated or the Chinese attempted to launch.

In just ninety minutes, General Nordish's ego, his quick temper and his unconstrained passion had brought two nations to the highest level of military tension that had ever existed between them. Each now teetered on the brink of a nuclear war. The US and China were facing their moment of terror.

Paradoxically, most wars were started this way. Throughout history, seemingly innocuous situations have quickly spiralled out of control, fuelled by distrust and cynicism. Since the dawn of time, ancient kings, latter day princes and Prime Ministers have rallied to the cause of war, grimly announcing to their countrymen that their nation was under threat and boldly declaring war. They have done so with calm alacrity; sometimes, when passions were hot, without so much as a ten-minute conference with their courts, their cabinets, their people or their Parliaments. At the onset of World War I, the assassination of an Archduke was sufficient to rally the failing European monarchies to the siren call of war, causing them to throw down metaphorical gauntlets and unleash unparalleled human carnage. When World War II came around, the world had forgotten the brutal lessons of WWI. Indeed, Colonial Prime Ministers in India, Canada, Australia, New Zealander and other Commonwealth nations routinely declared… *"Britain is at war… and, as a consequence, we, too, are at war."*

History's superpowers — the Romans, the Carthaginians, the Mongols, the Portuguese, the Spanish and the British — have each, in turn, risen to the siren call of war, spurred on by faux confidence in their military superiority and a need to project their power. Use it or lose it, so the saying goes! In contemporary times, US Presidents have widened the scope for war, informing successive congresses that 'dark forces' threaten and must

191

be opposed. Those two, politically charged words, 'dark forces', have been the precursors to dramatic, unilateral declarations by the United States that it was, once again, at war.

History's brutal lessons about war are quickly forgotten and the constraints those forgotten lessons impose are conveniently ignored. National indignation and political ego rarely give reflection a seat at their table. In times of crisis, those who plead the cause of peace are branded cowards, or disciples of appeasement. As the invasion of Iraq has shown, political passion and righteous indignation can ignite a primeval thirst for war, even when the facts justifying such a momentous act are lost in a fog of political rhetoric or, worse still, the product of doubtful provenance. Wars, once entered into, become a nightmare for the young men and women who tremble on their awful battlefronts, and for those charged with crafting disengagement, when national treasuries and voters have lost their taste for a continuation of the carnage.

In understanding and exploiting this recurrent human failing, Pushkin's covert operation, to plant false information about China's Electromagnetic Pulse Warheads, had achieved its purpose brilliantly, dramatically heightening tension between the US and China. As Shakespeare famously wrote - *"Oh, what a tortured web we weave... when first we practice to deceive!"*

Beijing, China

Commodore Lin Tin You paced nervously outside the Beijing office of Premier Wei Jintan. The Naval Chief's nervousness was understandable, as he contemplated how he might explain the disastrous collision of his Jin class 'Giant Turtle', the pride of China's nuclear sub fleet, with the American sub.

Immediately following the collision, Commodore Lin had received an encrypted report from the sub's Commander, Fu Gao Fung, stating that there had been an underwater collision with another sub, believed to be an American Virginia class sub on patrol. The Commander of 'Giant Turtle' had reported 'slight damage' to the hull of the huge Chinese sub, but had failed to report on the disposition of the US sub, suspecting however, but omitting in his report that the collision may have inflicted terminal damage to the smaller, US sub. Commodore Lin had relayed the report to Joint Services Command and the Chinese Premier's office, conscious of the explosive military and diplomatic consequences of the incident. He therefore expected, and had prepared for, a harsh interrogation from his political masters.

After waiting an eternity in an anteroom, Commodore Lin was ushered into the Premier's suite, where he found the Premier and General Zhang Ming Wei seated together at a circular table. Commodore Lin snapped to attention, bowed towards the political leader, then turned, straightened and delivered a respectful salute to the brilliant young General, who clearly enjoyed the personal confidence of the Premier.

'*Lin Xiansheng! Qing zuo* (Lin. Please take a seat!),' said the Premier, with little warmth in his greeting, as he beckoned the Commodore to a seat at his table.

'It seems that you and your navy have given me, and our nation, a large headache. How is it possible that two high-tech submarines could run into each other in a vast expanse of ocean?' he inquired sarcastically. 'And how is it that your report failed to mention anything about the fatal consequences for the American sub and its entire crew? Your 'Giant Turtle' has brought us to the brink of war, and your naïve report simply states that your sub collided with a US sub, as if it were an everyday event?'

'Dear Premier. I am painfully aware of the difficult political situation this unfortunate collision has caused. Upon learning of the collision and, later, that the American sub had gone to the bottom with all hands lost, I immediately suspended the Commander of the Giant Turtle, his XO and other senior mariners pending a detailed inquiry into this tragic event. The Giant Turtle is manoeuvring towards dry dock as we speak. We are making a thorough examination of its hull in the hope of understanding more about what happened. The on-board voice recorder will give us the conversations and commands on the bridge, minute by minute, in the lead-up to and aftermath of the collision. The entire crew will face a thorough grilling and be required to explain every detail of this affair. Many of them will face a court martial for their actions.'

'That is all very well, Commodore, but it does not help me address the immediate circumstances. The Americans are furious. They have called a special session of the UN Security Council to demand answers from us. We must ensure that our Ambassador to the UN, in New York, is thoroughly briefed on the circumstances leading to this debacle and given a basis to strenuously defend our position.'

'My dear Premier, as soon as the crew came ashore, I summoned the Commander and his XO and interrogated them personally. There may have been some hesitation on the part of our Commander in responding to this highly unusual encounter, as he digested the alarming sonar readings on their screen, but he insists that he followed engagement protocols precisely, and that caution was a far better option than precipitate action. However, his young XO, who recently underwent refresher training at the academy, was less defensive. He implied that, because of his commander's hesitation, our sub missed a critical window for avoiding the collision. He conceded

194

that the American sub must have detected our sub before we detected theirs. That would explain why they were able to use their time advantage to adopt a 'hide and hover' mode, a tactic calculated to make them invisible to our sonar, so that they appeared on sonar screens as part of the permanent seascape.'

'Are you telling me that Commander Fu was fooled by their clever evasion tactics or that he just ploughed straight into the under-sea landscape?' snapped the shrewd Premier. 'Is it your normal practice to collide with underwater objects?'

Commodore Lin looked pale and shaken. He had walked into an intellectual ambush and was clearly rattled by the Premier's clever question, with no room for escape. There were only two possibilities. Either the crew of *Giant Turtle* had been fooled by the American 'hide and hover' tactic or they had simply ploughed into the seascape. Either answer served to confirm gross negligence on the part of the Chinese crew.

'With respect, dear leader,' stammered the Commodore, 'it is not quite that simple. By the time our crew picked up the American's hull signature and identified it, the size and momentum of our giant sub and its closing distance made it impossible to change course in time to avoid a collision. In the cat and mouse game routinely played by opposing submarine forces, it is fair to say that they outfoxed us. If we accept what the young officer has reported, our defence is somewhat weak. But we have never had to manoeuvre such a large hull as Turtle's in such a confined space.'

'Gentlemen,' interjected the wily young General. 'Whether the young officer's account is correct or not is immaterial to the swirling politics. We can reach an internal view about what happened, but we must never cower publicly before our adversaries or admit weakness. The defence which we ask our Ambassador to deliver is simply this... that we were routinely patrolling our own waters when our vessel was intercepted by an interloper - a US submarine operating provocatively in unfamiliar waters, on our very doorstep. The actions of the US sub in patrolling our waters should be compared with the unthinkable act of China deploying its submarines in waters off the east coast of America – for example, off the coast of Miami – an action which the US would roundly condemn as highly provocative,' concluded the General. 'We must express our deep regret that the provocative action of the US in our waters has cost lives, but assert our right to patrol our own waters without foreign interdiction or harassment,' he added..

'Thank you, General Zhang. It seems, once again, you have come to our rescue. Is there anything else we have missed?'

'Just this,' replied Zhang. 'It is not my place to instruct you, Commodore, on how to run your navy. However, it seems that, in constructing the world's largest nuclear submarine we have failed to allow that its greater mass and momentum have resulted in slower manoeuvrability. I expect your final report will identify this and propose new training procedures to ensure this catastrophe is not repeated.'

With this withering indictment, General Zhang had achieved two objectives. He had demolished his naval counterpart in front of his political boss, asserting his superior command of events and, at the same time, elevated his position within the military political hierarchy, making himself indispensable to his political masters.

'Commodore Lin,' added the Premier. 'You may leave us now. I expect a full internal report, addressing all of the naval operational issues, and we will no doubt have more to say about those who contributed to this debacle. We must hope that the international tensions created do not escalate to unmanageable levels. That is all.'

Cowed and humiliated, the naval Commodore shuffled from the room and the Premier resumed a more intimate tone with his brilliant young military commander.

'This whole affair is the last thing we needed. The Americans are already hopping mad about the possibility that our Dongfeng missiles carry electromagnetic pulse warheads. Now they will be baying for blood because of this naval disaster. Our respective forces will automatically come up to higher defence conditions, creating the preconditions for a nasty situation unless cool heads prevail. We must act to ensure we have safe hands on the controls and seek to lower the temperature between our opposing military forces. What would you suggest, General?'

Mount Sinai Hospital, New York City

The tall, athletic frame of a naked Colonel Tom Grant emerged from the en-suite shower and stretched. The former SAS Officer's wrists were bandaged with loose gauze strips, which were now dripping wet. A patch on the back of his head was shaven, revealing stitches, where Peregrine's gun barrel had crashed into his skull. His left arm and right thigh carried angry ridges of pink scar tissue. These were a legacy of another, more deadly campaign, in Afghanistan, where he had braved a hail of Taliban bullets to rescue one of his troops, earning him the George Cross Medal, awarded for conspicuous bravery under fire. If one overlooked these warrior scars, Grant was a perfect male specimen. His abdomen rippled with muscle. Above it, a wide, muscular chest and broad shoulders were the signatures of a man whose daily fitness regime was an article of faith. The ruggedly handsome Aussie gave a hint of his keen analytical mind, measuring his surrounding world through intelligent, blue eyes. As if those attributes were not enough to ensure a commanding presence, the charismatic soldier exuded a strong aura, accentuated by a determined set of jaw, which told something of the quiet anger and steely resolve lurking within him, following his ordeal in the dark cellar. Tom Grant still rankled at the humiliation he had suffered at the hands of Russian agent, *Peregrine*. Now that he was recovered and back on his feet, he was keen to get back into the field, to run *Peregrine's* accomplices to ground and to make them pay for the ordeal he and Dr Maggie King had been subjected to.

Working through a well-practised routine, he arched his back, stretched down to his toes, twisted his torso through 90 degrees, and straightened. Then he pulled each arm, in turn, across his chest until his shoulder joints cracked, testing muscle tone and flexibility. Satisfied with this stretching regime, he unravelled the wet bandages around his wrists and tossed them

197

casually to one side. Finally, he turned to the neatly-pressed military uniform hanging from his bedside cupboard and began to dress. His aide-de-camp had smuggled his uniform in the night before, on Grant's strict orders, to permit his early, unexpected escape from hospital confinement.

Grant had received excellent care at Mount Sinai. CIA Director Frank Angiotti had insisted that he be given the best possible medical attention there, ensuring that his strength had been quickly restored. He marvelled at the large, private room provided to him at New York's most expensive private hospital and wondered how much it had dented Angiotti's and the US taxpayer's budget. The staff had worked a miracle. Immediately upon his admission, they had stabilised him, inserted a glucose drip into his wrist and plied him with vitamins and hydrating fluids. A normal regime of healthy food and hydration had quickly restored his physical well-being. Now, his three-day ordeal at the hands of the sadistic Russian seemed like a distant nightmare. Just twenty-four hours since his rescue, he was already champing at the bit to get back into the field. Looking furtively out of his window for signs of his aide-de-camp's arrival, he straightened his tie, squared his jacket and adjusted his military campaign ribbons, ready for a confident march towards the hospital's main entrance. His ADC, Mike Stephens, entered Grant's hospital room precisely on time, greeted his boss warmly and helped him slip quietly out of the room and down the hallway.

'You sure about this business of slipping out early, sir?' said Mike Stephens, concerned that his boss had blithely ignored the instructions of the medical and nursing staff, who did not want him discharged until the next day.

'Of course I am. They mean well, but I can't just sit here on my arse and do nothing. What news do you have of Dr King? Did she pull through?' he inquired, genuinely.

'They tell me that she was also admitted to Mount Sinai – this same hospital. Angiotti insisted that you both be held here in well-guarded, private rooms to minimise any further threat from the Russians, but no one would tell me where Dr King's room was located. I had to use diplomatic privilege to spring you from your room, telling Angiotti's security detail that the Consulate had obtained Angiotti's agreement to release you into its care. One of the guards told me that Dr King came through the ordeal in much better shape than you did and has already been released.'

'Good news, Mike. For now, we need to get back to my office as quickly as possible. Here's how our day will look. First, I need you to book a call to Frank Angiotti, so I can find out what his team have been able to discover from the Russian. Then we will need to prepare a despatch to Sir Robert Chandler and the ASIS blokes in Canberra, bringing them up to speed. After that, see if you can track down Maggie King and put me in touch with her. Finally, I need to talk to Ambassador Richard Bayliss in Washington, so that he is in the loop and doesn't have any surprises.'

By 10.00 a.m., Tom Grant was behind his desk at the Consulate, waiting for Mike Stephens to buzz through each of the calls. No sooner had he settled into his chair than the phone system on his desk lit up with the first call.

'Excuse the interruption, sir,' said Mike Stephens. 'I have CIA Chief Angiotti on line one. He rang us before I could initiate your call to him,' he added.

The two men had built a close rapport. They shared a plain-speaking manner, a pragmatism that transcended diplomatic formality and had bonded, as some males do, in a common cause. Tom Grant stabbed at the blinking light on his phone pad and opened the conversation with the CIA Director General.

'Frank! Good to hear from you, mate. I just got back to my desk here at the Consulate and I'm itching to know whether your forensic guys were able to get any leads on the Russian perpetrators. What have you got?'

'You Goddamn Aussies are somethin' else,' replied Angiotti, in familiar vernacular.

'My guys at the hospital tell me you did a runner on them. How you feelin'?'

'I'm fine, thanks to the great medical team at Sinai, but I don't want to just sit around a hospital ward while those Russians are still out there, playing with our national security and peddling misinformation about the Chinese.'

'What the hell do you mean by that?' shot back the wily CIA chief.

199

'Well, I think I got kidnapped to prevent me relaying explosive new intelligence about the murder of your Deputy Director, Charles Ritter. It was all in an intelligence analysis from our people in Canberra, which I was about to pass to you when they took me. The Russians must have learned that I knew about them falsifying Ritter's report. We think they falsified the report to implicate the Chinese and to set the USA and China at each other's throats, since China was growing too strong.'

'Late last Friday evening, I received the explosive intelligence from our mutual friend, Sir Robert Chandler, just before Dr King and I set off for our weekend outing in the Hamptons. Chandler's report passed on information from our London station, establishing links, back in the 1980s, between Charles Ritter, China's Dongfeng missile program and a Russian agent named Anatoly Pushkin. As you will know, Pushkin now heads up Russia's Secret Service, the FSB. When our people saw the connection between Ritter, the Dongfeng missile and Pushkin, the Russian agent Ritter had tortured all those years ago, they put things together pretty quickly.'

'My God, Tom! Are you saying that the Russians staged this whole thing to start a war between the USA and China? If that was their objective, they have made a damn good start! In fact, things couldn't be much worse. Our National Security Adviser, that crazy warmonger, Bill Nordish, swallowed the crap in Ritter's report about the Chinese having electromagnetic pulse warheads. On the strength of Ritter's report, he brought our forces up to DEFCON 3. As if that were not enough to make the hair stand up on our necks, yesterday the Chinese sank one of our nuclear subs while it was on a routine patrol in the South China Sea. That resulted in a further escalation, to DEFCON 2. There were no weapons fired, so our surface fleet investigators have not ruled out the possibility that the subs collided while stalking each other. Under normal circumstances, both sides would simply release public statements calling this a tragic maritime accident, like the French and British did when their subs collided in the English Channel. However, that hasn't happened. Instead, General Nordish raised our military alert condition, and that demanded an equal response from the Chinese. The underwater collision thus assumed the character of a more serious international incident. Both sides are jittery now. In fact, Nordish has demanded an emergency session of the UN Security Council and it looks like Secretary of State Rankin has no option but to oblige him.'

'We need to move fast if we hope to defuse what is fast becoming a highly volatile situation,' replied Tom Grant.

'I'll be damned! That crazy bastard, Nordish, has reacted just as the Russians hoped he would and brought us to the brink of a nuclear war,' said Angiotti.

'Yes, he has,' said Tom. 'Making it critical that we expose Russia's involvement in falsifying Ritter's report. These events have heightened China's distrust of American intentions. You need a circuit-breaker with the Chinese… a third country to act as an honest broker and lend credibility. I think my government could play that role. Our intelligence chief, Lazarus, wants this thing sorted. He wants us to find hard evidence that Ritter's report on the SEMP warheads was fabricated. Finding that evidence might just get us all off the hook and defuse this thing, before it spirals out of control.'

'You are reading my mind, Tom. Let me tell you what our investigation has revealed so far, because it strengthens your claim of Russian involvement. Our techs have been working on the mobile phone handsets we recovered from the farmhouse. They were able to trace calls back to some Russian guy in Boston, calling himself *Red Bear*. The calls were made by *Red Bear* to the dead guy, *Peregrine*, who kidnapped you and held you in the cellar. He also calls himself *Sergei*, and we found that the cell phone was registered to one *Sergei Kerin*, a real estate agent in New Jersey. We think the real estate business was a front for his real work, espionage on our soil as a member of the Russian Secret Service.'

'We have a third Russian in custody, the one you shot in the thigh when he turned up at the farmhouse. He is *Alexei Dolgorukov*, Second Secretary (Commercial), Russian Embassy. He is claiming diplomatic immunity and refusing to cooperate with us. We are holding him, despite his Ambassador's formal demands that he be immediately released, but we will have to let him go shortly,' concluded Angiotti.

'Releasing him might not be such a bad thing, Frank. If we get some eavesdropping and surveillance on him, he might just lead us to this *Red Bear*, who seems to be a central plank, running these covert operations from Boston.'

'I agree, and we've already made a start in that direction. Our technicians are analysing the *send* and *receive* signals from the cell phones used by the Russians. They hope to triangulate the cell towers and determine the locations of the calls. There seems to be a common thread. One particular cell phone, whose SIM is registered to a false address, was activated just three weeks ago, at La Guardia airport, and has since been used in Langley and, more recently, in Boston. We think *Red Bear* is the owner of this cell phone and is the Grand Poohbah directing the operation. It looks like he entered the United States three weeks ago. That's when the SIM card was first issued. Immigration at La Guardia is trying to produce an eye and thumb scan data base to be matched with foreign aliens with Russian names who entered the U.S. around that time. We should have something soon.'

'Can I somehow be made part of your investigation team, Frank? These blokes tried to kill me. That makes this personal. Apart from that, the tensions between you guys and the Chinese are increasing on a daily basis. My inclusion, as a neutral, third country representative, might help to take some steam out of that. However, I will need a formal request from your Government for me to participate in the investigation. If we can clear this thing up together, and my government can provide independent confirmation of Russia's involvement in a covert mission to discredit the Chinese, we will all emerge winners.'

'Consider it done, Tom. I will have you cleared with our internal security people, get you badged-up as a Deputy Director, and get advice to State that you are working with us on this thing. Meanwhile, we have a bigger problem to deal with; Lieutenant General Bill Nordish. The best way to defuse that reckless bastard is to have a quiet chat with the Sec-State, Liz Rankin. I'll set it up. Nordish won't listen to me. He has it in for me because my agency now has the President's ear and we out-manoeuvred him on a couple of recent issues, when we thought he had gone too far and needed to

202

be pulled back a peg or two. Liz Rankin is a seasoned diplomat and a quiet, reasonable voice within government. She has the President's ear on foreign relations and that makes her our best chance of calming the military chiefs.'

'I agree, Frank,' replied Tom Grant. 'Get me that audience so I can share our intelligence with the Secretary of State. Maybe Dr King could sit in?'

'Will do, Tom, and I support your suggestion that Dr King be included. Her views on East Asian affairs are widely respected and having her there might also help to calm the horses. I will call Rankin and set up the meetings. Could you contact Dr King and see if she can attend? If we manage this discreetly, in cooperation with Liz Rankin's office rather than Bill Nordish's, we might just persuade the Sec-State to moderate the government's response and prevent Nordish doing something stupid.'

'Agreed,' replied Grant. 'Can you give me Dr King's number? It seems you have her so well-guarded that no one can tell me where she is hiding.'

'You've got it, Tom,' replied Angiotti with a deep chuckle. I thought it best that we keep her under wraps for a while, until this thing blows over. I'll get one of our men to give you her details as soon as we're off the line,' he ended.

Less than thirty minutes later, Mike Stephens was able to contact Maggie King and patch her through to Colonel Tom Grant's office. Tom lifted the handset sheepishly. He felt a deep burden of guilt about the way his plan for a romantic weekend had turned into such a nightmare, and fumbled, clumsily, for an explanation.

'Maggie, darling! Thank God you are OK. I am desperately sorry that you were caught up in this whole bloody mess,' he said, sincerely.

'I'm fine, Tom, and I don't blame you in the least, although you could have warned me that you were a spook. This whole spy thing has been a bit of an adventure for a boring old academic like me. Incidentally, Frank told me about the nuclear sub collision in the South China Sea. Wow! That is explosive stuff! We'll have to manage that with kid gloves. It puts the whole relationship with China on a knife edge and makes it even more important that we expose the Russians before this ticking time bomb explodes.'

'I couldn't agree more,' said Tom. 'I have just finished that same discussion with Frank Angiotti, who has agreed to arrange a meeting tomorrow with the Secretary of State, so that we can brief her. We need to tell her what we have learned about the Russian attempt to implicate the Chinese in Ritter's death and to falsify his report. Frank Angiotti and I think you should sit in on this as well, to support our cause.'

'I'm in,' replied Maggie. 'Wouldn't miss it for the world! I don't suppose we could catch up sometime today, maybe this evening, to compare notes?' she added.

Tom Grant's spirits soared. She was clearly still interested, as he was, in exploring the intimacy they were beginning to find before their kidnapping by the Russians.

'I have a pretty solid diary,' he replied. I'm waiting for an update from our people in Canberra and I've also promised our Ambassador, in Washington, that I will bring him up to speed. Why don't we catch up later, say around 6 p.m. in the foyer of my hotel? We could try their happy hour. After that, I know a great little restaurant, just around the corner, where we can work through issues over dinner. My shout. I owe you big time, lady, having turned our romantic weekend into a damned kidnapping,' he added with a roguish laugh.

***

Later that evening, Maggie and Tom were ushered to a table in a private corner of the futuristic, black and red-themed *Bar Basque*. The Spanish bistro, located on 6th Avenue, was a venue where the tantalising aromas of Spanish paella and barbequed shrimp mingled with the clinking of glasses and reckless quaffing of 'bull's blood' wines. Earlier that evening, Maggie had arrived at the Andaz looking amazing in tailored white pants and a polo shirt. Even when she was dressed casually, she managed to achieve elegance. The outfit she had chosen for this date had achieved that beautifully. At the same time, it accentuated her slender figure. Hers was a natural beauty which needed no cosmetic assistance. On this occasion, however, a subtle hint of eye make-up and some lip gloss had added a special, feminine allure. The attraction Tom felt towards her was growing stronger with each meeting. Their shared ordeal in the Hamptons had added another dimension to their relationship, creating an additional bond. At the Andaz, they had enjoyed pre-dinner drinks in the lobby bar, choosing martinis to keep faith with the popular New York practice. Then they had pushed on, in the slightly ebullient mood which always accompanied a few martinis, to the trendy 6th Avenue bar and eatery, which had been highly recommended to Tom by the concierge.

Tom had been attracted to Maggie from the moment they had first met but now, as their relationship progressed, he was discovering new things about her which were not apparent from that first encounter. He found her totally engaging, not just because of her beauty but because of her complexity. Her sharp, analytical mind and the respect she commanded from her peers were aphrodisiacs, setting her apart from other women he had known. Only one other, Andrea Sloane, had attracted him in this way. Andrea had also been a beauty with a keen intellect, but had fallen victim to the dangerous trade she had plied, adding a dark chapter to Tom's life which he still struggled to forget. Tom promised himself that he would do whatever it took to protect Maggie from those same dark forces, which had almost cost them their lives.

They ordered drinks and began an easy conversation. As they were both keen students of international affairs, it was inevitable that their conversation would turn to the developing crisis between the US and China, and to the ways in which government and diplomatic resources might be mobilised to diffuse tensions. Tom had his Masters in Political Science, while Maggie had her Doctorate in Asian Studies, making them a formidable source of wisdom about how to handle the crisis.

They were furiously in agreement that the American response must be measured. The language chosen by each side would need to be conciliatory, allowing each side to manufacture a dignified retreat without appearing to give ground. The US would need to avoid slighting Chinese dignity or causing them a national loss of face, while the Chinese would need to offer the American side some political wriggle room, so important in a democratic, rather than autocratic environment. Maggie was certain about

205

one thing. Through their respective advisory roles, she and Tom would have to calm the hawks, particularly the National Security Adviser, General Bill Nordish, before he created a nightmare both sides would regret.

Intoxicated by the martinis, the wine, the night air and the bohemian mood at *Bar Basque*, their conversation finally lost its gravitas and gave way to a more personal exchange. Wanting to learn more about this alluring woman, Tom picked up the thread of her intimate confessions in the Hamptons, concerning her family and her father's tragic passing. A moment of quiet reflection followed, when Tom paused to stare into Maggie's eyes. Maggie, in turn, stared intently back at him, as each of them delved into the other's innermost feelings Then quietly, the big Aussie leaned across the table and wound his fingers into Maggie's. In that single, electric moment, a profound desire overwhelmed them both, attacking with power and fury. Maggie assumed a look of desperate need and instinctively responded by reaching across the table with her other, free hand, curling it around Tom's neck and pulling his face towards hers. Her lips sought his and found a hungry response, as they abandoned all pretence and allowed raw passion to take over. Their mouths searched out and discovered a powerful chemistry, as their kisses rolled smoothly, like waves on a tropical shore. Finally, uncertain about the next move, Maggie paused, caressed Tom's cheek with her hand and whispered:

'My God, Tom! What have we done?'

'Shshsh!' the big man replied, with a gentleness that surprised her. 'Let this moment take us where it takes us. We've found something pretty special, don't you think?' he added, stroking her cheek before continuing... 'Let's get out of here!'

They scrambled to their feet, settled the bill and made their way back to the Andaz. As they turned into 42nd Street, Maggie took ownership of her man, wrapping her arm around his waist as they walked and nestling into the crook of his shoulder. When she snuggled in under his arm, Tom felt as if Maggie had become a natural part of him and had always been there. He marvelled at the sensual heat radiating between them and knew, with absolute clarity, that they must be together for the rest of time.

Back at his hotel, the lift clunked to a halt on Tom's floor and they tumbled into the corridor, barely making it into Tom's room before their savage hunger returned. Tom wrapped his muscular arms around Maggie's waist and lifted her up to him. Maggie responded eagerly, wrapping her arms around him and straining on tip toes to reach his mouth and continue her desperate exploration of his lips.

There was no time, no space, and no consciousness as they carelessly threw off their clothes. Finally, unashamedly, they fell onto the bed and began a time honoured ritual, as their bodies rose and fell and their mouths gave expression to a need which neither of them could speak.

UN General Assembly – New York

Secretary of State Rankin's black limousine, accompanied by a small motorcycle escort, swept across the plaza, passed through a security boom gate and disappeared down a ramp leading into the bowels of the United Nations building. Located on the shores of Manhattan Island, the thirty-nine storey UN headquarters stood defiantly on the banks of New York's East River, its seventeen acre site proclaiming it an extraordinary piece of real estate and the building an especially important edifice.

Normally an astute politician and confident diplomat, Liz Rankin was unusually nervous this day, as she contemplated her difficult address to an emergency session of the Security Council, convened by the US government in response to the sinking of USS Delaware. US Naval Intelligence had reported the incident to the US Joint Chiefs and the President, just as China's naval command had reported the incident to its political leadership - but neither China nor the US had yet acknowledged the event publicly. Liz Rankin was therefore painfully aware that the content of her address would be explosive.

Her story would find its way to news-hungry outlets around the world. Reporters would devour it like vultures, translate it into emotionally-charged headlines and send their texts spinning around the world. Liz Rankin knew this would result in a further escalation of the diplomatic temperature between the US and China, something she had wanted to avoid, but she knew that her address would necessarily use strong language, drafted by a team of faceless foreign policy bureaucrats at State. This had been deemed necessary as a result of China's failure to provide an adequate response to America's diplomatic demarche and because of Bill Nordish's insistence that American honour, and its superpower status must be preserved.

As Rankin entered the forum, a hush came over the delegates, who were keen to learn the as yet undisclosed reason for this hastily convened emergency session. The first female Chair of the Security Council, Australian Foreign Minister, Jillian Pope, a confident and charismatic chair despite her diminutive, feminine form, called the assembly to order and invited her friend, US Secretary of State Elizabeth Rankin, to make her way to the rostrum.

'Madame Chair. Delegates,' Rankin began. 'Yesterday, at 10:28 Eastern Standard Time, America's newest submarine, *USS Delaware*, while patrolling in the deep layer of the Manila Trench, routinely reported contact with a Chinese *Jin Class* nuclear submarine. We have since identified the Chinese submarine as the *Giant Turtle.*'

'Shortly thereafter, at 10:34 hours, US Naval Command received a final transmission from the US submarine, indicating that it had lost forward thrust, that its hull had suffered a massive breach and that it was sinking rapidly towards implosion depth. All communications were lost, and subsequent search and rescue efforts confirmed that the vessel, too, was lost along with all hands. There were no survivors.'

Taken by surprise and alarmed by the gravity of this revelation, the assembled delegates issued a loud exclamation which reverberated around the large, circular forum. Some delegates stood, turned to their aids, and whispered urgent messages, to be relayed back to their Governments, while others simply gasped at the moment of the event, so that the Chair was forced to bang a gavel and call the meeting to order.

'Ladies and gentlemen, please resume your seats,' demanded the Chairperson. 'I ask delegates to show proper respect and to allow the US Secretary of State to finish her important statement. You have the floor, Madame Secretary. Please continue.'

'We now know from US naval intelligence sources,' Rankin continued, 'that this was no accident. They describe a naval practice, politely referred to as "shadow patrolling", but more vulgarly, as "stalking". This is a routine operational exercise employed by all NATO forces and by most other nations, to monitor the movements of opposing submarines in international waters. Our experts insist that Chinese passive sonar and hull signature technologies are as advanced as our own and should have given their submarine abundant capacity to detect and avoid another submarine over distances much greater than that applying in this case. *Interdiction*, otherwise described as physical engagement, they note, is a practice reserved for "hot" or wartime patrols and is never practised in peacetime.'

'Upon detecting the approaching Chinese submarine, Delaware's Commander stopped all engines and came to a neutral, "hover and wait" attitude. Only two of Delaware's torpedo tubes were armed, but its outer tube doors were closed, a routine, non-aggressive attitude for such peacetime patrols.

'I am assured that, at least three kilometres before it advanced upon Delaware's position, the Chinese submarine's sonar would have identified a large, stationary mass, interpreting it as another submarine or subterranean feature. Despite this, the Chinese submarine continued on a collision course towards Delaware, in what appears to have been a deliberate provocation, resulting in this tragic incident. Our *Eye in the Sky* surveillance satellites eventually obtained images of a damaged PRC submarine, clearly identified as the *Giant Turtle*, their latest Jin Class sub, limping back to its Shanghai mooring. This validates our reconstruction of events and the accuracy of Delaware's initial and final reports. There is no doubt that the Chinese *Giant Turtle* nuclear submarine collided with and sank the *USS Delaware.*

'In the final moments of its descent to the bottom, Delaware's Commander released the sub's data recorder, which our surface fleet has recovered. It faithfully records the underwater drama, just as we have relayed it. It ends with the brave Commander advising that a catastrophic implosion was imminent, which would tear the sub's steel hull and superstructure apart. I must also, therefore, reluctantly report that the reactor core of the Delaware will now, almost certainly, be exposed and releasing contaminants into the surrounding tidal currents in that part of the South China Sea.'

Upon hearing this further revelation, another volley of loud protestation echoed around the chamber. More experienced delegates winced at the wider implications - under International Laws, Environmental

Laws and the 'Law of the Sea' conventions - of the catastrophic event. Anticipating a strong, negative reaction, Secretary of State Rankin quickly sought to allay fears.

'While the loss of lives is tragic, the issue with the reactor core is not so serious. The small amount of radiation it will emit across a vast ocean footprint will ensure that environmental impacts are miniscule. Further, the inexhaustible volume of ocean waters surrounding the reactor core will, I am assured by our physicists, exclude any remote possibility of a meltdown. Indeed, the reactor was courageously shut down by our Commander in the final minutes of the sub's descent to the bottom. He did so in the full knowledge that his action would cause the engines to immediately lose thrust and condemn himself, his vessel and his crew to an eternal, watery grave.'

'Given the seriousness of this event, the US now calls upon the People's Republic of China to explain its breach of naval protocols, its failure to take appropriate evasive action and its apparent belligerence. It must do so immediately, to defuse a provocation which has seen twenty-eight US citizens lose their lives and the US and Chinese naval commands raise their defence conditions to *high alert*. Any continued escalation of events would clearly result in an unspeakable holocaust.'

A new wave of murmurs swept the chamber as these highly charged words, crafted by insensitive State Department bureaucrats, reached the ears of Rankin's anxious audience. Their accusing tone had clearly unsettled the Chinese delegates, who were now shuffling in their seats. A silence followed, which was finally punctuated by movement in one quarter of the forum, as the entire Chinese delegation rose to its feet and prepared to leave. Incensed by Rankin's strong rhetoric and frustrated by their inability to provide any response without direction from Beijing, they had simply gathered up their papers and turned towards the chamber exit, in a gesture calculated to make clear their unwillingness to support any US censure motion.

'I see that the Chinese delegation is preparing to leave the chamber,' Rankin noted. 'Madame Chair, I urge the Chinese delegation to remain. I have more to say - words which will, I hope, balance the angry tone of my government's initial response - and I wish these words to be communicated to the Chinese Government,' she continued. A seasoned stateswoman, Liz Rankin understood that her words had caused the Chinese delegates a huge, public loss of face and was angry that the government's speech writers had been so clumsy in making no allowance for that cultural trait.

In response to calm urging from forum attendants, the leader of the Chinese delegation turned, paused, and reluctantly moved back towards his seat, beckoning the other members of his delegation to do likewise. By now, Rankin was acutely aware of the hostile political atmosphere which her prepared speech, and its accusatory language, had created. She crushed her notes in a balled fist and threw them to one side, electing instead to choose her own, more conciliatory language.

'I would ask the Chinese delegation to understand that the loss of American lives carries a high political price in our western democracy. It requires, indeed demands, that my government deliver a robust response. However, at a personal level, I want very much to believe that this provocation may be simply explained as a tragic accident, perhaps an error of human judgement,' she added. 'My Government will see China's response as a signal of the importance it places upon its relationship with us and of its willingness to seek ways to lower diplomatic tensions.'

'We Americans, and many other nations around the free world, have long admired the Chinese people. Our high regard for China and its people is not a contemporary phenomenon. Rather, it is based upon China's contribution to humanity over many centuries. In this area, China has no peer. It has been a source of knowledge and inspiration for us all. Our Governments will always have differences on some issues, but the citizens of our two nations have forged strong cultural, business and familial links which transcend those differences, providing a foundation for growing cooperation and friendship. Let us strive to resolve this issue quickly and to restore trust. I ask, simply, that China provide a frank account of the circumstances surrounding this incident and call upon their officials to work with mine to find a peaceful pathway towards resolving this matter. Thank you.'

The Security Council comprised five permanent members, each with a power to veto resolutions, and ten non-permanent members. As Rankin concluded her address, the delegates from the USA, UK, France, Luxembourg and South Korea applauded, while the Chinese, Russian, African and South American delegates maintained a stony silence. These four remained uncertain what diplomatic posture their respective governments might choose. Then all eyes returned to the chairwoman, who addressed the assembly.

'Does the Chinese delegation wish to respond to Secretary Rankin's remarks at this time?' she inquired.

Under UN protocols, an invitation for a permanent member to speak at a security council meeting comes with no fetters upon time or content. It is a licence to say what one needs to say, and to take as long as is deemed necessary to address any volatile issue the council is charged with defusing. In this case, silence ensued, as translators hastily relayed the chairwoman's question to the headphones of the delegates, in their respective languages.

Mr Lin de Bao was not just China's Ambassador to the UN. An experienced head of mission, with numerous other postings in the west, he was a realist, possessed of an extraordinary intellect, a man of the world, and a man with a fine command of English nuances. Lin de Bao considered the chairwoman's invitation to speak, borrowing time, and making his audience wait, as he calculated his response. He was painfully aware that, had the US not insisted upon this emergency session of the council, it would, instead, have been convened to hear China's response to US allegations about its use of electromagnetic pulse weapons.

The nimble-minded old diplomat saw at once that he could use this postponement to wrong-foot his opponents, but he would need facts to back up his response. He shuffled papers on his desk to buy extra time, while instructing an aide to urgently retrieve the briefing papers sent from Beijing on the electromagnetic pulse issue. Delegates now shifted impatiently, as he began polishing his glasses. All the while, his busy mind was preparing an exquisite, diplomatic ambush. Satisfied at last, he rose to speak, and a respectful silence descended over the forum.

'Madame Chairwoman,' he began softly, lowering the tone and vitriol. 'My delegation will seek a recess, so that we may consult with our government on the matter of the unfortunate submarine collision. I propose that we reconvene tomorrow, by which time the People's Republic of China will have a response to the strong language used by the United States. However, since this matter has replaced other pressing matters of interest to China, which seem to have taken a back seat, I would offer the following observations.

'Over many centuries, the Chinese people have evolved their own unique culture, based upon pacifism, Confucian respect for nature and a reverence for scholarly pursuit. Throughout our history, foreigners have come to our shores - from India and Arabia, to trade with us, from the Steppes of Russia, with evil intent, from Europe, with the friendly arrival of Marco Polo, to be fascinated by the wonders of our civilization, and later, by self-seeking imperialists. Most foreigners came to learn from us, to absorb our practices and to take our technologies back to their homelands. However, when we were confronted by hostile incursions, from the Mongols and others, we built a Great Wall, not as an offensive measure, but as a *defensive* one, to protect our people and preserve the quiet enjoyment of our own culture.

'Later, as foreign powers developed their gunboat diplomacies and sought to expand their military and economic influence, we found ourselves increasingly besieged by foreign hegemony, which interrupted the quiet management of our own, domestic affairs. Western powers demanded territorial concessions along our eastern coastline and introduced a State-sponsored drug trade, which left many of our people in a drug-induced stupor. These things attacked our national self-esteem. Later, we suffered atrocities at the hands of brutal Japanese invaders. These negative experiences made us wary of contact with the west, and we retreated, for almost half a century, from their aggressive influence. Their actions left a permanent scar upon our psyche, which has always preferred peace. We therefore find the US assertion that this incident was somehow the result of Chinese aggression, highly offensive. Our Chinese navy is small compared to America's. It is evolving to enable us to take our place in a rapidly

214

changing world, one in which we are destined to assume a greater global leadership role. However, we see this as a heavy burden and have chosen to contain our naval and military deployment to our immediate, geographic area, in defence of our own, immediate interests. Our navy has rarely ventured beyond China's own, surrounding waters.

'I ask delegates to consider these facts and to answer one simple question: Would the United States and its allies tolerate Chinese naval patrols along America's eastern seaboard – for example, off the coast of Miami - in the same way as America feels free to patrol our southern seaboard, the South China Sea? Applying this test, I ask delegates to reconsider which nation – the US or China - is adopting an offensive, rather than a defensive attitude and I urge you to seek wise counsel before acting so quickly to condemn us.

'I now turn to the Security Council's previous business agenda, requiring consideration of America's demarche *'That China explain its possession of 'Electromagnetic Pulse Weapons (SEMPs)'*. This matter was to be heard today but was replaced by America's special request for an emergency session on the submarine collision. My government notes this political over-riding of the agenda but welcomes an opportunity to comment upon the previously scheduled matter.

'When, in the 50s, the US was testing its early nuclear devices in the Pacific, it exploded an A-bomb in the upper atmosphere, creating the first electromagnetic pulse, which destroyed electrical installations on its own island of Hawaii. America had unwittingly unleashed a potent, new force upon an unsuspecting world. As with the atomic bomb, America, not China, was the first to introduce SEMP weapons. Accordingly, America, not China, must now explain to the world where they believe that dangerous technology may take us.

'Instead of keeping its own magnetic pulse warheads under wraps, or rejecting them as sinister weapons of mass destruction, the US has lent further legitimacy to this WMD technology, having created its own 'Federal SEMP Commission' to undertake research into this dangerous technology. In doing so, it gave this technology a State imprimatur, raising grave questions about America's own military intentions.

215

'Indeed, since the Snowden affair, this technology is now available on the internet. Any nuclear country with an upper atmosphere launch-vehicle now has it. The US belief that China also has that capacity is correct, but this simply makes China a member of a broader community, including the USA, Russia, the UK, France, India, Israel, North Korea and Pakistan who have satellite launch vehicles. Moreover several other States have a capacity to bring SEMP technology on line quickly, including Germany, Japan and Iran.

'China therefore feels disinclined to bend to American demands on SEMPs, since they impose a moral and ethical standard upon China which the US itself does not meet. If America wishes to press the issue in the UN, China will gladly remind the world that the US invented the technology, that the US was the first to use the technology, and that the US gave legitimacy to it by establishing its own, Government funded, SEMP Commission. Moreover, delegates may be interested to learn that the US has also recently deployed what they call a 'surgical variant' of an electromagnetic pulse beam, which can focus on a discreet target - a high-rise building or a manufacturing facility - to strike surgically and take out all of its electronics. This heightens the hypocrisy of their position.'

The wily old Chinese diplomat had calculated his argument brilliantly. His speech would set a new benchmark in the national discourse between the east and the west, along with other, iconic speeches, like the one in which America warned Russia that Berlin would remain free, until "hell freezes over".

UN Ambassador Lin de Bao had enthralled his audience. His address was relayed to governments around the world, and to Beijing's 'Forbidden City', where Chinese Vice-Premier Wei Jintan and senior PRC leaders, including General Zhang Ming Wei, were gathered. The faces of the Vice Premier and his ambitious young General wore satisfied smiles, as they savoured the clever old diplomat's brilliant riposte. His words, beamed out to news programs hungry for any new, political nuance would usher in a new age of Chinese influence in international affairs and herald the end of half a century of American domination of international affairs.

National Security Advisor, Bill Nordish's unbridled passion and his clumsy handling of the Manila Trench incident had combined to create a perfect storm. He had been the catalyst for a subtle shift in power, as nations around the world witnessed the confident manner in which China had rebutted the American demarche and made them look ordinary.

America, not China, had suffered a national loss of face, one which would give voice to a volley of demands from the Congress to re-establish American global prestige... serving to further inflame an already volatile situation.

Secretary of State, Elizabeth Rankin, was furious. Having been thoroughly outmanoeuvred, she gathered her papers and strode from the auditorium, anxious to deliver a firm rebuke to her President about listening to the hawkish noises of the National Security Advisor. She would tell her President that, in her view, Nordish had become a 'loose cannon' on the deck of America's ship of state.

Orthopaedic Clinic - Boston MA

Anatoly Pushkin marvelled at the extraordinary improvement in his mobility, as he made his way with increasing confidence between the bars of the medical walkway, without needing to grip its handy guide-rails. He was concluding the second week of his outpatient rehab program, following a highly successful operation on his hideously disfigured knee. Dr Geoffrey Weir, the highly acclaimed American orthopaedic surgeon, had worked a miracle. He had implanted a revolutionary new prosthesis with characteristic precision and overseen a miraculous recovery program.

Pushkin's shattered knee had initially been a painful reminder of his torture at the hands of the CIA and the cause of a bitter determination to exact revenge. Over time, however, he was forced to admit that the theatrical limp it had left him with, had also brought special benefits. It had become a personality signature, giving him an eccentric presence and a special notoriety within the Russian intelligence community. His pronounced limp might even have been responsible for his rapid rise to the top of the Soviet hierarchy. It had made him unfit for field service and thus resulted in his transfer to a more strategic, head office role, where he had excelled. It had also given the intelligence boss extra style and panache, personified by his use of a finely crafted walking cane sporting the head of a growling bear.

Nonetheless, ever since his brutal ordeal three decades earlier in the dark warehouse on London's Isle of Dogs, Pushkin had dreamed of the day when he might walk normally again, upright and without pain. News of an American breakthrough in corrective surgery had made that dream a reality, and he had insisted he be allowed to travel to the USA to undertake the procedure, despite the obvious risks involved for a senior intelligence officer. Moscow had protested that his plan to visit the USA was insane, but the FSB chief had used his high rank and standing within the Politburo to gain approval to do so. He had booked himself into Dr Weir's Boston clinic and blithely entered the United States, just three weeks earlier, under the assumed name 'Vladimir Jurkiev'. Using this new identity, supported by papers expertly forged by his own agency, he had sailed through customs and immigration without incident.

The unsuspecting American surgeon had been delighted to welcome his first Russian patient into his prohibitively expensive program. He had found Pushkin an intelligent, articulate chap. Indeed, he hoped that Vlad's treatment might attract more of Russia's nouveau riche and open doors of opportunity for him to publish his papers in Russia's medical journals. His initial examination of Pushkin's knee cap, however, made it clear that a viable reconstruction would require all of the surgeon's genius. The patient's knee had presented with extensive atrophic degeneration and serious collateral tissue damage, exacerbated by years of medical neglect. Vlad would require a complete *autologous chondrocyte implantation*, some *tissue scaffold* and *mosaicplasty*, he decided, but these procedures, together, heightened the risk of tissue rejection. Undeterred, the surgeon had turned to an experimental technology he was pioneering in cooperation with the University of Washington. It combined an oxidized zirconium femoral component with a polythene tibial insert, forming an advanced bearing with amazing strength. Above all, the technology created a robust, mechanical scaffold, with flesh-like qualities, promoting tissue acceptance, making it superior to the usual, metal components and performing even better than the body's own, natural knee.

The timing of Pushkin's recovery could not have been better. His time spent convalescing - commuting as an outpatient from his Boston safe house to Dr Weir's clinic - had been used to advantage. It had given Moscow an important field asset in the USA, enabling Pushkin to personally direct the operation to plant false information about China's Dongfeng missiles and to kidnap the meddling agent, Tom Grant, to prevent him from exposing the covert operation.

Moreover, Pushkin's bold and risky plan had clearly succeeded, if the latest intel reports from Moscow were any guide. It seemed that the

Americans had swallowed the bait - hook, line and sinker - and fallen for Pushkin's little subterfuge. Contemplating these positive aspects with smug satisfaction, Pushkin came to the end of the walkway, where a nurse waited to catch him. His rapid recovery had made her support redundant so, instead, she handed him a towel and encouraged him to continue, unassisted, to the shower block.

'You have made excellent progress, Vlad. I think you can walk down to the locker room by yourself now. When you have showered and changed, I will meet you in the lobby to assist you into your cab,' she suggested.

Twenty minutes later, Pushkin's cab turned into his driveway, as it did every day. His Boston safe house was an impressive, Georgian mansion in a gated community. Moscow had agreed that he could rent the excessively bourgeois property, both because it reinforced the illusion that he was one of Russia's new business elite and because it created a perfect subterfuge, masking his real identity as the head of Russia's Secret Service. He strode across the lounge-room on his sturdy new leg, threw his keys onto his desk and fired up his laptop. It whirred into life and the screen lit up. Then he clicked on 'Outlook Express' and waited patiently for new email traffic from Washington station, with whom he had agreed upon a covert communication protocol, hoping to retrieve and trash any cryptic messages that had come in during his absence.

He was not disappointed. There, on his screen, was a simple, short example of the message protocol they had agreed:

To: Vladimir Ivanovich Jurkiev

Dear Mr Jurkiev. We are pleased that your treatment is progressing well. However, the Embassy has received advice that your Aunty Irina is not well and that you should contact her urgently. She will leave for the hospital at 11.40 a.m. today.

Uri Kastanov,
Second Secretary, Consular Affairs
Embassy of the Russian Federation, Washington DC.

The message appeared innocuous, but its reference to *Aunty Irina* was a call to action, requiring that Pushkin visit a pre-arranged *drop* site on the Boston Common to retrieve a communication. As his watch indicated that it was already 10.50 am, Pushkin immediately booked a cab, arranging for it to meet him at the gateway to his compound and take him to the eastern access pathway into the Common. He would instruct the cabbie to wait for him on the edge of the Common and return him to his residence. The Boston Common had been established in 1634, as America's first public park. Since then, it had become a magnificent, botanical walkway, linking the two hemispheres of the city. Indeed, its rambling pathways and lush vegetation made it an ideal place for the Russians to exchange covert messages.

On reaching the side access gate, Pushkin alighted from his cab and walked down a meandering pathway to the *drop*. Chosen for its urbanity, the drop site was, in fact, an isolated park bench surrounded by gardens on a bend overlooking a small stream, where patrons often stopped to feed the ducks. Being located on a bend between two long approach paths, the location was ideal for scanning ahead and behind, to ensure that there was no tail. Pushkin took a seat and waited.

Minutes later, a middle-aged woman approached, gestured towards the vacant space on the bench, and was invited by Pushkin to sit there. The dishevelled old lady placed a folded newspaper on the bench between them, retrieved a paper bag from her shopping trolley and began throwing its contents, breadcrumbs, to the ducks. Minutes later, she arose, nodded a polite farewell and continued on her way. Pushkin waited a respectable time before standing, gathering up the discarded newspaper and strolling back to his taxi. Once back in his safe house, he sat at his desk, unfurled the newspaper and scanned its contents. His eyes settled upon an article in the lift-out section, which was overprinted in scrambled text. He placed this section of the newspaper beside him and withdrew a cypher machine the size of a mobile phone and a *codex* book from a drawer in his desk. These would enable him to decode the message, which he would then destroy.

During his brief stay in the US, Pushkin's only communications had been with his field agents - *Peregrine*, in Langley, and *Dolgorukov*, based at the Russian Embassy in Washington. They had done a splendid job of intercepting Grant and the woman. However, communications from them had ceased abruptly, just twenty-four hours earlier and this new communication, coming from Mother Bear, was highly irregular, indicating a serious problem. Pushkin had already smelled a rat. His last discussion with *Peregrine* had confirmed that Grant and the woman were captive in the abandoned farmhouse on Long Island. Since then, neither *Peregrine* nor *Dolgorukov* had reported in, as they were supposed to, or responded to Pushkin's messages. Pushkin was thus certain that the two must have been compromised in some way. That meant that his cell phone must also now be a liability, and he would have to replace it.

While these developments were disconcerting, Pushkin remained confident that he was under no immediate threat. He had entered the country under a false passport, using the assumed name Vlad Jurkiev. A different surname, Krasnyeet (Mr Bear) had been used when he had paid for the SIM card for his mobile phone. He had given a fictitious address, so there was no prospect that he could be traced. Moreover, his cover role, as a patient at an exclusive medical clinic, took him off the radar of those looking for a foreign intelligence agent. The sudden loss of contact with his own field agents made him think that he should prepare for an early retreat back to Moscow but he was in no great hurry. Indeed, there was still a celebratory aspect to his mission. Moscow station had confirmed that the US government had swallowed his fiction about China's Dongfeng missiles. The gullible Americans had gone to DEFCON 2, making his bold, military deception an extraordinary success. The boys back in Moscow would be celebrating even now, as Pushkin uncorked a Californian wine and regretted having to join them back in Moscow, where the wine was like cat's piss. Both reassured and distracted by these thoughts, Pushkin returned to his desk and focussed upon the ponderous task of decoding the covert message. As its meaning unfolded, his brow creased and his fingers began to move more urgently across the key board:

'Mother Bear to Red Bear: Peregrine down! Kangaroo and Wombat have escaped. Washington agent compromised. FBI commencing national manhunt / investigation. Recommend immediate exit and return to den.'

Almost before he had digested these words, Pushkin, alias *Red Bear*, alias *Vladimir Jurkiev*, was on the phone to Aeroflot, booking the earliest possible return flight to Russia. His exit strategy had already been well formed in his cunning mind. He would take a domestic flight to New York, where he was least expected. There, he would transfer to an Aeroflot, international flight, taking him by direct route over the Arctic Circle to his beloved homeland and Moscow. If he were efficient in making good this strategy, he could be in international airspace within four hours and at his desk in FSB headquarters ten hours later, before the Americans could possibly imagine that he, the head of Russia's intelligence service, had ever been in the USA… operating right under their noses as he directed the Dongfeng deception.

No doubt the meddling Colonel from Australia would have relayed his theory about the corruption of Ritter's report on China's Dongfeng to his contacts at the CIA. That revelation would be explosive and require a careful diplomatic response, but the damage to US – China relations had already been done and a cold front in relations had already formed and was icing over. That was an excellent, if not a perfect, mission outcome which would earn him accolades back home. Satisfied with this logic, he completed the flight bookings and began packing, leaving no vestiges of his official persona or presence, either at the Boston Clinic or within the US homeland.

CIA Headquarters, Langley, Virginia

CIA Director Frank Angiotti drummed impatient fingers on his desk, before turning back to the file which Sally Ormiston had deposited in front of him. It had damning information about the SIM card in the mobile phone recovered from the deceased Russian, *Peregrine*, together with the call log of the mobile phone service provider. These silent, digital witnesses had yielded key fragments of information and these were now assembled for him. Peregrine's mobile phone had provided evidence of his involvement in Col Tom Grant and Dr Maggie King's kidnapping. When taken together with the intel provided by ASIS's London station, this combined evidence had also prompted Angiotti to reopen the investigation into CIA Deputy Director Ritter's death.

While the CIA and Homeland Security were the lead agencies on matters involving suspected foreign power activities on US soil, Angiotti had insisted that the FBI, which was essentially a domestic policing agency, also be included in the investigation team. This strategy had enabled Angiotti to multiply his resources. As the CIA boss, he would not only control the investigation, but influence its wider focus, subtly informing the FBI's search efforts and expanding inter-agency cooperation across a broader front. If the joint investigations enabled him to run 'Red Bear' down on US soil, the FBI would have authority to affect an arrest. Time was now critical. Tom Grant's heroic escape from his captors, his elimination of one Russian agent and his exposing of another, would have sent a danger signal to *Red Bear*, causing the Russian intelligence chief to flee the US as quickly as possible.

***

Investigations had confirmed that *Red Bear*, the enigmatic figure at the end of the covert phone calls, had been the brains behind everything. He was now exposed as the project puppet master, pulling the strings. Whenever he had identified himself as '*Red Bear*', he had commanded obedience and respect from his underlings, Peregrine and Sergei. They had addressed him as *Meed-Vyeht Krasnyeet*, Russian for '*Red Bear*', and always deferred to him as their 'chief', confirming that Russian agents were behind the elaborate and potentially explosive deception. If Angiotti could run *Red Bear* to ground, his capture would publicly expose the Russian attempt to falsely implicate the Chinese. That explosive, public revelation would likely see the Russian Government retreat into a phase of diplomatic denial, silencing their US intelligence network for a while. Ritter's assassination and the military tension caused by the manufactured evidence about China's use of electromagnetic warheads, were damning indictments of Russia's meddling in another nation's affairs, and could do much to relax tensions with China.

For that reason, Angiotti had assigned his best operative, Agent 'Macka' McKenzie, from Special Ops, to the team the FBI had established, with the same mission as the CIA – to track down the elusive *Red Bear* and bring him in. Macka's IT expert, Louis Ambrose, would be a key player in the investigation and Tom Grant would also be in the mix. To override inter-agency jealousies, the administration had instructed the FBI to respect Angiotti's team and the Aussie Military Attaché as trusted colleagues. They had even arranged for the CIA operatives to be issued with 'temporary special agent' passes, giving them authority to act with full FBI investigative powers, as if they were permanent FBI team members.

Tom Grant arrived early the next morning. Instead of joining as a mere functionary, Grant immediately took charge, instructing Macka to begin by enlisting the assistance of his contacts in the US Customs and Immigration Service. Macka was to ask his contacts there to scrutinize arrivals over US sea and air ports over the weeks leading up to and following the date, five weeks earlier, when the then unidentified Russian agent, Red Bear, must have initially entered the United States.

The data they collected was then 'washed' by Macka's IT expert, Louie, to reduce it down to those entrants with a Russian connection of any sort or with a seemingly incongruous or inconsistent purpose of visit. The shortlist would be further refined by narrowing it down to a range of arrival dates, countries of origin and purposes of visit, since these details were provided on flight and arrival declarations. This list was then further washed, using thumb print data, eye scan data and video footage, to eliminate or retain suspects, and would finally be processed against CIA, FBI and Interpol records for a possible match with known criminals or covert operatives.

Later that afternoon, after a tedious process of washing data, Louie handed Tom Grant a file containing the team's final shortlist of suspects. Tom Grant instructed Macka to immediately transmit a copy of the shortlist to Frank Angiotti, sensitive to the fact that he was only on the team as Angiotti's guest and had been stomping around other people's turf. The data was also sent to friendly intelligence agencies. It did not seem likely, however, that they or Angiotti could shed much light on matters until Macka and his team had further reduced the shortlist and eliminated suspects.

At 6.00 p.m. that evening, as the last rays of light were fading into darkness, Frank Angiotti was hunched over his desk, completing his tedious daily routine. He shuffled the 'action' and 'decision' files to one side and turned to the information sent to him by Tom Grant and agent 'Macka' McKenzie. He doubted they could have made much headway in their huge task of investigating the kidnapping plot, but he wanted to check progress and ensure that he was across all of the issues. He was therefore astonished to find that Grant's team had already produced a shortlist of suspects.

As he leafed through the data, which included images of immigration entrants over the span of likely dates, one particular image caught his eye and he paused to inspect it more closely. He clicked the 'resize' button on his computer, to magnify the image, then went into his photoshop software to refine the grainy image. All CIA operatives used this in-house software, which enabled them to generate leads, based upon enhancing digital images, and employing standard deviation and biological probability

226

techniques. Angiotti's attention had been particularly drawn to a passenger identified as 'Vladimir Jurkiev', company director, arriving from the Ukraine. Jurkiev had stated his purpose of visit as 'medical procedure'. . There was a haunting familiarity about the man, whose face was slightly disfigured, and Angiotti was also drawn to the familiar, narrow-set of the man's eyes. The man had a distinctive look, but it somehow seemed contrived. Angiotti studied the image again, racking his brains to place the features. Suddenly, he leapt up from his desk, slapped the file down, mouthed an obscenity and called out to his PA:

'Sally! If they are still here at this hour, get Tom Grant and Macka up here… now! Goddammit!'

Fortunately, Tom Grant and Macka were still at their desks when Sally Ormiston's call came through. Minutes later, they burst into Angiotti's office, followed by agents Louie Ambrose and Bill McCabe, who Grant had decided should join them.

'What is it, boss?' rasped McKenzie. 'Why the panic?'

Angiotti beckoned the men towards his desk, turned his computer around and showed them the digitally enhanced image. As he did so, he rolled his eyes triumphantly and pointed excitedly at the screen.

'Recognise this guy, Macka? Call me crazy, but I think we have a big fish on the line… the famous Anatoly Pushkin, Director General, Russian Joint Intelligence Services and head of the FSBR. Cunning bastard! All we did to enhance this image was add a full head of grey hair, and bingo, there he was. It might sound crazy, but I'm sure that is him, right here in our midst, operating right under our noses!'

Agent McKenzie struggled to place the image, while Tom Grant looked on quizzically, sensing the enormity of Angiotti's claim. Then Grant leaned over Angiotti's desk, turned the computer around and began scrolling through its data.

'According to the file, this bloke came in five weeks ago using the pseudonym 'Vladimir Jurkiev'. Your counter-intelligence guys must have a recent file photo of the real Pushkin. Can they do a facial scan? You know, look for twelve points of facial recognition, and confirm absolutely that he is the bloke you think he is?'

'They sure can,' replied Angiotti. Get on it right away, Louie, and work carefully. We don't want to get this call wrong, or we'll have the diplomatic incident of the century, but I'll bet my sweet arse on it. I haven't seen or heard of Pushkin since a meeting of the UN Security Council in New York about three years ago, when he was part of the Russian delegation. We followed him closely and kept tabs on him. He had just been promoted to head up the FSBR and we wanted to get a handle on the new boy. One side of his face was disfigured. One eye was damaged and he had a scar running from his eye socket down the side of his cheek. He had thick, grey hair back then and wore horn-rimmed glasses. He must have shaved his scalp and used contact lenses, to change his appearance, but that's his face alright! I'd bet my life on it. He also had a pronounced limp, so we should try to get some wide-angle security camera footage from the terminal to confirm that our suspect has a limp.'

Tom Grant stroked his chin thoughtfully, then turned to agent McKenzie and issued a volley of additional instructions.

'If that is Pushkin and he knows we're onto him, he'll be making a dash for an airport. You will need to alert your Homeland Security people, your customs, immigration and border protection people, airline personnel and port authorities. See if you can also get manifests of domestic and international airline passengers leaving for Canadian or European destinations. If he's smart, that's how he will leave.'

'Let's hope we're not too late,' chimed in Angiotti. 'Give all agencies the bald image of Pushkin entering over Kennedy three weeks ago, some digitally altered images representing how he might look in various disguises, and the most recent official photo of him you can find. Circulate them quietly. We don't want to scare the horses. If he's brazen enough to come into the States like a common tourist, he's brazen enough to leave on an international flight from a major airport. He might even reuse the same entry passport, in the name of Jurkiev, believing we haven't worked that out yet, but I wouldn't bet on it. It's more likely he'll have another passport, in another assumed name. I would also bet that he has assumed a different physical identity, but our face and finger-scan technologies at passport control points might still find enough points of comparison to raise an alert.

Focus on key features like nose, eyes, brow, cheek and chin points, etc. Tell your immigration guys that any vague match – say five points of matching data, should trigger a detention order. Get on it!'

'If he still has a pronounced limp, that will narrow the search effort dramatically,' added Macka, failing to allow that the declared purpose of the visit – 'medical procedure' - might have resulted in the limp being repaired.

Despite these thorough precautions, none of the investigative team could have anticipated that Pushkin, after receiving the best medical attention available in the west, now walked with the upright, confident gait of a fully functional pedestrian, nor that his facial scars had been removed and his face given a new symmetry. Nonetheless, the net was closing fast, as Macka and his team mobilised all of the resources at their disposal in their hunt for the elusive Russian intelligence boss.

***

Satisfied with the arrangements he had set in train, and not able to do much more as his work day drew to a close, Tom Grant placed a call to his aide-de-camp in New York to check on matters in his own office. Mike Stephens took the call and immediately relayed a message he had received just moments earlier.

'Hi, boss. Glad you rang. I've just received a message from Lazarus indicating that he will be arriving in New York at 21:00 hours and would like you to pick him up at the airport. He is on his way to London but will be making a brief stopover to meet with you. I will try to get you a short haul flight or a chopper back to New York and I'll be on standby to take you to Kennedy in time for Sir Robert's arrival.'

At 10 p.m. that evening, Mike Stephens was cruising along the freeway towards New York city, having collected his special cargo from Kennedy airport. In the rear seat, the shadowy figures of ASIO Chief, Sir Robert Chandler, and Colonel Tom Grant were occasionally illuminated by the passing glow of overhead streetlamps. The men's discussion was 'unter vier

Augen', as Sir Robert liked to say, and took place in the safe confines of Tom's Consular vehicle, which was regularly swept for bugs.

'At first,' Sir Robert began, 'this Dongfeng business was little more than a covert operation gone wrong. Now it has assumed a much greater dimension. Our American cousins have been very clumsy. The rebuke they delivered to our Chinese neighbours in the UN, in front of a global audience, was unwise. It made an initially small issue the touch-paper for a potentially global conflagration, after China's clever response. As an attempt at international diplomacy, the American bluster was a complete and utter disaster, which backfired spectacularly. That infernal collision of the American and Chinese subs didn't help either. Right in Australia's front yard! No one could have seen those things coming! Together, these things were rather like throwing accelerant instead of water onto a fire, don't you think? They seem to have ignited a much wider, political fire-front. Our Government – the Foreign Minister and the Minister for Defence in particular – are now worried that we might get some nasty bruises if those two elephants, China and America, let this thing get out of hand.'

Sir Robert had a wonderful way with words, highlighting the key issues with rich allusions and metaphors, so that their meaning was absolutely clear. He was a man possessed of a keen intellect, able to temper his wit by making shrewd assessments of the human condition and using them to build empathy with any discussion partner. This rare gift had earned him a wide network of admirers and the respect and friendship of colleagues across the global intelligence community.

'That may be so, Sir Robert,' said Grant, 'but I sense that your visit is more than just an opportunity for you and I to exchange pleasantries on US foreign policy. How does our Government intend to respond and how do I figure in it?' replied Grant.

'A very astute observation, my boy,' replied Lazarus. 'I have arranged a bit of a chat with our American mates, tomorrow afternoon. Our Ambassador will join us. We will all meet in Sec-State Liz Rankin's Office and I rather hoped you might persuade your very talented colleague, Dr Maggie King, to join us,' he added.

'Does she have to be involved in this?' replied Grant. 'She has been through so much - what with the kidnapping and associated physical trauma - and it was all because of her association with me. I feel really guilty about that,' said Tom.

'I would hardly call her an outsider, Tom. She is covertly employed by the CIA as an advisor on Asian affairs. With respect, old boy, I think you are underestimating the extent of her current involvement. I also think she might be genuinely angry about the whole Russian business and keen to help our cause in any way she can.'

'Well I won't be responsible for dragging her into this mess. You'll have to ask her yourself. I am already feeling guilty about involving her in this crazy business. For God's sake! We almost got her killed. Just leave her out of this!' he snapped.

'My dear boy,' replied Lazarus. 'Do I detect a chink in your professional armour? I do believe this woman has gotten under your skin and is distorting your judgement. You and I have become good friends, Tom, but we must never allow personal emotions - even friendships - to cloud our professional judgement. You are important to our soft diplomacy with the Americans, so we can't afford to have you compromising this new emergency in any way. I must urge you... indeed *instruct* you to reconsider.'

Grant assumed a pained expression, turned to Lazarus and fired a last, angry retort.

'You bastard, Lazarus! You know damned well that I never let anything personal interfere with my work. I will go this far. Dr King is visiting me in New York tonight. She was going to join me for a romantic dinner and stay over, before you happened into town at short notice. I will be seeing her after I drop you off. Maybe we can all sit down tomorrow, over breakfast, and make some more sense of this thing.'

Cnr 5th Ave and 42nd St - New York

A sporty-looking Maggie King jogged up the eastern slope of Bryant Park, opposite Tom Grant's 5th Avenue hotel. Her morning jogs had become a magnificent obsession. Maggie found that they cleared away the cobwebs and allowed her to process difficult thoughts, making the most complex somehow seem clearer. This morning, however, she was filled with mixed emotions, both guilt and euphoria, after another intimate night with Tom Grant. She had always been strongly independent, but that seemed to have changed. Now, when she was in his strong, reassuring arms, she became a weak, supplicant woman. For the first time in her life, she felt a conflict between her career ambitions and her feminine needs. Deep within, however, she knew that her career would always triumph over personal distractions, and this meant that she had to fight the urge to be subject to any man. Damn him! She needed him in her life and this need was growing stronger every day.

She rounded the final bend and came to a halt at the top of the rise, on the corner of 42nd and 5th. There, she bent down to rest her hands on her knees and gulp in deep breaths, a natural response to replenish her body's oxygen deficit. Her body tingled, as oxygenated blood rushed to her extremities, creating a physical euphoria which always accompanied the end of her strenuous runs.

When she had gathered her breath, she straightened and turned to make her way across the street to the hotel lobby. As she approached the level crossing, she became aware of a presence beside her. The silent intruder was a rotund, mature-aged man, wearing an immaculate suit, a bow tie and a spotted, silk pocket handkerchief. These made him look ridiculously formal on this New York morning, on a busy footpath and amongst a passing parade of early pedestrians, street people and casual joggers. He turned and looked quizzically at Maggie through elegant, blue-framed glasses, hoping to engage her in conversation. When she had assessed the stranger at her side and determined that he was not threatening, she addressed him.

'Can I help you, sir? You seem lost.'

'Ah, I must appear so,' replied Lazarus, 'but nothing could be further from the truth, Dr King. Indeed, I am *found,* as the bible says. Allow me to introduce myself. I am Robert Chandler, a senior Australian bureaucrat and close friend of Tom Grant.'

Lazarus rarely ventured out of his own, domestic jurisdiction, but this time he had risked a more adventurous course. His mission was becoming clearer. Following the report from the ASIS London station, he needed to confer with colleagues in London and get the Brits working in tandem with his own people on the Dongfeng affair. It was also increasingly clear that the US, with or without his support, must be made to engage with the Chinese positively, to defuse the increasingly volatile situation. A succession of unlikely events – the suspected manipulation of intelligence about the Chinese Dongfeng missiles, the collision of the nuclear submarines and the subsequent, clumsy US diplomacy at the emergency session of the UN Security Council – had conspired to bring the free world to the brink of a dangerous conflict; too close to home for Sir Robert's liking. He needed to find common ground and to persuade the Americans of the need for a more pacific diplomacy. The west needed to diffuse tensions, while his team gathered evidence of a sinister Russian hand in the affair. That strategy had been sanctioned by the PM himself, after consulting with his defence chiefs, and had resulted in Lazarus making this unusual, fly-in visit.

'I hope you will forgive this intrusion. Allow me to explain. When he is not engaged in our military exchanges with your country, your friend, Colonel Tom Grant, works for me. He is an important link in my national intelligence network. Your CIA chief, Frank Angiotti is my counterpart here and, may I say, a trusted and respected friend. As for me, I am en route to London for talks with the Brits, but I plan to spend a few days here venting some ideas with Tom, and with your own people. Tom is someone

233

we both value highly, but he is angry at me for wanting to involve you in a matter concerning both of our nations. I rather hoped, by this personal intervention, to persuade you to support me in this matter and to bring Tom around to accepting your involvement. I understand I will be joining you and Tom for breakfast, where I will explain the purpose of my visit, but I wanted to explain myself to you first. Tom does not know that I have chanced this advance encounter with you.'

'Go on,' said Maggie, intrigued by the eccentric gentleman's unfolding logic.

'What I am about to say will quite likely offend your national pride, as I explain my own, sincere need to protect both of our national interests. If you find my words offensive or presumptuous, I could not blame you. I simply ask that you hear me out.'

'Go on,' repeated Maggie, now more interested than ever.

'My country is no longer remote from the global discourse, though America may think it so. Indeed, the epicentre of global power has shifted markedly towards Asia, on my country's doorstep. China was once a sleeping dragon. Now it is well and truly awake, and its hot breath will soon blow over all of us. Indeed, we Australians will feel that heat before it reaches your shores. I will risk sharing some sensitive information with you and trust you to keep it between us... 'Unter vier Augen' ...as I like to say. Please don't disappoint me, dear lady. Your betrayal would cause me much pain.'

'You have my word, Sir Robert,' replied Maggie.

'Our people in London recently uncovered information that makes us believe there is a sinister, covert operation, here on American soil, to heighten tensions between the US and China. I recently gave Tom authority to share details with Frank Angiotti and, as a result, our respective intelligence assets are now jointly investigating the matter. We have code named this clandestine mission *Operation Dongfeng*, since it has its genesis in a strategic US defence document about a Chinese missile of the same name, which we think was intercepted by Russian intelligence operatives and changed, to imply a serious military threat. We still lack conclusive proof, but the document has already resulted in a strongly worded

234

demarche, from your Government to the Chinese, and a terse exchange between the US and Chinese Foreign Ministers at a recent session of the UN Security Council.'

'I see,' replied Maggie. 'I think I know what you are implying. I followed media coverage of that crazy exchange in the UN Security Council and it made my blood boil. And I think you're also saying that the Russians behind this Dongfeng affair are the same ones as those associated with Tom's and my kidnapping.'

'Quite so,' continued Sir Robert. 'But we need to prove-up our intelligence before setting hares running between your government and the Chinese. If you forgive me for saying so, your National Security Adviser, Bill Nordish, has much to answer for. His clumsy management of this *Dongfeng* affair has stirred up a hornet's nest and compromised our intelligence efforts. His clumsy diplomacy has been exacerbated by the unfortunate collision of one of your nuclear subs with a Chinese nuclear sub, creating a precondition for a major international conflict and a huge dilemma for my government, which is bound to stand with America under the terms of the ANZUS Defence Treaty between us. It has our PM and our defence chiefs on edge.'

Sir Robert paused, stroked his chin thoughtfully and continued...

'Dr King, you are widely respected for your grasp of international affairs. You are held in high regard by the academic and political communities alike, and are thus well placed to exercise moral authority on this issue. I think it possible that you share my concerns about Nordish, and about the tensions within your own administration that this buffoon has created. He has conjured a diplomatic nightmare out of a difficult, but otherwise manageable incident.'

'You must be channelling my thoughts, Sir Robert,' replied Maggie. 'Nordish is an ass... an accident waiting to happen. His fierce nationalism makes no concession to the way the Asians think or act. He has little understanding of the Asian psyche or of the impact of causing China a huge, international loss of face on the floor of the UN Assembly. Secretary of State Rankin has been forced to defend his clumsy diplomacy. She must be as furious about the situation he has created as we are.'

235

'My dear lady, you have understood me perfectly. I feel encouraged to explain the purpose of my visit more fully. Our Ambassador is arranging a meeting with your Secretary of State, Rankin, to propose a diplomatic initiative to defuse the situation. You speak Mandarin and are versed in the thinking of the Chinese. I am asking for your involvement in a peace mission to Beijing… a chance to work through issues with our diplomats and to help us find a way forward. Australia is a small nation; too small to represent any sort of political or military threat. But China depends on our resources and sees us as an important trading partner. We live in an Asian world, with greater cultural familiarity. Our diplomats are skilled in Chinese diplomacy and ideally placed to broker a peaceful solution of the issues, as a sort of middleman.'

'Well, Sir Robert, you have certainly got my attention, but why should the American administration want me to play any role? We have an ambassador in Beijing and an Embassy full of sinologists. These things are normally handled at that level.'

'Quite so. But as a great Chinese philosopher once said, one has to win each battle to win a war. I need your support to win over Liz Rankin, here, not in Beijing. I need a respected, independent academic voice to calm the horses inside your State Department and sway your President to our view. When I broach the subject over breakfast, Tom will insist that you have no part in it, because he has developed deep feelings for you. Tom's defensive attitude is understandable, but not necessarily in your nations' best interests. You will both have to balance personal feelings against your professional duties, which you both take quite seriously. What do you say?'

'I say you are one clever, manipulative son-of-a-bitch, Sir Robert. You have found the only chink in my armour. If I had been offered a voice in this affair by our own administration, without your intercession, I would have jumped at the opportunity to urge a more conciliatory approach. Now you have handed me that opportunity, I suppose I should thank you, even though my involvement might cost me my relationship with Tom. I am in, but I will need time with Tom to work this through.'

AirTrain depot, Newark, New York

Anatoly Pushkin – alias *Red Bear* - alighted from the Greyhound coach and mingled with passengers on the curb side, as bags were unloaded. His trip from Boston to New York had been uneventful. The coach had delivered him directly to the *AirTrain* terminus in Newark, where he planned to transfer to the new, fast rail link to JFK. He had calculated that the popular airport rail-link offered the safest, most anonymous approach to the airport, one which would not attract any particular attention. In light of the new security measures introduced after the 9/11 attack on New York's World Trade Centre, he had considered using a passport under an assumed name to exit the US. He had discounted that idea, electing, instead, to use his passport of entry, in the name of Vladimir Jurkiev, which he was confident remained routine as far as US security personnel were concerned. The new eye and finger scan terminals at immigration desks would be indifferent to his much-improved face, gait and bald head, since their focus was merely on facial and fingerprint points of comparison. Both processes would provide a match with his eye marble and fingerprint patterns on entry, supporting a routine approval of his documents.

He had chosen JFK because it was almost too obvious, too public and therefore unlikely to be the focus of any manhunt. JFK processed over 110 million passengers per year and life was about taking calculated risks. Immediately after 9/11, tighter security measures had brought America's busiest airport to a crawl and imposed significant stresses on its customs and immigration resources. Several years had since passed, and the practical dictates of processing large numbers had seen procedures gradually become lax again. Together, these factors had persuaded Pushkin to exit this way, relying upon his original entry documents. He had also chosen an early evening flight, so that he would be passing through customs and immigration formalities just as the day shift came to its end, when the officers staffing those functions would be jaded by a long day's work and their alertness blunted.

At the Aeroflot check-in counter, the process was routine. Pushkin accepted his boarding pass from Aeroflot's attractive hostess and contemplated, with satisfaction, a comfortable Business Class flight to Moscow. In Moscow, his colleagues would doubtless celebrate the genius of his mission and this gave him a smug sense of achievement. Having checked in his baggage he had nothing but a small briefcase as carry on. He found this strangely liberating. With time to spare, he strolled through the shopping mall in the departure area and flopped onto a sofa at a café. He ordered a coffee and began retracing steps in his mind, wanting to ensure that he had left no loose ends. The past weeks seemed to be fading in importance, becoming less real in his consciousness as his departure time approached. The events over the previous, frenetic weeks had been real enough, but had now given way to thoughts of his homeland and Moscow. His hand brushed over his reconstructed knee, reminding him of his three great, personal achievements - the successful plastic surgery to his face, the reconstruction of his crippled knee, and his clandestine mission to manufacture a crisis in relations between the USA and China, which had largely succeeded. Each of these missions had been accomplished!

He was now looking forward to a hero's welcome on his return. Mother Russia was stirring under its charismatic leader, Putin. His hard line politics had rattled the Americans, who were increasingly frustrated by Russian attempts to regain lost territories, starting with the annexation of the Crimea, populated by ethnic Russians who favoured a return to the motherland. Moreover, the US was now so thinly deployed across a number of different global theatres that it lacked the resources or political resolve to demand that Russia withdraw from the Ukraine. America was grappling with the politics of its awkward retreat from Afghanistan, with the rise of the Islamic State movement and with a consequent new wave of jihadist aggression across the Middle East. Overextended resources and domestic political pressures had made any further military escalation unthinkable. The Americans could not have expected a more complex alignment of

238

global challenges or a more difficult tax upon their dwindling political resolve. Growing more confident with each passing minute, Pushkin expected that his Dongfeng deception would provide his political leaders with welcome relief from the global outcry over Russian aggression in the Crimea.

Enjoying his coffee and now very much at ease, Pushkin delved in a pocket for a pen and began filling out his departure form. He entered the name 'Vladimir Jurkiev', the corresponding passport number and other details. Satisfied that he had completed all fields, he finished his coffee, stood and made his way to the departure gate. The queue before the counter was short, but he could hear his native tongue above the murmur of other, foreign conversations. Joining other Russians in this departure queue was reassuring. It highlighted the increasing number of his nouveau-riche countrymen who now routinely visited western destinations. His turn came, and he approached the immigration counter with renewed confidence. A tired looking US immigration official accepted his papers routinely, as those of yet another Russian tourist.

The official thumbed nonchalantly through Pushkin's documents before instructing him to press his finger into the finger-scan device and look directly into the camera. Nothing in the Russian's demeanour, or in that of the tired immigration official, suggested anything but routine process. Indeed, the immigration official picked up his stamp and thumped it routinely across the face of Pushkin's passport, then shuffled the papers together, ready to hand them it back to him.

Data matching software is generally fast, but airport software has to scan an international data base of millions to identify any inconsistency or menace. To make matters worse, the system is constantly refreshed, as new data from around the world is uploaded. The delay between the passing of Pushkin's documents back to him and the buzzing of the warning signal on the immigration official's monitor was no more than a few seconds, but long enough for Pushkin to have recovered his documents and continued his forward progress. The strident tone of the warning buzzer told the Russian espionage chief that he had a serious problem, but he continued past the immigration desk as casually as possible, praying that the alarm would cease. It did not. Before he had progressed ten metres, he was intercepted by two security officials, who emerged from an adjacent office in response to the alarm.

'Please come with us, sir,' they said, taking up positions on either side of Pushkin.

Pushkin was unarmed and the two athletic security personnel looked like they meant business. His brain raced frantically to calculate a means of escape. He knew that he must act quickly, that any delay would be costly and that things were bound to spiral out of control. Like all of Russia's clandestine field operatives, he carried a cyanide capsule with him, which would deny his adversaries the luxury of an interrogation, but that drastic measure would only be employed as a last resort. He fancied that he still had a slim chance of beating the odds, but his previous euphoria had now been replaced by a feeling of cold dread, making his heart beat faster in his chest. His initial angst then turned to a steely resolve, as his creative mind searched for a way through the impasse. Feigning complete cooperation, he stood to one side and asked the officers politely what the problem seemed to be. As the conversation unfolded, he noticed that both officers had standard issue, Smith and Wesson service revolvers hanging at their belts. They became the focus of his attention.

'I'm sorry, sir, but your passport check has resulted in a 'D' notice, requiring us to *detain* you and seek further clarification,' replied the older of the two officers.

'There must be some misunderstanding,' replied Pushkin pleasantly. 'But I am, of course, happy to answer any questions you may have.'

'Please follow us, sir,' replied the older officer. 'We will need to take you to an interview room and ask you some questions, while we await further advice.'

Underestimating the deadly resolve of their civilian suspect, the two officers naively turned to lead Pushkin off to an adjacent interview room for questioning. As soon as they turned their backs, Pushkin closed ground on the closest of them, clamped his left arm around the officer's neck and deftly pulled the man's service revolver out of its holster. Now armed, he pressed the revolver into the officer's back.

'Keep walking towards the interview room,' he demanded in a low but menacing growl. 'Any false move and I will shoot.'

Upon hearing this extraordinary demand, the lead officer turned towards Pushkin, and motioned towards his hip, where his service revolver was located.

'Bad move,' growled Pushkin. 'Trust me, I will kill you if you so much as flinch.'

The officer let his hand drop to his side, and the trio continued on to the interview room, which was located a short distance from the immigration check point. As soon as they entered the room, Pushkin became more strident. He was confronted by a female immigration officer and another, younger male, who turned casually towards the new arrivals, expecting nothing out of the ordinary, having been through the process many times before. Finding themselves confronted by a gunman holding their colleagues hostage, their eyes widened in disbelief. Pushkin's next action was swift and brutal. Waving his revolver menacingly, he pushed his captives roughly toward their two startled colleagues and barked at all of them to kneel on the carpet, facing the wall. When they had complied with his demand, he hammered the skull of the nearest officer with the butt of his revolver, sending him crashing into the wall.

That prompted the younger man to reach for his revolver. There followed a sharp report, as Pushkin's weapon fired at the rear of the young man's skull, catapulting him forward and sending a mist of grey matter from the gaping wound in his victim's head. A pool of crimson blood slowly pooled around the victim's corps and the female officer began sobbing hysterically. She was quickly comforted by the older security officer, who sought to calm the situation, respecting Pushkin's deadly intent.

'Alright, sir,' said the older security official in a quiet, reasoned voice. 'We don't want any trouble. No more killing... please! What do you want from us?' he asked.

'That's more like it,' replied Pushkin. 'Remove your side arms, slowly, and slide them across the floor to me. You... hand me your jacket and cap and then, all of you, lie face down on the floor. Don't move a muscle. Nobody needs to get hurt. When I am ready to leave, I want you all to remain still. Any attempt to follow me… or to raise an alarm… would be very foolish. Is that clear?'

'Very clear,' replied the older security official, unbuttoning his Customs jacket, removing his cap, bearing the insignia of his office, and throwing them to Pushkin.

Pushkin put on the jacket and cap, thrust a second revolver into his belt and moved towards the door, where he paused and asked - 'Who has the door keys?'

The female staff member mumbled weakly that they were on her desk. Pushkin asked her to retrieve them and throw them to him.

'Now, on the floor! Face down. All of you!' barked Pushkin.

When his hapless victims had complied with his demands, he opened the door to the interview room, slid out, closed and locked the door behind him and strode casually between the immigration control desks towards the airport's main arrival lounge. His immigration jacket and cap had given him an aura of unquestioned authority. Nobody found his movement through the barricades unusual and his progress therefore was unchallenged.

Once through the passport control area, he quickened his step and made his way to a lift, which would take him to the B level concourse leading to the long term public car park. There, he planned to hot wire a vehicle and make his escape. He was nearly free and clear, but there were lurking dangers. He knew that, once the alarm was raised, an 'all point's' call-out would result in road blocks on all the main arterial roads surrounding the airport. Timing would be critical, but the wily intelligence chief was an expert at his craft and the odds were slowly turning back in his favour. He would find a bolt hole, somewhere, and go to ground until the heat had passed.

Escape from Kennedy Airport

Anatoly Pushkin made his way through the airport carpark, keeping himself in dark shadows, farthest from the sun. His breathing was heavy, but his new knee was holding up remarkably well, as he maintained a brisk gait across the carpark. In the far corner, he found what he was looking for - a small hatchback, looking scratched and neglected. A vehicle like that would be unremarkable as it made its way out of the car park. Lacking time to toy with the door lock, he wound a handkerchief around his hand and smashed the side vent window with his fist. He pushed his arm through the broken glass and unlocked the driver's door. The impact of the blow made him wince, and he feared that he might have damaged his wrist, but his adrenalin was flowing and that small fact seemed unimportant. He pulled down a bundle of wires from under the dash and attempted to arc across the terminals, behind the key mechanism. After two or three attempts, a spark crackled and the starter motor growled. Then the small engine shuddered and turned over, running smoothly.

Pushkin jumped in, reversed out of the parking bay, accelerated through the car park towards the exit at the far end of the parking complex, burst through the security arm of the pay station and launched the little vehicle down the exit ramp, joining the regular traffic flow. Once outside the car park, he slowed to a modest tempo, conforming to the general traffic speed to avoid drawing attention to his vehicle.

Although he was clear of the airport precinct, Pushkin knew that he was by no means free. He knew, with absolute certainty, that his assault upon the airport immigration officials would have sparked a massive police response and he realised that he would need a miracle to escape the police dragnet. He calculated the odds of making an escape down the long freeway

243

corridor leading back to New York, but ruled that out as too risky. The police would have broadcast their *all-points* alert, calling for road blocks to be set up on all airport approach and exit roads. The freeway would be crawling with patrol cars. It seemed unlikely, however, that his battered little stolen vehicle would have been identified yet. If he could park it somewhere close and go to ground, he would buy time to regroup and plan an alternative escape. Those odds were worth taking. He had no other options.

Pushkin had two fake passports stitched into the lining of his carry-bag. These would have been helpful, but the bag, and his computer, had been confiscated at the airport, and his new identity was no longer a secret. The immigration officials and the surveillance cameras had also captured his new image at the checkpoint. He would need a radical disguise... a hat or a bandana. Above all, he needed somewhere to lie low... a bolt hole, where he could calculate his next moves. Moreover, it needed to be close to the airport, inside the perimeter of the road blocks.

As he drove onto the ramp leading from the airport towards the distant freeway, he could see the flashing lights of police vehicles ahead. That rang huge alarm bells.

Thinking quickly, even while his vehicle was climbing the ramp from the car park to the freeway, he wrenched the wheel to the right, threaded his way across three lanes of protesting traffic and turned, instead, into the 'Best Western' airport hotel. There, a large number of airline passengers were being offloaded from buses and assisted out of cabs. This provided a perfect subterfuge, distracting attention from his arrival. Pushkin's adrenalin was coursing, but his survival instincts remained strong. Logic told him that the situation demanded calm indifference so, despite his angst, he forced himself to drive calmly through the hotel forecourt to the underground car park.

Once inside the dimly lit car park, he manoeuvred the little car into a corner, with its damaged window facing the wall, parked it and made his way to the lift. The lift led to the foyer, so he calculated that he could take it to lobby level and exit into the large, anonymous space of the hotel lobby. When the lift jerked to a halt at lobby level, however, a large group of guests were waiting to enter it, so he chose to remain in the lift. As it rose towards the 3rd floor, he realised that the overcrowded lift was, in fact, a valuable accident of fate which he could exploit.

The lift came to a halt, and he stepped into the corridor, waited for others to alight, and watched the lift doors close. If he took time to study the passing parade of guests entering and leaving this floor, he reasoned, he could select a suitable, lone guest to overpower and take over his or her room at gunpoint. The safe sanctuary of a hotel room would buy him extra time, particularly if he set up a 'do not disturb' sign.

Pleased with this solution, he stationed himself on a sofa opposite the bank of lifts, browsing a magazine, while actually assessing guests as they alighted from the lifts. Most guests seemed to be with partners. Others were in groups. He needed a single guest. Eventually, a dapper, elderly gentleman, who appeared to be alone, emerged from the lift-well. He was sporting a neat bow tie and blazer and brandished a stylish walking stick. Despite the man's elegant attire, Pushkin's attention was particularly drawn to the man's ill-fitting toupee, which struggled to sit on his bald head. This suggested a frail man, but one with financial means. Sensing this as an opportunity, Pushkin arose and followed the man along the hotel corridor. The man walked stiffly, in the stilted way that old men do, to his hotel room, then paused to fumble in his pockets. He entered his key-card, a green light came on and the door clicked open.

At the same instant, Pushkin moved up behind the old man and pushed him brutally through the doorway, sending him sprawling onto the room's carpet. The door clicked shut behind them as the old man turned to view his assailant, his eyes reflecting astonishment and indignation. Before the old man could mouth a protest, Pushkin pointed his Smith and Wesson at his forehead and pulled the trigger. An angry, red hole appeared between the startled man's eyes, as his body twitched violently, then slumped, and slowly ceased all further movement.

Pushkin grabbed the old man's corpse by the legs and dragged it into the bathroom. He then struggled to deposit it, head first, into the bathtub, so that the blood escaping liberally from his victim's head could be contained. Then he returned to the lounge area, switched on the TV and tuned into the latest CNN news. There was the usual economic and political news, but nothing about the airport incident. Were the media under instructions not to cover the incident, he wondered? Was it too soon? Perhaps the morning papers would have a story. They would have a field day with this thing, exposing Pushkin's identity and sparking a diplomatic nightmare.

Despite this worrying truth and the reality of his brutal attack on the old man, Pushkin maintained a steely resolve and a distorted sense that his actions were just – that they were a necessary part of the war against western hegemony. This bankrupt logic was a rationalisation easily reached by Pushkin. Like all psychopaths, he had no capacity to feel emotion or guilt. Indeed, if he felt anything, it was disgust at the proximity of the old man's corpse in the bathtub. For some reason, it made him feel unclean. 'I'm growing soft,' he thought, as he returned to the bathroom, stripped off and prepared to step into the shower. However, standing naked beside the bloody corpse made him uncomfortable, so he retrieved a spare blanket from the closet and covered the old man's body and face with it, before resuming his shower.

***

Five hours later, as the hands on the bedside alarm clock approached 11 p.m., Pushkin awoke from a deep slumber. He had decided that his next move would need to be under cover of darkness and had set the alarm for this hour, when the hotel precinct was bound to be at its quietest. He yawned, surveyed his unfamiliar surrounds and smiled. He was always surprised that sleep came so easily, even after such brutal episodes. His ability to shut out all emotion and calmly calculate his next move was the thing which, more than anything, set him apart and had propelled him to the top of his clandestine profession. He was a psychopath, but a cool one.

Thoroughly refreshed after his shower, he rummaged through the old man's bags for items of clothing that would aid his disguise. He chose a striped shirt and bow tie. Next, he retrieved the old man's academic-looking glasses, toupee and well-worn felt hat. These contributed an image of geriatric frailty and the hat and toupee covered his bald pate perfectly. Pushkin's own briefcase, including his passport and wallet, had been confiscated at the airport immigration check point. However, he had been delighted to discover the old man's car keys and wallet, which contained the old man's driver's licence, cash and some credit cards. With the old man's toupee, shirt and bow tie, he had achieved an uncanny likeness, closely matching the old man's security ID, which he pocketed. Next, he opened the coat closet and removed a wire coat hanger, which he flattened and shoved down one leg of his pants. Finally, he switched off the room lights and gazed back into the darkened hotel room.

Through the open bathroom door, the old man's corpse was illuminated by an intermittent, blue neon light, which penetrated from the street below. Disturbed by this unnerving image, he returned to the bathroom and closed the door. Then he left the hotel room, attached the 'Do not Disturb' sign and walked to the lift foyer.

One lift was designated to deliver passengers directly to the hotel's below-ground car park. He boarded that lift and rode it to the basement carpark. There, he surveyed a rich bounty of vehicles, looking for one which would spirit him away from the airport before daylight. The little old vehicle he had taken from the airport car park would be reported stolen before long and would become an unacceptable liability. A modern vehicle, with digital locking and burglar alarms, would also be a risky choice, should he disturb its alarm system. Then it struck him that the old man must have a vehicle parked somewhere in the hotel car park which might suit, so he fumbled for the old man's car keys, pressed the clicker and saw blinker lights flash on an old Landcruiser parked nearby. The old cruiser would be a perfect escape vehicle, barely attracting attention and matching the owner's ID details. He strode to the old Landcruiser, climbed in and started the engine. Delighted with this elegant solution he made his way quietly out of the car park towards the freeway. As he mounted the on ramp, a pair of police vehicles came into view, their blue lights strobing in the dark. He continued smoothly towards them, slowed his approach, pulled to a halt, and wound down his driver-side window. Experience had taught him that a confident manner would mask any suspicions, so he seized the initiative, addressing the policemen before they could speak to him, in colloquial American.

'Evening officers! You fellers still lookin' fer those bad guys?' he said with a smile.

'We sure are,' they replied. 'We hate to impose, sir, but we've got some formalities to go through and I'd be obliged if you could help us out with a few answers.'

'Delighted to help, son,' chirped Pushkin. 'But you guys should get some shut-eye. I've already been through this process half an hour ago, on my way *into* the airport.'

'Sorry to subject you to this again, sir, but could I please ask you to identify yourself and explain your presence at the airport?'

'Why sure yer can, boys. Name's Gerry Watkins, from Newark. Had to bring my sister, Maddie, ter th' airport to catch th' 11 p.m. shuttle to Denver. She's gettin' a bit frail these days and I didn't want her struggling with her heavy bags. You know how it is when a body gets old,' he finished, simultaneously flashing his fake ID.

'I sure as hell do. Thank you, sir. You may proceed,' replied the policeman, giving Pushkin the excuse to smile, wave goodbye and chug off in the old Landcruiser. Pushkin's escape had been crafted perfectly. He would be well out of range by the time the officers at the road block enjoyed the first rays of morning light.

***

Back in Langley, news of Pushkin's detection at the airport, and of his subsequent escape from the clutches of the airport Customs and Immigration officers, had simultaneously been passed to CIA head, Frank Angiotti's desk, thanks to the interdiction protocols which Colonel Tom Grant and 'Macka' McKenzie had put in place. Upon learning of the incident, Director General Angiotti had instructed the two men to arrange an urgent rendezvous with FBI officers at the airport terminal, where they were to set up a joint command centre to direct the hunt for the elusive Russian. Because of the international ramifications of the incident, CIA officer McKenzie was given seniority over the FBI staff and jurisdiction. Tom Grant would contribute to field decisions. A tight perimeter had quickly been established around all airport exit roads, but there had been no sighting of the Russian.

Tom Grant was initially convinced that the Russian, whose identity was now on the monitors of FBI agents and local police across the state, remained somewhere within the lock-down perimeter. Seven hours later, as dawn broke, Tom was no longer so sure. His task force had established a dragnet around the entire airport precinct, but there had still been no sighting of the Russian. Tom was no longer confident that the Russian was somewhere close by, and finally instructed a group of officers to check all the hotels, motels and residential buildings within the perimeter. That required a court order and the issuing of warrants, which would cost valuable time. Grant and McKenzie were aware that they would thus exceed the critical, 24-hour time frame, beyond which the chances of success became much thinner. However, Pushkin could only lie low for so long. He would have to come up for air and when he did, Grant and McKenzie would be waiting for him.

Always thorough in his approach, Tom Grant then contacted Frank Angiotti to report the disappointing lack of progress at the airport and to request around the clock surveillance of the Russian Embassy in Washington, where he thought it possible Pushkin, if he had eluded the dragnet, might pop up. Grant would, himself, be travelling to Washington later that day, in response to a request from Ambassador Bayliss to drop by for a briefing on new intelligence concerning the Chinese.

While Tom had little other progress to report, he was able to tell Angiotti that a laptop computer had been found in Pushkin's possession, which the Customs officers had confiscated at the airport. The rugged Australian SAS officer recognised that this was a critical breakthrough and had asked Angiotti to immediately arrange for a CIA computer specialist to forensically examine the computer's hard drive for evidence that agent Ritter's report had been altered. If that could be proven and evidence of Russian involvement handed to the Chinese, the diplomatic pendulum would swing back in America's favour. More importantly, China's silence on its magnetic pulse weapons capability would be shown to be a clever ruse, and the resultant loss of face would, surely, open the way for a speedy normalisation of relations.

State Department-Washington DC

Dr Maggie King approached the reception desk at Liz Rankin's State Department office, after navigating several security checkpoints. Though she was still a young woman, she was widely acknowledged as a leading and respected voice on international affairs and was thus already favourably known to the Secretary of State. The two had met briefly at public forums, but never really spoken. However, Maggie's request for an audience with the Secretary of State had been readily acceded to. It had come with support from Richard Bayliss, Australia's Ambassador to the US, and from CIA boss, Frank Angiotti, whose intercession had given special gravitas to the request. As the Ambassador had put it, *"Dr King has a matter of strategic importance to our nations which she wishes to discuss in strict confidence."*

Within minutes of Maggie King's arrival, Elizabeth Rankin appeared in the reception area to personally greet the young academic. She did so with characteristic warmth.

'Ah, Dr King, how good to have this opportunity for a confidential chat... for I gather that is what you have in mind. I follow your expert analysis of Asian affairs quite closely and have always hoped that we might have an opportunity for a personal meeting like this. I often feel you are my only ally in a policy area which is becoming increasingly difficult for me within the administration. Do come in. Coffee?'

After they had settled into armchairs and taken delivery of their coffee, Secretary Rankin dismissed her staff and instructed that they be left alone and not interrupted.

'Thank you for agreeing to meet with me, Secretary Rankin,' Maggie began. 'I want to talk to you about our deteriorating relationship with China. Not just about the submarine collision. That was unfortunate, but it was an accident waiting to happen… one which some commentators think is a consequence of our own sloppy foreign policy, rather than China's. I don't know if you share this view, but I am certain that our National Security Adviser, General Bill Nordish, does not. Frankly, our nation's clumsy naval exercises on China's doorstep have added an unnecessary layer of complexity to our relationship. I sympathise with the Chinese view that the US would find naval exercises by their navy off the coast of Florida equally provocative.'

'I agree,' said Rankin. 'And you are right about Nordish. Between you and me, he is a bull in a china shop. We will have to manage his strident behaviour very carefully. But if your visit is not to discuss the submarine disaster, what is it about?'

'My purpose, Madame Secretary, is to address a much more sinister matter; a matter of national security which must be protected at this stage. I have been authorised by the CIA to share with you intelligence provided by a close ally, on a top secret basis, to our government. It affects our relationship with China in a fairly dramatic way and even more so, our relationship with Russia. As we speak, CIA Director Frank Angiotti is passing this same intelligence to President Kennelly. It casts new light on our demarche which, as you know, accuses China of arming its *Dongfeng* Intercontinental Ballistic Missiles with electromagnetic pulse warheads. The new intelligence, from Australia, challenges our factual and moral authority for that assertion. If the Aussie's north Asian and London intelligence sources are correct, we need to move quickly to cool things down, before they spiral out of control.'

'Go on,' said Rankin, now hanging off Maggie King's every word.

'You will be aware of the recent rash of seemingly unrelated, violent events, including the murder of CIA Deputy Director, Charles Ritter, and my recent kidnapping. We now know that those events had one, common purpose; to undermine our relationship with China. The Australian Security Intelligence Organisation — ASIO, as it is known — and its sister organisation, ASIS — through their London station, were able to join the dots and expose this sinister plot. They uncovered a covert operation by the Russians, right under our noses, to implicate China in what seemed like a provocative ramping up of its military threat. With our demarche, their covert mission to increase tension in our relationship with China has largely succeeded.'

'Are you saying that Russia has been conducting a covert operation on US soil, with the sole aim of poisoning our relationship with China?' replied Rankin.

'That is precisely what I am saying, Madame Secretary, and if we don't extract ourselves carefully from this dangerous situation, we will have egg on our faces and have to stare down some serious military consequences,' replied Maggie.

'Here is what we think happened,' she continued. 'You may have read media reports about the recent demise of the former Deputy Director of the CIA, Charles Ritter. We believe he was murdered by the Russians. He was preparing a report on China's *Dongfeng* missiles, which our military experts had previously considered obsolete. We believe the Russians kidnapped Ritter as he made his way home with the report, intercepted his report, and altered its contents by adding their own, creative content to implicate the Chinese. Ritter's report held that the Chinese had re-armed their Dongfengs with electromagnetic pulse warheads. To implicate the Chinese, the Russians even burned the Chinese characters - 'Dong' and 'Feng' - into Ritter's forehead, so determined were they in their sadistic plot to deceive us. Later, when they learned that the Aussie intelligence agencies were onto them and planned to expose their treachery, they kidnapped the Australian Military Attaché, Colonel Tom Grant, and me, to prevent us delivering the ASIO report to your Government.'

'Good God,' replied Rankin. 'You can't be serious! If what you say is true, this will shake the foundations of our relationship with Moscow and return us to a cold war era. You say you were also kidnapped,' continued Rankin. You poor girl! Why so?'

'I was what one calls 'collateral damage' - simply in the wrong place at the wrong time. I was spending a weekend in the Hamptons with the Aussie Military Attaché when they struck. They took us both captive, heavily drugged us and held us in a remote farmhouse. They planned to kill us later, when the heat had died down, and dispose of our bodies. We were lucky to escape with our lives,' she concluded.

'Have we been able to run the perpetrators to ground?' inquired Rankin.

'The FBI and CIA are now embarked upon a secret, national manhunt for the ringleader of the Russian operation, none other than the head of the Russian FSB, their national spy agency. He was intercepted at JFK airport as he attempted to flee the country, but he managed to overpower our people and escape.'

'That is an amazing story. What an incredible web of deception and intrigue,' exclaimed Rankin. 'If word of this gets out, it will send diplomatic shock waves around the western world. Where do you suggest we go from here?'

Maggie began cautiously. 'My own view is that, with some well-crafted, clever diplomacy, we could turn this thing around... to our own diplomatic advantage.'

'I like your instincts. You sound like a girl after my own heart,' replied Rankin, genuinely impressed by her younger counterpart's positivity and beginning to feel a close bond with the intelligent academic. 'How might we achieve that?'

'What we need, Madame Secretary, is a circuit-breaker... a face-saving initiative that lets both China and the US off the hook. I believe we should enlist the support of our Australian allies. China sees Australia as a non-threatening, middle-ranking power. The two have strong economic ties. Indeed, China depends upon Australia for a number of critical resources, including iron ore and coal. The Aussies are thus much closer to the Chinese than we are. We could seek their intercession on our behalf — as a sort of third country arbitrator — to arrange a private, tripartite peace conference with the Chinese leadership in Beijing. The Australians could brief China in advance on Russia's convert operation to discredit China and build tension. That would clear the air for us and enable us to negotiate a joint, Chinese-US response.'

'How will China react to a third party arranging the meeting? Surely they would expect a superpower like us to manage our own affairs,' replied Rankin.

'I think there is a mutual need for a circuit-breaker and some face-saving. We also need a neutral agency to arrange these talks. Both sides need to step back a bit and sheath their swords, as it were. The Australians could arrange the meeting on the basis of their need to hand over intelligence important to China's national security. Having a neutral, third party explain Russia's involvement in the Dongfeng business will provided much needed credibility and buy us a seat at the table on other sensitive issues. I think we could orchestrate this scenario by inviting our respective Ambassadors in to smooth the diplomatic path. What do we have to lose?'

'I buy that logic. It might just work,' said Rankin. 'Please go on.'

'If I were in your shoes, Secretary Rankin, I might even swallow a bit of humble pie, as a peace gesture,' added Dr King, realising that she must tread warily on this issue. 'You could indicate that the US is prepared to sign a joint protocol with China banning the use of electromagnetic pulse warheads. We could make this a win-win situation; for the US, for China and for an increasingly cynical world. In the process, we would be offering China an opportunity to join with us in proposing what we would both describe as a global peace initiative. Everybody is a winner... excepting for the Russians, of course, who would receive the strongest possible international rebuke.'

'We might even agree protocols around joint naval exercises off the waters of our respective nations, and trade these off against China's agreement to protect free navigation and fly-over rights in international waters, neutralising the present conflicts with Japan and others over disputed Islands in the Straits of Taiwan.'

'Maggie... I hope you don't mind me calling you that... I don't know how to thank you enough,' replied Liz Rankin, leaning towards the young academic and touching her wrist affectionately. 'Your analysis has brought rare clarity to these complex matters, and your proposed solutions are nothing short of brilliant. It gives me great hope for the future, that our nation can rely upon young women of your character and intellect. Let's you and I make this thing happen, girl. Will you agree to work as my special counsel on this, and lead my staff in setting up this tripartite meeting?'

'Of course, Madame Secretary! I would be honoured to do so.'

CIA Headquarters, Langley, Virginia

In the light of the additional intelligence provided by Colonel Tom Grant's North Asian and European sources, CIA Director General Frank Angiotti now found that he was fighting intelligence fires on a number of different fronts. The suspicious circumstances surrounding the death of his deputy, Charles Ritter, had initially required a small, special investigation team. Following the subsequent kidnapping of Colonel Grant and Dr Maggie King, and the discovery that Russian security chief, Anatoly Pushkin was likely involved in Ritter's death, the CIA's initially small team had been much expanded. It now comprised a cross agency, CIA-FBI-Immigration effort and had morphed into a full blown national manhunt for the elusive Russian.

The hunt for Pushkin, however, while it was the highest priority, was not the only focus for the Agency. There was a wider operation, involving friendly intelligence agencies around the world and Pentagon armaments experts, to more clearly define the threat posed by China's hitherto dormant Dongfeng ICBM arsenal. The blustering intervention of Nordish, the hawkish National Security Advisor, who still stubbornly insisted that Ritter's report was accurate, had compelled the US administration to determine the facts, once and for all. It was now imperative that they know whether the Dongfeng really had the capacity to reach the north American stratosphere and, from there, create an electromagnetic pulse wave over the US and Canada. The President had personally mandated this work, with 'whatever resources it takes'.

The additional pressure coming from National Security Advisor Nordish's office was becoming an irritant. The aggressive warmonger was now also baying for blood over the collision of the nuclear subs in the South China Sea. In an effort to appease him, the President's office had instructed

255

Angiotti's team to work with the Secretary of State, her foreign counterparts in the EU, Japan and Oceania and the US Joint Chiefs, to better direct and coordinate diplomatic efforts on the submarine crisis. Together, these things were straining Angiotti's resources beyond breaking point.

If this melange of crises were not enough, Angiotti had just received new advice that the Chinese were mounting another territorial challenge off the coast of the Philippines. The Japanese were apparently frothing at the mouth. This was therefore the issue to which the intelligence boss now turned his attention, as Communications head, Samantha Green, entered his office to deliver a report on the subject.

'OK, Sam. What have you got for me on this latest Japanese outrage?' he asked.

'It's an urgent inwards from the Japanese Ambassador, sir, who advises that his Government is alarmed about a new territorial incursion by the Chinese, in the South China Sea. The Japanese are demanding that our Government intercede.'

The fatigued-looking Comms Officer sighed, blinked despondently at the report she carried from East-Asian Ops, marked "Urgent – DG's Eyes Only", and handed it over.

She then watched patiently, as the CIA chief's eyes scanned each line of the message. As they did so, his body language indicated mounting frustration:

SITUATION REPORT
Classification: **Top Secret – DG's Eyes Only**
Chinese Intentions - Scarborough Reef – South China Sea

On Monday, by means of an urgent diplomatic communique delivered to the State Department by Japanese Ambassador Dairoku Takahashi, the Japanese Government reported the detection of new Chinese naval activity in and around the Scarborough Reef, a hotly contested coral Atoll, 140 miles off the Filipino coast. This information was also transmitted to our NATO and Pacific allies, for their information.

Yesterday, Australia's intelligence agency, ASIO, responded with the explosive news that it had intercepted a Chinese military directive, outlining plans to plant explosives on the western face of the coral Atoll. Their Office of National Assessments believes this indicates plans to create a deep-water channel and mooring facility for Chinese naval vessels. If this intel is correct, China has stepped up its opposition to our 'Asian Pivot' strategy, involving a beefed-up naval presence near the Philippines.

On the back of dramatically increased tensions following the collision of the Chinese and US nuclear submarines in the Manila Trench, heightened sensitivities between China and the US and across the Asia-Pacific basin, it is imperative that the west find a diplomatic initiative to calm the adversaries and for calm logic to prevail.

An overt, undisguised initiative of this sort by China will send shock waves around Asia, impacting our South Korean, Taiwanese, Japanese, Filipino and ANZUS alliances. China's land reclamation activities on the contested Spratly Islands have already created a very tense atmosphere. Their new base there has given China a capacity to project far wider power than that projected by the US Pacific fleet.

A second naval base on Scarborough Reef would give China overwhelming control over the South China Sea and the ability to project its military footprint across a host of adjacent national borders. The Australian intelligence boss, Sir Robert Chandler, advises that Japanese intelligence services have since verified ASIO's intelligence.

As a consequence, Sir Robert advises that the Australian Ambassador will shortly request urgent meetings with Secretary of State Elizabeth Rankin, and with your office, to formally hand over its latest intelligence and discuss its consequences.

The Ambassador will convey Australia's concerns that any further escalation in tensions between China and the USA will have consequences for Australia. China is Australia's largest trading partner and is dependent upon Australia's industrial raw materials. It looks upon Australia's substantial mineral resources with jealous eyes.

China has demonstrated time and time again that it will not baulk at using economic diplomacy to discipline disloyalty, and this sort of

257

commodity diplomacy has already cost Australia billions, through the cancellation of iron ore and other contracts.

The Australians fear that this latest Chinese initiative will redefine the military balance in North Asia, with serious consequences for Australia's future defence. It will sorely test the US administration's commitment under the ANZUS defence pact.

The Australian Ambassador will carry with him a diplomatic communiqué - a 'Note Verbal' - for Secretary of State Rankin, offering to broker peace negotiations with the Chinese. As a vitally interested, medium power, with strong economic links to China, Australia believes it can be an effective emissary, helping to dampen any further rise in the temperature of relations between the US and China. Finding a diplomatic solution assumes additional importance following the worrying Dongfeng missile affair and the collision of the US and Chinese nuclear subs in the Manila Trench.

The Australian Prime Minister and his National Security Committee of Cabinet are following these developments closely and wish to be advised of the outcome of our Government's consideration of these matters.

MESSAGE ENDS

'Goddammit! That's just what we need,' barked Angiotti. 'I gotta try to contain this thing, before the media… or worse still, that crazy bull-in-a-china-shop, Nordish… get hold of it. Give me a line to Secretary of State Rankin, Sam, and then track down Dr Maggie King. Tell them I want an urgent meeting with them in my office to pass on sensitive information about new Chinese intentions in the South China Sea.'

'I'll get right on it, sir,' replied the comms officer.

'Thank you, Sam. That will be all.'

Office of National Security Advisor, General Bill Nordish

General Bill Nordish was in a foul mood. He paced about his large Washington office, muttering obscenities and venting frustration that the President's closest advisers, who were working on difficulties with China, seemed to be intentionally keeping him out of the loop. This was not an imagined, but rather, an accurate assessment of the situation. His bombastic manner had done nothing to endear him to senior colleagues, who found it easier to work around him. On this overcast Washington morning, news of the Chinese incursion around the Scarborough Reef had just arrived on his desk. His face flushed scarlet as he read several despatches containing the explosive information. When he had finished reading them, he slammed them down and bellowed through the doorway at his personal assistant.

'Kelly, get me a line to the air and naval chiefs – one at a time,' he bellowed. 'And when I'm finished with them, I'll need a line to the Secretary of State. She's sitting on this thing like it's hers alone to manage. I should be across every detail... managing our national security risks. While you're at it, get me Barbara Scully at the office of the Secretary of the Airforce in DC. I need to ask her why the hell she has still not responded to my request for another naval sail-past and a B-52 flyover of those damn Spratly Islands, to enforce freedom of navigation and passage,' he barked.

These demands rolled easily from the lips of General Nordish, as if they somehow implied a simple, uncomplicated process. In fact, multiple layers of highly codified protocols were required for any such undertaking, for very good reasons. Operations like this were risky. They could be a touchstone for wider conflict, so the raft of approvals required for them provided important checks and balances. The Joint Chiefs had first to brief the President on all associated risks. Then the Secretary of Defence and his

259

Defence Appropriation Committee had to provide input on force deployment issues and overall hardware and deployment costs. To provide advance operational data in support of any aerial or a naval operation, a targeted surveillance and reconnaissance mission would be required, employing one of the Air Force's sixty-three military satellites. Leaving aside the naval pass, the request for a B-52 flyover required the involvement of all Air Force commands. It began with the Air Force Chief of Staff, General Arnold Medbury at the Pentagon, interrogating his hierarchy of command. He would call for mission briefs and ops input, in turn, from Lt. General Bill Foxall's Intelligence and Reconnaissance Command, and from General Martin Edwards' Air Combat Command, at Langley-Eustis, Virginia.

These checks and balances were comforting. They prevented precipitate action by any one commander. However, a number of recent developments in China had raised the risks associated with any such operations and these were currently being reassessed. Following both the strident diplomatic exchanges about the Dongfeng EMP capability and the collision of the nuclear subs, China's political rhetoric had become more assertive and the deployments of both the US and Chinese military forces in the South China Sea had been ramped up. These had created a climate in which any miscalculation might trigger a dangerous tit for tat exchange, either in the air over the disputed islands or between the naval forces, as each side enforced its own interpretation of the freedom of navigation and overfly zones.

International convention on ADIZs (Air Defence Identification Zones) and FNOPs (Freedom of Navigation Operational Zones) were a work in progress. Theoretically, they were regulated by clear geographic data, defining sovereign airspace above a country's national borders and using law of the sea conventions to define sovereign waters surrounding national borders. While these were clear in most cases, they had become complex in the South China Sea. Firstly, the air and sea sovereignty of closely adjacent nations, like Vietnam and the Philippines, did not neatly fit a standard international model. National interests and geographical claims to territories overlapped in some sectors. Secondly, the islands lying in open waters, between the overlapping sovereign boundaries, and disputed claims about their historical use and ownership, required tortuous international adjudication.

That process had dragged on for years. China was adamant that its fishermen and traders had, for centuries, enjoyed uninterrupted use of certain islands in the South China Sea. Applying common law logic, they asserted that their history of landfall and use had made them sovereign to China. China's physical annexation and use of the islands had, however, been brutally interrupted, they argued, following Japan's invasions of China and the Philippines in the 20th Century. The recent claims of those near neighbours were, in China's view, therefore an historical aberration… a blip on the historical horizon… and China's long-standing claims, they insisted, overrode contemporary claims. There was some justification for this view, but there could be no adjudication of it as long as China refused to sit at the adjudicator's table.

In fact, General Bill Nordish's request for a naval and aerial operation to enforce freedom of sea and air passage had been strongly supported in the past, by similar requests from the Philippines, Japan and South Korea, and the President had approved the idea in principle, subject to clarifying risks. General Nordish's plan had all seemed on track until the previous week when, at the eleventh hour, General Bill Foxall's Intelligence and Surveillance Command had reported a disturbing new development, prompting an urgent rethink of that strategy.

***

Back at Langley-Eustis, Bill Foxall received the latest message from the bombastic, National Security Advisor that he should call back urgently. He knew immediately what this was about. Nordish was pissed-off that Foxall's reconnaissance command had urged caution about the 'freedom of air and sea passage' operation, in light of new intelligence just received by them. Foxall was a polite and highly professional officer, but no weakling. A tall, commanding build of a man with strong, natural leadership qualities, he had demonstrated both his sporting prowess and a capacity for achieving academic excellence, during his young days at the academy. Later, he had developed an impressive service record. He was highly respected across his command and unstinting in his defence of his men. He neither took, nor gave any quarter in his infrequent, fractious exchanges with Nordish and would not truck any bullying by him now. Always a calm professional, he would let the potency of the intelligence reports speak for themselves. To ensure no misrepresentations of his discussion with Nordish, however, he had invited his XO to be present and would conduct the discussion on speaker phone. That would ensure that he had a witness to the exchange and also that it remained civilised. He and his deputy, Lt. General Laurie Dunlop, listened to the dial tone and waited for General Nordish to pick up.

'Nordish here! Damn it Bill, I have left a number of messages for you requesting feedback on the fly-overs. What the hell is delaying your report?' he barked.

'Mornin', General,' replied Foxall in a languid, easy tone, calculated to disarm Nordish. 'I got all of your messages, but I wanted to make sure I had all the facts before I went shooting my mouth off. You know better than most of us how important it is to be thoroughly prepared, before launchin' into an operation like this,' he added, delivering the subtle message that Nordish was, in fact, shooting *his* mouth off and should shut up and listen to good advice. 'Before we proceed,' he added, 'you should know that I have you on speaker phone. My number two, Lt. General Laurie Dunlop is here with me. He has been coordinating the cross-agency work on this operation.'

'Alright, Bill,' Nordish responded in a more conciliatory tone. 'I'll give you a chance to explain the delays, but nothing you can tell me will diminish the need to get this thing done immediately. The Chinese are runnin' rings around us while we twiddle our thumbs. We are still their military masters, and they need to be reminded about that!'

'With respect, General, our first obligation is to weigh the risks of this operation – both political and military - to our relationship with China and to the lives of the boys who serve in our military – before we embark on this course. Our surveillance work, backed up by Frank Angiotti's intel work at CIA, have confirmed a disturbing new development which changes

262

the military balance in and around the South China Sea. General Dunlop agrees with that conclusion, don't you Laurie.'

Lt General Laurie Dunlop responded in the affirmative, throwing Nordish off guard. Foxall was using the speaker phone masterfully to remind Nordish that he had an audience. Suitably chastened by this, Nordish invited General Foxall to explain.

'Last week, China added two batteries of new, surface to air missiles, to its recently developed Spratly Island outpost. At first, we thought they were the old HQ9 SAMs – a variant of Russia's S-300. That was quite concerning. However, we have since learned that the new Chinese SAMS are what they call HQ10s - a reverse-engineered and improved version of the Russians' 400. This missile can engage targets at a 400-kilometre slant range, which out-distances and neutralizes our on-board missile-arming detection equipment. These new SAMs are super quick and give the Chinese a commanding new coverage of air encroachments over the Spratlys. They will probably also be deployed to the Scarborough Reef.'

'You mean to tell me that these Chinese, who only just got out'a their Mao suits, are better equipped than us?' Nordish stammered. 'I don't buy that!'

'That's about it, General,' replied Foxall respectfully. 'And it gets worse. As you know, they have been rapidly rearming and have made some astonishing strides forward with their air technology... just as we discovered by accident when their huge, quiet *Giant Turtle* nuclear sub snuck up on our US sub, in the Manila Trench.'

'How so?' said Nordish, struggling to find a rational objection.

'Well,' continued Foxall, 'The new HQ10 SAMs will outmanoeuvre any on-board counter-measures we have on our B-52s... or for that matter, our F-16s. That makes an aerial overpass very risky if anything goes wrong. When their missile is launched from so far out, our radar can't detect the launch. By the time their missile appears on the horizon and we detect it, our counter-measures are too slow to effectively intercept. It's a beauty. As for your proposed freedom of navigation operation, we now know that China has also acquired the YJ-62 anti-ship cruise missile. This is a sea-skimming cruise missile with a 300-kilometre range and a 300 kg warhead.

263

It out trumps anything of any of China's rivals - including our own US fleet vessels of up to 9,000 tons - have deployed in that theatre. They could sink any vessel in our Asian Pivot fleet at will. Simply put, they've got us licked on the water and in the air, so we need to tread carefully. I will be passing this intelligence to the President, as my Commander in Chief, with my recommendation that we abandon your requested fly-over and sail-past operations.'

'If you do that, Foxall, you will only show weakness. Your military logic is bad. Let me tell you why. The Chinese may have a home ground advantage in the South China Sea, but they know that we would trounce them in any serious, full-on stoush. That's why it won't come to a stoush. We need to show these Commies that they can't push us around. That is what I will be telling the President... and I will be recommending that we proceed with the fly-over. That is all!' concluded Nordish, before clicking off.

Wisconsin Ave., Washington DC

The Russian Embassy, with its stark, white, high-rise apartment complex and low-rise Chancellery, stood at number 2650 Wisconsin Avenue, clinically aloof from most other Embassies. Massachusetts Avenue, better known as 'Embassy Row', was located on the other side of Observatory Circle, and was the broad thoroughfare along which most other Embassies were located. On this overcast morning, the spear-like prongs of the Russian Embassy's perimeter fence pointed skywards, towards scudding, grey clouds, as if snarling at the heavens and challenging any unfriendly incursion. Indeed, the Russian Embassy's secure perimeter could only be accessed through one large, portal-gate at the centre of the complex, where a sentry box and three armed security guards stood defiantly, protecting the private diplomatic complex with a mission to interrogate every approach.

'Macka' McKenzie and his surveillance team stared indifferently at the Embassy's lacklustre architecture, but were grateful for the barren, moon-like landscape which surrounded the structure, since it afforded a commanding view of all movement to or from the single point of entrance. Macka had stationed his surveillance team in a van, opposite the main entrance to the Embassy. High resolution cameras enabled them to zoom in on any visitors, whether on foot or in vehicles, with astonishing facial clarity. Macka had with him two so-called tech-execs, for the surveillance aspects. In unmarked cars, half a block away, two FBI tactical assault vehicles were parked at the curb. Their mission would be to respond to any call from Macka's surveillance team and intercept Pushkin should he try to seek refuge in his Embassy.

At 1601 Massachusetts Avenue, Colonel Tom Grant was simultaneously concluding discussions with the Australian Ambassador, Richard Bayliss, about China's efforts to construct new naval moorings on

Scarborough Reef and deploy its new, superior interdiction missiles in the Spratly Islands. Having completed that discussion, their conversation turned to the search for Anatoly Pushkin.

'How confident are you that you can run him to ground, Tom?' inquired Bayliss.

'He is a slippery customer, your Excellency... that's for sure. We thought we had him cornered, when we staked out all ports of exit, but he managed to overpower the airport border staff and make his escape from the complex. We had every access route to and from the airport tightly patrolled, but he simply vanished into thin air. Frank Angiotti's guys are working with the FBI to door-knock every building around the airport, but our chances of success diminish with every day. It is starting to look like he has evaded our airport dragnet, so we now have a surveillance team watching the Russian Embassy, in case he makes a dash for asylum there.'

'Even if he makes it through his Embassy's gates,' replied the Ambassador, 'his asylum only protects him while he is on their sovereign soil. The moment he attempts to leave the Embassy, he will be back on US soil and vulnerable to arrest, under the new diplomatic protocols which waive immunity in the case of a criminal act or felony,' he said. 'He will be trapped... in a *Julian Assange* sort of dilemma.'

'That's right. Our surveillance team tells me he faces a tough task running the gauntlet to the Embassy gates. The Embassy is set well back from the street and all approaches to it are across open territory. This landscape was intended by the Russians to maximise their security, but in this instance, it works for us, allowing us to zero in on all approaching pedestrians and vehicles and to intercept,' said Tom.

'How will you recognise Pushkin,' asked Ambassador Bayliss. 'I mean, you have fresh surveillance images of him... from security cameras at the airport... but he is a cunning bugger, and he will almost certainly have fashioned some new disguise.'

'I agree, Ambassador, but we have very strong antennae when it comes to this man. We can feel him... almost smell him. We will just have to be alert and hope that we can suss him out if he attempts to approach the gate. As a matter of fact, I will be going directly to Wisconsin Avenue from here.

I told Frank Angiotti I would call in on his team there, headed up by a very smart guy called 'Macka' McKenzie. Macka has set up surveillance in a van opposite the Russian Embassy. He has a high-tech team monitoring movements and some swat team muscle, in case Pushkin shows up.'

***

Even as Tom Grant and Ambassador Bayliss were completing their discussion, Anatoly Pushkin emerged into open parkland from the leafy folds of Washington's Dumbarton Oaks Park, which stretched to the edge of Wisconsin Avenue. He brushed a gnarled hand over his stubbled chin, pulled his jacket tightly around his shoulders against the chill, and adjusted the toupee acquired from his latest victim. It was a loose fit and had proven difficult to control, so he repositioned it and secured it by pulling the old man's felt hat down tightly, so that its brim almost covered his eyes. He had since acquired a walking stick, to exaggerate his geriatric appearance. He advanced in a stilted walk towards a bench under a tree, sat and retrieved a mobile phone from his pocket – one he had stolen from the centre-console of an unlocked vehicle at the nearby shopping mall. He used this handpiece to prepare an anonymous SMS message, alerting his Russian Embassy contacts to his approach. Having crafted the agreed text, he paused to review it and then pressed SEND...

Pushkin's message, sent in simple, phonetic Russian, said... '*Red Bear on approach. Pass following text to Moscow station (Victor Svetlana) for interpretation: Recovery procedure identical to Beirut extraction. Same time interval to pick-up!*'

Satisfied with the clarity of his message, Pushkin crushed the stolen mobile phone under his boot and tossed its remains behind a bush. He then added to his disguise by attaching a yellow lapel rose (the identifier used when the Russians had extracted an agent from Beirut, fifteen years earlier). Having completed this preparation, he turned towards the parkland skirting Observatory Circle and began making his way towards the Russian Embassy. He had a long walk ahead of him, and his attempt at feigning a geriatric gait would make it a slow one. He decided he would keep to the folds of the dense shrubbery lining one flank of the park and find a suitable position to lie low until his Embassy counterparts were ready for him to make his final approach.

Within seconds of its transmission, Pushkin's message was intercepted and downloaded for analysis by the cyber machinery of the US Signals Intercept Service, which routinely monitored all communications to and from the Russian Embassy.

Pushkin's message was simultaneously relayed to CIA director, Frank Angiotti, who forwarded it to 'Macka' McKenzie's van, warning him that Pushkin might approach the Russian Embassy - either as a passenger or on foot. Angiotti immediately instructed his field staff to be prepared to intercept, arrest and detain the suspect… even though that course of action would mean breaching normal diplomatic protocols.

Forty minutes later, as Pushkin continued his tenuous way towards the parkland adjacent to the Russian Embassy, Tom Grant's driver dropped him off next to the nondescript FBI surveillance van. Tom alighted and knocked on the van's rear door. The door opened and Macka McKenzie appeared, his thumbs working busily on a coded text to Frank Angiotti, advising that his surveillance team were '*in position*'. Macka then assisted Tom Grant into the crowded surveillance van, introduced him to his tech guy and briefed him on latest developments. A hush then returned as the surveillance team continued to scrutinize all approaches to and exits from the Russian Embassy. McKenzie was not confident that anything would happen soon and had arranged for his team to be rotated every six hours, as complacency was an ever-growing danger for any surveillance team cooped up for a long period. Tom Grant and Macka then speculated about how Pushkin was likely to make his approach.

'Here's the problem, Macka,' he offered. 'Pushkin will never make it undetected across that expanse of open ground in front of the Russian Embassy, so it seems likely that he will have arranged a discreet pick-up, from a closely adjacent location, in an embassy vehicle. If he does that, we have a problem. How do we pull over and detain a vehicle with diplomatic licence plates, about to enter its own Embassy? That would make the Russians scream 'foul' under diplomatic protocols.'

'I agree,' said Macca. 'I have raised that possibility with Angiotti and he reckons we should still risk the diplomatic fallout from a vehicle intercept. Whichever way we handle this thing, we are bound to have a major diplomatic incident, but the downside is much greater for the Russians when we expose what they are up to, and Ivan knows that. I have two unmarked FBI pursuit vehicles parked just down the road and they will move to block any suspect vehicle, once we are sure it is attempting to pick up Pushkin. We have major jurisdiction on our own streets, but we had better not get this wrong, or there will be hell to pay.'

'Hang on a minute,' said Tom. 'I have an idea. When I got my diplomatic plates, your protocol guys told me that all foreign missions on US soil have agreed to waive diplomatic immunity for minor civil offences, like parking fines and motor vehicle accidents, committed on public roads. If that still applies, we could ram the pick-up vehicle, so that the collision becomes a traffic accident... you know, a local civil matter... and no immunity applies. We could even arrest the occupants for a motor traffic offence,' he added.

'That's an interesting idea,' agreed Macca. I will pass that on to our intercept team.'

Another quarter of an hour passed, and Tom began questioning the merit of his remaining at the surveillance site. It might be hours before anything happened, if it happened at all. He was taking up room in the small van and would add little should the team need to react. 'I think I'll leave you guys to it and get back,' he said.

Just as they were completing this exchange, a message flashed up on the surveillance van's monitor...

'FBI agents report discovery of corpse in bathtub at Western Airport hotel. Suspect may have assumed corpse's ID. Hotel registration identifies room occupant/deceased as Newark resident Gerry Watkins, 76, vehicle registration WSB 862. The vehicle is a 1989 Toyota Landcruiser. No evidence of vehicle in hotel car park, suggesting our suspect used vehicle and deceased's ID to escape road block. Forensics team investigating further. Maintain vigilance and prepare to intercept - end'

Field agent McKenzie turned to Col Tom Grant and smiled. 'That's got our suspect's signature all over it. Cunning bastard, this Pushkin, and I'll bet my arse he will have arranged that pick up we talked about. I reckon we can count on it.'

Tom Grant had only planned a short visit to Macca's surveillance truck. However, the FBI alert suggested that Pushkin was on the move and might make a dash for the embassy at any moment, so he changed his mind and elected to wait it out with Macka. His decision was soon rewarded. Both men settled back in their seats and studied the screen images above their heads. These were projected by two Zeiss telephoto lenses with zoom function, mounted on the van's exterior panels. Two screens offered different images of the target. One offered a wide-angle lens shot and the other focussed upon the entrance gates to the Russian Embassy. As McKenzie and Grant looked on, a black Mercedes with diplomatic plates backed out of its parking spot inside the Embassy forecourt, straightened and accelerated through the gates, causing the sentries to snap to attention as it passed through.

Reacting spontaneously, Macka snatched his comms handpiece from its cradle and barked a message to the adjacent FBI intercept vehicles.

'Hawkeye One to Rover One: Embassy vehicle on the move. Black Mercedes with Diplomatic plates. Start engines and prepare to intercept the embassy vehicle if necessary. Ram the bastards if you see any attempt to stop and pick up Pushkin, or any third party – over.'

The embassy vehicle turned left out of the Embassy gates and cruised sedately along the wide avenue. Almost simultaneously, the figure of an old man, wearing a yellow flower in his lapel, floppy hat and carrying a walking stick, emerged from the thick parkland scrub on the opposite side of the road and approached the curb side. Upon seeing this, the Russian Embassy vehicle spun its wheels, executed a sharp U-turn, and accelerated towards the emerging figure. It skidded to a halt beside the figure and two men jumped out, grabbed the old man and pulled him into the vehicle.

'Go! Go! Go!' barked Macka into his handset, prompting the two FBI vehicles to rev their engines and race towards the scene from their covert positions, some 100 metres further down the avenue. Pushkin was still clambering into the back seat of the embassy Mercedes, as it screeched off in a frantic attempt to make it to the safety of the Russian Embassy gates before the approaching vehicles could block its path. As it approached the Embassy at speed, the Russian vehicle skidded across the median strip, exposing its flank. Sensing a close race, the first FBI intercept vehicle gunned its engine and slammed into the flank of the Russian vehicle, T-boning it and jolting it sideways, as the second vehicle screeched to a halt across its nose, halting the vehicle's progress just metres from the Embassy gates.

Four FBI agents leapt from the two intercept vehicles and rushed to the undamaged flank of the Russian vehicle, brandishing pistols and screaming at the occupants, their voices ringing with authority and urgency. Though he carried no side arm and was technically an observer, Colonel Tom Grant simultaneously threw open the rear door of the surveillance van and sprinted towards the tangle of vehicles, as Macka McKenzie followed, fumbling for his service revolver.

'FBI! Out of the car! Now! Show me your hands! Out! Out!' screamed the FBI agents, waving their weapons menacingly at the occupants. In response, the driver and an accomplice began to emerge from the front seat of the Russian embassy vehicle, their hands raised, as the driver ushered an unbroken string of profanities.

In the rear seat, Pushkin was hemmed in by a second man, who struggled frantically with the door handle on his side. Pushkin could see that their vehicle had been forced to a halt just metres from the Embassy gates and that the American intercept team was on the opposite side of the vehicle. The Russian's eyes widened as he struggled to find an escape. He reasoned that, if he could prise his door open wide enough, he could squeeze through and make a dash across the short distance to the threshold of his Embassy, where he would be on Russian soil and immune from any further threat.

'On the ground! On the ground! Down! Now! barked the FBI team, grabbing each suspect by the scruff of the neck as they emerged from their vehicle and pushing each of them, in turn, down onto the road surface, into a prone position.

Tom Grant's military background had given him keen spatial awareness. While the FBI officers were doing their job well, Grant could see that they had left an open flank on the damaged side of the vehicle, offering Pushkin an escape option.

He quickly moved to that side of the Embassy vehicle, just as Pushkin forced his damaged door open. Following his surgery, Pushkin was no longer a limping ambulant, and the urgency of his predicament had given him new strength as he leapt free from the rear seat and pushed off towards the Embassy gates. Grant knew that he must act or they would lose their man. He dived towards the lower half of the Russian's body, bringing him crashing to the bitumen in a perfectly executed rugby tackle, and pinning him down inches from the Embassy threshold. Russian guards standing at the embassy gates were waving their weapons menacingly, but were unable to act with any authority while Grant and his captive remained on US soil.

Although Grant and Pushkin had been hunter and prey for months now, they had never come into close personal contact. The Russian's furious eyes now drilled into Tom Grant's, above an angry grimace, as their eyes locked for the first time.

'Got you, you bastard,' said Grant, and smiled triumphantly at the defeated Russian.

In the near distance, the sound of approaching sirens could be heard, as larger FBI vehicles with flashing lights arrived to reinforce the intercept. As they did so, another line of security guards emerged from the Russian Embassy's portico and dashed across the courtyard, brandishing weapons. They then congregated at the huge portal gates, uncertain how to proceed in the face of an overwhelming FBI presence.

Agent McKenzie marched through the chaotic scene toward the prone figure of the Russian intelligence chief, whose wig and hat now lay beside him, where they had fallen from his bald head. McKenzie looked down at his pathetic captive and addressed the Russian calmly, as Tom Grant looked on.

'Anatoly Pushkin. I am placing you under arrest for crimes committed on US soil. For espionage and murder. You have the right to remain silent. Anything you say may be taken down and used in evidence against you. I

272

am also taking your colleagues in for questioning for a number of road traffic offences. Cuff 'em, boys, and let's get 'em back for interrogation.'

***

Pushkin, once the lordly Chief of the Russian Foreign Intelligence Service, was then cuffed, assisted to his feet, and firmly but politely ushered into an FBI police van... this time, without his creative disguise. Beads of sweat gathered on his bald pate, as his foolish wig and absurd hat were bagged as evidence, linking his DNA irrefutably to the DNA of the dead corpse at the airport hotel.

Pushkin offered little protest, choosing instead to adopt a stony silence. He displayed no emotion or remorse, save for grimacing whenever he was handled, however politely, by the arresting officers. When he had been secured in the police van, agent McKenzie immediately contacted his boss, CIA Director Frank Angiotti, to discuss the sensitive modalities around Pushkin's capture, further handling and prospective interrogation. Too much was at stake. It would be inappropriate to treat him as a common felon, given the likelihood of a serious diplomatic protest, and each of the arresting officers had been briefed that they must exercise restraint, cross their 't's and dot all of their 'i's carefully, so as to make their case against Pushkin stick.

'Great job, Tom,' said 'Macka' as his cell phone vibrated and he answered it, anxious to receive final instructions from his CIA field controller in Langley.

'Frank Angiotti has decided that we should take Pushkin to FBI cells in McLean. Once there, the FBI have agreed that you may lead the interrogation, Macka. We have State officials and the President's office up our arse on this, so don't fuck up!'

After several hours in the police holding cell, during which Pushkin was well treated, McKenzie was given a protocol for the handling of Pushkin, which had been agreed with each of the other agencies. On instructions from White House National Security Advisor, Bill Nordish, Macka would be given unfettered powers to interrogate the Russian. In

273

seeking Nordish's approval for this, Angiotti had played the belligerent General like a grand piano, confident that he would demand answers. However, the immediately provable offences - the murder of the Customs Officer and the murder of the elderly hotel guest at the Airport Western Hotel – were police matters. Together, CIA and FBI forensic teams would work with local police to validate that charge, based upon prints, DNA and other evidence.

While the FBI had jurisdiction for domestic crime, the J Edgar Hoover facility, where the FBI was headquartered, was a largely administrative facility and lacked the necessary holding cells and quiet sequestration required for intense interrogation. Moreover, Pushkin was a controversial and politically embarrassing custodian. The Russians would certainly protest the manner of Pushkin's arrest, at the gates of their embassy, and seek diplomatic immunity, so every step had to be well planned. The FBI holding cells would be a neat, out of town solution and Macka could use that solution to advantage by piggy-backing off the FBI's jurisdiction in the domestic crime, while conducting his own interrogation and opening other lines of inquiry.

***

Colonel Tom Grant stood in a dark annex, looking through one-way glass at the Russian intelligence chief as he sat impassively at a desk in the interrogation room.

His feet were manacled, but his hands had been freed to the front of his body, and loosely chained to a bracket on the desk. This was possible because, following his arrest, Pushkin's cyanide capsule had been located and removed from his possession. As Grant looked on, Macka and two FBI officers entered the interrogation room. McKenzie took the lead in the interrogation.

'OK, Anatoly. It's time to dance. You comfortable?'

No sign of recognition or response was forthcoming, as the Russian intelligence chief turned his head contemptuously away from his interrogator, towards the wall, and began to play, nonchalantly, with his thumbs.

'Alright, Anatoly, have it your way. You have been read your Miranda rights. Your Embassy has elected not to be present for this interview. We have offered you, and you have declined State-funded legal counsel. I am thus free to begin questioning you and to record your answers. Do you understand this?' continued Macca.

Again, Pushkin ignored this statement and retreated into himself.

'Let the record show that I have explained and offered all rights and privileges to the prisoner preparatory to commencing this interview. Can I get you anything, Anatoly? ...A drink maybe, or a smoke, before we continue?'

As no response was forthcoming, Macka sighed in frustration, pressed the 'record' button on the wall panel of the interrogation room and began carefully...

'This interview is now being recorded.' 'For the record, it is now 10.45 p.m., on Thursday evening, 15 June. 'I am Officer McKenzie, special Field Operations, CIA, Langley, Virginia, in the company of officers Burke and Gentle, from the Washington FBI. We are here to question a person of interest, assumed to be Anatoly Pushkin, who has not yet acknowledged that identity. Again, for the record, the interviewee was found in possession of the ID of another, deceased person, believed murdered. He has been charged in connection with the murder of that person - Newark resident, Gerald Watkins, and is also being held in relation to suspected espionage activities, injurious to US national security interests, and of occasioning, or commissioning, other deaths on US soil.'

It had been a very long day for both agent McKenzie and Col. Tom Grant, but a longer one for Anatoly Pushkin, whose worst nightmare had commenced two days earlier, as he had attempted to evade airport security. The strain of his predicament was now clearly etched into Pushkin's face and his shoulders had slumped in a defeated attitude. Experience had taught interrogators that leaving suspects in a holding cell for hours, prior to their interrogation, induced anxiety and made them more inclined to cooperate. In this way, tiredness was the interrogators best friend.

'You are here because we have irrefutable evidence that you have committed a murder on US soil. You refuse to identify yourself as Anatoly Pushkin, but we are confident that will be confirmed shortly. We will nevertheless proceed, treating you at law as an unidentified felon, whose fingerprints and DNA have been found at a murder scene, both on the victim and on your own person, linking you to a capital offence, punishable in this State by lifetime imprisonment. Is that understood?'

Again, the stoic Russian simply averted his eyes and ignored McKenzie's words. After another twenty minutes of futile interrogation, McKenzie drew proceedings to a close, addressing Pushkin, this time by his Christian name:

'Anatoly, I am going to give you some time for serious reflection. We have you cold on the murder of Gerald Watkins, an innocent US citizen, who found himself in the wrong place at the wrong time and died at your callous hands.

'As we speak, our technical experts are conducting a forensic examination of the hard drive on your computer. We both know that those investigations, supported by your cell phone communication with the Russian Embassy, will provide the evidence we need to seriously embarrass your government and put you away for a long time. You will now be returned to a holding cell, but you will be woken and interrogated throughout the night, as your actions are a matter of national security. As evidence grows linking you to wider espionage activities, you will feel our noose tightening, including evidence linking you to the murder of CIA Deputy Director Charles Ritter, and the alteration of his intelligence report on China's Dongfeng missile installations.

'I'll save the best for last, Anatoly. If you choose to cooperate and help us with these investigations, we will consider a plea bargain reducing your likely charges. If not, I might put you back on the street, where your Russian mates will do our work for us. On the street, I reckon you would have a half-life of about twelve hours, if you are lucky.

'Your comrades don't want you back in Moscow, unless it's in a coffin!'

276

These last words seemed to penetrate the consciousness of the wily old Russian spy chief. For the first time, his eyes widened and he turned his steely gaze towards McKenzie, understanding the final humiliation he would face if he were released.

'This interview is concluded at 11.06 p.m.,' concluded Macka, with a sigh. 'Take the prisoner back to his cell.'

The two men, McKenzie and Grant, then left the building together, grateful that they could at last fall into a welcome bed. As Tom Grant made his way back to his hotel, his busy mind was already formulating his report to Lazarus, bringing Australian intelligence up to speed with these tectonic developments.

Office of National Security Adviser

From the proximity of her office alcove, Personal Assistant Cassandra Oliver could hear a storm brewing. She knew immediately that her boss would soon explode through the door and start issuing angry directives. It was going to be one of those days. Then, true to form, General Bill Nordish uttered another expletive, loud enough for the sound to escape through the heavy timber doors of his office. She winced, as the bombastic General burst through her door, brandishing a copy of a memo from Liz Rankin to the President, proposing a meeting with the Chinese in Beijing.

'Goddammit Cassandra, that woman is driving me nuts. The friggin' Chinese develop a crazy new weapon, then they sink one of our subs. Right now, they're deploying SAM missiles on their jumped-up island real estate, threatening our air and shipping passage in North Asia and makin' the Japanese jumpy, and all Rankin can think about is kowtowing to 'em, when we should be makin' em back off.'

'Get me a line to the President's office. I gotta head this off. It's makin' us look like pussies when the rest of the world wants a show of strength.'

While his young PA had security clearance, Nordish's careless disclosure of such sensitive information to her, from a cabinet Secretary's internal communication with the President, was typical of Nordish's brash disregard in such matters. Despite this, he had a point. The news that China had deployed Dongfengs with EMP warheads had sent shock waves through the NATO establishment. Prime Ministers and Foreign Ministers around the world had called on both sides to show restraint, but were jumpy about where this new international military threat was heading. The collision of the Chinese and US nuclear subs, sending American submariners to a watery grave and the pride of the US submarine fleet to the bottom of the Manila Trench, had added new fuel to the fire. Indeed, tensions between the US and China had never been so strained, and any small incident could now become incendiary.

Rankin's request for a meeting with the Chinese was well founded. It followed her receipt of Angiotti's report that a Russian covert operation might have distorted the Chinese Dongfeng missile threat. There was also the report from the Japanese, supported by Australian intelligence, about new Chinese construction activity on Scarborough Reef. The Scarborough Reef incursion was another act of belligerence on China's part, but if it could be proven that the Dongfeng report had been distorted by Russian interference, as a cynical attempt to heighten tension between the two superpowers, both sides might find a way to save face and avoid a major military confrontation. All the bases were loaded. All the triggers cocked, as time ticked on.

The naval collision and renewed global fears about Chinese hegemony had led to a dangerous escalation of tensions between the two powers, adding urgency to Secretary of State Rankin's request for a meeting to win breathing space. A meeting with the Chinese, whose forces were now facing off against US naval and air forces, both of them on high alert in the South China Sea, needed a circuit-breaker such as that proposed by Rankin. The meeting would also give Angiotti's team extra time to investigate and affirm the explosive intelligence about Russian espionage on US soil.

For several reasons, however, the tenuous intelligence about the Russian espionage had not yet been proven beyond all doubt and had not travelled beyond a tight circle, comprising the CIA Director, Secretary of State Rankin and the President. It had not yet been shared with Nordish. Given his belligerent mood and hawkish behaviour, doing so would have been like throwing accelerant on a fire, making things worse.

In the absence of this extra knowledge, Nordish had strong grounds for his view that a show of strength was necessary in light of the exchange in the UN Security Council, when the Chinese Ambassador, given the opportunity to refute claims about the Dongfeng's EMP warheads, had failed to do so. Nordish's anger at Rankin's calming initiative ran counter to this logic and was bound to force another stand-off with the President. That, in turn, would require that Nordish be fully briefed on the CIA intelligence. The President would then have to choose whether the meeting with the Chinese, jointly arranged with the Australians as intermediaries, should proceed.

In due course, this is precisely what transpired. Rankin found herself summoned to the oval office for a conference with the National Security Advisor and the President. Angiotti was also required to attend, to update the President on his agency's latest investigations into the Dongfeng affair. The four met in the oval office, where the President opened and gave Secretary of State, Elizabeth Rankin, the floor.

'Mister President, you will have read my request for a meeting with the Chinese. It comes at the urging of the Australian Government, which has offered to act as an intermediary to secure the meeting and attend as an observer. They have strong connections with Beijing and are particularly vulnerable to any flare up in relations, as they are dependent upon China for over 50% of their exports. In the event of a conflict with the US, they are bound by the ANZUS treaty to support any US position and fear this could potentially have serious economic ramifications for them. As a middle-ranking power, chairing the Security Council, they are an ideal mediator.'

'The proposal is that we meet with Chinese officials in Beijing to discuss recent developments in North Asia, and the tensions between us. I would not normally urge such action, but the current atmosphere is highly charged and I believe we should continue to favour diplomacy over a more aggressive response, at least until CIA Director Angiotti and his team have completed their further investigations.'

Almost before Rankin had completed her sentence, Nordish interjected.

'Damn it, Liz. We have had this discussion before. History is riddled with examples of how appeasement just opens the way for the other side to ramp up, believing they have us rattled. Neville Chamberlain learned that lesson the hard way, when he returned to Britain with a smile on his face just before Hitler invaded Czechoslovakia.

'It's time we toughened our stance, not weakened it.'

'I am inclined to agree,' said the President thoughtfully stroking his chin. The western world's eyes are upon us and they look to us for leadership on this issue.'

'With your permission,' offered Angiotti, 'there have been further developments which lend weight to our suspicions that the Russians are behind this whole Dongfeng thing. If we are right about this, the entire scenario changes and we have a chance to recalibrate our position and defuse this dangerous escalation.'

'Go ahead.' said the President. 'But the whole spy thing seems a bit fanciful to me. Doesn't change much, either, following the naval collision in the Manila Trench.'

'With respect, sir, I think it does,' said Rankin. 'The Defence Department's report confirmed that we were patrolling in their waters, that there was no locking on of weapons… no attack scenario. Indeed, it appears that their sub was simply quieter and bigger than ours, and that we were not smart enough to get out of its way.'

'Jesus, Elizabeth…' said Nordish, but before he could continue his stormy protest, the President raised a hand to quieten him and deferred to Frank Angiotti.

'I am interested in what you have found, Frank. Why don't you fill us in?'

'Thank you, Mr President. While you are across most of the earlier details, General Nordish is not, so I think it time we brought him up to speed,' he said.

'I absolutely agree,' said the President. 'Please carry on.'

'Our suspicions were first raised when our Deputy Director, Charles Ritter, was found murdered in his apartment. He had been working on a report into the Chinese Dongfeng ICBM silos, and the potency of the missiles, which we believed were an obsolete design *borrowed*, if I may use that term, from the Russians some years ago. The Friday before his body was found, Ritter had confided, in a casual discussion with me, that he had considered the threat from the Dongfeng silos minimal, that they were a cumbersome missile which we could easily interdict, and that they were barely capable of making it to our shores. None of that rhetoric was found in Ritter's final report, which was recovered from his personal computer, taken from his home following his death. We were very puzzled by the whole tone of his final report. He had technically breached security protocols by taking his report home with him, as he had wanted to finish it over the weekend. His final report was wildly at odds with the verbal assessment he shared with me, and we began to smell a rat.'

'That may be so,' said the President, 'but if we cannot prove Russian interference, how does that change the predicament we now find ourselves facing?'

'I am coming to that, sir, and I agree. Without clear evidence of the Russian espionage and their tampering with Ritter's report, we have nothing. However, our quiet investigation into the matter proceeded, and we were amazed to discover footage, at an airport immigration control point, of the head of Russia's spy agency entering the United States under an assumed name. He has since been linked to communications with Russian field agents, and with his embassy. More recently, he was intercepted by immigration officials as he attempted to leave the US. He made a run for it, with our CIA and FBI units in hot pursuit, and was captured two days ago. We were able to link him to a murder at an airport hotel, where he stole the ID of his victim. His involvement in the murder of a US civilian has been clearly established, as his DNA was found on the victim and on the victim's personal effects, in his possession. If you think the Dongfeng issue is a problem, sir, try explaining to the Russians why we have arrested and detained the head of their national spy agency.'

'My God,' said the President. 'What a damned mess we have here!'

'Let me retrace the sequence of events, because they are significant in determining which side began this dangerous escalation,' continued Angiotti. Following Ritter's alarming report that the Chinese Dongfengs carried electromagnetic pulse warheads, we accused the Chinese, in the UN Security Council, in front of all of the delegates, of using a weapon of mass destruction to threaten our security. Their Ambassador would neither confirm nor deny deployment of the EMP warheads, and things started spiralling out of control. If we could prove Russia's role in a deception of this magnitude, we may enable the Chinese to save face and take the steam out of this whole affair. I therefore strongly support the Secretary of State's initiative.'

'Truth is, however, you don't have any solid proof yet, do you?' said the President.

'No sir, we don't. But we have the Russian spy chief in custody and are interrogating him. We are confident we can join more dots and that he will finally crack.'

'Alright everyone,' said the President. 'Here's my decision. I cannot allow the Secretary of State's initiative to proceed at this point... not until I have a watertight case against the Russians. Things are very tense with the Chinese at present, so I also have to consider how the world is watching our response to this extraordinary chain of events, resulting in this dangerous escalation. I am going to support Bill Nordish's request for continued naval and air passes to preserve freedom of air and sea navigation in the South China Sea. The UN will support that. God help us if an incident arises from which we cannot pull back. Meantime, I want all of our CIA and FBI resources to focus on resolving the Russian espionage thing, as a matter of priority over any other agency work. Bill, you will advise the Secretary of Defence of our decision and have him prepare his freedom of navigation patrols. That is all.'

Elizabeth Rankin gave her reluctant assent to this approach and quietly left the oval office. She would now have to suspend arrangements for the peace mission to Beijing. She was therefore dejected, and could only find agreement with one phrase the President had uttered – '*God help us if an incident arises.*'

150 East 42nd Street, New York

Colonel Tom Grant was seated at his desk in the Australian Consulate General, New York, completing a coded despatch to Sir Robert Chandler (codename *Lazarus*) about the capture and arrest of Anatoly Pushkin and the likely consequences of his interrogation. He had earlier reported the entry of Pushkin into the US under an assumed name, the suspected clandestine activities associated with his presence, and the manhunt to run Pushkin to ground following his attempt to leave the US.

Tom Grant was certain that Pushkin was behind the Long Island kidnapping of himself and Dr Maggie King and was able to support this theory by describing the callousness of the Russian spy chief in the murder of the old man at the airport hotel, and the Custom's Officer at the airport

He concluded his report with information on Angiotti's meeting with General Nordish and the President, at Australia's urging, to consider a meeting in Beijing to take heat out of the situation, and the President's reluctance to approve such an initiative without irrefutable proof of Russian involvement in the Dongfeng affair. He transmitted his coded message, signing it with his codename *Archangel*, and turned his attention to other routine matters he needed to tie up, before leaving his office.

Tonight would be special. After a long week in Washington working through issues with CIA chief Frank Angiotti and agent Macka McKenzie, he was looking forward to catching up with Maggie. She had agreed to accompany him to a diplomatic cocktail party at the WestHouse Hotel, in Manhattan. His jovial aide-de-camp, Corporal Mike Stephens, would pick them up, take them to the cocktail event, and then return them to the Andaz Hotel for dinner. Maggie had preferred to stay over, rather than make the trip back to her digs at Princeton, where she was now an important member of the academic team. This decision had romantic overtones and Tom was overjoyed.

Tom Grant found his vehicle and driver, with Maggie already on board, standing at the curb side as he exited his building. She shuffled over, creating space for him to join her in the back seat. Tom slid in beside her, leaned forward, planted a kiss on her cheek and broke into a wide grin. Maggie looked resplendent in a white evening gown, wearing simple pearls and smelling of fresh soap.

'Maggie darling, you look amazing,' he said.

'You don't look too bad yourself, soldier,' she replied, affecting a *Mae West* accent. 'Although I do prefer a man in uniform. You are starting to look like a diplomat, in those business suits, Tom, but you need some advice on your selection of ties!'

'Thanks for the fashion lecture, mate. How's is life at Princeton?'

'Well, I've got my senior lectureship sorted and have been offered tenure. With the Masters and PHD behind me, I suppose I will need to work towards a professorship, but I think I need to chill for a bit. It's been hard work. How was Washington?'

'That's a long story. Lots happening, and some of it a bit hot for general discussion. I'll tell you as much as I can over dinner, later tonight. For now, I have to catch up on some Defence Attaché duties, although tonight's bash is just a regular get together for western diplomats in New York. I could strangle a nice cocktail!'

They arrived at the portico of the salubrious WestHouse Hotel and joined a throng of happy people mingling in a large function room adjacent to the foyer. A drinks waiter offered a tray of assorted drinks, and Tom grabbed a martini while Maggie chose a white wine. As they looked about for a familiar group to join, a gregarious matron in a tropical shift beckoned Maggie to join her and her colleagues.

'Hi Maggie. How about introducin' me to this tall stranger you got with you?'

'Tom, let me introduce Professor Susanna Duffield, from Princeton. She runs our Political Science program. Susanna, this is Colonel Tom

Grant, the Australian Defence Attaché. Tom's here under our military's exchange program with Australia.'

'Nice to meet you, Tom,' replied the voluble academic, examining the tall, athletic Australian closely. 'Nice hunting, Maggie. You an item, Tom?' she added, with a mischievous twinkle in her eye.

Maggie looked decidedly embarrassed as she struggled for an answer that fell short of commitment. They both knew that Tom's attachment under the military exchange program would end in a couple of months, and had avoided that difficult issue.

'Let's just say he's growing on me. Not like a fungus. More like a comfortable shoe at this stage, but he still needs a bit more training.'

Susanna roared with delight, while Tom hid his discomfort, trying to look equally amused by Maggie's off the cuff joke at his expense.

'Say, I have been meaning to congratulate you on your new appointment,' said the matronly political scientist, whose contacts in the state department ran deep.

Tom Grant looked at Maggie with raised eyebrows. This was news to him.

'Something you forgot to tell me Maggie?' he asked, puzzled by the remark.

'It's something that came up while you were in Washington,' she replied, 'with some twists to it. I'll fill you in later.'

***

The cocktail party was fun, and Tom's reaction to the gregarious academic's remark had faded in his consciousness. Maggie had woven her arm through Tom's and kept it there throughout the event, publicly owning their relationship as a bounteous quantity of grog and food flowed, leaving them in a warm, slightly tipsy mood. They made their way to the exit and found Mike Stephens parked under the portico, ready to transport them back to Tom's hotel, where he dropped them off and sped away.

'I don't need to eat, Tom, after all that cocktail food. Let's just grab a nightcap in the lobby bar and then go on up,' said Maggie.

They settled onto stools at the Andaz bar and ordered wine.

'So, Washington was interesting, was it Tom?' said Maggie.

'Yeah. I called on Defence and signed off on some Military Attaché business. Most of it was hush-hush stuff at CIA, where they were still trying to firm up intelligence on a suspect. A big fish who had entered the country under an assumed name. Our suspect made a run for it and I found myself involved in bringing him down.'

'How so, Tom? You're not an authorised US law enforcement officer. You are only a foreign interloper who is supposed to observe and report.'

'It's complicated, but that is exactly what I was doing when the suspect made a bad move. Had to help the local guys bring him down. No big deal,' he added, careful to protect the wider context and respect the secret intelligence aspects of his role.

'Enough about me, Maggie. What's all this about congratulating you on your new appointment?' said Tom, wanting to end his interrogation.

'It came out of the blue. Elizabeth Rankin contacted me for my views about the strained relationship with China, and I agreed to meet her to discuss it. That is my area of expertise, after all. At the end of the meeting, Rankin surprised me by asking whether I would accept a more permanent, advisory role with her office... not full time, but whenever she needed a fresh set of eyes on a sensitive issue. It's extra money, and it lends a bit of extra curricula status, so I said yes.'

'So, you also travelled to Washington while I was there and didn't bother to tell me?' said Grant.

'It was a professional matter with some confidential aspects. I was in and out on the same day, so it didn't seem right to distract you with it,' added Maggie.

'I smell a rat!' said Tom. 'This is Sir Robert Chandler's doing, isn't it? I know for a fact that he wanted to set up a meeting with the Chinese, and he told me he thought you could help him persuade Rankin to support the idea. Trust me... this whole military escalation is becoming very dangerous. I told him to leave you the hell out of it!'

'It really had little or nothing to do with Sir Robert,' she lied, 'and I don't have to explain myself to you every time I take on a project,' she added defiantly.

This seemed to placate Tom, and he backed off. He had pushed her too far. Tonight was about being together, and he didn't want anything to spoil that. Their conversation mellowed and their night caps encouraged a more languid mood. Finally, they made their way to the lifts, heading for Tom's room. As they waited for the lift, the physical bond between them was suddenly more palpable. When they alighted on his floor, he took her hand and gently guided her to his door. Once inside, the tall Australian circled her waist with his big hands and drew her to him. She seemed to melt at the quiet power of his command and her breath quickened when he sought her lips. Their deep, lingering kiss opened a floodgate of sexual desire, quickly becoming a torrent of physical need, requiring no logic or explanation.

'Oh, my darling… I have missed you so much,' she moaned, and they tumbled onto Tom's bed, tearing at each other's clothing in their search for urgent release.

CIA Headquarters, Langley Virginia

The next morning, Frank Angiotti was back at his desk. He was deeply engrossed in a National Security Agency (NSA) report dealing with Russian and Chinese cyber intrusion, which outlined much increased activity by those two foreign powers, both in hacking into western servers and in signal interception. It noted that sophisticated new software had been installed at the NSA to deal with this growing cyber threat and had greatly improved the agency's ability to trace activity back to source. Just as he was concluding that task, his PA entered and delivered an urgent message:

'Sir. I have just had a request from agent McKenzie and his IT guy for an urgent meeting. They think they have found something big. According to agent McKenzie, they have found clear linkages that confirm Pushkin's identity, that provide evidence of his wider espionage activities and that may lead to a string of other charges. Macka thinks this will put a noose around Pushkin's neck and force him to deal.'

Angiotti needed no prompting. This was the breakthrough he had been waiting for.

'Send him up immediately, Julie! Hold all calls and see that we are not interrupted.'

Several minutes later McKenzie appeared, with a bespectacled young talent he had recruited to interrogate technical devices and track down covert cyber activity.

'Julie tells me you're onto something big, Macka. Tell me what you've got.'

'Where do I begin?' said Macka. 'We were struggling with our investigation until this young man here stumbled onto something seemingly innocuous, which gave us the break we were looking for. Then the rest began unravelling like a ball of string.'

'You remember that Pushkin entered the US using an assumed identity... that of one Vladimir Jurkiev. It turns out a man using that name... Vladimir Jurkiev... checked into an orthopaedic clinic in Boston, Massachusetts two months ago. It was the clinic of one Dr Geoffrey Weir, a world leading orthopaedic surgeon. He remembers his Russian patient well and describes him as an intelligent, well-spoken man of about sixty-eight, who had limped into his practice with difficulty, aided by a walking stick. Jurkiev had been booked in for complex surgery to a shattered knee. Here's where it gets interesting. The Aussie Secret Service's London station had been separately looking into the death of Charles Ritter on our behalf, and was able to confirm that Ritter was once one of our London field operatives. At the same time, a much younger Anatoly Pushkin was serving as Second Secretary at the Russian Embassy. Back then, Ritter had *made* him – discovered that he was a KGB agent.

'We now know that Ritter then intercepted him and interrogated him roughly. The Brits told the Aussie station chief that Ritter had taken Pushkin in for interrogation, found that he would not talk, and had broken his kneecap with a hammer. The Brits say he had been left for dead on the Isle of Dogs, where they found him. The Ruskies delivered him into intensive care and then repatriated him to Moscow.

'Way back then, when our London station learned of the brutal interrogation, Ritter refused to admit that he had conducted it, in breach of all accepted protocols. However, he was forced to submit to a psych test, which revealed that he had sadistic tendencies, so we pulled him from the field and gave him a desk job back here. The rest is history. He became Deputy Director of this agency and was working on the Dongfeng missile when he was killed. Looks like Pushkin wanted revenge and managed to intercept Ritter's report on the Dongfeng missile, setting us all up.'

'God in heaven!' said Angiotti. 'Do we have enough now to hang him out to dry?'

'There's more. My clever young techno-wizard here was able to examine both email and cell phone traffic. He triangulated cell towers around Jurkiev's Boston apartment and found SMS messages, code signed 'Red Bear', which we think were from Pushkin, directing operations. They went to the Second Secretary, Russian Embassy. We knew that the Second Secretary was an intelligence officer and we think he was directing the operations of the two Russian thugs who kidnapped and worked over Colonel Tom Grant and Dr Maggie King. They must have arranged the kidnapping to prevent Colonel Grant relaying the British intelligence to us and blowing their cover.

'Finally, we now have compelling physical evidence. We have Pushkin's medical records, which will tie him to the surgery on his knee. Dr Weir has agreed to testify to that aspect if we need him. We also have his eye scans, DNA and fingerprints. They will assure Pushkin's conviction for murdering the old guy at the airport hotel, and can also be used to confirm his identity. The Russians will know that he has been made, so he is a dead man walking. He is out in the cold. All that we have to do now is to play him like a grand piano, 'til he cracks and tells us everything!'

'Great work, Macka,' said Angiotti. His excitement at the new evidence was palpable as he said, 'Patch me through to the White House. I am gonna enjoy sharing this with the President, and with that bellicose arsehole General Bill Nordish.'

In short order, Angiotti and Macka found themselves on a secure line to the Oval Office. The President himself was on the other end, wanting to review developments. Angiotti gave him unvarnished details of their investigation, provided complete confidence that the Russians had undertaken a covert mission on US soil and were directly implicated in the murders of three people and the kidnapping of two, including a member of the diplomatic service and a respected academic.

'I am flabbergasted that they would dare to undertake such a venture, right under our noses,' said the President. 'I will call an emergency meeting of our security and foreign relations team, informing them of your great work. Frank, this nation is indebted to you and your team, for stopping this thing in its tracks. Thank God we didn't have to raise our military alert to the final level, and stare down the Chinese. This whole thing could have gone pear-shaped, and we have to clean this up.

'Meantime, you have my full authority to order the arraignment of Pushkin and to seek any bargain you can reach with him, to identify others

291

associated with this heinous crime. I will make sure National Security Advisor Nordish is apprised, though I expect he will not want to eat much humble pie. Oh, and I will, of course, give Secretary of State Rankin immediate authority to go ahead with arrangements for an urgent meeting with the Chinese, to explain the Russian involvement in raising tensions between us. I understand the Australian Government will send their Ambassador in, as a mediator, to attend to modalities and set up the meeting.

***

Agent McKenzie had Pushkin returned to the interrogation room, manacled to the desk and prepared for another interview. This time, he was well armed with damning evidence which Pushkin could not refute. He strolled into the room, glared at the stonewalling Russian spy chief, smiled and activated the recording system.

'For the record, it is 15.00 hours on Monday 19th June. I am Agent McKenzie, head of field operations at CIA headquarters, Langley Virginia, and I am interviewing the suspect who alleges he is Vladimir Jurkiev, but who we now know is Russian SFB Chief Anatoly Pushkin. He stands charged with the murder of Gerald Watkins and of conducting covert espionage activities on US soil, affecting US national security.'

Pushkin, who had heard this a dozen times before, continued to avert his gaze and assumed a bored demeanour, refusing to acknowledge his interrogator's presence.

'Listen up, Anatoly, 'cause what I say this time will require your undivided attention. You are now charged with all of the above crimes. We now have firm evidence supporting each charge. I will outline what our agencies have discovered about you, so that you are in no doubt as to your criminal status and the penalties that they each attract. As I speak, the same details are being conveyed to your Government by our Ambassador in Moscow, preparatory to our disclosing them to a full sitting of the UN Security Council. You're gonna become famous, *Red Bear,*' he concluded.

At the mention of the codename *Red Bear*, Pushkin's eyes widened and he turned to face his accuser, beads of perspiration now forming on his troubled brow.

'You entered the USA using an assumed identity... that of one Vladimir Jurkiev. You then used that name... Vladimir Jurkiev... to check into an orthopaedic clinic in Boston, Massachusetts, two months ago. You limped into the surgery of Dr Geoffrey Weir with difficulty, aided by a walking stick. That image has been captured on his clinic's CCT footage and matched with your arrival into the US as Vladimir Jurkiev. Dr Weir will identify you as his patient and testify that he performed complex surgery on your shattered knee. We even have the *before* and *after* CAT scans.

'We also know that, in 1981, you served as Second Secretary at the Russian Embassy in London, at the same time as CIA field agent Charles Ritter. We know that you had a run in with Ritter, and that he smashed your kneecap with a hammer. X-rays from the intensive care ward in London, dated 1981, confirm the identical bone and cartilage damage as you presented with at Dr Weir's clinic. I will therefore, now address you by your real name, Anatoly Pushkin, Chief of the Russian Secret Intelligence agency, otherwise known as the SFB.'

Pushkin's demeanour had now radically changed. He was perspiring like a pig, swallowing hard as the brutal clarity of these statements hit home.

'There is more, Anatoly. After examining both email and cell phone traffic, obtained by triangulating traffic over cell towers surrounding your Boston accommodation, we found messages, code signed 'Red Bear', from you to the Second Secretary at the Russian Embassy. We know that the recipient is an SFB agent and was directing the operations of two Russian agents – one now deceased - who kidnapped Colonel Tom Grant and Dr Maggie King. It is clear that you ordered that action to prevent Grant relaying the British intelligence to us, which would have blown your cover.

'Finally, we now have compelling physical evidence, leaving no doubt about your commissioning of these crimes on US soil. We have your medical records, which tie you to the surgery on your knee. Dr Weir has agreed to testify to that aspect if we need him. We have your eye scans,

DNA and fingerprints. Your colleagues in Moscow now know that you have been made, so you are a dead man walking.

'It's over, Anatoly. You will be on the front page of every newspaper shortly and the world will know what a sadistic prick you are. With the charges you face, your life is over, but if you will agree to a guilty plea and cooperate in confirming these facts, I am authorised to offer you a much-reduced sentence, a new identity and a more accommodating incarceration than the isolation cell you might otherwise face on death row. Is that clear?'

State Department, Washington DC

At the President's direction, the wheels of government had turned remarkably swiftly. Secretary of State Elizabeth Rankin was in a buoyant mood, her judgement having been vindicated, and she had rapidly set wheels in motion for the meeting with the Chinese. As a matter of accepted diplomatic protocol, she had called in her good friend, the Chinese Ambassador to the USA, Liu Qixin. She had briefed him confidentially on her Government's desire for a meeting with Chinese leaders, so that the Americans could share confidential information about a new development, offering a way out of the present impasse. Rankin knew full well that the Chinese had suffered a major loss of face, impacting their international standing, and was confident they would favour any rational means of avoiding a full out conflict, which neither side could win and with lasting, bitter consequences for both nations.

To preserve the international reputation and standing of both governments, Rankin had explained to Liu that the US had invited Australia, a middle-ranking power with close ties to Beijing, to act as the author and mediator of the meeting. The meeting would thus be viewed as an Australian initiative, with no suggestion that either side had backed down in the tense dispute between the two nations. Liu had found that solution elegant, and promised to use his full influence to support the initiative.

Encouraged by her meeting with Liu, Rankin had then assembled a team, largely drawn from her close advisors, to prepare for the meeting and, concurrently, asked that Special Advisor on Asian Affairs, Dr Maggie King, be included in the travelling party and told to be prepared for an imminent departure for Beijing.

Rankin had then summoned Australian Ambassador, Richard Bayliss, to her office and informed him, confidentially, of the President's approval of Australia's mediatory role.

Bayliss, in turn, had immediately notified the Australian Foreign Minister, Jillian Pope, who had the added advantage of being the current Chair of the UN Security Council. The Australian Minister for Foreign Affairs had already been briefed for this eventuality and was delighted that her portfolio, and her Government, would benefit from her nation's positive mediatory role, as an anxious world looked on. She had immediately briefed the Australian Ambassador to China, Michael Lightowler, that they had a green light from Washington to make the necessary arrangements.

As details of the meeting unfolded, Sir Robert Chandler, Australia's ASIO chief and Col Tom Grant's close mentor, learned with satisfaction that his initial proposal had now found its way through the complex machinery of government and resulted in this most pleasing outcome. Recalling his secret meeting with Dr King to recruit her support for the initiative, against the wishes of Tom Grant, Chandler had elected not to brief Grant on these developments yet, until the mission was well underway.

Chaoyang District, Beijing, China

A black Mercedes bearing diplomatic plates, with two flags flapping from its front mudguards, cruised through the Chaoyang District of Beijing towards the Chinese Foreign Ministry, followed by two Australian Embassy vehicles. The lead vehicle pulled into the Ministry's imposing portico and slowed to a halt at the front stairs. Australia's Ambassador to China, His Excellency, Michael Lightowler AO, alighted from the vehicle. Simultaneously emerging from the vehicles behind him were his deputy, Charge d 'Affairs, Ranald Maddock, and First Secretary, Dr Jocelyn Choy. They were greeted by protocol officers from China's Ministry of Foreign Affairs.

As Secretary of State Rankin had briefed China's Ambassador to the US in advance of the Australian approach, the Chinese were well prepared for this meeting and understood its intended purpose. Lightowler would, they expected, reiterate what they already knew - that he was calling upon the Chinese as a mediator, with a brief to arrange a meeting between US officials and the Chinese leadership. The meeting would review tensions, in a frank and fearless way, and the Americans would share new information with the Chinese. Lightowler had an additional agenda. He would use the meeting to protect his government from potential trade or economic fallout.

Ambassador Lightowler and his team were ushered into a large room, with a long conference table at its centre. They were directed to seats, designated by rank, along one side of the long table. Green tea and face towels were then provided, while the Australian diplomats admired the magnificent antique scrolls, alter tables and timeless ceramic objects which decorated the room, in elegant, traditional style.

'Xie Xie Nimen. Tai Kequi! (many thanks, you are very kind)' said the Ambassador to the protocol assistants, as they attended to these rituals. Michael Lightowler's Mandarin was impeccable, but he rarely spoke Chinese during formal negotiations, preferring to speak through a translator and keep his fluency a matter of conjecture. Interpreters were always used by the Chinese side during formal negotiations, and Lightowler preferred to exploit his language fluency to advantage, by digesting what the Chinese officials were actually saying, and editing the sanitised version, so often delivered by Chinese interpreters. Maddock's Mandarin was even more fluent than his Ambassador's, so he would interpret for the Ambassador and politely correct any nuance, should the Chinese interpreter fail to communicate accurately.

As the Australian team waited for the Chinese Minister to appear, Ambassador Lightowler reviewed his briefing notes. Each Ministerial visit required such notes, providing insights into the character and career background of the Chinese Minister, and an outline of issues currently plaguing his portfolio.

Yang Lin was an experienced and wily campaigner. He had been a provincial politician and had enjoyed a period, as a visiting scholar, at Yale University. His fidelity to leaders on the Central Committee had earned him an appointment as Ambassador to Japan. He had handled that tricky assignment with great finesse. Ever since the famed Nanjing massacre, when the Japanese had butchered Chinese citizens in the 1930s, China had harboured deep resentment towards the Japanese. In the 80s, that discord had been amplified when the Japanese Government attempted to whitewash their war crimes. Lin had found words to soften the dialogue between the two nations, signalling to the Japanese that there was a new will to forgive. He had since risen to become a member of the Central Committee.

Then, just as relations were normalising, Japan had elected a fiercely nationalistic Prime Minister, who immediately advocated rearmament of Japan, a move forbidden by its surrender treaty with the Americans. Since then, the political atmosphere had changed further, as Japan had reacted to new Chinese ambitions in the South China Sea. The US had removed the treaty handcuffs upon Japan, explaining that they were no longer appropriate for a modern ally in the Pacific, who could provide a counterpoise to growing Chinese military strength. Under the leadership of its charismatic, new Prime Minister, Japan had since stridently opposed China's territorial ambitions, particularly their occupation of disputed islands in the South China Sea — the Spratlys and Scarborough Reef — and Yang Lin had found himself regularly called upon to steer difficult exchanges between the two nations.

These events had shaped the mind of the middle-aged politician, with both positive and negative implications for the discussions which Michael Lightowler would now lead. On the positive side, the Chinese Minister was thoroughly versed on regional issues and had been a calming voice within the Chinese leadership following the submarine collision. On the negative side, he seemed less patient on difficult issues with the US over North Korea and Taiwan, and aggressive in his response to the 'freedom of navigation' politics being pushed by the US. Was his strident defence of Chinese sovereignty over the disputed islands a sign of toughness? Together, these issues had led to the current escalation of tensions between the two nations. But was Yang Lin a conciliator, or a hawk? That had not really been tested before.

After a short wait, a small contingent, led by Chinese Foreign Minister Yang Lin, entered the room. The Australians rose to their feet and turned politely to recognise the Chinese Minister's entrance. Lightowler extended his hand and smiled. He enjoyed a warm, personal relationship with the Chinese Minister, having organised and hosted three visits, by his own Foreign Minister, Jillian Bishop, to China.

When both parties had taken their seats on opposite sides of the table, with Foreign Minister Lin and Ambassador Lightowler in the centre and their respective support teams and translators seated around them, The Chinese Minister began the dialogue.

'Hen gui-de Au-da-li-ya Dashi! Wode Zhongfu… gen ninde Zhongfu… duo dasuan nege zhende He Ping…'

'Dear Mr Australian Ambassador! Our Governments – yours and mine – both aspire to a genuine peace between the American and Chinese people. But why does Australia jump so eagerly to America's tune. We are close

299

friends, but America and China are now adversaries. Great adversaries should talk directly to each other, as the lion must sit down with the tiger. Why have the Americans sent you to do their bidding, and what is your Australian position on these issues?' he opened.

Ambassador Lightowler listened patiently to the English translation of the Foreign Minister's opening remarks, allowing a moment's pause before responding.

'Dear Minister, we are a small, middle-ranking power, with no involvement in the present difficulties. However, we are not here at America's urging. Quite the opposite! We have acted alone, as a good friend might act when two friends quarrel, to avert a major conflict which would collaterally harm our nation. When dancing with elephants, one must be careful not to be trampled. Australia increasingly finds itself an 'innocent pawn' in this separate, more distant dispute between China and America. I wish we were neutral, like Switzerland, and could remain aloof from it all.'

As these words were translated into Mandarin, the Chinese Minister nodded sagely.

'Australia considers itself a close neighbour of China's, while America views our part of the world through a more distant lens. Our two nations have built a unique trade and investment partnership. Australia feeds China's thirst for raw materials, while China is our largest export market. We must work to preserve peace in our region, because if conflict erupts between our two friends, there can be no winners. We will all be losers. However, we also understand that both our American and Chinese friends are proud nations, and do not wish to appear weak. That is why my Government respectfully sought this meeting, as a friend of both sides, to act as a mediator, as we believe that people of good will can always find a solution.'

'My dear Ambassador,' replied Yang Lin, 'Wo mingbei ninde yisa... (I agree with your sentiments). I appreciate your noble intentions, and will pass this proposal on, with my strong support, to President Zhi Xiaoping and his close cabinet colleagues for consideration and a more formal response.'

Yang was well aware of the true purpose of Australia's intermediary role. It would provide the elegant diplomatic face-saver that both sides needed.

'Should my Government agree to this meeting with the American leaders, how do you propose that this be communicated to the world?' asked the wily Minister.

'Minister Yang,' said the Ambassador. 'If your government is able to accede to this request, we will of course liaise with your public media offices, the CPD (Central Propaganda Department) and the CAPP (Central Administration of Press and Publication) to prepare releases acceptable to both you and the Americans.

'We will be at pains to inform the global press that Australia acted alone in calling this meeting, as a mediator, so that an anxious world does not sense any weakness on either side. Australia will be shown to be a logical mediator, as our Minister for Foreign Affairs, Jillian Bishop, currently chairs the United Nations Security Council. We will stress that neither China nor the USA promises anything from the meeting, but that both sides hope that it may be a small step towards peaceful reconciliation.'

***

Two days later, Foreign Minister Yang Lin was summoned to a meeting with Chinese President Zhi Xiaoping. Also in attendance were Premier Wang Bao, Vice Premier Wei Jintan, General Zhang Ming Wei, Chinese Ambassador to the US, Liu Qixin, who had been recalled for the purpose, and two members of the Central Committee.

The discussion between them on the matter was brief, as each of them had received background papers. In particular, they were keen to understand what the curious new information, or intelligence, might be, which the Americans and Australians had indicated was so important that it would change the dynamic of the discussions. All of those present at the leadership meeting were agreed that there was nothing to lose from the meeting, and that it was imperative that they learn whatever they could from it. One voice, however, had offered an additional twist. It was the rich baritone voice of the young, confident and resourceful tactician, General Zhang Ming Wei.

'Tongshimen,' he began. 'Colleagues, I am in favour of the meeting. It is always better to glean whatever intelligence we can from our adversaries, if only to better inform our own strategies. However, if we are astute, we can use this meeting to project strength, not weakness. We will be asked to provide a venue for the meeting.

'I propose that the meeting be held on the deck of the new 'Shandong' aircraft carrier, recently launched by you, Mr President. The carrier will, after all, project power in our region. General Douglas McArthur used the same device - his aircraft carrier's deck - to project US power in the Pacific, when he took the surrender from the Japanese.'

The elder statesmen in attendance nodded sagely at this suggestion. Once again, the brilliant young military tactician had chartered a masterful course forward. 'One other thing, comrades,' he added. 'The leadership team must not include our President, or our Premier, but rather those immediately below that rank, as the US President will not participate at the meeting. If the meeting fails to achieve anything positive, both of our national leaders will be immune from any political fallout.'

That same afternoon, the Australian Ambassador's motorcade repeated its familiar procession to Foreign Minster Yang Lin's office, where the Ambassador was warmly received and informed that the Chinese leadership had agreed to the meeting. Ambassador Lightowler was also informed that arrangements for the meeting should begin immediately, and that the meeting would take place in Dalian, on board the 'Shandong', a venue cleverly chosen by China for its masterful symbolism.

The 'Shandong' was a 70,000 tonne, Type 001A-class aircraft carrier, a new design with radical improvements upon the Russian Kuznetsov-class. While final electrical and other small fit-out work had yet to be completed, military experts around the world had hailed it as 'a brilliant variant', which had closed the gap with the US Navy in a spectacular way. Some experts had even suggested that the Chinese hybrid, based upon technology 'obtained' from Russia and the USA, surpassed the US technology. Indeed, it was rumoured that the Shandong employed electromagnetic catapults - far stronger and more reliable that the conventional, US steam catapults.

Ambassador Lightowler was elated at the news that the Chinese had agreed to the meeting, but greatly troubled by the proposed venue for it. He reported the outcome of his meeting with the Chinese Foreign Minister, including his satisfaction that the meeting would proceed, but setting out plainly his reservations about the venue.

In Canberra, Foreign Minister Jillian Bishop expressed the view that the meeting itself was more critical than the venue, and her counterpart in the US, Elizabeth Rankin, immediately agreed. Officials then began building the architecture of the meeting. In Washington, State Department officials began polishing their briefs and this process was mirrored by their Chinese counterparts in Beijing. Despite the vastly different political systems of the two sides, the processes of government were remarkably similar. Each of the American and the Chinese Ministers would receive a 'general brief', supported by a Q and A, prepared by senior policy advisors, guiding the dialogue; '*If the Chinese should raise xyz .... you should respond as follows…*'

In Washington, Rankin began assembling her team for the meeting. It included herself, as Minister of State, and her trusted personal staff. Dr Maggie King, senior department officials, a team of approved journalists and a team of security personnel would also be included. The US delegation numbered a staggering seventy-eight people. They would travel together on Airforce Two, frequently used by the Secretary of State on such occasions. The flight plan for Airforce Two's journey to Beijing included a stopover in Manila, to confer with that nation's controversial President, who had requested US support to help him contain Islamic separatists in the southern part of the Philippines. The delegation would then fly on to Singapore, for an ASEAN meeting, which would consider the sensitive issue of Chinese naval and military expansion in and around the South China Sea, which had made ASEAN nations increasingly jumpy. The final leg, from Singapore to Beijing, would symbolically take Airforce Two near to, but a safe distance from the 'no-fly' zone imposed by the Chinese over the Spratly Islands, to reassert freedom of sea and air navigation along that key trade corridor.

In Canberra, Australia, the Minister for Foreign Affairs and Trade, Jillian Bishop, assembled a much smaller team. She would rely principally on the support of her Ambassador and his staff, but would also travel with her department head and her First Assistant Secretary (FAS) for North Asia, from Dept of Foreign Affairs and Trade. This much smaller delegation, with no supporting security personnel, would fly to Beijing on Australia's low budget version of Airforce One – an RAF A330 Airbus especially equipped with high tech communications and administration facilities, including a conference room.

A most unusual aspect of Australia's mediation role would be their conveying of sensitive intelligence to the Chinese, concerning the Russian covert activity. The Chinese would be handed a report which had concluded that the Russian activity had been calculated to embarrass the Chinese Government and divide the two superpowers. The detention of SBF Chief Anatoly Pushkin, who had been arrested for his role in directing the covert operation, would also be communicated, along with a proposal that Russia's interference in the affairs of both nations be raised at a special meeting of United Nations General Assembly.

America's CIA chief, Frank Angiotti, America's FBI chief, Australia's ASIO chief, and Britain's MI6 chief would jointly sign a carefully-worded intelligence report, containing the results of their joint investigations into the matter. Such a diverse national source of intelligence would give the report international status and lend important, non-secular credibility with the Chinese for its contents. Security officials from both sides would attend separate meetings in Beijing, to work through details of the covert Russian operation and discuss each national response. However, this would occur *after* the meeting between the three Foreign Ministers, so as not to detract from it.

With luck, this would result in four nations - China, the USA, Britain and Australia - condemning the Russian action, and so, paradoxically, bring the parties together.

Airforce Two - Over South China Sea

Secretary of State Elizabeth Rankin sat with Dr Maggie King and two of her personal advisors around a conference table on board US Airforce Two. The group was working through protocol aspects surrounding the Secretary's arrival in Dalian situated on China's eastern seaboard. Airforce Two would land on the edge of the city, from whence the American delegation would journey to the port precinct in a convoy of cars provided by the Chinese Foreign Ministry and, finally, be ferried by naval barge to the huge aircraft carrier standing in the bay. The historic talks would then be held on board the carrier. Rankin wanted to be sure that the number of supporting officials matched that of the Chinese party, maintaining minimum standards of respect but absolute equanimity of status.

Their silky-smooth variant of the 757, with its sophisticated comms, quiet luxury, long haul capability and missile avoidance technology, cruised smoothly through the night along a corridor over the South China Sea, leading in a straight line from Singapore to Dalian. The aircraft's anti-missile capability would not be required at the present altitude of 38,000 feet, more than seven miles above sea level and well out of range of SAM systems. The flight had been uneventful, so after completing formalities, the two aids left Rankin and King to themselves. Elizabeth Rankin offered Maggie King a glass of wine and the two women began an easy, personal conversation.

'I know about your academic achievements, Maggie, but not much about you, the person. I see that you recently visited Australia as keynote speaker at their Institute of International Affairs,' she said. 'How did you find the Aussie's? What are they *really* like, and what do they think about us - meddling in the politics of their region?'

'Madame Secretary,' said Maggie, 'just like our early British settlers, the Aussie's are mostly Anglo-Celts – with a strong Irish Catholic influence. But their early settlers were convicts - considered refuse by the British establishment. They were whipped and beaten and made to provide free labour, just as our African slaves were. They sweated on empty stomachs, in a harsh environment, to build a nation. Nowadays, they are different. They are worldly, educated and have morphed into a Eurasian society, with a lot of hybrid vigour, and an exotic mix of immigrant influences. That makes their politics different. They have fought with us and the Brits through every major global conflict, but we constantly demand that they balance their European heritage against their new Asian geopolitical reality. They have a huge dependence upon China - for about 50% of their foreign trade. That's why they make such a brilliant intermediary for our difficult meeting. But we have to tread carefully. Subtly, unwittingly, we are forcing them to decide between China and their US alliance.'

'But are they, as people, like we Americans, or somehow different,' asked Rankin.

'What struck me most was the Irish larrikin in their national culture, which is so infectious that even the Asian population – who now make up 38% of the genetic soup - behave like Aussies. They acquire the same broad accent. They have a keen anti-establishment streak that keeps politicians on their toes. To put it somewhat crudely, you can't bullshit an Aussie voter... but I sense that they are loyal beyond comprehension. If I were in trouble, I would want an Aussie covering my back.'

'And is there a special man in your life... any kids in prospect?' she lied, in a motherly tone, having already viewed Dr King's security vetting documents.

'There is one guy... or should I say a *bloke*... who I met in Melbourne. He is now the Australian Military Attaché here, in New York, where we met again by accident.'

'Was that the guy who was kidnapped with you, and the man who has been working with Frank Angiotti to break this whole Russian thing wide open?' she asked.

'That's the guy. A tall, athletic hunk, with a couple of honours degrees and a medal for valour in Afghanistan. He's kinda' protective… wraps his big arms around me and makes me feel safe. He would kill me if he knew I was on this mission. I think he's that special one, and I think he feels the same way about me, but we both struggle with career and geographical issues. That makes commitment difficult.'

'Do you love him?' asked Rankin simply, risking an intimate woman's question.

'I do, and we will have to address that issue soon. His military exchange program ends in a couple of months. We would be great together, but one of us will have to make a big concession. Probably be me, because I can't imagine life without him.'

***

Just as Elizabeth Rankin and Maggie King were finishing this intimate exchange, their aircraft lurched sideways. The first violent, side-shuffle movement was followed by a sequence of jumps and shudders as the aircraft entered a pocket of severe air turbulence. So violent were the aircraft's next movements that Rankin and King, in unrestrained armchairs, were thrown sideways out of their seats, as their wine glasses clattered to the floor. Without belts to restrain them, the pair had to grab desperately for the conference table, which was bolted to the floor, and clung to its legs for support, as the bucking aircraft continued its crazy, shuddering progress.

In the cockpit, Wing Commander Bob Fergusson immediately disengaged the autopilot system and took the yoke, fighting to control the wide-bodied aircraft and search for calmer air. He immediately switched frequency to a channel which would give him mid-course communications with air traffic controllers in Banda Seri Begawan, Brunei, some 600 kilometres off his starboard wing, and with Ho Chi Min City, 500 kilometres off his port wing. Unknown to him, transmissions would also be heard by both Chinese and Vietnamese air commanders on their respectively claimed and developed Spratly Island bases. Despite protestations from the Chinese that installations on their Spratly Islands

307

were non-military, and only intended to support marine research and commercial fishing, US satellite images had confirmed that the Chinese had recently deployed CIWS (close-in weapons systems), including deadly accurate radar guided anti-aircraft batteries.

As Wing Commander Bob Fergusson wrestled with the aircraft's heavy yoke, his number two, Second Officer Bill Landers, clicked his handset to SEND mode and began the first of a long series of transmissions:

'This is US Airforce Two, calling Banda Seri and Ho Chi Min controllers. Come in please,' he said calmly. His transmission met with no reply, but rather, a blanket of loud hissing and crackling. He was within transmission range, but realised that there was excessive electrical interference, when bolts of lightning suddenly lit up the entire cloud landscape below his cockpit window. The storm's electrical activity was making communications unclear, if not impossible. He tried again. No response.

'Sorry skipper. Looks like heavy electrical interference. I'll keep trying, but I can't promise anything 'til we get through this electrical stuff and the fierce air turbulence settles. I don't fancy our chances of avoiding a lightning strike in this thick soup.'

'No problem on that score, number two. Our aluminium fuselage is a magnet for lightening, but it is a Faraday cage, providing an electromagnetic shield. That should not be a problem... unless a direct strike disables some external component. Keep trying for the local control towers,' said the skipper. 'We might just get lucky.'

After another fifteen minutes of futile transmissions, a faint reply could be heard over the cockpit comms system.

'Banda Seri... to US Airforce Two,' came the hissing reply through the static. 'We hear you. We have been asked by Ho Chi Min and Hong Kong traffic controllers to broadcast an urgent weather alert to all commercial aviation in the area. A massive low... a cyclone, that is... with a huge eye, which was supposed to be located much further west, has quickly moved to the east and is projecting very high winds and lightning activity over the South China Sea. Hong Kong has gone to Typhoon level 5. Satellite imagery reveals a huge spiral of white turbulence, extending over an area of some 2,000 square kilometres, stretching from Kunming, in the west, to Hainan Island in the east and south to the Spratly Islands, and stacking over 40,000 feet.

'Descend to 15,000 feet and attempt to fly around or under the cyclonic mass. Over.'

'Roger that, Banda Seri. Try to stay in touch. Do you have us on radar? Over.'

'Negative. We... and you could... (static)...' Then the faint controller's voice was drowned out by a blanket of louder hissing and static interference.

In the main cabin, aircrew worked frantically to secure loose items and ensure that all passengers were tightly belted in. At the same time, a smaller team of aircrew struggled through the Secretary of State's private Conference Room door and made tenuous progress, hand over hand, towards a row of jump seats located along one side wall, which they began to fold down. They then assisted Rankin, King and other State Department officials into them, one by one, and strapped them in.

'Once we have you all strapped in,' said a male crew member, 'we will close the conference room door and activate the *secure pod* mode. You will be as safe as houses once that is done,' he added reassuringly. 'And we'll get you safely down in Dalian.'

The conference room had been modified in this air force variant of the 757, making it a secure pod, capable of breaking off from the main fuselage as one section in the event of a catastrophic event. It was designed to protect senior commanders and officials, but provided little comfort as the aircraft bucked, jumped and shuddered.

'Let's take this bird down to fifteen thousand and see if we can get below this mess,' said the number one. He tilted his heavy yoke to port, and gradually pushed the control column away from his chest, sending the large jet into a roll to the left and banking its nose towards the boiling sea below. Even with hydraulic assistance, the jet continued to buck and roll, threatening at any moment to break apart. Passengers gripped the sides of their seats with white knuckles, as the turbulent descent continued along an uncertain, jumping and bucking path. Lightning now flashed all around the fuselage, making further communication with the ground futile.

Then, quite suddenly, the heavy jet experienced a spectacular free fall, as it was caught in a massive downdraft. Its free fall was so fast that it induced a sort of weightlessness. Passengers and crew gasped as they felt their bodies float out of their seats, only remaining in them because of their tight harnesses. Someone's mobile phone drifted down the aisle at eye level. Stomachs heaved as the aircraft twisted and dropped though space. Each passenger sat in wide-eyed astonishment and silence - a helpless captive to the extraordinary circumstances. Faces grimaced in angst as the ghostly storm harbinger shook them and took charge of their destiny.

'I can't control her, number two. Get on the other yoke and help me! No. No. That's a bad idea. We are veering steeply towards port and my radar show us approaching the Chinese Spratlys. Get on that damn mic and issue an urgent mayday. It may not get through, but if it doesn't, we will be pushed by this system right into the Chinese no-fly zone and have those bastards shooting missiles at us,' he barked.

'Right skipper,' replied the number two, as he grabbed the mic from its cradle, pressed SEND and began transmitting.

'Mayday! Mayday! This is US Airforce Two to ground stations. We are in free fall and losing control of our rudders. Mayday! Mayday! We might have to ditch. Coordinates roughly over the Chinese Spratly installations. We are a civilian airliner on a diplomatic mission. Not adversaries. Do not... repeat do not interdict. Over.'

'Good job, Bill. Send again and keep sending!' barked the number one as he continued to wrestle with the yoke to bring his aircraft out of its steep bank to port, already aware that it had ventured into the Chinese no-fly zone. 'Just keep sending, or we will be dead ducks,' he said.

On the man-made Chinese Spratly Island, a young military commander, Lieutenant Wu Zhou Ting, received a report from his radar operator that an unidentified aircraft had entered the Chinese no-fly zone. His orders, in such an event, were clear. He was to protect Chinese sovereignty at all costs against any foreign attempt to enter the disputed air space. In doing so, he was to follow international protocol, which required that he issue repeated warnings to the errant aircraft that it must immediately bank and manoeuvre to leave the no-fly zone. This warning was to be repeated over and over again, during a five-minute window for diversionary action. Any failure to comply, identify or divert would trigger automatic interdiction.

The Chinese comms officer immediately began transmitting this warning.

'Chinese Spratly Command to unidentified aircraft... you are violating Chinese sovereignty and flying within our no-fly zone. Please respond, identify yourself and take immediate diversionary action! You must return to international air space! Over!'

This message was repeated again and again, but its transmission and the urgency of it, were lost in the swirling teeth of the cyclone, swallowed by its electrical ferocity. Only intermittent, unintelligible words made it to the flight deck of Airforce Two.

Simultaneously, the piercing noise of a Chinese siren began whining above the furious white noise of the cyclone, sending anti-aircraft personnel, in heavy weather gear, scrambling towards their CIWS batteries. They entered command codes and their dashboards lit up. Digitally-controlled fire systems on each battery, guided by a sophisticated radar scanner, would automatically lock the Chinese guns onto the rogue aircraft. As the Chinese teams arrived at their respective batteries, the boiling sea exploded over the breakwater installations surrounding the island and a furious wind and vertical barrage of rain whipped at the Chinese gunners grim faces.

Above them, spiralling downwards towards the island batteries, Wing Commander Bob Fergusson and Flight Officer Bill Landers now wrestled with their respective control yokes, as an intermittent voice call... just a few broken words... indicated that the Chinese were trying to communicate with them.

'We can't hear them, and they probably can't hear us. But you have to let go the yoke, Bill, and keep repeating that Mayday. Tell 'em we are out of control and that the cyclone has caused us to stray. And remember the protocols. We have to identify first, deliver our mayday and then explain our inability to control the aircraft. Do it! Now! And keep on, while I try to level this baby in case we need to ditch. We may still find a way through this,' he barked.

On the ground, the Chinese comms officer, his fluent English a necessary prerequisite for his role, listened intently for any acknowledgement and reply from the unidentified aircraft. Through a blanket of hissing and crackling, he heard only a smattering of intelligible words of response, as radio reception faded in and out.

'…US Airforce…''…US Airforce…'

After repeated warnings, the comms officer turned to his commander and advised that he had identified the aircraft as a US Airforce jet; that it had failed to take evasive action; that it continued its path towards the Chinese installations and that the required time for response and diversion had now been well exceeded.

'Bu haole,' he groaned (this is not good). 'Instruct batteries one and two to engage. Action stations! Action stations!' said the young Chinese commander, understanding fully the moment of his brave decision and wishing he did not have to make it.

As Airforce Two emerged from the swirling mass of cloud around it, bright flashes suddenly appeared on the horizon, signalling that the anti-aircraft batteries had locked onto the US aircraft and commenced firing. Within seconds of each flash appearing, explosions erupted around the aircraft's fuselage, their shock waves shaking the heavy-bodied jet and adding to the chaos of its uncontrolled descent.

'Holy shit!' exclaimed Bob Fergusson. 'They don't get it! The bastards are firing upon us. We are very slow compared to a fighter jet, so they are bound to hit us, that's for sure. No point in evasive action. I'm gonna try to drop this baby onto the deck, though attempting a belly landing on these mountainous seas doesn't look good. Instruct the cabin staff to have everyone assume crash positions!' he barked.

As soon as he had completed this command, Fergusson eased the yoke forward and the aircraft's nose dropped into a steep, evasive dive. Despite this, the fuselage suddenly shuddered violently, as it took a direct hit from the Chinese batteries, tossing the huge aircraft onto its side. Terrified passengers shrieked as they fought against gravity. Seat belts cut into shoulders and bellies as everyone struggled to oppose the forces pulling them to the left wall of the cabin, now located below them.

'What the hell was that?' screamed the flight engineer, struggling in his pilot's harness. Let me quickly assess the damage.' He consulted his instrument panel, which included a fisheye lens projecting back onto each wing. 'Kill the port engines, skipper! The left wing's been hit and one of the turbines is hanging off, creating drag. A large chunk of wing is missing. Looks like the hydraulics are cactus…' he roared '… and I can see a thick stream of aviation fuel spewing from the port tank.'

The aircraft then began to roll, in a slow, spiralling motion which eventually placed it upside down, before continuing through that perverse attitude back towards a level plane. Inside the cabin, most people sat in horrified silence, gripping armrests and fighting gravity with each roll, while others simply screamed in terror. The rolling fuselage was now beyond any response, making normal flight impossible, and a final descent into the boiling ocean inevitable. The angle of impact would be a lottery. 'Hang on,' said the pilot. 'We're going in! I have no response from the left flaps. I'm gonna ignore the wing flaps and try to use the tail flaps to bring her back level!'

Before the pilot could complete these words, dark mountainous waves, their crests foaming in protest against the gale-force winds, appeared in his cockpit window. The ocean surface rushed towards him, as everyone tensed, sensing their last moments of life. As if they were resisting the final few yards, the aircrafts hydraulics groaned, like the cry of a dying beast, as the wide-eyed pilots wrestled desperately with their unresponsive yokes to raise the aircraft's nose. The last thing anyone heard was a deafening blast, as the wide-bodied 757 smacked into a heaving, mountainous wave and broke apart. Then everything went black.

***

The young Commander of the Chinese Spratly Island battery instructed his communications officer to patch him through to the PLA's Southern Air

Command, based out of Guangzhou. He was eventually connected to a Captain Liu, described as *Senior Duty Officer*. The young battery officer gave his report with exaggerated confidence and authority, realising that its explosive content could cost him his job.

'Sir! I regret to report that our Spratly Island anti-aircraft batteries have just fired upon a US Airforce jet, which entered our airspace, violating our no-fly zone,' he said. He then allowed time for this sinister news to fully register, before continuing...

'The aircraft appeared on our radar screens at 20.05 hours. In line with international protocols, we issued instructions for the aircraft to immediately return to international airspace. These warnings were repeated, well beyond the minimum period required, prior to engaging. We received no response from the aircraft, apart from two, brief aircraft communications – both identifying the aircraft as a US Airforce jet. Our radar-guided batteries then engaged it, and the aircraft disappeared off our radar screen, confirming that it was brought down. We have despatched a tug and three rescue launches to determine if there are any survivors, but our vessels are struggling with huge seas and cyclonic winds, and will not reach the site for some time.'

There was a brief pause while the Southern Command officer absorbed this alarming information. He attempted to respond in a calm, measured way, but a slight tremor in his voice betrayed his clear sense of horror and disbelief.

'Tongshi (comrade),' he began. 'Are you *sure* that this was an armed, military aircraft? Were its systems locked on, or did they remain in passive flight mode?'

'Commander, electrical interference and the sideways tramping of the aircraft caused by the cyclone made it impossible to determine those things. Our radar was unable to determine whether it had locked on or not. However, while we were demanding that the aircraft change course, we were simultaneously plotting its progress. It was on a direct heading for the Island's military installations. When it was three kilometres out and contact was inevitable, I instructed our batteries to engage, in line with orders from Beijing to defend our sovereignty over the Chinese Spratlys at any cost.'

'You have done well, comrade, but I will have to take this up the line… urgently, as it is a very serious situation. I hope for your sake that you did not fire in error.'

The Guangzhou officer immediately relayed his message to Beijing Air Command who, in turn, passed it to the National Military Command, the Security and Defence Committee of the National People's Congress and the Chinese Foreign Ministry. A joint strategy would be required, combining appropriate diplomatic and military responses, so a national leadership group was convened just hours later and began work on this task. Their deliberations were led by the brilliant and mercurial young Military General, Zhang Ming Wei, who took just fifteen minutes to join the dots.

'My God!' said the US educated Chinese General. 'The ground crews did not know that *Airforce Two* is a civilian airliner, an air force passenger jet used by the Vice President and the Secretary of State of the USA. It seems they have shot down the American Foreign Minister, Elizabeth Rankin, and all of her diplomatic delegation, en route to what is essentially a peace mission… one which they proposed. Despite their violation of our airspace, due to the ferocity of the cyclone, the world will hold us accountable for this! There will be all hell to pay! Gentlemen, we must immediately go into damage control, and come up with some swift diplomacy to avert a disaster!'

UN Security Council, New York

When news broke of the downing of Airforce Two with the anticipated loss of all lives, the US President, his cabinet and people around the world were shocked. The public at large were outraged that China could perpetrate such an evil act. Ignorant of the true facts, and never allowing facts to get in the way of a good story, the *Washington Post* summed up the public mood in its strident, front page headline:

'China Downs Airforce 2. America on Brink of War!'

This headline was repeated around the world, and reactions began flooding in. The American President addressed an anxious world press from his Oval Office, expressing outrage and demanding that an emergency session of the UN Security Council be convened immediately. With his Secretary of State presumed dead, he instructed his Ambassador to the UN to lead the diplomatic response and to explain that the US stood ready to counter any Chinese threat and would not baulk at military intervention if the Chinese did not explain their actions fully and immediately stand down. The UN Ambassador, Jonathan Rubenstein, was a calm and confident diplomat, but he was left in no doubt by his President that he should *'not mince words when issuing this ultimatum to the Chinese'*. The US Asian Pivot fleet and the Air Command were ordered to come up to DEFCON 2, the second highest level of war preparedness, also referred to as FAST PACE mobilisation – a readiness to go to war within six hours. DEFCON 1 was the last, desperate Defence Condition, also described within the military as 'Cocked and Ready – Nuclear War Imminent!' NATO allies with forces adjacent to the theatre also mimicked the US defence readiness.

Meanwhile Jillian Bishop, Australia's Foreign Minister, had arrived independently in Beijing. Her delegation had landed several hours ahead of the Americans and had not yet departed for the domestic flight to Dalian, where she would join the US party for the meeting with the Chinese. She was informed by a polite Chinese protocol officer of the tragic events and advised that there would be no American party to the bilateral talks she was expected to mediate. Being in China, she was also now unable to chair an emergency session of the UN Security Council. On her advice, the US therefore used its numbers to elect an alternate chair - the highly respected British diplomat and member of the Security Council, Sir Nigel Ashby.

***

As his vehicle motored along 42nd Street, Colonel Tom Grant shook open his morning newspaper and read the headlines. Gobsmacked by news of the horrendous events, he immediately asked his driver to step on the gas and switch on the car radio, so he could listen to commentary as he sped towards his New York Consular office.

'Mike, when we get in, get Dr King on the line for me. There is war in the air, and I will be fascinated to hear what she has to say about all this. You should be able to reach her at her Princeton office, although she's probably fielding lots of questions from the media right now. This stuff is right in her area of expertise,' said Grant.

After Grant had ridden the lift to his floor and settled into his office, he instructed his ADC to focus on tracking down Dr King. However, after nearly forty minutes, his ADC had still not been able to contact her. Then, suddenly, the ADC appeared in Tom Grant's office doorway with a stony, anxious face.

'I have some very difficult news for you, sir,' he began. 'The people at Princeton kept stuffing me around... you know, avoiding answering my questions and duck-shoving me to other desks as I tried to contact Dr King. I smelled a rat, and eventually contacted the executive secretary at the Department of State. Turns out Maggie King was invited to accompany the Secretary of State to China as her personal advisor for the mediation. For

317

obvious reasons, the composition of the official party and the timing and arrangements for their departure had to be kept secret. It looks like she was on board... and went down with Airforce Two, sir. I'm terribly sorry!'

Tom Grant felt as if a sledgehammer had hit him in the chest and knocked the wind out of his body. His mouth fell open and he stared, uncomprehending, at his ADC, struggling to digest the horrific news he had just received.

'Bloody hell!' he bellowed. 'What the fuck was she doing on that flight?' I told her to avoid that meeting like the plague... that it involved dangerous espionage matters and could put her at risk. That damn Lazarus must have put her up to it. Get him on the line!'

The next morning, grim faced UN Security Council delegates made their way into the UN chamber, took their seats, and spread out their briefs, in preparation for their responses to the explosive events. Some whispered to closely aligned neighbours, while others adjusted their headphones, anxious to hear translations of addresses.

Finally, a hush descended upon the forum, and all eyes turned towards the chair. Sir Nigel Ashby adjusted his bow tie, banged his gavel and called the assembly to order.

'Distinguished delegates, ladies and gentlemen, I will not prolong these proceedings by expanding upon the events which have brought us to this emergency session. The tragic downing of a civilian airliner, US Airforce Two, on a peaceful mission to China, will already be known to you. The fact that it was transporting the US Secretary of State and her delegation, who were embarked upon a peace mission, makes this event more highly charged, both politically and militarily, and has moved many of you to roundly condemn it. When calm logic becomes a hostage to outrage and emotions boil over, we risk acting precipitously. With so much at stake, that would be extremely foolish, so I urge all delegates to exercise restraint, and respect all views, as we work through these difficult issues,' said the sober British diplomat. 'You will have been working through the night, with your respective Embassy colleagues and intelligence services, to piece together the tragic chain of events which have, it seems, brought us to the brink of a nuclear war. Five decades ago, a distinguished American stood in this same chamber and said, *"a doomsday clock is ticking, and it is three seconds to midnight"*. At that time, sanity prevailed, and a global holocaust was averted. Let us hope and pray that sanity can prevail again.

'This emergency session was convened by the United States, so I would normally invite the US to speak first. Overnight, however, our Secretary General received a most unusual, personal request from a Head of State - from the President of the People's Republic of China. He asks that China be permitted to speak first, so that our debate might be informed by facts just to hand in Beijing. This request has been acceded to by the President of the United States, and by Australia's Foreign Minister, who is on the ground in Beijing as a mediator. As the current Chair of this Security Council, she was uniquely placed to guide our judgement of this request.

'I therefore call upon China's Ambassador to the UN, His Excellency Mr Lin De Bao, to address us. Before he does, I caution delegates that this usually *closed* forum will today be *open;* albeit to a small number of accredited TV and print journalists. An anxious world is looking to us for answers, and the fragile situation demands that we give our world audience complete transparency,' he said. 'Ambassador Lin, you may proceed.'

In the space of a few short months, the affable, much-loved elder statesman had felt a growing coolness, as tensions between his nation and the US had escalated. He had no illusions about the hostility he now faced. Indeed, his government had made clear the kind of presentation they expected from him. He must buy time, at all costs, until emotions cooled, and give transparency to all of the facts. He was to display appropriate humility and remorse, despite China's conviction that it had complied with all international protocols and was innocent of any wrongdoing. In short, to avert a war, he was to eat humble pie if necessary, something which most Chinese found extraordinarily difficult to do. He shuffled his notes, then threw them philosophically to one side. He had learned his prepared, formal text off by heart but preferred his own, sincere words to the doctrinaire language crafted by cautious speech writers in Beijing. He adjusted his round reading glasses, raised his sombre head and began:

'Mr Chairman, delegates. I come before you with a heavy heart. My hands tremble with emotion, and I can find no words to describe the deep sadness that I feel. It is a sadness which the people of China and the leaders of my nation share, as we all search for answers to this horrendous event. My heart, and that of my nation, goes out to the families who have lost loved ones. Their loss is more painful and more futile than we can ever understand, because each passenger on Airforce Two was, in his or her own way, an ambassador for peace. That makes this tragedy doubly sad. Those heroes did not deserve an unjust and ignominious end to their lives.'

At this point, Lin De Bao choked, bowed his head, and genuine tears began to run down his dignified cheeks. He continued, with a distinct tremor in his voice.

'Most of you know me personally. You know that, despite our differences, Elizabeth Rankin and I were close friends. Forgive me for allowing my emotions to affect my composure. I will miss her terribly and her passing will leave a giant hole in our lives.

'Friends, Elizabeth's death must not be in vain. She was a peace-maker, lighting our path. Her death teaches us that the greatest achievements of man are not found in the mind-boggling technologies he has developed, or in the awesome power of his war machines but, rather, in his simple humanity. That is what sets us all above those cold, mechanical things. We know this to be true, but our human fallibility continues to tear our nations apart. Our land, naval and air forces shadow each other daily. We troll cyberspace for secrets about each other, and strive to be one step ahead, as if a final conflict between us were inevitable. We robotically follow identical command and control procedures, whenever our forces brush together on oceans and in skies at the edges of our overlapping worlds. These close brushes have become routine, but this time our protocols have let us down catastrophically. Our actions today will define us as humans, not machines, and will be judged by all of mankind.'

With these passionate and moving words, Lin De Bao now held every delegate in his thrall. Around the chamber, solemn diplomatic faces were now trained intently upon the frail old Chinese diplomat, whose nationality and ethnicity had become irrelevant, dwarfed by his giant human persona. He composed himself, and continued:

'Colleagues, today's electronic media feed us their spin at the speed of light. It travels at warp speed over global superhighways, turning fiction into fact, even before the truth is uttered. We must not risk a global meltdown simply because we are too quick to anger, too quick to judge or too impatient to consider the facts.

'I will not attempt to whitewash the events which led to the downing of Airforce Two. Nor do I want, by labouring over them, to cause you further pain. I simply ask that you examine the material I am about to share with you. Meteorological data, showing the ferocity of the cyclone into which Airforce Two flew. Radar-tracking data, showing the flight path of Airforce Two, as it veered way off course. Voice recordings of the frantic exchanges between our ground forces and the errant US aircraft pilots.

'Use these to judge objectively. Try to understand how a freak combination of circumstances has conspired to deceive us all. Each delegate, each United Nations member state, and each of the accredited journalists, will be given copies of these documents and recordings, for they expose the raw truth, and must provide the evidence upon which we base an objective and just examination of these events.

'Quite simply, a fatalistic convergence of events has conspired to alter history. The first of these was the enormous weather system, which dominated the whole South China Sea on that fateful evening. Winds gusted at over 200 kilometres per hour and the sky crackled with fierce electrical activity. The power and fury of that huge, electrical storm made communications between our ground forces and the US aircraft impossible. The voice tapes now prove that the only intelligible transmissions received by our Chinese ground crews from Airforce Two were those which identified it as an American Airforce jet. They show that the cyclonic conditions had made the aircraft impossible to control and blew it savagely off course. Indeed, in the chaotic conditions, it veered some eighty kilometres west of its published flight plan, crossing into our no-fly zone and continuing on a direct line of approach to our Spratly Island batteries. The voice tapes show that our Chinese ground crews followed international protocols precisely... the same protocols which the US employs when an unidentified aircraft enters its airspace. They show that our Chinese crews issued "turn-back" warnings, again and again, for a much longer period than that normally mandated, before our ground forces engaged what seemed to be an approaching, hostile military aircraft. They did so when the aircraft was just four kilometres, or to put it more graphically, just ten seconds short of its apparent target. Together, these facts speak plainly. With the benefit of hindsight, we now see the string of fatalistic follies that, together, produced a tragedy - one which neither side contemplated or desired.

'Mr Chairman, Sir Nigel... esteemed friends and colleagues, I should now like to move two motions:

'One - that this assembly reconvene in twenty-four hours' time to give member states an opportunity to examine the documentary and other evidence we have provided, and...

'Two - that the mediation - proposed by Australia - between China and the United States - be allowed to proceed, with the US Ambassador to China representing America, supported by advice from his State Department.

'With our agreement to these two motions, dear friends, we may yet have a chance to avert a holocaust and to boldly write our names in history, alongside Elizabeth Rankin's – as peacemakers, not warmongers. Thank you.'

***

Following a brief silence, the French delegate rose to his feet and began to applaud. He was joined by the Brazilian, then the German and, progressively, by a host of other delegates, until a thunderous applause made it clear that this was the sanity everyone had been waiting for. A motion from the Chair proposed that first the Chinese, and then the US forces stand down from their DEFCON 2 status, to a lower level of military preparedness, as a sign of good will and a step towards peace. It was agreed that the Security Council would reconvene in forty-eight hours' time. It would do so armed with new facts, and with a new resolve to find a peaceful path forward.

Two days later, the immaculately-attired Australian Foreign Minister, Jillian Bishop, having flown back from Beijing, marched across the

322

Security Council floor towards her place at the centre of the table fronting onto the assembly. In short order, she congratulated delegates on their mature management of the crisis, and called upon the US Ambassador to the UN, Jonathan Rubenstein, to take the floor. Rubenstein rose to his full height, turned towards the chair, and acknowledged Bishop. His address would be broadcast around the world, and excerpts from it would appear in millions of lounge rooms, as families across every religious and ethnic divide turned on the evening news, so he had prepared particularly carefully.

'Madame Chair, distinguished delegates, ladies and gentlemen! Two days ago, we stood on the brink of a global holocaust. Today I stand before you in a celebratory mood. *Good* has, it seems, triumphed over *evil*. I will shortly deal with issues surrounding the collision of the US and Chinese submarines, and more recently the tragic downing of Airforce Two over the Spratly Islands. Our negotiations on these two issues, mediated by our close friend and ally, Australia, and the outcome we have achieved, will surprise and delight even the worst pessimists amongst you.

'But first, it is my difficult duty to share with you a dark and sinister matter,' he said.

Upon hearing these curious words, delegates around the chamber leaned forward in their seats, anxious to learn what events deserved such a grave introduction.

'Delegates, you will recall that my esteemed colleague, Ambassador Lin De Bao and his US counterpart, faced off across this chamber some months ago, as the United States accused China of arming its Dongfeng missiles with electromagnetic pulse warheads. Our own intelligence reports had confirmed that these missiles were capable of bringing the entire North American continent to its knees. Well, I am reluctantly obliged to advise that British and Australian intelligence agencies, working closely with our own agencies, have uncovered a covert act of espionage, on US soil, calculated to discredit the Chinese Government and create a dangerous military stand-off between China and the USA. Which nation, you ask, might be so foolish as to attempt such a cynical, ill-advised act of espionage, on US soil, under the world's noses? We now have incontrovertible evidence that the covert mission was directed and approved by no less an authority than the Government of the Russian Federation. President Petrov, this time you have gone too far.'

Even as Sir Nigel turned the page of his notes to continue his speech, accredited media representatives began rushing for the exit doors of the chamber, determined to be first to market with news of the damning claims against the Russians. Equally, there had been a renewed sense of unity about condemning this cynical interference in another nation's affairs, which had served to bring the Chinese and US delegations closer together and forged a joint determination to usher in a bright new morning of peace and reason in global relations.

EPILOGUE
Forest Hills Hospital, Queens, New York

Tom Grant looked nothing like the tall, self-assured Special Forces officer he had once been, as his haggard figure emerged from his staff car. He moved uncertainly towards the front steps of the Forest Hills Hospital in Queens, made his way into the foyer and took an elevator to the second floor, where he was met by Professor Sussana Duffield. The normally garrulous, middle-aged academic from Princeton was ashen-faced and appeared emotionally drained. She had spent several hours at the bedside of her close friend and colleague, Dr Maggie King, having rushed there after news of Dr King's ocean rescue and repatriation, on an Airforce medical flight from Hong Kong, where she had been in intensive care for the previous four weeks.

Against all odds, Maggie King had been one of only three survivors of the Airforce Two disaster over the South China Sea. All three survivors had defied incredible odds, assisted by their unique position on the aircraft inside the executive suite's reinforced survival pod. The pod had done exactly what it had been engineered to do, detaching itself from the main fuselage on impact and skating across the pitching ocean surface, before breaking open and continuing to bob violently on the surface of the boiling sea. Despite its ingenious design, such was the force of the crash landing that most of those in the survival pod, including Secretary of State Elizabeth Rankin, had perished. Some had been dashed against the pod's metal superstructure, while others had survived the initial impact, but succumbed later to their injuries or drowned as they struggled in the foaming seascape.

Maggie King's survival owed much to her extraordinary fitness and her dogged determination. She had clung for hours to a piece of floating debris until her arms were aching in their sockets, and she was finally plucked from the sea by a Chinese rescue launch. For the first hour of her ordeal, the sea around her had been an inferno. Burning aviation fuel had danced across its surface and licked at her head and shoulders, which were exposed above the water line. After clinging to life, barely conscious, and eventually being plucked from the water, she had lapsed into a deep coma. Colonel Tom Grant had yet to appreciate the gravity of her condition.

'Hi Tom,' said Sussana. 'I am so sorry we have to meet again under such tragic circumstances. Are you sure you are up for this?'

'Do I feel ready to see the woman I love, lying comatose in a hospital bed? Of course not! But I have to face those demons and be there for her when she pulls through,' he replied, choking out his final words.

'When, if, she pulls through, I would say, Tom. I admire your optimism and I wish I shared it. Don't get your hopes up too much, Tom. She has a massive mountain to climb. Have they told you about the extent of her injuries?'

'What do you mean? All I know is that she survived… that she is alive. Is there something else I need to know before we go in?'

'Yes, Tom, there is. Let me explain. The person you will see in that hospital bed is not the beautiful young woman you remember. Much of her hair is missing, her scalp and the side of her face was badly scarred by burning aviation fuel. Half of the bones in her body are broken. She is in a coma from which she may never recover, and the only noise you will hear from her is the aspiration of air from the ventilator, which keeps her artificially breathing. Her chances of survival are slim, and of regaining consciousness, even slimmer. You still think you're up to seeing her like that?'

'I'll have to take that chance,' replied Tom, as they made their way to the private hospital bed, where Maggie's life support systems were generating a series of repetitive graphs and whirring noises, as they mechanically kept her alive.

Tom Grant made his way to the bedside, and struggled to contain raw emotion, as he looked down upon the broken remains of his lover. Her badly scarred face made her unrecognisable, and tubes and wires invaded her nose, her thorax, her chest and her wrists, like the tentacles of an elaborate, man-made octopus. The whoosh and hiss of the ventilator added a surreal, robotic quality that robbed the human form in the bed beside him of its humanity, reducing it to its basic, clinical components.

He reached for her hand, felt its coldness and sensed the lack of any warm or live response. Then he dropped his head and turned away. Desperate to remain stoic, he mumbled… 'I'm sorry, Sussana. You were right. I can't do this.'

As Colonel Tom Grant made his way towards the exit, a rogue tear escaped and rolled down his chiselled jaw. As he approached the exit, he felt a crushing force invade his chest, as his huge frame shuddered and he dropped to his knees. Finally, unable to contain his emotions, he issued an anguished bellow and wept like a baby.

Earlier that day, Lazarus had informed Tom Grant that his mission in America had ended and that he must return to Canberra for reassignment. He had dreaded this moment, and the decisions it would force upon him and the woman who had become his special soul mate. Somewhere in his shattered dreams lurked the happy image of that woman accompanying him back to Australia as his bride, but that was now nothing more than a vacuous fantasy. He would not be granted an opportunity to hold her or bid her farewell, though he would remain in daily touch with her doctors for news of any signs of recovery. It seems that the greatest dreams of men are reduced to rubble, when fate intervenes to dash them upon the rocks of despair.

***

Federal Correctional Facility Otisville, New York

As Tom Grant made his melancholy way out of the Forest Hills Hospital in Queens, on the other side of the same city, Anatoly Pushkin was seated in the rear of a New York State prison van, as it made its way through the industrial quarter of New York towards the Otisville Correctional Facility. The Otisville facility was also referred to as 'Club Fed' because of its relatively soft conditions, being a special facility for felons guilty of white-collar or non-violent crimes. Pushkin had made a deal with Angiotti that he be sent to this comfortable facility for corporate criminals, where he would spend a minimum of five years, in return for testifying against his colleagues in Moscow and exposing their part in the Dongfeng deception.

The Ford Econovan in which he travelled was lightly armoured, with bullet-proof glass, window bars and reinforced side panels. Its driver and another security guard lounged comfortably on the front seat, enjoying their short outing on a sunny day to the nearby correctional facility. In the rear of the van, Pushkin lounged back in his new, orange prison uniform, with his hands and feet manacled, but otherwise relatively unfettered. As the van made its way down the narrow roadway skirting behind the industrial precinct, a large removal lorry suddenly reversed out of a side street, blocking its path. The driver of the prison van stood on his brakes and skidded to a halt, just feet away from the intrusive, larger vehicle.

Immediately sensing an ambush, the security guards drew their pistols and scanned the alleyway for any encroaching threat. Acutely aware that he was a sitting duck in a stationary vehicle, the driver quickly threw his van into reverse gear and accelerated backwards down the roadway. Before the prison van had retreated more than twenty metres, the rear tailgate of the removal lorry swung open and a figure emerged carrying a shoulder-mounted, rocket-propelled grenade launcher. This potent, anti-tank weapon had a serious punch and was more than equal to its task of completely demolishing the light, civilian vehicle. A missile fizzed from its barrel, slammed into the prison van and blew its front chassis to pieces. As flames and smoke engulfed the front of the prison vehicle, two men in balaclavas leapt from the lorry, sprinted to the rear of the prison van and packed plastic explosives around its rear door hinges. In quick succession, they inserted detonators, blew the rear doors off and leapt into the smoking van, brandishing pistols.

Anatoly Pushkin lay dazed and bleeding on the floor of the van, barely alive, but still conscious enough to understand what was happening. This was an execution… *his* execution! He would not be allowed to humiliate mother Russia or disgrace the office he held, as head of its Secret Service. He would make the ultimate sacrifice. Through a swirling blanket of smoke, Pushkin's last two experiences were the sound of a Russian saying 'Dasvidaniya, Anatoly!' and the sight of his anonymous assassin's pistol being placed against the centre of his temple, an instant before it blew his aqueous brain matter over the remaining walls of the prison van.

Other bestsellers by the author:

At the time of publication, the author was battling cancer. He leaves this epithet, quoted in his prophetic *'The Plato Prophecy'*, which warned a complacent world about the rise of autocracy and growing democratic dysfunction, published just prior to Russia's invasion of the Ukraine …

'All that is required for evil to flourish is for good men to do nothing'

'A Briefcase in Transit' (Published by Amazon KDP)
'Code Sentinel' (Published by Amazon KDP)
'The Plato Prophecy' (Self-published and available on Books Online Australia)

At the time of publication, works in train included:

'The Forbidden Mandate'
(a fiction about China's ambition to conquer the world, which completes his Tom Grant, spy thriller trilogy for potential serialisation / dramatization), and …

'Reflections: One man … one life'
(reviewing his life's journey, the world he witnessed from 1948 to 2022, lessons learned, values embraced, and aspects of his cancer journey, to shares with others).